Until
the
Dawn

Books by Elizabeth Camden

The Lady of Bolton Hill
The Rose of Winslow Street
Against the Tide
Into the Whirlwind
With Every Breath
Beyond All Dreams
Toward the Sunrise: An Until the Dawn *Novella*
Until the Dawn

Until the Dawn

ELIZABETH CAMDEN

BETHANYHOUSE
a division of Baker Publishing Group
Minneapolis, Minnesota

© 2015 by Dorothy Mays

Published by Bethany House Publishers
11400 Hampshire Avenue South
Bloomington, Minnesota 55438
www.bethanyhouse.com

Bethany House Publishers is a division of
Baker Publishing Group, Grand Rapids, Michigan

Printed in the United States of America

Library of Congress Cataloging-in-Publication Data
Camden, Elizabeth.
   Until the dawn / Elizabeth Camden.
     pages ; cm
   Summary: "In 1898, an abandoned mansion overlooking the Hudson River Valley proves a refuge and resource for Sophie van Riijn in her volunteer work for the Weather Bureau until Quentin Vandermark, a long-lost heir of the estate, shows up"--Provided by publisher.
   ISBN 978-0-7642-1720-3 (softcover)
   1. Family secrets—Fiction. 2. Man-woman relationships—Fiction. 3. Hudson River Valley (N.Y. and N.J.)—Social life and customs—19th century—Fiction. I. Title.
   PS3553.A429U58 2015
   813'.54—dc23   2015024516

Scripture quotations are from the King James Version of the Bible.

Cover design by Jennifer Parker
Cover photography by Mike Habermann Photography, LLC

15 16 17 18 19 20 21   7 6 5 4 3 2 1

Blessed are the pure in heart:
for they shall see God.

—Matthew 5:8

1

The Hudson River Valley
Summer 1898

"THAT'S WHERE THE BODY WAS FOUND, floating face-down in the river," an ominous voice intoned. "He was stone-cold dead."

Sophie sank behind the blackberry brambles to avoid being seen by the people ambling down the old pier toward the shore. She had hoped to take advantage of the river's low tide to gather oysters but had paused as a tour guide led a group of sightseers closer to the infamous spot in the river. The village needed the income from the tourists, and it would be best not to have the wild splendor of the spot spoiled by the sight of a local girl gathering oysters. She scooted a little higher up the hillside to remain hidden behind the bushes.

Every morning, steamboats left the bustling city of New York, only forty miles downriver but a world away from the primeval splendor of this isolated inlet in the Hudson River Valley. The steamboats always stopped so the tourists could admire the famous vista looming just behind Sophie, where one of the oldest mansions in America looked like a medieval fortress perched on the edge of the harsh granite cliff. Dating all the way back to 1635, when Dutch settlers arrived in North America, the gloomy sight of the Vandermark mansion had dominated this windswept cliff for centuries. Built of rough-hewn stone with steep gables and rambling wings, it had the grandeur of a Renaissance painting.

"There wasn't a scratch on him," the tour guide continued. "Karl Vandermark was in the prime of life, and no one could explain what caused his death. Was it murder? Suicide? The Vandermark curse? Karl Vandermark was one of the richest men in America and beloved by everyone in the village. It's been sixty years since his body was found on this very spot, but there are still no answers."

Sophie sighed in resignation. Why was everyone still fascinated by the Vandermark death so long ago? Perhaps it had something to do with the foreboding appearance of the Vandermarks' mansion, which had been made famous by painters and photographers who couldn't resist the gothic appeal of the isolated estate on the edge of a cliff. Named Dierenpark after the old Dutch word for paradise, the mansion was a familiar sight to tourists from all over the world.

The steamships usually stayed for only an hour, just long enough to let the visitors stretch their legs and buy a few trinkets from the stands set up near the Vandermark pier. In a few minutes, the sightseers would reboard the ship and be on their way farther north up the river.

It was an unusually large group of sightseers this morning. Most of them clustered around the tour guide at the base of the pier, but there was a group of ominous-looking strangers gathered close to the base of the cliff.

Marten Graaf was the most colorful of all the tour guides who led visitors up the river, and he was in fine form this morning, layering dark excitement into his voice as he told the tale directly to a young boy he pulled aside to point to the infamous spot in the river.

"The dead man's son found the body," he said. "Young Nickolaas Vandermark was only fourteen years old when he found his father floating in the river. Legend says the lad never got over it, but others suspect that the boy killed his own father, for he inherited forty million dollars the day his father died. There was no sign of foul play, but what would cause a healthy man to keel over in the prime of life? No one ever dared accuse Nickolaas Vandermark directly to his face, but something very bad was afoot. All the Vandermarks have come to terrible ends, and most of the folks around here think it was the Vandermark curse."

Even from a distance, Sophie could see the young boy Marten was speaking to flinch and withdraw. Most tourists loved the spooky tales about the old mansion, but this boy seemed unusually apprehensive.

"The house has been empty since Karl Vandermark's death," the guide continued. "A lawyer swooped in to take the young lad away, and not one Vandermark has set foot in the house since. They didn't take a stick of furniture or even a change of clothing for fear the curse would travel with them. Their clothes still hang in the closets; the papers are stacked on the desk as they were when the family fled all those years ago. Everything inside the house is exactly the same, like it's frozen in time. That house has been sitting empty for sixty years, with only a few servants to keep the place from being plundered for the treasures still inside."

"Why don't they sell it?" a sightseer from the back of the group asked.

"Who would buy such a house?" Marten burst out, startling a flock of crows into flight. The crows rode a wind current high above the cliff, where they wheeled around the mansion, their raucous cries echoing on the wind.

"Anyone who spends too much time in that house is likely to be tainted by the curse, as well," Marten continued to the spellbound tourists. "The first groundskeeper died when he stumbled over a rake. The next died after his joints took on a disease that twisted his body so he could barely walk. Even now, the housekeeper who tends to the inside of the house has turned into a hunchback. And the girl who brings them food each day? Well, she was the prettiest lass in the whole village, but the curse has tainted her, too."

Sophie blanched, stunned that Marten would draw her into the spooky tale told to the tourists. Mortification flooded her as she shrank even farther behind the blackberry brambles and prayed Marten wouldn't spot her. She wouldn't put it past him to point her out, just like any other attraction on today's trip up the river.

"Oh yes, even Miss Sophie van Riijn, who spends only a few hours each day in the house, has been afflicted," Marten continued. "She's had three fiancés and every one of them came to a bad end. The last one died just a month before the wedding. His lungs seized up so bad he could no longer draw a proper breath of air. Now no man in the village will come within a yard of Miss Sophie for fear of the curse."

Sophie averted her eyes, wishing she could block her hearing, as well. It was infuriating that Marten was exploiting Albert's death this way. Her heart still ached for Albert, a kind and gentle man who never put any stock in the curse. They had been planning a life together, and Sophie had such hopes for becoming a wife, a helpmeet, and a mother. Instead, she helped tend Albert during his final painful months.

If he were alive, Albert would tell her not to let the rumors dim her spirit, but to go out and find another man to love. But it was getting hard. She was twenty-six years old, and her string of broken engagements might be an intriguing tale for the tourists, but it was a deep and unrelenting ache for her.

"Did he go to a doctor?" The timid boy's question broke her dismal train of thought. "The one with the bad lungs? Did he go to a doctor?"

"Well of course he did!" Marten exclaimed. "He was dying, boy. The curse had gotten ahold of him and there was no hope. The man was a goner."

Even from a distance Sophie could see the boy's eyes widen in horror, and she ached with sympathy. This boy appeared to be terrified and, oddly, it seemed he was alone.

Sophie stood. She'd rather stay hidden than risk being pointed out as the tragic victim of three failed engagements, but she wouldn't let Marten terrorize a child in order to boost his tips. Her skirts brushed through the cattails as she made her way to the sandy shoreline and straight to the boy's side. The tour guide looked stunned to see her, and a guilty flush stained his cheeks.

"Ease up, Marten," she muttered as she passed him and drew the boy aside. He was a handsome lad, no more than eight or nine years old, with dark hair and enormous gray eyes that remained locked on the house at the top of the cliff. He barely reached her elbow, and she crouched down to be on eye level with him.

"There now," she soothed. "You know that man is just spinning tales in hopes of getting more tips, don't you? There's nothing to be frightened of."

"It looks like a scary place to live," the boy said tightly.

Sophie laughed. "But you don't have to live there, right? Tonight you'll go home with your parents and sleep safe and sound in your own bed. Everything will feel better once you're home, don't you think? What's your name, lad?"

11

"Pieter," he said. "Pieter spelled with an *I*."

"Pieter with an *I*! What a fine Dutch name, just like the saint. Even when he was afraid, St. Peter was a good man, wasn't he? There's no shame in being a little scared now and then."

The boy's gaze remained riveted on the mansion. His lower lip wobbled, and tears pooled in his eyes, on the verge of spilling over. This sort of trepidation seemed unnatural. Something was wrong with this boy.

"Come now, what's got you so upset?" she asked softly. "It can't all be about that silly old house. I always feel better when I talk to someone about what's worrying me. You can tell me anything. I promise not to laugh."

The boy glanced over her shoulder, and she turned to follow his gaze.

Oh dear . . . they were being watched.

The gang of tough men stood only a few yards away, glaring at her with hard eyes. There was only one woman with them, a timid-looking young lady who seemed as anxious as the boy. The half dozen men in the group looked like prizefighters, with massive shoulders and no necks. One of the men wore a fine gentleman's suit, but he looked no less fierce as he scrutinized her. There was no family resemblance between this boy and the hard strangers. Something was wrong. She turned back to the boy.

"Are you with those people behind me?" she whispered.

He nodded.

"Are they your family?"

He shook his head, and a trickle of ice curled around Sophie's heart.

"Where are your parents?"

"My mother is dead, and my father went back to the village. My father is really angry."

A man from the gang of strangers started heading their way.

12

He was dressed in flawless attire, but dread settled in the pit of her stomach as she eyed the man coming toward them. "This isn't your father?" she asked as he drew closer.

"That's Mr. Gilroy. He's my father's butler. He always watches me."

Sophie stood, moving to stand in front of the boy. This boy seemed frightened beyond all reason, and if he was in danger, she wouldn't stand aside.

Mr. Gilroy seemed taller and more daunting as he stood before her. For all his fine clothing and starched collar, a sense of barely leashed power radiated from the imposing man.

"Thank you for comforting the boy," Mr. Gilroy said in a gentle voice with a hint of a British accent. "I'm afraid young Pieter doesn't care for ghost stories, and your kindness is much appreciated."

Had there ever been a more courteous voice? It had a velvety, calming quality that set her nerves at ease.

"You're welcome. Most of the tourists enjoy tales about the old Vandermark estate, but some of us are more sensitive. Your group is touring the river, I take it?"

There was a slight pause. "Not precisely."

She waited for Mr. Gilroy to elaborate, but he said nothing. Tourism had been their village's salvation ever since the Vandermarks had abandoned the estate and closed down their timber mills, paper mills, and iron mines. The fishing and oyster industry had helped fill the void, but even those had collapsed in the past decade.

When Sophie's Dutch ancestors had come to America in the seventeenth century, the Hudson River was so bountiful that a basket dipped in the river could scoop up striped bass, perch, and bluefish. But all that was a thing of the past now. As Manhattan filled its riverfront with factories, the fish farther up the river died off and the oyster beds failed. Now the village needed revenue from the tourists who flocked to the Hudson River Valley to catch a glimpse of the unspoiled wilderness north of the city.

Sophie brushed back a strand of her blond hair that had broken free in the morning breeze. "Well, I hope you have a nice visit to New Holland. It's a lovely village, and most travelers enjoy the shops and cafés."

Pieter kicked the ground, scattering a spray of sand. "My father won't enjoy it. He never enjoys anything."

"That's enough," Mr. Gilroy said firmly but not unkindly. "Your father has been very sick, but he is doing what's right. He isn't doing this to punish you."

To her horror, the boy's face crumpled, and the tears finally erupted. "I just want to go home," he sobbed. "I want to go live with Grandpa again. Please, Mr. Gilroy, please, can't you take me back home?"

She couldn't help herself. Never had she heard so much misery in a voice, and she gave in to the urge to console him. Hunkering back down, she slid an arm around the boy's narrow shoulders. "There now, go ahead and have a good cry if it will make you feel better," she soothed.

There was something terribly wrong with this boy. He was too old to be blubbering in public, and none of the adults who traveled with him seemed interested in extending comfort.

She looked up at Mr. Gilroy. "Will the boy's father return soon? If you arrived on that steamboat, I don't know how much longer it will be here."

"We didn't come on the steamboat," Mr. Gilroy said. "The carriage we arrived in can't scale the hill, so my employer has gone to the village to get a lighter one."

She blinked in confusion. "Why do you want to scale the hill? There's not much up there but the Vandermark estate, and it isn't open for visitors."

14

"It will be open for us," Mr. Gilroy said.

"No, I'm afraid Dierenpark is entirely closed to the public. It has been for the past sixty years."

"It will be open for us," Mr. Gilroy repeated, not so gently this time. A note of steel lay beneath the velvet of his voice.

Oh dear, this was going to be awkward. This wouldn't be the first group of people disappointed they couldn't tour the mansion, but it was impossible. The narrow, rutted lane leading up the cliff was treacherous, and even though the Vandermarks had supplied funds to maintain the house and keep it safe from troublemakers, it was in no condition for visitors.

"There's not much to see," Sophie hedged. "The crows have taken up residence in the east wing and have a nasty habit of attacking strangers. There are some postcards for sale if you are curious about what the Vandermark mansion looks like up close."

"Thank you, but we will tour the mansion shortly and have no need of postcards."

Sophie took a step back. The staff hired to maintain the estate had been walking a fine line for decades, and strangers were almost always discouraged. Almost . . . but not always. Any group that traveled with a butler must be people of means, and Sophie sometimes made exceptions for people willing to pay ridiculous sums to take a peek inside the house. The village needed all the revenue it could get.

"On rare occasions, arrangements can be made for a very select type of visitor," she said. "It takes some time to arrange, for the estate is never open to visitors who arrive unannounced."

"We're not visitors," Mr. Gilroy said in an implacable voice. "We are the Vandermarks. And we've come home to stay."

<hr />

Sophie scrambled up the steep footpath, heedless of the vines and shrubbery that slapped at her skirts as she raced toward the top of the cliff. Rutted with centuries of maple roots and corroded by runoff, it was a treacherous path, but she had to hurry. Mr. Gilroy had told her that Quentin Vandermark, the great-grandson of the man found floating dead in the river, intended to take up residence in the house immediately. Today!

Which was a huge problem. No one had expected the family to ever return, and well . . . over the years, certain liberties had been taken with the house. Mostly by her. Some of it could be hidden, but she'd have to hurry. She hiked her skirts in one hand, using the other for balance as she scaled the hillside with careful steps. With each step higher, the air got sweeter and the leaves grew greener.

Despite the blather told to the tourists, Dierenpark wasn't haunted. Quite the opposite, in fact. Sophie had no explanation for it, but every square inch of the Vandermark estate bloomed with health and abundance. It seemed like the blossoms were more vibrant, the grass softer and greener, and the fruit grown on the estate sweeter than anything harvested in the village.

A screen of weather-beaten juniper trees provided a wind-break at the edge of the property, sheltering Dierenpark and creating an isolated haven of beauty and peace at the top of the cliff. Built of granite block, Dierenpark was a sprawling mansion with gables, turrets, and mullioned windows. The oldest portion of the house had been built in 1635, but over the centuries, it had been expanded to become a rambling mansion, one of the largest private homes in America.

Tearing across the meadow, she burst through the front door and barreled down the center hallway to the sun-filled kitchen at the rear of the house. It was in the newest part of the mansion, with plenty of windows to let in natural light. A fire burned in the brick hearth, and bundles of herbs hung alongside copper pots dangling over the scrubbed wooden work table.

"The Vandermarks are here!" Sophie gasped, doubling over

16

from her frantic dash up the side of the cliff. "Quick, get the merchandise out of here, and hide everything else."

Florence Hengeveld pushed herself off the stool where she'd been bagging up Dutch cookies to sell to the tourists. With a face withered like a dried apple and a widow's hump slowing her walk, Florence had been the estate's housekeeper for forty years. She was the "hunchback" mentioned by the tour guide. But Florence wasn't a victim of the Vandermark curse. She was merely old, and old women often had a widow's hump.

"What do you mean?" Florence asked. "The Vandermarks' lawyer is here?"

For the past sixty years, the only contact they'd had with the Vandermarks was from a series of attorneys who paid their wages and settled the annual tax bill. So why had the family suddenly returned? Sophie bit her lip, praying they hadn't heard rumors about the equipment she'd installed on the roof of the mansion.

"They're here in person," she said. "Quentin Vandermark and his son. I thought they were living in Europe, but they're back, and they intend to take up residence today. Their carriage can't get up the hill, so they've gone to get a lighter one and will be here any moment. Quick! Hide anything having to do with the tourists. I'll find Emil to help."

"He's working on the garden fence," Florence said as she shuffled to a cupboard, dumping the bags of Dutch cookies and shortbread out of sight.

Sophie ran outside, calling for Emil Broeder, a simple-hearted man with a rapidly expanding family, including twin boys and a baby daughter only two months old. He and his family lived in the old groundskeeper's cabin a few acres away.

She found him repairing the fence that kept deer from plundering Sophie's herb garden. In short order she dispatched him to the house to hide all evidence of their tourism business.

But the biggest problem was on the roof, and it wasn't exactly something Sophie could hide. She would just hope the Vandermarks wouldn't notice until she could smooth the waters. Surely, with so grand an estate, they'd never even notice the paltry structures Emil had helped her erect on the roof, would they?

Because in her long line of failed engagements and thwarted dreams, her tiny weather station on the top of the Vandermark mansion was what gave meaning and purpose to Sophie's world. In a dying village where economic opportunities dwindled by the year, Sophie was part of a grand, national experiment to create the first system of accurate and reliable weather forecasts for anyone who chose to buy the morning newspaper. She'd never asked permission to install the weather station, but the roof of Dierenpark was now one of three thousand monitoring stations manned by volunteers who gathered climate data in hopes of creating accurate weather predictions that would make the world a safer place for everyone.

And she prayed Quentin Vandermark would not interfere with that.

Sophie heard the Vandermarks before she saw them. The clopping of horse hooves and the bumping of carriage wheels across the rocky front drive sounded like impending doom. Florence had put a kettle on to heat, and a bowl of Sophie's blueberry muffins and a Dutch sweet cake were at the center of the table, still warm from the oven and lending a comforting aroma of sweetened vanilla to the room.

Sophie sat at the kitchen table, rotating a mug of tea between her suddenly icy fingers. Why was she so anxious? They hadn't done anything wrong . . . or at least, they hadn't done anything the Vandermarks explicitly forbade them to do. It had been easy to feel like she belonged in this wonderful old house, but all that would change now that the real owners had returned. Sixty years—it had been *sixty years*—how was she supposed to know they would return with no warning?

Footsteps thudded up the porch steps. She had already unlocked the front door, since it would seem presumptuous to force Quentin Vandermark to knock for admittance into his own house.

He didn't knock. The front door banged open, and more heavy footsteps clomped on the hardwood floors.

"Where is she?" An angry voice roared through the old house, echoing off the walnut paneling in the grand foyer and hurting her ears.

Sophie sprang to her feet and headed to the entrance hall, where the group of imposing men trudged into the house. Mr. Gilroy passed her a tense smile, but the man whose bellow had shaken the rafters was a stranger to her. He was a slender man who leaned heavily on a cane as he lurched around the entrance hall. With dark hair and stormy gray eyes, his lean face was drawn tight with anger.

"Where is she?" he roared again as he limped toward the formal parlor, raising his cane long enough to strike at the draperies. Dust motes swirled in the air, and she feared the fragile silk might rip and come tearing down.

"Are you looking for me?" she asked calmly. Fighting fire with fire was rarely a good idea, and Sophie refused to do it.

He whirled around, shooting her a scorching glare. "Are you the one who has been telling ghost stories to my son? The one who terrified him so badly we can't get him out of the carriage?"

His voice lashed like a whip, and he was so daunting it was hard to look him in the face. Even the burly men in the grand foyer seemed cowed.

"Somehow I doubt I'm the cause of the boy's anxiety, Mr. Vandermark."

The man's eyes narrowed as he plodded across the parquet floor to scrutinize her. He would be a handsome man were he not so ferociously angry. With a lean face and high cheekbones, he looked like something straight out of a Brontë novel, and apparently he had the temper to match.

"Are you the person responsible for turning my home into an obscene tourist attraction? The one selling postcards and cookies down by the pier?"

"My name is Sophie van Riijn. I provide meals to the staff at the house, but I am not on your payroll, nor am I the cause of whatever has put you into a foul mood. I'd be happy to welcome you inside and get you all something to eat and drink. I imagine you are tired after your journey."

Mr. Gilroy stepped forward, unruffled by the raging tantrum of his employer. "Thank you, Miss van Riijn. We would be grateful."

Quentin Vandermark acted as though he hadn't heard. Leaning both hands on his cane, he scanned the impressive rooms on either side of the entrance hall. He seemed particularly fascinated by the portraits of a dozen Vandermark ancestors from earlier centuries, their powdered wigs looking strange to modern eyes. What must this man be thinking as he saw his ancestral estate for the first time? Sophie had been coming to this house since she was a child, but everything was new to Mr. Vandermark. He would need a guide just to find his way through the forty-room mansion.

"If you'll follow me to the kitchen, we have a kettle warming and some fresh blueberry muffins. I'm sorry we did not know of your arrival or we'd have prepared the dining room. Will Pieter be joining us?"

Mr. Vandermark tore his gaze from the old portraits. "He is in the carriage with his governess. I don't want him in the house until we establish the ground rules. My son has had a difficult year and is prone to fits of anxiety. Filling his head with tales of his ancestors floating dead in the river and people turning into hunchbacks from setting foot in this house is going to stop at once. Is that clear, Miss van Riijn?"

"Perfectly."

"And whoever is selling postcards with photographs of this home will cease and desist immediately."

Sophie tilted her head. "Artists and photographers have been featuring this house on their postcards for decades. We aren't responsible for that."

Reaching inside his coat, he grabbed a postcard and waved it in her face. "This postcard shows the *inside* of the house. Someone let them in to take those photographs, and I demand to know who."

Sure enough, the postcard he clenched in his fist was of the drawing room, sunlight streaming through the windows and fresh flowers in vases placed about the room. For scale, a little blond girl stood beside the fireplace, a bouquet of tulips in her hands. The photograph had been taken by her father more than twenty years ago, and Sophie was the little child, but she doubted Mr. Vandermark would recognize her.

"I believe that photograph was taken decades ago," she said. "I doubt you'll discover who is responsible. There has been a lot of turnover here at the house."

"So I gather. Dead people stumbling over rakes and dying of terrible diseases. Such charming tales you tell."

"Mr. Vandermark, the tour guides on the steamboats are all from Manhattan. If you have a complaint with their services, you will need to return to the city and take it up with them. All we do is tend to the house. Florence has the tea ready, if you'd like to follow me to the kitchen."

She didn't wait for a reply, but given the lumbering footsteps behind her, the men followed. Both Florence and Emil rose as they heard the group approach. Emil swept the cap from his head, brushing his straw-colored hair from his forehead with a nervous hand.

"This is Florence Hengeveld, the housekeeper here for more than forty years. And Emil Broeder has been keeping the grounds ever since he took over for his father two years ago."

"Tea?" Florence asked, lifting the copper kettle. The scent of Earl Grey filled the kitchen as Sophie began slicing a loaf of *ontbijtkoek*, a Dutch sweet cake spiced with cinnamon, ginger, and nutmeg.

Mr. Vandermark kicked out a stool from beneath the work table and twisted around to sit. His teeth clenched as he rubbed his knee, but he ignored the basket of blueberry muffins Florence pushed toward him.

"And what is *your* role here?" he asked, piercing Sophie with narrowed eyes.

She hedged. Apparently none of them had noticed the weather station on the roof, and now wasn't the time to discuss it. "My mother was the cook here before she died. There really isn't need for a permanent cook anymore, but I've always loved cooking, and Florence lets me use the kitchen to prepare a few meals for the staff each day. I also do a little baking now and then."

He reached inside his coat and then threw a packet of Dutch cookies on the counter. "Are you responsible for those?"

Her mouth went dry. She wasn't the only one to sell goodies to the tourists who stepped onto the pier each morning, but Sophie's baked goods were always the most popular. She sold cookies and sweet cakes to the vendors who manned the stalls near the pier and then gave the proceeds to her father. That money had paid for the town's only telegraph station.

"I am, but I haven't done anything wrong," Sophie said. "I don't use Vandermark money for the ingredients, and there is no crime in selling food to hungry travelers."

"Then let me outline the *crimes* for which I have evidence," he said in a clipped voice. "The servants at Dierenpark have participated in exploiting my home as an obscene tourist attraction. You have fueled malicious slander about the tragedies in my family. You have used this house in a manner I never authorized. You've done nothing wrong? Miss van Riijn, let me count the ways. Your wrongs surpass the depth and breadth and height a soul can reach. . . ."

His ability to mangle the immortal sonnet of Elizabeth Barrett Browning would have been amusing if she weren't so intimidated by him. She forced her voice to remain calm.

"I've never met someone who can take one of poetry's most remarkable passages about the purity of love and twist it into embittered screed on the spot," she said.

He quirked a brow, and for the first time, she saw a gleam of respect light his handsome features. "We all have our talents," he said dryly. The flash of humor was fleeting. His face iced over again as he fired another question at her. "How many tourists have you allowed into my house?"

"We don't allow tourists inside," Sophie said, wincing at the memory of telling Mr. Gilroy that on special occasions some tourists were welcomed in. Mr. Vandermark rose from the stool and stalked down the hall leading to the parlor where they relaxed once their daily chores were finished. It was an impressive room, with a bank of windows overlooking the river and a fire burning in the brick fireplace. A table beneath the window was full of antiques—a large Delft platter from the seventeenth century, a silver soup tureen embellished with arching dolphins for handles, even a few candlesticks from a medieval monastery. At the front of the table was a small card printed in Sophie's own handwriting.

Please don't touch.

It was proof they had allowed visitors into the home.

Mr. Vandermark stiffened as he glared at the note. He picked it up and carried it toward her, leaning heavily on his cane as he approached.

"If you allow no visitors, which of the servants need a reminder such as this?" he asked in a tight voice.

Heat flushed her face. She needed to confess what they'd been doing, but there wasn't an ounce of compassion or kindness in his expression. "On rare occasions we invite a select type of visitor—"

He cut her off. "And *on rare occasions* I believe the staff at Dierenpark are conspiring to violate every principle of loyalty on earth. You're fired. You're all fired. You have ten minutes to get off my property, and don't ever come back."

Sophie flinched. This estate was her refuge, her paradise on earth.

Mr. Gilroy stepped out of the shadows. "Quentin, perhaps we should wait . . ."

Sophie held her breath, praying for a reprieve. Mr. Vandermark seemed to sag and weaken as he hobbled toward a kitchen stool, easing onto it with a grimace. His face was ashen and drawn in pain. Perspiration beaded on his face, and when he dabbed at it with a handkerchief, Sophie noticed his hand trembled. Perhaps it was her imagination, but it seemed he was barely ahead of an avalanche of pain and sorrow gathering behind him. When he finally spoke, his voice was devoid of anger.

"Loyalty is important to me," he said with an exhausted, hollow tone. "I need to make this house a safe place for my son, and I don't trust any of you. It is clear that the misuse of Dierenpark has been occurring for decades. I want you out of here. The lot of you."

Behind her, Emil let out a mighty whoosh as though he'd been punched in the gut. Emil had lived his entire life on this estate. How was he going to get his wife and three children out in the space of ten minutes? Where would they go?

But even worse was Florence. The old woman had crumpled into a chair, her head sagging on her hunched shoulders. Florence had lived most of her life in this house. She started to quietly weep.

Sophie blanched as two of the fearsome men lumbered toward her. Instinctively, she stepped back. She'd never had such menacing glares directed at her, and it was intimidating.

"All right," she said quietly, picking up her cloak and folding it over her arm. "You'll find plenty to eat in the larder, and there is firewood on the back terrace. I'll help Florence collect her things, and we will be on our way."

But she would be back first thing tomorrow morning. There had to be a way to defuse the acrimony simmering inside Quentin Vandermark, and she just needed a bit of time to plan her attack. Her weapons wouldn't be menacing bodyguards or seething anger. She wouldn't fight on his level. But that didn't mean she intended to surrender. The real battle would begin tomorrow morning, and she wouldn't be put off easily.

2

"I'M SCARED of the dark."

Quentin tensed but wouldn't let frustration leak into his voice. "I know you are, Pieter, but we'll find the candles soon and light up the entire house. Come sit beside me."

They were in the kitchen, where the sunset filled the room with an eerie pink glow. Pieter was sullen as he flung himself onto the bench, and Quentin winced when the boy accidentally kicked his bad leg. Pain shot up from his shin, through his knee and thigh, finally hitting his spine. Dizzying pain swamped him, but he let no sign of it show before Pieter.

"Mr. Gilroy has gone on a hunt for some lanterns," he said as soon as he could deliver the sentence in a normal voice. "We'll stay here until he finds them."

Although it would be a good idea for Pieter to learn how to confront the dark sooner rather than later. There were no goblins or ghosts looming in the shadowy corners, but Pieter's imagination was likely to conjure them up at the least provocation. Pieter had been sleeping with a small light in his room ever since the incident last summer, and nine-year-old boys shouldn't need such crutches.

He ran a hand through Pieter's silky hair, leaning in to kiss the boy's head. Raising this child was the most important responsibility of his life, and so far he'd been failing. Coddling Pieter's fears hadn't worked. Neither had the parade of specialists and physicians hired by his grandfather. The only thing they had yet to try was forcing Pieter to directly confront his fears, and Quentin's time to pull the boy back onto a solid footing was growing short.

Because frankly, Quentin probably wasn't going to be alive much longer. His leg was getting worse with each operation, and his last doctor had warned he probably had no more than two years before his body finally failed him. How was he to raise this boy to manhood when the time was so short?

The day had been a catastrophe from beginning to end. For months he'd been preparing Pieter for this day, trying to erase the ominous tales Pieter had heard from his grandfather about the family curse and the haunted mansion that was the cause of it all. Pieter had become convinced he was destined to fall victim to the string of bad luck that plagued their family with each generation. The boy had wept a little this morning when he'd realized today was the day they'd be moving into Dierenpark, the mansion his grandfather had taught him to fear. Quentin had taken the boy onto their hotel balcony that overlooked Central Park and carefully explained there was no curse haunting their family. It all sprang from the jealous ramblings of people who took delight in the misfortunes of rich people. It had taken almost an hour, but Pieter finally relaxed enough to be willing to leave the hotel.

Then there were the problems getting the carriages up the hill. When Quentin went to town to arrange for another carriage, some morbid tour guide filled Pieter's head with dark tales that aroused every one of the boy's old fears. Then Quentin had stupidly fired the servants before he'd learned where the food, the privy, or the candles were.

At least they weren't hungry. A pot of stew had been simmering on the stove, and it was an explosion of flavorful seasoning, tender vegetables, and succulent beef unlike anything Quentin had ever experienced. Over the years, he had dined at the finest restaurants in Europe, but nothing compared with that stew. Perhaps they were all overtired and starved, but the moment they tasted the stew it was as if they were eating ambrosia from the heavens. And that Dutch sweet cake . . . with eight hungry men, Pieter, and a governess, each of them got only a single slice of cake, but it was sublime. Tensions had eased, people relaxed, and for a few moments it had felt like he'd made the right decision.

Then the sun started setting and Pieter's fear of the dark made him realize they didn't know where the lanterns were. The deepening gloom seemed ominous, but Quentin insisted they remain at Dierenpark even if they couldn't find the lanterns. This journey to the ancestral Vandermark estate was too important to turn away before their mission was complete.

"There is no reason to fear the dark," Quentin reasoned. "The earth has rotated away from the sun so that the people in China and India can enjoy the light. There is nothing evil in the dark. In a few hours the sun will be back."

"Grandpa says that at night goblins come out of the swamps to look for children who got caught outside. They dance around in circles on the lawn."

"And you believe such things?"

Pieter nodded. "That's why mushrooms spring up in circles overnight. That's what Grandpa said."

Quentin sighed. His grandfather had cared for Pieter for most of the past year while Quentin recuperated following his latest

29

surgery, and Nickolaas Vandermark had planted the seeds of superstition about the family curse into Pieter's gullible mind. Nickolaas was actually Pieter's great-grandfather, but it was a mouthful and simply easier for the boy to call him Grandpa. Pieter embraced his grandfather's endless superstitions far too easily, and now Quentin had to undo the damage.

"Pieter, I want you to repeat after me. If I can't see it or touch it, it doesn't exist."

Pieter did as instructed, his voice heavy with skepticism.

"The world is a predictable and rational place," Quentin continued. "Science can tell us precisely when the sun will rise and set. There are no goblins lurking in dark corners or hereditary curses that afflict innocent people for no earthly reason."

"Then why did my mother die?"

Quentin turned away to gather his thoughts. The last thing he wanted to discuss was Portia's death, sparked in part from her own irrational fears of the family's curse. He had to wash these poisonous superstitions from Pieter's mind before they ruined the boy. He had so little time remaining to guide Pieter into manhood, and he'd sit here until sunrise if it helped Pieter conquer his fears.

"Your mother died from cholera, not because of a ridiculous curse," he said patiently. "Repeat after me again. If I can't see it or touch it, it doesn't exist." The world operated on scientific principles, and he would allow Pieter no crutch of superstition in learning how to survive in it.

It was dark now, and Quentin braced himself for the long night ahead. It seemed that ever since his wife's death eight years ago, his life had become an endless night of darkness and despair, waiting for a dawn that never came. In a perfect world, he could promise Pieter that their lives would be filled with joy and sunlight. He wished he could teach Pieter that all it would take was integrity and faith to guide them into a safe and blessed world, but Quentin had long since given up believing in fairy tales.

By morning, Quentin was exhausted. During the night, Pieter had startled awake at every creak made by the old house. Quentin had tried to explain the effect cooling temperatures had on the expansion and contraction of building materials, but Pieter suspected it was ghosts or burglars. And just when they'd finally settled into a restless sleep, a thunderstorm had rolled through the valley, keeping them both awake until sunrise.

Thunder was one of the many things that terrified Pieter. "If you look in a mirror while it's thundering, you'll see a ghost," Pieter had said in a trembling voice. "Grandpa said so."

Quentin was bleary-eyed and exhausted as he dragged himself from bed. Pieter had finally slipped into a restless sleep, but Quentin was eager to explore Dierenpark.

The house was comfortable despite its imposing size. As an architect, he could immediately spot the places where some daring ancestor had tacked on a room or wing. The seventeenth-century rooms had low, wood-beamed ceilings and a coziness that came with their smaller dimensions. The rooms added in the eighteenth century had a stiff formality, with plaster walls, high ceilings, and an imposing scale. At some point, an orangery had been attached to the house, and the abundant glass panels captured the sun and regulated the heat to permit growing tropical plants and orchids.

As much as Quentin resented the staff who had been profiting off his family's tragedies, he couldn't criticize their care of the house, for the interior was in pristine condition. The bookshelves were filled with antique volumes, their leather bindings cleaned and oiled. The china cabinets displayed silver and crystal, all polished and in gleaming condition. The desk in the library was filled with paperwork that had been untouched for the past sixty years.

After he'd explored most of the ground floor, it was obvious the best place to work was going to be the large parlor adjacent to the kitchen. It was an older room with a low-beamed ceiling and a few settees and tables scattered about. A row of diamond-paned windows overlooked the river. The glass was slightly rippled, as was common of glass from the seventeenth century. The slight distortion made the river below seem to sparkle even more in the early-morning light.

Mr. Gilroy helped him lay out drafting paper on one of the tables close to the window, and he quickly sank into the day's work. He bid Mr. Gilroy to send Pieter to him as soon as the boy had dressed for the day.

"Are you sure you want Pieter to help with this?" Mr. Gilroy asked, his tone the embodiment of civility. "He seems a little young to learn the art of demolition."

"It is important for Pieter to see me at work," he said. Especially since Quentin had spent so much of the past year trapped in a convalescent hospital like a useless cripple. "I won't allow my son to join the class of the idle rich. He can choose any profession he wishes, except a life of leisure."

Despite his illness, Quentin had always been capable of gainful employment as an architect. He could no longer get out into the field to supervise construction, but he had been capable of drafting plans from his sickbed. Now that he was walking again, he'd mentor Pieter in the principles of architecture and scientific reasoning for as long as he could.

He took a sip of lousy coffee. None of them knew how to operate the percolating apparatus in the kitchen, and although Mr. Gilroy eventually got the contraption to work, bitter coffee grounds infused every sip. He took another taste, sucking on the grounds and trying not to laugh. How could two intelligent men be defeated by the simple task of brewing coffee?

A sudden peal of bells shattered the quiet of the morning, making him choke on the coffee. The bells came from a few feet behind him, buried somewhere in the walls. A doorbell? Mr. Gilroy looked equally startled but headed to the front door to check.

"The Vandermarks are not at home," he heard Mr. Gilroy's polite voice intone to whoever had the gall to ring their bell at eight o'clock in the morning. With his refined British accent, John Gilroy sounded proper enough to be butler to the queen.

"I don't need to see the Vandermarks," a sweet voice said. "I just need to pop up onto the roof for a few minutes."

It was the voice of the blond woman from yesterday. As much as she irritated him, he couldn't deny that she was probably the prettiest girl he'd ever seen on either side of the Atlantic. With flaxen blond hair and deep blue eyes, she looked like she ought to be flouncing through an alpine meadow in a flowy white blouse with a lace-up bodice. She had a heart-shaped face and a slim little nose and was the closest thing to an angel he'd ever seen. He'd been an angry brute yesterday, but nothing he'd said seemed to fluster her.

"You'd better talk to Mr. Vandermark about that," Mr. Gilroy said. "He was quite insistent that the household staff had been severed from employment."

"But I'm not part of the household staff. I work for the government. And I need to get onto the roof."

"Gilroy, send her back here!" Quentin hollered from his seat at the table.

A moment later she arrived, sadly minus the charming alpine costume but looking every bit as lovely in a simple gown with her hair in a casual braid worn over one shoulder. It annoyed him to see her looking so pretty first thing in the morning.

"Miss van Riijn, correct?"

"Yes, but everyone calls me Sophie."

"Fine. You're fired, Sophie."

Smiling, she set a covered basket on the table. "I brought some fresh scones. They're almond."

"Excellent. Leave the scones, but you're still fired." It aggravated him that she found his comment amusing.

"But I've never worked for you, so you can't really fire me, can you?" She drifted closer to the table, gazing through the window with a wistful expression on her face. "I always love this time of day. I like to stand at this exact spot, where I can see the goldfinches playing in the birch trees while I drink a cup of coffee and watch the sun rise. It is a perfect place to gather my thoughts and count my blessings."

He fought not to roll his eyes. "Miss van Riijn, please be aware that I am violently allergic to your brand of doe-eyed sentimentality. That much sugary optimism spilled into the atmosphere this early in the morning is liable to render us all comatose."

She cocked her head at a charming angle. "I don't understand what you just said, but I think it was an insult. Are you sure you wouldn't like a scone?"

He schooled his face into an impassive mask. It took a barrel of gall to waltz in here after being fired yesterday, and yet she'd slipped past Mr. Gilroy with ease and kept him nattering like a magpie. She was either a master of subversive tactics or was exactly what she appeared to be: a lone, naïve daisy standing in a field, begging to be shot for target practice. He normally did not feel much sympathy for people who exuded bottomless good cheer, but there was something oddly attractive about her. Not that he would let it soften him.

"I'm still waiting for you to explain your entirely unwelcome visit."

"I need to get up onto the roof to check the weather station. I take measurements every morning, and there was a storm last night, so it's especially important for me to check the rain gauge right away."

"A weather station? Explain yourself."

"It's very exciting," Sophie said. "The government has a new agency called the Weather Bureau, and they've set up thousands of stations all across the country where volunteers keep track of the climate. After I take the readings, I telegraph the information to Washington, where scientists chart all the data onto huge maps and try to predict the weather. They've gotten very good at alerting people when trouble is on the horizon."

Admirable, but he was still peeved this had been taking place on Vandermark property without their permission.

"What exactly is up on my roof?"

For the first time, she had the good sense to look a little apprehensive. "Just a metal shed to keep the equipment dry and protected from the wind. There's a barometer, a thermometer, a weather vane, and a rain gauge. I'll just step upstairs and be a few moments."

"You'll do no such thing, other than make arrangements to get that equipment off my roof. It was presumptuous of you to set up a private business in my house."

"But it's not a business, I'm a volunteer. There are three thousand weather stations in this country and the government can't afford to pay us, so we do it for free."

"Then you're an idiot. If the government valued your work, they'd find a way to pay for it. I don't want you tromping through my house every morning, so you'll have to find another place to work your acts of goodness and mercy. Now get out of here. You're trespassing."

A blush stained her cheeks, a sign he was getting to her, which was good. She had participated in a gross misuse of his property and ought to feel at least a little shame.

Instead, it appeared she was ready to challenge him.

"Sir, I have been coming to this house to take climate readings for the past nine years. I have come every single morning without fail. Through ice storms and floods. On every Easter and every Christmas. I came when I had influenza and could barely walk a straight line. I came on the day my mother died and on the day she was buried." Her voice wobbled a little, but instead of dissolving in tears, she straightened her spine and got stronger.

"Maybe some people don't understand loyalty," she continued, "but there are thousands of farmers and sailors who need me to take those measurements and get the data to Washington. They depend on accurate weather forecasts based on something more than irrational and superstitious guesswork. Our predictions are based on a solid foundation of scientific fact. I won't let a rich, privileged outsider dissuade me from that duty."

Quentin didn't move a muscle. Didn't let a hint of emotion show on his face. He stared at her until she lost a little starch and started to fidget.

"Go upstairs and take your measurements," he said quietly.

The way she sucked in a quick little breath indicated she was surprised, but she shouldn't be. If she knew the first thing about him, it was that his entire life was devoted to the triumph of science over superstition and quackery. He knew very little about the Weather Bureau, but if the men in Washington were basing their findings on real data rather than superstition, he would support it.

"Go on," he prodded.

She flashed him a little smile and darted for the hallway. He clenched his fist, irritated that her smile appealed to him. A girl like Sophie van Riijn probably had healthy young men all over the village lining up for her affections. The last thing she'd welcome was a crippled, embittered recluse who couldn't stand on his own two feet without the aid of a cane.

The moment the door closed behind her, he glanced at Mr. Gilroy. "Follow her. Find out what's up there."

3

SOPHIE DASHED UP TO THE ROOF, grateful for the brief reprieve from the dangerous man downstairs. He looked like he drank vinegar for breakfast, and she wasn't sure how to get on his good side. Or if he even had a good side.

She didn't want to move her weather station, for the government was exacting in their requirements for site selection. The stations needed to be high off the ground, with no neighboring buildings or natural impediments to interfere with wind readings. The roof of Dierenpark was perfect, and the fact that she loved this old estate made it a natural choice.

A wide section on the roof had been created as a widow's walk with a fine view of the river. There was a time when ships laden with furs and timber left from the Vandermark pier to transport their goods to the mighty trading ports of Rotterdam, London, and the West Indies—but that was long ago. The Vandermarks had moved their shipping empire to Manhattan, and now the pier was only a shadow of its former glory.

She was surprised when the butler joined her on the roof, but he seemed to be a kind man, despite his imposing appearance.

"Is Mr. Vandermark always so difficult?" she asked the butler. She didn't want to seem rude, but she needed to know what she was up against in order to help Florence and Emil get their jobs back. Last night, Sophie had found space for Florence and Emil at her father's hotel, but that couldn't last for long. The hotel was barely surviving on the thin trickle of tourists, and they couldn't offer the rooms to non-paying guests for very long.

"It has always been a privilege to work for the Vandermarks," Mr. Gilroy said, his smooth voice the epitome of diplomacy.

"Yes, but what's it *like?*" she pressed as she marked down the rain measurements in her journal.

"It has been interesting," Mr. Gilroy replied. "Mr. Vandermark's work as an architect has taken us throughout the world. We've lived in Hamburg, Cairo, and Amsterdam. We rarely stay anywhere more than a year, so I've seen most of Europe, Scandinavia, and America. We lived for a year in Moscow and spent a week in the czar's palace."

It was hard to imagine living in so many interesting places, but the Vandermarks were one of the richest families in America and had homes and estates all over the world. She'd spent her entire life within a few miles of this spot, but she liked it that way. She felt at peace here and had no ambition to leave it.

It seemed Mr. Gilroy appreciated this view, as well. "It's so tranquil here," he said as he braced his forearms on the ledge, his face wistful as he surveyed the miles of rolling hills blanketed by pine, sycamore, and spruce trees. An eagle soared on an updraft, hovering on the wind before peeling away to the wilderness below.

She joined Mr. Gilroy at the overlook, closing her eyes to feel the soft breeze on her face. "I love it up here," she said. "Somehow it feels like I am at the edge of something very special, with all of creation spread out before me. I feel closer to

God here. When I'm troubled, there is no place I'd rather be than right here at Dierenpark."

"Forgive me, Miss van Riijn, but yesterday the tour guide mentioned a young woman and her three fiancés. I presume he was referring to you?"

"That was me," she admitted. "I've been ready to walk down the aisle three times but never quite got there. Losing Albert was the hardest."

Over the next hour, Mr. Gilroy listened as she poured her heart out. Albert was a widower who'd owned the apothecary shop in town, and he'd been almost twenty years older than she. At first he was reluctant because of the difference in their ages, but over time the affinity between them became impossible to deny and they got engaged after only three months of courtship. Then Albert began having difficulty with his breathing. They'd thought it would pass quickly, but the lung specialist he'd consulted in the city had told him otherwise. Within five months he was dead.

Albert had been her third fiancé and, in hindsight, the only one she'd truly loved. It had been more than a year since he'd died, but she still thought of him daily.

"And the other two? How did they die?" Mr. Gilroy asked gently. For a moment she was confused, but then she remembered Marten's ghoulish assertion that all her fiancés *came to a bad end*.

"They're both still alive," Sophie answered. "But Roger Wilson is in prison and probably will be for at least another year."

Roger had been her second fiancé, and they'd become engaged when she was twenty-two. He was a clerk at the bank, and she'd thought he would be a good father and provider. She desperately wanted children, and Roger adored her, bringing her endless presents and painting wonderful pictures of what their life could be like. Later she learned that all the presents were bought with funds he embezzled from the bank. He claimed it was because he wanted to please her and a clerk's salary would never be good enough for a girl like her.

"Roger never really knew me," Sophie said with a sad smile. "Money doesn't matter to me nearly so much as needing to feel safe. What girl doesn't want to feel safe and protected? Marriage to a man who lined his pockets by stealing was a guaranteed lifetime of insecurity. I'm lucky to have learned the truth before we married."

Mr. Gilroy said nothing, but his gentle face radiated sympathy, which was a relief after the way others in the village had treated the scandal. They had whispered behind their hands and snickered as she passed. It was mortifying to have been dazzled by Roger's gifts and flattery. She rarely talked to anyone about the shameful incident, but something about Mr. Gilroy's kindly demeanor made her feel like she could share anything with him.

The wind ruffled his hair, and he looked at her with compassion and waited to hear the tragic tale of her third fiancé.

"My other fiancé was Marten Graaf, the tour guide who was so gleefully recounting the story yesterday morning."

The way Mr. Gilroy blanched summoned a bubble of laughter from Sophie. "Marten and I were childhood sweethearts. We were promised to one another forever and were supposed to get married when I was eighteen. Six days before the wedding, he got cold feet and fled to New York City. The only *tragedy* about Marten is that he's making a living by exaggerating stories to appeal to the tourists."

"I thought I caught a whiff of hogwash arising from him," Mr. Gilroy said.

She had to laugh at that. "It was a lucky escape." Although it hadn't felt so at the time. Sophie had always believed she was meant to be a wife and a mother, and she couldn't understand why God had given her this longing if she was to be forever disappointed. Her entire being churned with hope and the need to be useful. Maybe that was why she put such stock in tending the weather station.

"Who are those people watching the house?"

Sophie followed Mr. Gilroy's gaze. Nestled in a clearing on the edge of the property, a handful of artists had set up easels and were laying out supplies.

"Artists come here all the time to paint or take photographs."

The way Mr. Gilroy scrutinized the group of artists was odd. He looked as fierce as a hawk ready to pounce.

"They're harmless," she assured him, hoping this wasn't going to be a problem. Most tourists came through on the steamboats and lingered for only an hour, buying a few trinkets or something to eat. Sophie was proud of how she'd managed to convince the steamboat companies to stop at Dierenpark. It generated a modest revenue, but it wasn't enough to support the people of New Holland. The artists were different. They flocked to the Hudson River Valley to paint the natural splendor and the gothic beauty of Dierenpark. Sometimes they came for weeks or months, living in her father's hotel and patronizing the local establishments. The town needed the patronage of the artists.

"Do these people come regularly?"

"Almost every day," she admitted. "The house tends to be their favorite subject, but they also paint landscapes, and the water lilies at the base of the cliff are especially popular."

"Show me."

Mr. Gilroy's tone was tense, and his concern still seemed odd, but she'd humor him since it was important to have him on her side. He seemed to be the only one of the group that had arrived yesterday with an ounce of compassion.

"Do you see that crook in the river where it curves in closer to the house?"

Mr. Gilroy nodded.

"That inlet has always been called Marguerite's Cove, named after the original settler's wife. It's a strange little cove where oysters thrive, even though they've died almost everywhere else in the river. And over the oyster bed there are water lilies. Normally lilies only grow in fresh water. We are forty miles from the ocean, so the water is brackish, and science says it shouldn't be possible for those lilies to grow, and yet they thrive. They bloom every morning and release a heavenly fragrance. Nothing seems to kill them."

Mr. Gilroy braced his hands on the ledge, peering over to study the bend in the river as though hypnotized. "That's the spot where Karl Vandermark's body was found."

"Yes." She'd rather not dwell on the mysterious death of Karl Vandermark. It had happened sixty years ago and they'd probably never learn what caused a healthy man in the prime of life to die for no apparent reason. "It's a lovely spot, and aside from the house, the lilies are what the artists who come here love to paint."

"They'd have to be on Vandermark land to see the lilies," Mr. Gilroy said.

"I suppose so." She never discouraged the artists from setting up their easels, even when they strayed onto Vandermark land. It was a lovely spot and it seemed petty to chase them away.

"Quentin won't like it. You'll need to tell the artists they can't trespass on private land."

She turned to face him. "I understand he is entitled to privacy, but if Mr. Vandermark intends to live in New Holland, he shouldn't alienate the town by banishing the artists. The artists and tourists who come here are this town's lifeblood."

"We haven't come here to live," he said.

"Then why are you here?"

Mr. Gilroy's face was a little sad as he scanned the natural splendor of the countryside, the wild gardens, even her little weather station.

"It seems a shame," he said sadly, "but we've come to tear the house down. Mr. Vandermark is drawing up the demolition plans as we speak. A pity, but in a month this house will be nothing but a pile of rubble on the ground."

It couldn't be true. Even Quentin Vandermark couldn't be so pointlessly cruel and nasty as to destroy a house that was a landmark for the entire Hudson River.

Sophie grabbed the banister railing as she whirled down another flight of stairs, her feet barely touching the treads. This house dated all the way back to 1635, when the first Vandermarks traded with the Indians on this land. The cannon used to battle the French was still propped up on the edge of the cliff. This house was a microcosm of American history, and that horrible man wanted to waltz in and tear it down for no earthly reason?

She raced to the ground floor, following voices back to the kitchen, but she drew up short, stunned at the sight before her. Pieter sat at the old kitchen dining table where the staff took their meals. His father sat on the bench beside him, his arm draped affectionately around the boy's shoulders as Pieter read in halting words from a fat volume laid out on the table. The boy spoke in Dutch, his father's finger tracing along the page and correcting his pronunciation. It was a poignant sight, triggering a wellspring of deep longing and unfulfilled dreams.

Sophie froze, bewildered by this rush of unwelcome attraction. It was embarrassing to feel such things for a surly man like Quentin Vandermark, but he looked kind and protective with his arm around Pieter. Handsome, too. She swallowed hard and tried to smother this strange sense of yearning. Pieter looked up from the book, sending her a wide smile.

"Look at you, reading the old language just like a real

Dutchman," Sophie said with an approving nod. "My family quit speaking Dutch generations ago."

"My father does business in the Netherlands," Pieter said. "He's a famous architect who builds things all over the world."

An architect who seems to prefer destroying things rather than constructing them. "So I hear." She tamped down the bitter sentiment, scrambling for a polite way to ask what germ of insanity had warped Quentin Vandermark's mind into thinking the demolition of a national treasure was a worthwhile use of his skills.

"I've heard rumors about the long-term fate of this house that I find difficult to believe," she said, hoping her choice of words would fly over Pieter's head, but the boy understood her perfectly.

"We're going to blow the house up," Pieter said, pride in his voice. "My father knows how to use dynamite."

Dynamite? This was even worse than she'd imagined. "Now, why would you do such a thing?" She tried to sound lighthearted, but this was awful, a desecration of something wonderful and rare.

"Because the house is cursed, and I hate it," Pieter said.

His father sent him a sharp glare. "Pieter . . ."

The boy cleared his throat. "Um, we're doing it because Grandpa asked us to. The house belongs to him, not us. We're just doing it as a favor."

"We're doing it out of *loyalty*," Mr. Vandermark said pointedly to his son. "We both owe Nickolaas a great deal, and it is his wish to return this piece of land to its natural state, without a house on top of it."

She clenched the back of a chair so hard her knuckles hurt. This house was everything to her. It was beauty and mystery and a tiny piece of paradise. This man didn't know the first thing about Dierenpark or he wouldn't be so cavalier about tearing it down.

"You can't," she said weakly. "The town depends on this house. It would be wanton destruction to tear it down. An unimaginable catastrophe . . ."

There was more she wanted to add, but Pieter interrupted. "Do you know where the lanterns are? We couldn't find them, and it was dark last night."

A guilty pleasure took root, for if Mr. Vandermark hadn't fired the servants so abruptly, they wouldn't have been in the dark. Nevertheless, Pieter wasn't to blame for what had happened, so she sent him a smile.

"Do you want to come hunting for them with me? I suspect I can find a few lanterns in short order."

Pieter glanced back at the table. "I have to finish my breakfast first."

The only thing on the kitchen table was a half-eaten apple that looked like it had been plucked off the tree outside. "All you've had is apples?"

Neither answered, but given the way Mr. Vandermark's mouth tightened, she'd guessed right.

"We didn't bring any food with us," Pieter said. "And I don't think anyone knows how to cook."

Well, at last. A chance for her to become indispensable. "There are eggs in the larder outside, and some cheese, as well. Why don't I fix you all a nice breakfast?"

Pieter's delight was comical. "Yes, please!"

She motioned for Pieter to follow her to the larder and help carry in the food, but Mr. Vandermark's voice stopped her.

"Wait until I have one of my men accompany you."

"But the larder is right outside the back door."

"You will wait for one of my men to accompany you."

The demand didn't seem odd to Pieter, but it seemed a waste of time to Sophie. The larder was visible from the window, a mere twenty yards away.

A bull-necked man finally arrived and introduced himself as Ratface. Sophie tried not to blanch. A disfiguring scar tracked across the middle of his forehead, through his eyebrow, and continued down his cheek, where it disappeared behind his ear. It was hard to even look at him, but surely he didn't deserve such a horrible name.

"I only need to go to the larder outside the back door, Mr. Ratface."

"Just Ratface," he growled, leading the way.

Pieter didn't seem to mind the surly man, and as they gathered eggs and cheese from the larder, he peppered her with questions the entire time. How long had she lived in New Holland? Why wasn't she married? Would she come back to cook them lunch and dinner, too?

Sophie fielded the questions with good-natured aplomb but felt the horrible scrutiny of Mr. Ratface the entire time. Why would Mr. Vandermark have such rude servants? She had stored some cranberry muffins and a bowl of cherries in the cold larder. They wouldn't last much longer, so she scooped them up, as well.

Things didn't improve once they returned to the kitchen. The rude servant plopped himself on a stool in the corner of the kitchen, watching her every move as though she might be preparing to steal the silver. From the dining table, Mr. Vandermark also watched her.

She would not let these men disturb her. After lighting the oven, she popped the muffins inside the warming compartment to take the chill off. Cracking eggs into the bowl with practiced ease, she added a bit of cream, salt, and pepper and then began the soothing, rhythmic whisking of the eggs.

Preparing and serving food had always been a joy, for it made her appreciate the abundance of the world. It took over a year of sunshine and water for a tree to produce the cherries gleaming from the china bowl, and Sophie imagined she could smell those endless hours of sunlight distilled into the small piece of fruit. The black pepper came all the way from the wild Malabar coast of India, yet the tiny fragments of cracked pepper still carried an intense kick of flavor reminiscent of the land where it had been grown. The honey she drizzled over the cranberry muffins was a miracle of nature, gathered from thousands of wildflowers and transformed into this amazing substance so sweet it tasted like a summer day.

Pieter seemed eager to help and drew near as she poured the eggs into a cast-iron skillet sizzling with melted butter.

"See how the heat causes the bubbles to rise in the mixture?" Sophie asked. "I need to keep the eggs moving so the proteins in the eggs don't burn, but you can't stir too hard. That will cause all the air to escape. I spent a good two minutes whisking the mixture, and we want these eggs to be light and fluffy, right?"

"Can I stir?" Pieter asked.

It was an easy task, but the skillet was on an open flame and the handle was hot. She glanced to Mr. Vandermark for permission. His face was stern, but he gave a quick nod of consent.

"I'll hold the handle, and you can use the spoon to keep the eggs moving." She loved the way the boy slid in front of her, so trusting as he took the wooden spoon to nudge the eggs around the pan. "Perfect!" she said. "I'll bet you've done this before."

The boy seemed to grow a little taller. "Nope! This is my first time."

"Well, you're doing wonderfully. Keep stirring while I drop the cheese in."

Two more of the brutish-looking servants and the governess joined them in the kitchen. With the scents of herbs and warm cranberry muffins permeating the house, it wouldn't be long before the rest were here.

They were an imposing lot, all of them grim, suspicious, and rude, but Sophie wasn't going to let them spoil her morning, for there was something about sharing a meal that automatically brought people together. It was hard to resent someone you were breaking bread with. Forcing lightness into her tone, she glanced at the men and asked, "Who is going to set the table?"

They looked as confused as if she'd asked them to begin square dancing, but she refused to back down as she nodded to the top shelf. "The plates are over there, and you'll find a cloth for the table in the sideboard."

A couple of the men reluctantly moved toward the sideboard, and Sophie tipped the eggs onto a serving platter. Within minutes, a cloth was spread, the plates and pewter forks laid out, and Sophie carried platters of food to the table.

Sophie was not a perfect woman. She hadn't been brilliant in school, she had a catastrophic history with romantic relationships, and her only sense of purpose in the world came from gathering and reporting weather statistics each day. But for all her shortcomings, she was an extraordinary cook, and everyone in New Holland knew it.

Soon Quentin Vandermark would know it, too.

It didn't take long for groans of satisfaction to rise as the men began wolfing down the eggs. The governess was more restrained, but she allowed a grateful smile as Sophie brought the basket of warm cranberry muffins to the table.

"Those smell so delicious I think I'm about to faint," the governess said as she reached for a muffin. The men around the table grunted and nodded as they reached for the basket.

Then she noticed Mr. Vandermark remained rigid in his chair across the room, glowering at her. "Aren't you joining us?" Sophie asked him.

All the heads swiveled, forks paused in midair. Everyone looked guilty, as if they hadn't realized they dove into their meals without waiting for their employer to join them.

"I've already eaten," Quentin said bluntly.

"Are you sure?" Mr. Gilroy asked. "Apples aren't very satisfying compared to this feast. This may be the best breakfast I've ever had." The butler lifted a heaping forkful of eggs to his mouth and moaned with pleasure.

Mr. Vandermark's face looked like it was carved from stone. "Food is a commodity," he said. "A product that is bought and sold to fuel the human body, nothing more. I've got work to do."

The vinegar in his tone stifled the merry conversation from moments ago. All that could be heard was the scratching of his pencil and the clatter of silverware against the plates as the guards ate in silence.

Sophie returned to the kitchen, systematically cracking another round of eggs and seasoning them with practiced hands. Quentin Vandermark was going to be a challenge. He didn't seem to have a trace of warmth or compassion in his entire body. He wouldn't even accept *food* from her—how was she going to convince him not to destroy Dierenpark? Or perhaps coax him into rehiring Emil and Florence?

All her life, Sophie had tried to look for the good in people. No matter how surly, disrespectful, or difficult, she believed there was a spark of goodness inside each person, but she had never met anyone quite like Quentin Vandermark. He seemed clouded by an iron cynicism he hid behind like a shield.

Would it be possible for such a ferocious man to ever soften? She sensed there was a seed of humor and decency buried deep inside, but it would take professional mining equipment to dig it out and drag it to the surface, and he would probably fight tooth and nail to stop it from happening. Sometimes unhappy people were like that. It was easier to remain locked in their fortress of discontent rather than risk the pain associated with emerging into the light of day.

She finished breakfast quickly, for it was important to get

back to town and telegraph today's weather data to Washington by noon. Each time she sent off the messages, she liked to imagine the men in Washington as they added her data alongside the messages from thousands of other volunteers. The scientists would transfer her information onto their giant maps and try to make sense of it all. Perhaps it was pathetic that her entire sense of self-worth was based on this simple duty, but most women her age had husbands or children to give them a sense of purpose. She had daydreams of anonymous scientists in Washington who breathlessly awaited her daily messages.

She couldn't bear to think what would happen if Dierenpark was torn down. She had to convince Quentin to leave the house alone, but how did one appeal to a man who had no curiosity, no desire, no kindness?

She would have to think of a way. She could not let Dierenpark be destroyed.

⁂

Sophie's father was equally horrified at the prospect of the great mansion's demise. Sitting alongside him behind the mahogany front counter in the hotel lobby, she could barely wait until he finished telegraphing her climate data before recounting everything she'd learned that morning.

Her father was the perfect ally to help save the house. Not only was he the mayor of New Holland, he was also an attorney who was prepared to use those skills to thwart Quentin Vandermark.

After the Vandermarks had left New Holland sixty years ago, the timber mills closed and industry dwindled. The village survived on fishing, but over the decades the fish stocks declined and the fishermen were forced to leave. There was no longer enough business to support an attorney in the village, and since serving as mayor paid nothing, her father poured his life's savings into this hotel in hopes of encouraging the tourist industry. He pressured journalists to write favorable articles about the climate and scenic beauty of New Holland. He took out advertisements in Manhattan publications touting their close proximity to the city and a balmier climate than the Adirondacks. Sophie had used her friendship with Marten Graaf to encourage the steamships to add Dierenpark to their stops along the Hudson before heading up toward the more popular tourist destinations in the Catskills and Adirondacks.

Her father had helped fuel the legend of the Vandermark family's tragic history, although he hadn't made it up from whole cloth. Despite their staggering fortune, the Vandermarks had been visited by tragedy in each generation, beginning with the first two brothers to emigrate from the Netherlands. While one brother worked on building the house and constructing the pier, the other traveled far and wide to form alliances with the various Indian groups in the vicinity. It proved to be his downfall when he was murdered by one of the Indian tribes only five years after arriving. That tragic death seemed to have set the tone for the bad luck, suspicion, and bitterness that grew with each generation. Even after the family fled Dierenpark, tragedy seemed to follow them, with a string of untimely deaths and scandals that happened no matter where they lived.

Her father paced the lobby of the hotel, rubbing his jaw in concentration. Whenever there was a problem, Jasper van Riijn could usually solve it. The hotel lobby was a perfect example. Five years ago, her father decided that cultivating a lively sense of community would help dissuade people from moving away from the village. He redesigned the hotel's lobby with decorative moldings and fresh paint, filling the space with comfortable seating and tables for people who wished to socialize or play cards. Ferns in brass planters helped warm the space, and the room had become so popular it now doubled as the town hall. Sophie took a seat at one of the tables as her father paced.

"What about the mills?" he asked. "Do you think they'll reopen the timber mills?"

"I don't think they intend to stay for very long. After destroying the house, they plan to return the land to its natural state. They didn't give any indication of wanting to stay in New Holland beyond that."

"You said the house belongs to the grandfather, not this Quentin fellow. Perhaps we can take some legal cover there. Unless they have a written affidavit from the old man, I intend to stop it."

Sophie shook her head. "They claimed to be demolishing the house on the grandfather's orders. I'm not sure the village has a right to tell them what they can or can't do on their own property."

"Sophie, there won't *be* a village if that house goes," her father retorted.

"What if the Weather Bureau decides to build a climate observatory here?"

Her father sighed. "Not that again," he said, and Sophie winced at the frustration in his voice.

In recent years, the Weather Bureau had begun building upgraded facilities along the coastlines and rivers of the eastern seaboard. The new stations were far more prestigious than the volunteer weather station Sophie manned on top of Dierenpark. Each observatory would have at least ten employees, and Sophie desperately wanted one of those jobs for herself.

Ever since hearing of the new climate observatories, Sophie had been steadily working to get one located in New Holland. She had already written to the Weather Bureau, asking how to nominate a prospective location. She began compiling a proposal that explained New Holland's key location for transmitting news up and down the Hudson, and had started a petition to demonstrate the town's support. She even used her modest savings to fund a geographical survey of the surrounding area to tout the location.

"We are on an important river." Sophie hoped her voice didn't sound too defensive. "We've got high altitude, which will make our signal lamps visible for miles in all directions. If I could only—"

"Sophie, they'll never hire you," her father said. "I can't bear to see you longing for something that will never happen. It's time to give up this fool's dream."

She swallowed hard. It hurt that even her own father didn't believe in her abilities. Over the past few months, her work to collect signatures for the petition had made her something of a laughingstock in town. The postman pointed out two spelling errors in the petition she drafted. Marten reminded her that she'd failed natural science in school and questioned why the government would trust her judgment.

No one believed in her. No one thought she should even try.

In a perfect world, she would already be a wife and a mother, but she'd failed three times to land that dream. She had to do *something* with the rest of her life, and over the past few months she had drafted and rewritten her proposal for an upgraded climate observatory at least a dozen times—but had yet to submit it. She didn't know anything about how to write a proper business proposal and was groping blindly in the dark. Maybe in fifty years she would be an old spinster still fiddling with this outlandish proposal, but it was better than giving up, for nothing was more debilitating to the human soul than the loss of all hope.

Sophie didn't have much to brag about in this world, but her ability to nurture the flame of hope in the face of despair had been her salvation all her life. And that meant she intended to fight to win a climate observatory for New Holland, just as she was going to fight for Dierenpark.

4

QUENTIN SCRUTINIZED THE TRAPPINGS in the formal parlor. Altogether, there was probably a million dollars' worth of artwork, silver, Turkish carpets, and imported furniture in this mansion, and his grandfather was convinced the curse would somehow survive unless it was all destroyed, which was an obscene waste. The old man was growing more paranoid and irrational with age, but loyalty drove Quentin to carry out his grandfather's wishes to the letter. After all, he owed Nickolaas a debt that could never be repaid.

He wandered to an identical room on the other side of the entrance hall. In the home's glory days, these rooms surely hosted lavish balls and splendid gatherings. Just looking at the portraits gracing the walls was testament to the long line of generals and merchant princes in his family's history. Their faces were somber, grim even, but weren't all portraits from that era gloomy? Something about those faces staring at him was disconcerting, as if they knew what he intended to do. Would they approve? Even in the seventeenth century, the legend of the Vandermark curse had begun to haunt their name.

In the kitchen at the rear of the house, he could hear Pieter and his governess bickering about dinner. Mr. Gilroy had driven into town this afternoon to buy food and hire a cook but had returned with only a sack of groceries. Apparently, cooks were scarce in New Holland, and Quentin had ordered the governess, Miss McCarthy, to do her best preparing the food for their evening meal.

It wouldn't rival what Sophie had cooked for them this morning, which smelled so good he'd been hanging on to his seat by his fingernails to stop from lunging across the table and devouring everything in sight. He was a rational man who controlled his baser instincts, and everything about Sophie van Riijn rubbed him the wrong way. She was too cheerful. Sunny. People like that had no conception of what the real world was like, and he'd survive on apples before he'd eat a morsel of food she cooked.

"We'll have bread and cheese for dinner tonight." Miss Mc-Carthy's voice sounded from the kitchen. "I won't risk our lives by trying to light the fire in that stove. We'll just have to wait until your father hires a proper cook."

"But I'm hungry," Pieter whined.

Miss McCarthy's reply was too soft to hear, but Quentin hoped she wouldn't tolerate that sort of petulant behavior. Pieter had grown soft and spoiled while living with his grandfather, and it was time for the boy to grow up and start acting his age.

Quentin moved closer to the kitchen to listen in. Miss Mc-Carthy was trying to tempt Pieter with the fresh fruits and vegetables Mr. Gilroy brought from town. "These carrots are perfectly fine eaten raw. And the mushrooms, too. There's plenty to eat."

"I don't eat mushrooms," Pieter said. "They spring up overnight where the evil fairies dance in circles on the lawn. If you come too close, the fairies will trap you inside and you'll never get out."

Miss McCarthy laughed. "How right you are! My grandmother used to say that if you run around the fairy ring nine times, it confuses the fairies and the people trapped inside can get away."

Quentin stalked into the kitchen as fast as his bad leg allowed. After months trying to undo the damage done by Nickolaas, the last thing he wanted was a silly governess reinforcing Pieter's irrational beliefs. He stood in the doorway to the kitchen, and the governess looked up in surprise.

"Miss McCarthy, you may collect your belongings," he said bluntly. "Mr. Gilroy will provide you with two weeks' severance pay, and then you will be escorted back to New York. Tonight."

"Did I do something wrong?" she gasped.

"You were warned that my son often indulges in harmful superstitions, and that when he voices them you were to require him to say that if he can't see it or touch it, it is not real. You have not done so. I will inform Mr. Gilroy of your imminent departure."

There was no need. Mr. Gilroy was leaning against the doorframe on the opposite side of the kitchen, watching the incident with disapproving eyes. It didn't matter. If Mr. Gilroy didn't like it, he could quit.

Which might be a good thing. It was hard not to like Mr. Gilroy, but the man was nothing more than a spy for his grandfather. Mr. Gilroy didn't even bother to deny it anymore, but Quentin tolerated it because if he got rid of the butler, Nickolaas would figure out how to slip another spy into his household who might do considerable damage before Quentin spotted him.

After Miss McCarthy was hustled from the kitchen, Quentin glanced at the bowl of freshly washed mushrooms amid the vegetables on the kitchen work table. Limping forward, he scooped one up and popped it into his mouth. The mushroom was raw and flavorless, but he locked eyes with Pieter as he chewed and swallowed. The boy looked mortified, as though Quentin had just swallowed a live goldfish.

"You know what you're having for dinner," he said firmly.

Pieter shrank two inches, and his eyes grew wide. "Please don't make me," he whispered.

"Mushrooms are a perfectly healthy food. They grow quickly because after a heavy rain they expand with water at a rapid rate, and that's why it appears they spring up overnight. They are an outgrowth of decayed tree roots, which explains why they grow in circles. It's science, Pieter. It has nothing to do with fairies or magic or anything else your grandfather told you."

Three of the bodyguards loitered in the hallway outside the kitchen, waiting for dinner. Quentin pushed the bowl of mushrooms toward Pieter then used his cane to pull the bread, fruit, and cheese to the opposite side of the table.

"When you get two mushrooms down, you can eat anything else you want. Otherwise you'll go to bed with nothing."

Pieter's face froze in revulsion, but Quentin wasn't going to coddle the boy. He left the kitchen, pushing past the men gathered in the hall.

"Seems a little mean, sir," Ratface muttered as Quentin passed.

He stiffened. Ratface was the toughest of his bodyguards, plucked straight from the squalid underbelly of New York where he ran interference for Irish street gangs. He'd hired Ratface because he was a sharp-eyed man capable of forecasting the behavior of gutter rats. The Vandermark family was a perpetual target for kidnappers, lawsuits, and blackmailers, and he needed ruthless men to be on constant surveillance. To be labeled *mean* by a man like Ratface was nothing to be proud of.

But the biggest danger to Pieter wasn't kidnappers. It was the paralyzing fear that had been planted, nurtured, and reinforced by Nickolaas Vandermark. How was Quentin supposed to undo the damage his grandfather had embedded in his son? Patience wasn't working. Neither was logic or distance from Nickolaas. When he took custody of Pieter back from his grandfather last month, they both agreed it was best for Nickolaas to be scarce while father and son became accustomed to each other again. The Vandermark name carried vast burdens and responsibilities, and it was his duty to ensure that Pieter would be strong enough to shoulder them. It was unlikely either he or Nickolaas would be alive to see Pieter into adulthood, and it was time for the boy to overcome his childish fears and superstitions.

"If that boy eats a morsel of food before he finishes the mushrooms, you're all fired without references."

He slammed the door behind him.

~ ❧ ~

The first thing the next morning, Quentin hobbled outside to sit on the front portico of the mansion, his head leaning against the stone balustrade, his leg stretched out before him. It had been impossible to sleep last night, and he was exhausted as he rose before dawn and staggered outside, hoping the morning air would revive him.

He shouldn't have been so hard on Pieter last night. The boy had refused to eat a single mushroom and had gone to bed hungry. A little stubbornness from a nine-year-old could be forgiven, but superstitious nonsense was dangerous. Generations of Vandermarks had come of age believing their family was uniquely cursed, and he had to stop any hint of pointless superstitions from taking root in Pieter.

He covered his face with his hand, remorse consuming him. The truth was—and it shamed him to admit it—he didn't know how to be a good father. Both of his parents had died when he was a baby, and being raised by Nickolaas Vandermark hadn't exactly shown him the model of a wise and loving father.

The ache in his chest swelled, and he squeezed his eyes against the pain of remorse. All he'd ever wanted in life was to be a solid man and a good father, but he was failing at both.

He still remembered with aching clarity the morning of Pieter's birth. It was the most perfect day of his life. He'd been in the room for it all, for nothing could drag him from his wife's side that day. As the time drew near, the doctor ordered him to a far corner and draped a privacy sheet across Portia's knees, but Quentin watched her face as she labored to deliver the child they both desperately wanted. She'd been so brave, crying out only at the very end when her head rolled back on the pillow as Pieter slipped from her body. Then she started laughing and weeping in joy, Pieter's cries joining hers.

The proudest moment of Quentin's life came only seconds later when Pieter was placed in his arms, a tiny, wriggling infant wrapped in a towel and still wet from birth. His little face was wrinkled, his eyes squeezed shut. He was twisting and whimpering in despair, and Quentin's entire heart split open.

"Hush, baby," he soothed, rocking the tiny infant against his chest. "Hush now. Don't you know I would do anything in the world for you?"

And he would. He would lay down his life to protect this miraculous gift that had just been placed in his arms. As if sensing the love radiating from him, Pieter's muscles eased and his eyes opened, staring up at him with a solemn gaze. Quentin was struck speechless with wonder, the bond growing by the second. Through eyes swimming in tears, he looked to Portia, propped up on the bed, watching them both with an exhausted smile on her face.

Moving to the bed, he sat on the mattress, tilting the baby so Portia could see. "Look at him, Portia. Just look at him . . ."

He wanted to say more, but there were no words to describe how happy and proud he was.

Portia reached for the baby, and he set Pieter in her arms. Portia turned her face into the column of his throat. He held her as they both wept for joy, and for that brief moment, he knew that he and Portia would overcome the chasms in their marriage and become a real family.

It hadn't worked out that way. Portia died before Pieter's first birthday, and then he broke his leg less than a year later. The descent into sickness and depression had been swift. Not that his life had ever been perfect, but the nascent stirrings of hope had been extinguished by a series of catastrophes. And despair of the soul had proven so much harder than the pain in his body.

Quentin scrubbed a hand across his face, forcing the memories away. The only logical way to proceed was to try doing better by Pieter in the future.

He drew a deep breath and scanned the meadow before him. A stand of ancient juniper trees encircled the meadow, creating a haven within its sheltering rim. The grounds were overgrown, with grasses and wildflowers flourishing in profusion. A pair of butterflies fluttered through the overgrowth. Blackberry vines twined through a fence that protected an herb garden. The call of a meadowlark sounded from a nearby apple tree laden with fruit.

He blinked, realizing this might possibly be the most beautiful place he'd ever seen. There was a tranquility here, made of warm earth and dappled sunlight and a green, soothing scent. It looked like a primeval kingdom, a lost paradise, a memory of ruined perfection.

He'd never been here before, but it seemed oddly familiar, as though he had dreamed it once, or perhaps seen it in a grand painting. It seemed . . . well, *magical* was the only word he could think of for it.

Which was nonsense. He was here on a mission, not to squander time waxing poetic over a long-neglected meadow. That irksome Sophie person was likely to arrive soon. Pieter would be famished by now, and perhaps he'd have Sophie cook breakfast for them again. He sensed she'd be willing to cook in exchange for permission to keep tending that weather station on the roof.

As though answering his thoughts, Sophie emerged from the dense screen of trees, ambling toward the house with a smile as bright as the morning. Her blond hair spilled over one shoulder in a loose braid, and she carried a cloth-covered basket. A single daisy was tucked behind one ear. Decades of training required him to rise to his feet. It was ungainly, but he managed to stand and brace his cane beneath him before she reached the portico.

"I've brought an orange loaf," she declared with a smile as she halted before him.

His cane shot out and blocked her entrance. "I suppose you'll be wanting to get up onto the roof."

"Your powers of foresight have me in awe." Humor underlay her words and it was contagious, but he refused to give in to the impulse to laugh with her. The orange loaf in that covered basket smelled so tempting it made him weak. It smelled of butter and citrus and endless Mediterranean skies.

"My son is hungry," he said bluntly.

"Hence the orange loaf. It's got dried cranberries and a vanilla glaze."

His stomach started to growl. "We will require another round of scrambled eggs like you made yesterday. Mr. Gilroy has already purchased the ingredients. After you make breakfast, you may have access to the roof."

She hesitated. "It is important that I gather the data at the same time each morning. All the volunteers are asked to take their readings before nine o'clock. The data is more meaningful if it is standardized. I'll go take the weather readings then get breakfast started."

He conceded, more out of respect for science than any kindness on his part. He did not want to stress his leg so early in the day, so he lowered himself to sit on the front step. It annoyed him that she felt free to sit beside him.

"What do you do with the data once you collect it?" he asked.

"There is a telegraph machine at my father's hotel, and he wires it to the Weather Bureau. In exchange, the town gets free weather predictions for the Hudson Valley wired to us each evening."

"But what do *you* get out of it? You're the one who is doing all the work."

She answered without hesitation. "I get immense satisfaction. It is a privilege to be a part of this endeavor. Last year there was a week of terrible storms upstate and we were notified of a flood heading our way. Farmers were able to move their livestock to higher ground and get their hay inside well ahead of the storm. Without that warning, thousands of cows and sheep would have drowned."

"And you do this for free," he pressed.

"We all do it for free." She said it like *he* was the simpleton, not she.

"Then you are being taken advantage of. If the warnings issued by the Weather Bureau saved the valley's livestock, you ought to be compensated. The system will only work on goodwill for so long before it breaks down."

The music of her laughter rivaled the birdsong in the distance. She uncovered the basket, the warm scent of the buttery cake rising from within. "Would you like a slice of orange loaf? I baked it even before I knew you intended to haggle over access to the roof like a real robber baron. People aren't always motivated by money. Sometimes they do things just to be kind."

She tilted the basket toward him. The cream-colored loaf was drenched in a vanilla glaze and flecked with bits of dried fruit and lemon zest. His mouth watered. He hadn't been hungry until she'd started waving that basket in his face. He folded his arms and narrowed his eyes.

"So you consider yourself *kind*, do you?"

"I hope so." She seemed a little miffed he wanted nothing to do with her fancy bread and withdrew the basket.

Her naiveté was appalling. People like Sophie van Riijn smiled while allowing the government to exploit her goodwill, and that kind of gullibility annoyed him. He couldn't deny there was something appealing about her, even as he was exasperated by her foolish benevolence.

A worm dropped onto his lap from the portico above and he reared back, brushing it onto the steps in disgust. He used his good leg to kick it farther away, but Sophie swooped in, laughing as she plucked it away from harm.

"Goodness, don't tell me you're frightened of a little caterpillar," she said, holding the wiggling green and yellow worm between two slender fingers. He'd never seen a woman gladly handle an insect before, and it was a little humbling.

"I assure you, ma'am, it takes more than a caterpillar to alarm me." No man who had allowed his leg to be broken, rebroken, and submitted his body to a live vivisection ought to be squeamish about such a thing. "Just toss it aside," he said grimly.

She carried it to a cluster of wildflowers and set it on the ground. "It's a monarch caterpillar," she said as she rejoined him at the portico. "They eat milkweeds, so he will be fine over there. I always love watching the caterpillars go through their transformation every year. They are truly a miracle of nature."

They were a pest and annoyance, especially when they dropped on unsuspecting people without provocation, but Sophie seemed to have an endless supply of patience and goodwill. Perhaps he could put that cheerful nature to good use.

"Can you tell me what causes thunder?" he asked.

"It's an acoustic shock caused when air gets superheated by a burst of lightning. Why?"

"I was curious about what you'd say."

Pieter liked Sophie. She was soft edges and soothing tones and radiant warmth. Pieter was accustomed to rejecting anything Quentin had to say about science and the rational world, but what if the message came from Sophie?

For the first time since arriving at the mansion, a smile curved his mouth. Sophie might be good for Pieter. And Quentin would be willing to put up with her teeth-grating cheerfulness if she could help ease Pieter into a more logical frame of mind. It would be a challenge, but he'd pay her a fortune if she would do it.

"Aside from letting the government take appalling advantage of you, what else do you do with your time?" he asked.

The question seemed to hurt her feelings. She looked away and fiddled with the lace at her cuff. "I help at the hotel."

"What would it take to get you to agree to be our cook for the next few weeks?"

A flash of exhilaration lit her eyes, but it was quickly masked. "Well, I've never cooked for money before . . ."

That surprised him. She seemed so competent he'd assumed she must have worked in her father's hotel.

"I need more than a cook," he admitted. "I've decided my son would benefit from a course in meteorology, and I'd like you to teach him. Show him the scientific method. How you gather data and pass it on to scientists who use it for research. I'll pay a great deal in exchange for such tutoring."

"You want to pay me to be nice to your son? I'd do it for free."

For such an intelligent woman, her repeated willingness to

let people take advantage of her was exasperating. "I don't like to be obligated to people. I would prefer to set a salary."

"You'd want me here every day?"

"Every day. I will tolerate no superstition. If my son inquires about fairies or goblins, or God or Jesus, I want you to squash the discussion."

"You lump God and Jesus in with fairies and goblins?"

"Yes," he said bluntly, hoping she wasn't going to be one of those tedious religious types. "If something cannot be experienced by one of the five senses, it is not real. I won't have my son instructed in anything else."

"Are you . . . ?" Her face flushed and she lowered her voice, so soft he had to lean in to hear. "Are you an atheist?" she whispered.

She sounded so appalled she might have been asking if he carried bubonic plague. "Yes, Miss van Riijn, I am an atheist. Or as I prefer to think of myself, a free thinker. An intelligent man unfettered by the chains of folklore, superstition, and oppression."

She pondered the words as she scanned the meadow before the house. "I've always felt my faith liberated rather than oppressed me. Knowing there is a kingdom of God has been very reassuring. I can't imagine what it must be like to believe we are alone in the world." Sophie looked at him with a bit of humor in her eyes. "No wonder you're so grouchy."

The laughter began deep in his chest, but he masked it as a cough rather than letting it escape. He cleared his throat until he could regain his composure and present a straight face.

"Well, this *grouchy* man is prepared to offer you a salary of one hundred dollars a week for cooking our meals and instructing my son in the basics of meteorology."

"One hundred dollars?" she gasped.

"One hundred dollars," he affirmed. It was an outrageous

price, but it was worth it if she could make these weeks easier for Pieter. "And your discussions shall be limited to the scientific principles of the universe, kindly omitting mention of catastrophic floods, stone tablets delivered to mountaintops, or snakes offering apples to foolish women."

As he'd suspected, she looked tempted. People would do anything for money, and she'd pitch her godly principles into the deep blue sea if the price was right. She plucked a strand of grass peeking through the slate tiles at her feet. She methodically shredded the grass to pieces before she turned to face him.

"I won't deny my religious beliefs," she finally said.

"So long as you don't foist them on my son, I'll be satisfied."

She smiled, and it was irritating how much her radiant face appealed to him. A girl this pretty and innocent had no understanding of the dark clouds that haunted the world. She had never known pain or fear, and her simplistic belief in God only underscored her naiveté.

"You've got a lot of people with you, and cooking for them all is too big a job for one person. And frankly, I don't think my father would consent to letting me be here without some sort of chaperone. It would be best if you rehired Florence, as well."

"The old housekeeper with the humped back? She's too old to be working."

"She's tougher than she looks."

He shifted in discomfort and stretched out his leg, rubbing the failing muscles in annoyance. Just thinking about the old woman made him uncomfortable. "I don't like being waited on by someone so old and feeble. If she needs money, I'll give it to her."

"What she needs is to feel useful. She's only sixty-two and wants to work."

That was surprising. The old woman looked eighty, not barely into her sixties, but what Sophie said was correct. A vocation was important for sustaining the spirit. There had been times when work was the only glimmer of hope he could cling to when the darkness overtook him. He wouldn't deny the dignity of work to a housekeeper who had served his family for four decades.

It didn't escape his notice that Sophie was manipulating him, subtly bargaining for exactly what she wanted before consenting to his plan. "Oh, very well," he said sourly. "You can bring the housekeeper back."

"And you will be nice to her."

"I'm always nice."

Her laughter rang out over the meadow. Her amusement could probably be heard in Manhattan, but he had no intention of joining in.

"Florence is a sensitive soul. You scared her within an inch of a heart attack on your first day here, so I'd like to assure her that you can be trusted to comport yourself like a gentleman."

"Save me from the tender sensibilities of women," he muttered. "They are the death warrant for all logic and reason in the universe." He looked at Sophie and conceded. "In the future I shall treat Florence as though she is made of hand-blown glass. Or perhaps nitroglycerine."

She graced him with a blinding smile. "When do I start?" she asked in that annoyingly cheerful voice.

"Now. I'll go wake Pieter and send him to you on the roof."

"You aren't coming?"

It was humiliating that he lacked the ability to climb two flights of stairs, but his physical limitations were none of her business so he dismissed her question. "Pieter will join you shortly. He will be accompanied by a bodyguard."

Sophie's brow wrinkled in confusion. "I can assure you no harm will come to the boy on the roof. The widow's walk is surrounded by a railing and is perfectly safe."

"Pieter never goes anywhere without a bodyguard."

"But why?"

"My son will someday inherit eighty million dollars, a fact that is widely known. Last summer he was kidnapped by a team of thugs while I was convalescing after surgery. For nine days he was held blindfolded in a closet while awaiting ransom."

Sophie sucked in a horrified gasp, her hand flying to her mouth. She finally seemed to grasp that the world was not a cozy dollhouse ruled over by a benevolent Christian father. Pieter had been so traumatized by the incident that Quentin had summoned his grandfather to take custody of the boy. Too ill to leave the clinic where he'd been hovering between life and death following a string of experimental surgeries, he'd trusted Nickolaas to abide by their agreement not to subject Pieter to the rot about a family curse.

"We got him back, but it was a traumatic ordeal from which he still has not entirely recovered. He is afraid of the dark and afraid of strangers. The constant presence of bodyguards helps him feel secure."

"I see," she whispered, her lovely face seeming to show genuine regret, which was nonsense. Pieter was practically a stranger to her, and she didn't need to pretend sympathy. She tossed the pieces of grass away and looked at him with a little more understanding. "I'll be waiting for Pieter on the roof."

He managed to stand while she excused herself, but the instant the door closed, he lowered himself onto a step again to lighten the weight on his leg, which had begun to ache.

He needed to eat. If Sophie was going to be their cook, he couldn't keep subsisting on apples out of irrational stubbornness. Dragging the basket of orange loaf closer, he cut a large wedge and ate with his fingers, too impatient to even carry the basket inside.

He nearly went dizzy from the tangy bread dissolving in his mouth in a combination of sweet, tart, and cream. Were he a praying man, he would thank God he'd completed the negotiation before he ate a morsel of Sophie's food, or he would have been a puddle at her feet. No wonder Pieter adored her.

He wolfed down the rest of the slice quickly, eyeing the remainder of the loaf as he chewed. This was the best thing he'd tasted in years, and it wouldn't take much effort to make the rest of that loaf disappear, but he needed to rouse Pieter now, before Sophie was finished with her work on the roof.

As he headed back into the house, he realized that for the first time in years—for a few precious moments while bantering with Sophie—he had been free of the relentless pain that darkened his world.

5

TUTORING PIETER would give Sophie an excellent excuse to visit Dierenpark every day. She still needed to find a way to get Emil re-hired, but for now her primary objective would be figuring out the Vandermarks' motivation for tearing down the mansion. She hadn't been able to sleep last night. Every time she began drifting off, hideous images of Dierenpark being consumed by fire and earthquakes, or of snakes invading the gardens to poison every living creature, jolted her awake time and again. She didn't find much relief upon waking. If poisonous snakes didn't ruin Dierenpark, Quentin Vandermark's dynamite surely would—unless she could persuade him otherwise.

This meant more to her than simply saving the town's most notable landmark. Dierenpark seemed almost holy to her. It was a place of serenity and enchantment she felt compelled to protect. As she prepared breakfast, Sophie tried to eavesdrop on the bodyguards to glean some insight, but it was hopeless. The moment she came into view, they all stopped talking and scrutinized her with suspicious eyes.

The pantry had been replenished following Mr. Gilroy's trip into town, and she prepared a hearty breakfast of fried potatoes, crispy bacon, and heaping mounds of scrambled eggs with freshly grated cheese. She added some fruit she plucked from the trees around Dierenpark and was pleased to see Quentin join them for breakfast this time, eating in silence at the end of the table, listening to Pieter gleefully recount his adventure on the roof with Sophie.

After breakfast, Quentin retreated to the orangery, a splendid building added to Dierenpark in the early nineteenth century. Built mostly of glass panes enclosed with gothic white arches, it was capable of keeping trees and plants flowering throughout the year. It was located only a stone's throw from the main house, and from the kitchen window she watched Quentin cross the short distance to the orangery. It was a slow journey. His entire body tensed each time he put weight on his damaged leg, and twice he paused to catch his breath.

What was his interest in the orangery? Whatever it was must be important for him to make the painful journey. As she cleaned the kitchen, she saw no one else join him, and it would be an excellent time to speak with him in private. Now that they had established a modicum of civility between them, a direct conversation would be the best way to understand his motives for tearing down the house.

She headed to the orangery as soon as the kitchen was tidy. Inside, he sat on one of the benches near the potted lemon trees, scribbling in a notebook. She knocked on the door, waiting until he bid her to enter. The air was warmer inside, perfumed by the scents of citrus, lavender, and viburnum.

"How long has this orangery been here?" he asked.

"I think it was added by Karl Vandermark," she said. "Sometime in the 1820s, I suspect."

"Hmmm." He sounded entirely displeased as he went back to scribbling in his notebook.

"Why? Don't you like it? Most people love the orangery."

"I didn't know about it," he said. "All this glass will be a danger during the demolition process. So no, I am not particularly dazzled by this orangery."

"Mr. Vandermark," she began hesitantly, "can you tell me why you wish to tear down Dierenpark? Your family's history of benign neglect seems to have served everyone quite well. And if you no longer wish to carry the financial burdens of the estate, why don't you simply sell it?"

He didn't even bother to look up from his notebook as he continued making notes. "My grandfather wants the land turned back to its natural state. Some kind of nonsense about healing the land and beginning anew."

"But why?"

He gave a snort of derision. "Who knows why eccentric old millionaires do anything? He wants the building torn down, so that's what will happen."

"Your grandfather was the boy who found his father floating dead in the river, right?"

He folded his arms across his chest, watching her through speculative eyes. "*Found* his father in the river? That's a kind word for it. Most people think he killed Karl Vandermark in order to get his hands on the family fortune that much sooner."

"I don't believe it. He was only a child."

"He was fourteen," Quentin challenged. "Old enough to pull it off."

"I still don't believe it."

Although plenty of people in the village did. The Vandermarks' insistence on privacy only fueled the wagging tongues. After the tragedy, a team of lawyers immediately surrounded fourteen-year-old Nickolaas until his estranged mother came racing back from Europe to drag the boy to France and away from the reach of the American justice system. Over the decades, Nickolaas refused to speak of what had happened to his father, and rumors filled the void. Sixty years later, a cloud of suspicion still hung over the old man.

Not that it mattered. Sophie merely needed to know how to stop Quentin from demolishing Dierenpark. "But why you?" she pressed. "How can you let yourself be drawn into something so irrational?"

His pencil froze. His face suddenly seemed haunted, possibly the saddest expression she'd ever seen.

"Because I am loyal," he finally said. "I owe my grandfather more than I can ever repay, and he's rarely asked me for anything. I won't turn him down now."

"Perhaps the best way to show your loyalty would be to stop him from making a terrible mistake."

He gave a wry smile as he turned back to his notebook. "I'm not sure someone as cheerful as you can ever understand, Miss van Riijn. The people in my family often suffer from fits of melancholia so profound it can become hard to even breathe. My grandfather has dragged me back from the precipice of despair more than once."

She looked away, for she did understand grief. When Albert sickened and died, she had been devastated. It was only her faith that kept her anchored in the real world when a part of her wanted to follow Albert into the grave, but Quentin was an atheist. The world was surely darker for someone like him.

"When my wife died, I was ready to give up," Quentin continued. "Pieter was a baby, and I had responsibilities, but it didn't matter to me. Rumors reached my grandfather that I wouldn't leave my room, that I'd quit bathing, that I neglected Pieter . . . all of which was true, by the way. My grandfather appeared with three tickets to board a steamer to sail to Egypt, convinced that standing at the pyramids could somehow cure me. He said the pyramids were the source of an ancient, mystical energy convergence that might spark healing."

"That doesn't sound very Christian."

Quentin's laughter was so sudden it took her by surprise. "No, my grandfather is not a Christian. Over the years he has dabbled in Buddhism, Shamanism, Transcendentalism, even the rites of the ancient Druids. Utter nonsense, but that's just the way he is. In any event, he dragged me from bed and put up with my foul temper the entire journey across the Atlantic. And the trip was priceless. Pieter was only a year old, but the three of us saw the desert in all its vast, arid beauty. There is something about baking in that hot sun that started to get through to me, and I was able to finally breathe again."

He tossed down his pencil. "Look, my grandfather is a difficult and eccentric old man, but he is the only family I've ever known. My parents and older sister were killed in a hotel fire when I was an infant. The only reason I survived was because I was in a different wing of the hotel with the nursery maid. Nickolaas raised me from the cradle. It wasn't easy, and we rarely get along . . . but he has saved me time and again. And if he wants me to tear down Dierenpark, that is what I will do."

The resolve in Quentin's voice was unshakeable, and appealing to him would be pointless. What she needed to do was figure out why Nickolaas Vandermark wanted the house destroyed, and how was she to do that? The elder Vandermark was a famous world traveler who was rarely in the United States. Pieter had told her only this morning that while living with Nickolaas they'd visited Stonehenge, the Acropolis, and the old Moorish castle guarding the Strait of Gibraltar.

"Where is your grandfather now?" she asked.

He shrugged. "I have no idea. Probably off in search of the golden fleece."

"Would Mr. Gilroy know? He seems quite knowledgeable about everything and very generous with his time."

"So you've fallen under Mr. Gilroy's spell, have you?" Quentin asked, a hint of humor back in his voice. "You'll need to watch out for that, as Mr. Gilroy is an unabashed spy for my grandfather."

She must not have heard him properly. "He's a *what*?"

"Mr. Gilroy is a spy," he repeated. "I certainly hope you didn't share any heartfelt secrets, because if you did, that information is already on my grandfather's desk."

The blood drained from her face, and she felt lightheaded. Oh heavens, she had spilled her heart out to Mr. Gilroy! Everything about her humiliation when she'd fallen for Roger Wilson's flattery and gifts, and Marten's betrayal only six days before the wedding.

"I did!" she sputtered. "He seemed so kind and sympathetic . . ."

"Don't take it too hard," Quentin said. "Mr. Gilroy is a professional. He's been on my grandfather's payroll for a decade. He specializes in ferreting out secrets, gaining unsuspecting people's trust, and entrapment. Someone like you didn't stand a chance."

"But why does your grandfather spy on you?"

"Because we don't trust each other. Nickolaas Vandermark is as cunning as any Borgia prince, and twice as rich. He feasts on intrigue as though it were mother's milk. If anything you told Mr. Gilroy is of interest to my grandfather, Nickolaas will have hired a team of private investigators to uncover every detail of your life. He probably knows the color of your undergarments by now. That's just the way he is. You need to watch what you say around Mr. Gilroy."

She still couldn't accept it. Mr. Gilroy seemed so caring, and she instinctively trusted him. "But he seemed so nice . . ."

"That's because he *is* nice. He is also a man who has amassed a small fortune by working for my grandfather while simultaneously drawing a salary from me."

It didn't seem possible that such a genteel man could be so underhanded. "So you are saying that Mr. Gilroy will always put Nickolaas Vandermark first, no matter what?"

"No, I'm saying Mr. Gilroy will always put *himself* first. He is quite clever at playing me against Nickolaas when it suits his purposes. Mr. Gilroy lives by his wits. Don't give him ammunition to shoot you with, because he won't hesitate if it suits his purpose."

"I think that's terrible."

Quentin pushed himself to his feet, grasping his cane and using careful steps to close the distance between them. There was no cynical mockery in his face, only a hint of wistfulness as he studied her.

"I worry about you, Miss van Riijn," he said quietly. "You are simply too sweet-natured to survive very long in the real world. You think that God and Jesus set the rules, but it's really people like my grandfather and Mr. Gilroy who are pulling all the strings."

What must it be like to view the world through such a dark glass? Being attuned to God's presence in the world did not make her fragile; it made her stronger. But how strange that Quentin Vandermark, a virtual stranger with a ferocious reputation, echoed her father's sentiments exactly. Her father repeatedly tried to block her from anything that might put her feelings at risk, and it was humiliating that everyone underestimated her. She raised her chin a notch.

"I'm not a Ming vase," she said. "I've been knocked down a time or two, and I've always survived."

For some reason, the comment appeared to trouble him. He returned to his bench, all trace of warmth gone from his voice.

"My son *is* a Ming vase," he said ominously. "Handle him with care, Miss van Riijn, for he is the only thing in the world I treasure, and I won't let anyone damage him."

She didn't doubt it, for she'd already learned from the body-guards what had happened to the men who'd kidnapped Pieter last summer. After paying the ransom, Quentin hired a team of mercenaries to track the money, hunt down the kidnappers, and bring them to justice. Those who resisted did not survive to make it to trial.

No, she didn't doubt that Quentin wanted to protect his son. She merely didn't think he knew how to do it.

6

THE NEXT WEEK WAS EXHILARATING as Sophie undertook her first professional job, tutoring Pieter and cooking for the Vandermark household. Although she had yet to figure out a way to get Emil re-hired, Florence had returned to her position as housekeeper, a blessing considering the amount of food these men devoured at every meal. It was hard not to be flattered by the enthusiasm they showed as they consumed the meals she set before them each day.

There was nothing magical about her cooking, but she loved sharing the recipes that had been handed down through generations of her family. She used the same roast duckling recipe her grandmother once cooked for her father. As she seasoned the cherry sauce with a dash of cider, she liked to imagine her grandmother looking on with approval. As she rolled out dough to make Dutch cookies, she imagined countless generations of housewives back in the old country, pleased to see their recipes had been remembered and carried all the way to the New World. Cooking these recipes was harkening back to a collective memory, passed down from mother to daughter for centuries, then shared by their families gathered around the table. Perhaps someday she would have daughters and granddaughters who would make and serve her own recipes. Food was more than just a combination of starches and proteins to fuel the body. It was comfort and celebration and joy.

Collins, the scariest of the bodyguards because he had a set of frightening metal teeth instead of real ones, went into town daily to fetch groceries. When he laid a slab of pork shoulder on the wooden counter, she dared to ask the question she had been fearing.

"Mr. Collins, are you able to eat something like pork with those teeth? If you need me to prepare something softer . . ."

The smile that spread across his face was a little chilling, as it exposed plenty of the shining metal. "No baby food for me, ma'am. But thank you for asking."

She wasn't quite so terrified of him after that. As the aromas of simmering chowders, meat, and baking bread permeated the house, it was secretly satisfying to watch each member of the household drift past the kitchen, surreptitiously peeking at the dishes as they emerged from the oven. Collins even politely asked for a cookie.

But Mr. Vandermark had not softened in the least. She couldn't understand why, but he seemed to actively dislike her. Whenever she entered a room, he made an excuse to leave it. On the few occasions they spoke, he consistently had something rude to say.

But no matter how frustrating his father, working with Pieter was a joy. He smiled more when she was near. He laughed and asked questions, losing the timid streak that clung to him at other times. Each morning they went up to the roof to gather climate data while Sophie explained the principles of temperature and humidity, how heat affected rainfall, and what caused the winds to shift. After the first few days, Sophie let Pieter take the measurements while she carefully looked over his shoulder to ensure he was reading the thermometers and gauges correctly.

"Excellent," Sophie murmured in approval the day Pieter completed an entire set of readings with no help from her at all. "Your father will be so impressed at how quickly you're catching on."

Pieter closed the front cover on the case protecting the thermometer, taking an unusually long time as he fastened the latch. "I'm always afraid I'm going to make a mistake. I never do anything right."

It hurt to see a young child already riddled with such crippling anxiety. It didn't help that Quentin constantly berated him, but all Sophie could do was try to give the boy a few tools to cope with it.

"Being young and afraid is a normal part of life," she said gently. "It doesn't feel good, but I don't suppose a tulip bulb feels good once it's buried in the cold, dark soil . . . but it works out in the end, doesn't it? When the time is right, the tulip will grow to its full potential. It obeys the rules of science, just like your father always talks about. Maybe right now you are going through a difficult time, just like the tulip bulbs, but you'll be okay. Just have a little faith."

Pieter fiddled with a button on his shirt and chewed on his lip. She could tell by the way his face was screwed up that he was wrestling with a question, and she waited patiently while he searched for the words.

"Aren't you afraid of my father?" he finally asked.

She was, but it would be cruel to admit it. And the anxiety in the boy's voice was heartbreaking.

"Why? Are you afraid of him?"

Pieter nodded. "He's mad all the time. I can't ever do anything to make him happy."

It was impossible for one person to *make* someone else happy, especially someone as grim as Quentin Vandermark. Pieter was a sensitive boy, and it was crushing that he blamed himself for his father's surliness.

"You aren't to blame for your father's unhappiness, Pieter, and there is nothing wrong with being a little worried or afraid every now and then. It's a normal part of life."

She had been warned not to proselytize to Pieter, and she would honor that agreement, but it didn't preclude her from talking about her *own* faith. "I was raised to believe that Jesus is with me always, even though I can't see or touch him. I can feel him in my heart, and he's never led me wrong." She hunkered down so she could see him better, took his hand, and smiled into his eyes. "I believe he's looking out for you too, Pieter," she whispered.

To her surprise, Pieter launched himself at her, hugging her with all the strength in his spindly arms. "It's going to be okay," she whispered, rocking him gently.

"Did you know a bunch of bad men kidnapped me last year?" he asked in a muffled voice.

"I heard about it."

"I was so scared, and I prayed the whole time. I don't even know how to pray, but I just kept thinking, *please, please, please . . . someone help me and I promise to be good forever*. I don't know who I was talking to, but maybe it was Jesus."

"Maybe," Sophie said with a gentle smile. It wasn't right this boy was being deprived of a religious faith, but if she directly countermanded Quentin's orders, she'd be shown the door as abruptly as the unfortunate governess, and then she'd never see Pieter again. Her heart urged patience, and to keep teaching Pieter by example.

She had time. Quentin had said it would take a month to create a detailed floorplan of the house, complete with measurements for the depth and density of the walls, the strength of the structural supports, and the dimensions of each room. He filled pages with mathematical equations to determine the extent of dynamite needed to bring down the walls. Most ominously, he had begun drawing large *X*'s on support columns, and circles where he wanted Collins to begin drilling holes in the walls. As soon as his plan was complete, sticks of dynamite would be inserted into those holes, and then Dierenpark would be demolished.

It had been ten days since the Vandermarks had returned, and the sight of those *X*'s and circles drawn on the walls chilled her. The only real hope she had was figuring out why Nickolaas Vandermark wanted the house destroyed, and she still didn't even know if the man was on the American continent. Unless she could somehow persuade the eccentric old millionaire to spare Dierenpark, Quentin intended to demolish a rare treasure.

Sophie returned to the hotel every evening as soon as dinner was on the table at Dierenpark. It made for a long day, but her father had been scandalized at the prospect of his innocent daughter sleeping in a household of nine men with only an old woman as chaperone, so she still made the journey home each night.

This evening, she sat at the hotel's kitchen work table, decorating Dutch *gevulde koeken*, an Old World recipe for almond cookies passed down through generations of Sophie's family. Marten Graaf, her childhood sweetheart and former fiancé, kept her company. Marten still had a crippling weakness for her *gevulde koeken*, and whenever he was in town she sent him back to the city with a large tin of freshly baked cookies.

Their ongoing friendship seemed strange to many people in the village, but not to Sophie. Marten had been her fondest friend since childhood, and despite a difficult few years following his abandonment, they were friends again. Sometimes she sensed he regretted jilting her, but Sophie would never take him back. She had grown into a woman, while Marten still seemed trapped in his impetuous, carefree youth. He seemed such a pale man compared to Quentin Vandermark.

Where had *that* thought come from? Quentin was a bad-tempered man with no faith, no manners, and a cynical streak wider than the Hudson River. Aside from intelligence and a sense of humor, he had no redeeming qualities whatsoever. She couldn't even credit him with being a good father. She didn't doubt that Quentin loved his son, but he was depriving Pieter of the comfort the boy needed so desperately.

"Do you want a raspberry or blueberry topping?" she asked Marten. She had a jar of each from canning preserves last weekend, and it would take only a few moments to put a dollop on each cookie.

"Can I have both?" Marten asked with his typical audacity.

The back door to the kitchen banged open and her father clomped inside, a tower of boxes balanced in his arms.

"Marten, I need you to look the other way," Jasper said, dumping the boxes on the wooden countertop with a thump. The way her father's hand covered the label on the box closest to Marten immediately put Sophie on alert.

"Literally or figuratively?" Marten asked as he leaned in for a closer look. Her father scooted the boxes to the far side of the table.

"I need you to literally leave this kitchen before I figuratively annihilate Quentin Vandermark."

Sophie held her breath. The way her father covered the labels on the boxes indicated he was up to no good, but if he had a plan to save Dierenpark, she wished Marten would leave quickly. She scooped the still-cooling cookies into a tin and pressed them into his hand.

"I'll have blueberry *gevulde koeken* next time you visit."

The moment Marten was out the door, she whirled to face her father. "What are you doing?"

"I've already searched through all the court records and documents relating to the title of that house," her father said. "I've spent the past week looking for anything that would call their ownership of the house into question. I even consulted with descendants of the local Lanape Indian tribe to see if I could prove the original Vandermarks cheated them out of the land."

"And?" Sophie asked.

"Adrien Vandermark paid a princely sum for it back in 1635. Which was a shame. Most of the early Dutch settlers bargained with glass beads for huge chunks of land, while Adrien paid in gold, along with bolts of cloth and some iron cooking equipment. One of the Lanape elders still had a kettle that was said to be from Adrien Vandermark."

This gave Sophie pause. Adrien Vandermark was known to be a friend to the Indians, and yet only five years after he arrived he was killed by an Algonquin raiding party that swept down from the north. It was his brother Caleb who ultimately created the Vandermark legacy and fortune in New Holland.

"Nothing in the courthouse archives will help us," her father continued, "but the Vandermarks had a personal vault stored in the basement of the bank on Main Street."

"Like a safe deposit box?"

"Precisely. They didn't call them such back when Karl Vandermark established it, but that's what it is, and these boxes are what I found inside the vault."

"Father! You can't poke through their safe deposit box."

"Why not? It's been abandoned for sixty years. I don't intend to steal anything; I just need to see if there is something of interest here. Why else would Karl Vandermark have locked up these boxes?"

She could think of plenty of things he'd want secured in a safe place. Bars of gold? Antiques from the Old World? People as rich as the Vandermarks surely didn't store all their wealth in one place, and there could be any number of curiosities stored in those boxes. She didn't know how her father had gotten the key to that bank vault, but the fact that he made Marten leave the room was a sure sign it wasn't aboveboard. She shouldn't have anything to do with this, but as he lifted the lid off the first box, it was impossible not to peek.

Old papers.

The same with the next box and the next. On some level, Sophie was disappointed not to see golden Spanish doubloons or a stash of pirate treasure, but her father seemed delighted.

"Never underestimate the power of a paper trail," he said with relish as he lifted the first set of documents from a box. They were loose pages written in the spindly handwriting of the eighteenth century.

Paper trails might fascinate a lawyer, but Sophie just wanted to save Dierenpark, and it was going to take more than old pieces of paper to do it. It was going to require figuring out the strange, hidden, and deeply complex attitudes of Quentin and Nickolaas Vandermark, and given Quentin's determination to avoid her, she still didn't know how to accomplish it.

Sophie wished that dealing with Quentin Vandermark were as easy as dealing with the twenty thousand honeybees that lived in the eight-frame beehives on a patch of land at Dierenpark. She had no idea who first built the hives, but they seemed to have been here forever, tended by generations of Broeders, who had served as groundskeepers at Dierenpark for as far back as anyone could remember.

The groundskeeper's cabin was the first structure at Dierenpark, built by the original Vandermark brothers in 1635. Caleb Vandermark soon began building the main house, eventually turning the cabin over to the groundskeeper. Until last week when Quentin had fired Emil, members of the Broeder family had lived in that cabin for centuries. Emil lacked the patience for beekeeping, so Sophie had taken over the task years ago.

Beekeeping required care to establish a mutually beneficial relationship, and over the years it seemed the honeybees had become accustomed to her. She never dropped her guard around the bees and always treated them with the respect they deserved, and in return, they supplied Dierenpark with golden, sweet honey.

Complete concentration was needed to extract the honey, and she welcomed the chance to take her mind off the questionably obtained Vandermark documents her father thought might be the key to saving Dierenpark. While her father might be willing to wade into the legal quagmire, Sophie wished she could merely find a way to live peaceably alongside the Vandermarks, much like she had learned to do with the bees.

Wearing a gauzy veil to cover her face, she waved a smoker beneath the hives to lull the bees into complacency. It was a delicate task to lift each frame and drain the golden sweetness from the honeycomb, but she soon had a small bucket of honey still warm from the hive.

As she approached the mansion with her honey, she spotted Quentin sitting on the front steps of the house, peering into a small mirror while he dragged a razor across his soapy face. It was a little unnerving to see a man at such an intimate moment.

"What were you doing back in the woods?" he asked, distrust heavy in his voice.

"Gathering a bit of honey. We've got a couple of eight-frame beehives behind the juniper trees."

"Bees?" he asked. "You've been harboring a colony of dangerous *bees* on my property without permission?"

She supposed it was natural for people to fear things they didn't understand, but the alarm in his voice made her worry he'd try to dispose of the hives. "Honeybees are a wonderful blessing," she said calmly. "If you treat them gently and with respect, they are usually harmless. And look around you! None of the apple trees, the cherries, the roses, or the herb gardens could propagate without the cooperation of the bees. They are one of the reasons the plants at Dierenpark have always been so abundantly healthy. And their honey is divine."

"Miss van Riijn," he said tightly, "do you actually believe that if you smile for the bees they will not sting you? That you can appease them with the force of your sweetness and light?"

He was mocking her, but yes, she actually did believe it was possible to live in harmony with the bees. "I usually say 'good morning' to them whenever I open up a hive," she admitted. "But I'm not stupid about it. I put them in a drowsy mood by waving a smoker beneath the box for a few minutes. I've been doing it for years."

"And you've never been stung?"

She shrugged. "I've been stung a few times, but I survived. I really do believe that if a person treats all living things with respect, eventually the enemy will soften and we can all live together in peace."

She looked him directly in the eye, the veiled challenge obvious. Since arriving in New Holland, Quentin Vandermark had banished the servants, fired his governess, and threatened to demolish a cherished landmark, all without patience, understanding, or bothering to ask anyone's opinion. He was a smart man and knew exactly what she was implying. His eyes glinted with cynical humor.

"Then heaven help you," he said brusquely. "One of these days the world is going to clobber you flat."

"I thought you didn't believe in heaven," she teased.

"I don't. It is an expression of sympathy for a naïve woman who thinks the world is populated by benevolent enemies and friendly bees."

She smiled as she stepped around him and up onto the landing. "I'm sorry, Mr. Vandermark, even your surly words can't dampen my mood today." After all, the morning was dawning bright and clear, the scent of jasmine perfumed the air, and she was going to bake a delightful honeycake this afternoon.

No matter what, she was going to try kindness to soften Quentin. If that didn't work, perhaps her growing affinity with Pieter might buy her some goodwill. Or three hearty meals a day. It would take time and patience, but she intended to establish a rapport with Quentin, just as she had done with the bees.

But it wasn't going to be easy. She returned home that night to find her father grim-faced and holding a letter for her.

"You've had a message from the Weather Bureau," he said as he turned the note over.

A trickle of anger awakened as Sophie read the letter.

We have been informed your station needs relocation due to improper installation on private property without the owner's consent. Please select a new location immediately and re-read the manual for station volunteers. Unauthorized intrusion on private property is a violation of the bureau's standards and will not be tolerated.

She'd never been reprimanded by the Weather Bureau before, and it hurt. A slow burn began to build, for this was Quentin Vandermark's doing. The man had a lot of nerve to tattle on her, especially given that she was using Weather Bureau equipment to mentor his son. Even worse, this did not show her in a good light for persuading the government to build a climate observatory in New Holland.

Why did he dislike her so much? Although Pieter and the bodyguards appreciated her presence, Quentin found endless fault with her. He criticized the way she sang in the kitchen, the happy faces she drew with icing atop her spice cookies, even the way she skipped up and down the staircases.

It was one thing for him to be rude to her face, but she couldn't let him damage her reputation with the Weather Bureau. She wasn't going to let him hobble away like he typically did whenever she was in his presence. Sometimes a person had to stand up to a tyrant. Sophie would much rather bake her enemy a nice blueberry pie and soften him with kind words, but she'd been trying that ever since the Vandermarks arrived, with little to show for it.

It was time to try a bit of justified outrage.

7

THE FOLLOWING MORNING, Sophie found Quentin in Dierenpark's library, measuring the columns that supported the wraparound gallery above them. It was a long, narrow room with books running the length of one wall and a series of arched windows marching along the opposite side. Quentin's brooding face was in sharp contrast to the morning light pouring in from the windows as he jotted down the measurements in the small notebook he always seemed to have with him.

"Did you complain to the Weather Bureau about me?"

His pencil froze as he glanced up at her. "I sent a telegram suggesting their illegally installed equipment needed relocation. I also wanted to verify that you were indeed associated with the organization."

"You think I would lie about that?"

"At the time I did. Now that I know you better, I understand you are perfectly willing to let people exploit your foolishly naïve disposition."

She squared her shoulders and took a few steps closer. "Don't you understand that people sometimes do things simply for love?

I know I was in the wrong when I set up that station without permission. I didn't think the family would ever return, and the station causes no harm, but I still should have asked one of your lawyers and I'm sorry I didn't." She paused to catch her breath so her voice would stop shaking. With his complaint to the bureau, he'd done so much more damage than he realized.

"I've spent the past year working to get the Weather Bureau to invest in an upgraded climate observatory in New Holland," she explained. "I've done it all on my own without a bit of help or encouragement from anyone. I've drafted proposals and circulated petitions. I've listened to people tease me for being idealistic and irrational. No one, not even my own father, thinks I have a chance at persuading the Weather Bureau to plant that research station here, but I've worked so hard. And in one afternoon, you've stained my reputation with them out of pure meanness." She rarely spoke so harshly, but it didn't put a dent in the iron expression on his face.

"Why does this mean so much to you?"

How could she explain years of feeling useless and adrift? A man born with the Vandermark name had opportunities showered on him since birth, while people like her had to go find them—and that wasn't easy in a dying village.

"Because I want to have a sense of purpose in this world." She should know better than to expose her feelings so freely, for it hurt when he smirked at her answer.

"Odd, it seems like you've had a purpose for quite a while." Grasping his cane, he limped toward the walnut desk on the far side of the library. "Come here. There's something I want to show you."

After plopping into the desk chair, he slid open a drawer and tossed a photograph at her. It was the postcard sold to the tourists that showed Sophie as a five-year-old, standing in the grand salon and clutching a bouquet of tulips almost as tall as she.

"My goodness, what a charming little girl you were," he said coolly, but his eyes were dark with accusation.

Sophie stiffened but didn't move. She'd been only a child when the photograph was taken and could hardly be accused of wrongdoing, but she didn't like where this conversation seemed to be heading. "What would you like me to say?"

"Who took the photograph?"

My father. She had no intention of telling Quentin that. Given his hard-eyed expression, Quentin was out for blood.

"I was five years old. You don't really expect me to remember, do you?"

He pushed himself to his feet, grabbed his cane, and lurched around the desk in that lopsided gait she was coming to know so well. She felt like an insect trapped in a web as the spider drew closer. Her mouth went dry, and she took a step back, but he didn't seem angry, he seemed . . . curious.

"The rest of the world may think you are an innocent lamb in the woods, but you are twice as clever as you let on. I doubt anything escapes your notice, despite your wide-eyed innocence. Who took the picture?"

She blinked, surprised at the dubious compliment. "Why should I tell you?"

"Miss van Riijn, the statute of limitations for trespassing on private property has long since expired, so the photographer is in no danger of criminal prosecution. Since you tell me you were five years old, this corresponds with when your father first became mayor of New Holland. A coincidence?"

Any attempt to quibble would only antagonize him. "You know it's not," she admitted.

His smile of satisfaction was a wolf's smile. "My men have learned a great deal about this town and its quixotic mayor. It appears the intrepid Jasper van Riijn set about the town's salvation while watching how the tourists sailed past New Holland on their way to the more famous resorts farther north. The Vandermark house was his linchpin to coax them to linger in the village, and he decided to exploit every conceivable angle."

"Why are you so hostile? Not everyone was born with millions of dollars at their disposal. My father is only trying to protect the town he loves."

"Then it is likewise perfectly legal for me to initiate a lawsuit for punitive damages against your father. He has two decades of ill-gotten gains from exploiting my family's ancestral home—"

"But what about the statute of limitations? You just said that photograph was too old to be used against him."

"For taking the photograph, yes, but the exploitation continued until two weeks ago when I returned and threw out the staff that had been selling photographs of our house and allowing special tours without authorization. *That* I can still sue over. You have been making free with this house for the past twenty years. I've learned you grew up playing with the groundskeeper's children. Playing hide-and-seek in the meadow. Picking our wildflowers and harvesting our oysters. As you got older, you read almost every book in our library."

Her face heated with embarrassment, for everything he said was true. Yes, she'd plundered his library. Those books gave her wings, and she wouldn't apologize for having dared to crack open the abandoned volumes.

"The novels of Ann Radcliffe were always my favorite," she said, her chin held high.

"It shouldn't surprise me that even your choice of reading material is quaint and overly sentimental."

She turned her face away. Dierenpark had seeped into her soul and spirit, but he was making it impossible to stay here. Instead of saving Dierenpark, it seemed she was only putting her family in danger.

"Mr. Vandermark, I don't believe it is wise for me to continue tutoring your son if I am exposing my father to litigation. I will make arrangements to relocate the weather station immediately, so at least one of your concerns will have been addressed."

"No need to be so hasty," he said in a rush.

"In the brief time we've known each other, you have threatened me with a lawsuit, tarnished my reputation with the Weather Bureau, insulted my faith, and attacked my taste in literature. I think I've overstayed my welcome. I will prepare lunch for the household then head into town to find a new location for the weather station."

It hurt to even say the words. She expected Quentin to gloat in triumph, but he pushed to his feet, his face alert and eyes fierce.

"You can't quit!" he thundered. If she wasn't so upset, the incredulity on his face would have been comical. He looked like he wanted to lunge across the desk and manacle her to the floor to stop her from leaving.

"You can't *force* me to cook for you."

"I didn't hire you to cook. I hired you to mentor my son."

"Pieter is welcome to join me wherever I establish a new monitoring station, for he shouldn't be punished because you can't look at a person without threatening a lawsuit."

It was hard, but she managed to keep her composure as she turned to leave the library, closing the door softly behind her.

Quentin waited a solid ten minutes before pursuing her. Which was a struggle. He fought the impulse to follow her to the kitchen to continue their argument, but that would tip the scales in her favor. It would betray how much he enjoyed her company and wanted her to stay.

Everything about her fascinated him. Her charm, her beauty, her bizarre combination of intellect and innocence. She looked as sweet as a newly unfolded daisy, but he suspected she might actually be tough enough to repel bullets with her untarnished dignity. Her buoyancy annoyed him at the same time as it attracted him.

It was bewildering, but Sophie's cheerful disposition and quick banter managed to worm beneath his defenses each time he saw her. He wasn't used to enjoying a woman's company. He'd ignored that piece of his soul ever since Portia died, but Sophie's presence made him cognizant of the hollow place that had been empty for so long. It was easy enough to ignore when she wasn't around, but when she traipsed into his line of sight, it summoned up old yearnings for the sparkle of a woman, for summer evenings at the seashore, for lying on a blanket to watch cloud formations overhead and hoping the world was more profound than what he could see and touch.

A woman of Sophie's attractiveness would never be interested in someone like him, so it was frustrating that he couldn't stop these flights of the imagination, but he wasn't going to let his son be deprived of her company over a little snit. He didn't really intend to sue her father over those photographs, he just wanted to goad her a little. He didn't expect her to quit.

He remained seated behind the desk, clenching and unclenching his fists as he planned his strategy. This was . . . well, this was suddenly and unacceptably galling. If Sophie realized how much he needed her, she'd raise the stakes and probably start haggling over the preservation of this house, which was the only thing he could never offer her.

After ten minutes, he forced his features into a smooth mask of disinterest as he approached the kitchen. He heard her before he saw her. The thumping sounded like she was attacking a punching bag. Rounding the corner and staying partially concealed in the kitchen archway, he watched her turn a wad of dough on a floured countertop, using her fist to punch a large hole in the center.

"Your attack on that bread dough is reminiscent of the way Rome went after Carthage. I certainly hope I'm not the cause of your surge in brutality."

She pretended not to hear him, but the tightening of her mouth betrayed her. Even as he crossed the kitchen, she refused to acknowledge his presence. He stood beside the window that had been cracked open to allow a weak breeze to filter into the room.

"It looks like it might rain this afternoon," he said casually.

"It won't." She gave the dough another turn then flipped it with practiced hands into a stoneware bowl and covered it with a damp cloth. "It will be cloudy all day and won't rain until this evening. After that, we will have two, maybe three days of clear weather."

She said it without looking at him, but with such confidence he couldn't resist taking a little dig. "Then I see no reason why you can't tutor my son for two, maybe three days on the roof here at Dierenpark."

"Possibly because I am under threat of a lawsuit here." She carried the bowl to the windowsill, still not looking at him. She rinsed her hands in the basin then dried them in an economy of movement he found oddly attractive. Such simple motions but graceful and timeless in a way that appealed to him.

He clenched his teeth. Was he truly attracted to a woman because of the grace with which she washed her hands? It was appalling, but true.

She began stemming a bowl of strawberries, and he gaped at her quick and efficient fingers flying through the task. He leaned closer for a better view, and his eyes widened.

Well, he had just discovered the one part of the fragile, willowy Sophie van Riijn that was not beautiful. She had the hands of a farmer's wife, with trim nails and tough calluses. The backs of her hands were heavily nicked with tiny burns and scars.

He supposed all cooks had such scars, but for some reason he hadn't expected to see them on Sophie. They made him like her even more.

"What if I promised not to sue your father over those silly pictures?" he offered.

"Not good enough," she said without looking up as she grabbed a knife and began dicing the strawberries. "You'll find some other ancient offense to sue him over."

"There have been a lot, have there?"

She dropped the knife. "You see? That's exactly what I mean. No matter what I say, you manage to twist it and use it against me. I can't trust myself around you, and the sooner I'm away from this house, the better."

This would never do. Instead of persuading her to stay, he was pushing her away faster. Most of his life had been spent among hard-hitting corporate industrialists who didn't flinch at a little blunt language. He wasn't used to apologizing to anyone, and it made him feel exposed and weak. He couldn't look at her. How ghastly to be at her mercy, but he liked her and didn't want her to leave. And Pieter needed her. He swallowed hard, prepared to do whatever it took.

"I have been short-tempered and rude," he admitted. "I promise to refrain from any lawsuits for violations committed at Dierenpark prior to my return, provided that your father stops circulating rumors about my family. And stops selling the photographs, as well."

That should have pacified her, but she scooped up the strawberry stems and dumped them into a waste bowl and headed outside. He watched through the open doorway as she tossed the stems onto the kitchen dump, her mouth still a hard line. He parsed his words carefully as she returned to the kitchen.

"I've often heard that women are like elephants in that they never forget an offense, no matter how genuine the apology."

"That was an apology? I'm sorry, I mistook it for another legal salvo."

"It was an apology. I'm not accustomed to delivering them, so I may be a bit clumsy."

Her lips twitched. He was going to crack her composure if it killed him, but she was still sulking as she began slicing a loaf of bread, and he still hadn't won her agreement to stay and tutor Pieter.

"King Solomon had seven hundred wives," he said. "I'll bet he had a lot of practice delivering apologies. Women can be so fussy about these things."

She kept slicing the bread without looking at him, and he started to feel like an idiot. He had been in the wrong, and she deserved an honest apology.

"Please," he said, dropping every trace of cynicism and looking her squarely in the face. "I have no desire to sue you or your father, and my son truly needs you. *I* need you. I can be a bad-tempered fool, and I'm sorry. What will it take to convince you to keep tutoring Pieter?"

More money, shorter work hours . . . whatever it took, he intended to provide it. She said nothing as she continued slicing the bread with breathtaking speed, but she performed the task fearlessly. Such a simple gesture yet so classically Sophie, the way she handled everything from the surly bodyguards to taming the bees with grace and ease.

"I'll agree on one condition," she finally said.

He cocked a brow, curious why she suddenly seemed so nervous.

"There is an abandoned timber mill on the outskirts of town," she said.

"I know. My great-grandfather operated it until the day he died."

"And it's been shuttered ever since," Sophie said. "I'd like to show it to you."

The way she held her breath and the hungry expression in her eyes put him on alert. She was up to something. "Why?"

"I think it might be suitable for turning into one of the up-graded climate observatories the Weather Bureau is starting to build. They would pay you handsomely to lease the space."

He had no interest in amassing more money, but he sensed this was important to her. She briefly outlined her ambition to apply for a full-fledged climate observatory here in New Holland and how she hoped to use the mill as leverage. It was fascinating to watch the way energy sparkled in her eyes as she talked. Sophie seemed to harbor a wellspring of dreams and ambition just waiting to be tapped, even if she aspired to something as improbable as this.

He squeezed the handle of his cane, wishing her expression didn't remind him so much of a young architect who once aspired to equally far-fetched dreams. "If I look at the mill, you'll continue to tutor Pieter?"

"I'd want you to do more than just look at it," she said. "I've been putting a proposal together outlining the merits of locating an observatory in New Holland. If I can offer a ready-made building for the site, it will make the proposal even stronger. I'd like you to look at the mill and consider giving your approval in my proposal. If you do that, I'll be happy to keep working with Pieter."

"Has bribery worked for you in the past?"

"This is my first try," she said, a bit of humor dancing in her eyes. "But I have hopes."

"We'll go this afternoon."

He turned away from the eagerness blossoming on her face. He didn't like the prospect of being dragged into the wilderness with her. The rest of the people in this town might underestimate her, but he'd quit doing so on that second morning when he'd recognized Sophie's purity of spirit that never seemed to fade. Her sort of luminous hope was dangerous for him. It cast a spotlight on the grim limitations of his life. He could only watch, never participate, in Sophie's bright optimism and faith in a perfect world.

She would be appalled if she ever sensed his attraction to her, but he would keep it tightly contained. His son needed her too much to risk frightening her off because of this wild, unwieldy, and unwelcome fascination he harbored for her.

8

THE ROAD WAS BADLY RUTTED and overgrown, jostling the carriage springs that squeaked and groaned with each bump. Sophie felt a little awkward being confined so tightly beside Quentin in the carriage, but she'd endure anything if she could win his agreement to transform the abandoned mill into a climate observatory.

A deep, fragrant forest surrounded them on all sides. Most of this land had been cleared when the mill was in operation sixty years ago, but forest could overtake the land quickly. Brambles thwacked against the side of the carriage, and the scent of deep, loamy soil pervaded the air.

"This is far enough," Sophie said to Mr. Ratface, who drove the carriage. They had arrived at the promontory that jutted out toward the river, where the old mill once funneled tons of timber toward cities all over the world. Forest surrounded them on three sides, but straight ahead was a rambling old building that would have covered a city block had it been built in town. It was two stories tall, with a bank of large windows, mostly broken, running along the top floor.

"I know it looks bad from the outside, but the building is structurally sound, and it's ideally placed to take advantage of the river." She spoke quickly, her words tripping over one another lest he cut her off. Quentin's face was closed and shuttered as he clung to a leather strap, gingerly stretching his good leg out the carriage door. He looked embarrassed as Mr. Ratface stepped forward to brace a shoulder beneath Quentin's outstretched arm and gently lowered his employer to the ground. Sophie averted her gaze and waited for Quentin to adjust his clothing before turning to face him.

"Let's go inside," Quentin said, already heading toward the building. He was probably eager to get this over with as quickly as possible, and she scrambled for ways to make this deal look attractive to him. The lock on the door had rusted through ages ago, and Quentin was able to push the squeaking door open with ease.

It didn't seem so bad inside. Sophie watched as Quentin waved away a gnat that pestered his face, scanning the interior of the mill with curiosity. He didn't seem bored—rather, he seemed to be assessing the building with an architect's eyes, perusing the timber chutes and network of flywheels overhead.

"You can see how spacious the building is," she said. "If we clear out the band saws, there will be plenty of room for all kinds of table-sized maps. And the best thing is the miles of timber chutes through the forest. It means we already have a path cleared that will be suitable for laying telegraphic wires."

A patter of sudden rain on the roof punctuated the silence. "I thought you said it wasn't going to rain until this evening," Quentin commented.

"Weather prediction is still a bit of an estimate," she admitted, looking out the window with concern. The drops of rain were fat and heavy, indicating a healthy downpour was only moments away.

"I hate to think of Mr. Ratface getting wet. Should we ask him inside?"

"His name is simply Ratface," Quentin replied, a hint of amusement in his voice. "I can assure you he takes it as no sign of disrespect if you call him such."

"That can't be his given name."

"It is how he chooses to identify himself." The rain was falling steadily now, fast and heavy, and it didn't seem right to make a man stand in the rain when it was perfectly dry inside the mill.

"Nevertheless, I hope he isn't getting wet."

"Of course Ratface is getting wet. Ratface gets paid double what most men in his position earn, and he is glad for the work."

Sophie darted to the door to peek outside. The rain fell so hard it looked like sheets of white. The bodyguard stood huddled beside the carriage, holding a horse blanket over his head. She didn't care how big and scary he was, he looked absolutely pitiful hunched under that dripping blanket. Without thinking, she dashed outside, yelping as cold water spattered her hands and face and streamed into her eyes. It was so cold! She sprang around the rapidly forming puddles, and it didn't take her long to reach Mr. Ratface.

"Come inside," she shouted, chilly water tracing rivulets down her neck. "Come inside—you'll drown out here!"

Mr. Ratface didn't have to be asked again. Pushing away from the carriage, he reached out to share part of the horse blanket with her and jogged toward the safety of the mill.

⁂

Quentin looked in exasperation as Sophie dashed through the rain. All he wanted was to win her agreement to keep tutoring Pieter, but now he was stranded in the middle of nowhere during a rainstorm. Damp weather always made his leg ache down to the marrow of the bone. He took a swig of the concentrated willow tea he kept in a flask for just such an event. It tasted like tree bark, but sometimes it helped with pain.

The door banged open and Sophie rushed inside, her skirts soaked. The air was cooling from the downpour, and she'd probably catch pneumonia and infect everyone at Dierenpark. They'd all be dead before the week was out because she couldn't resist taking Ratface under her wing. Shrugging out of his coat, Quentin handed it over to her. "Put this on, you're freezing."

She laughed and brushed it away. "Let me dry out a bit first." She bent over to squeeze water from her skirt.

"I'm sorry we left you out there to get soaked, Mr. Ratface," she said, smiling up at him as she finished wringing her hem.

Ratface shifted uncomfortably. "Umm . . . just Ratface, ma'am."

"I'd feel better calling you *Mr.* Ratface."

Ratface looked at him, bewilderment apparent on his face. Then he cleared his throat and faced Sophie. "My real name is Pureheart, ma'am. I'd truly prefer it if you called me Ratface."

Quentin spewed out a mouthful of tea, choking on laughter.

If possible, Ratface looked even more uncomfortable as he provided an explanation. "My mum was a fan of that Bible verse, the one about the pure of heart and seeing God."

Sophie perked up. "'Blessed are the pure in heart, for they shall see God?'"

"That's the one," Ratface admitted. "My mum was a good woman, but to the bottom of my soul, I wish she'd given me a normal name."

Sophie winced in sympathy. "My real name is Sophronia. I understand. But come, let me show you the mill."

She proceeded to point out where the offices could be built and which areas would be suitable for the giant, oversized maps used by the meteorologists. She spoke in a breathless voice, a blinding smile on her face the entire time. She must be cold, miserable, and wet, and still she smiled. Everything about Sophie was warm and cheerful, transforming this abandoned millhouse by her mere presence.

She continued rambling while he and Ratface trailed after her, but Quentin had stopped listening. Her desire to transform this abandoned mill into a climate observatory was admirable but not his problem. He was only here because it was her condition to keep mentoring Pieter. Outside, the rain poured down in sheets, and the wind buffeted the trees so hard it flipped up the silvery undersides of the leaves. They would probably be trapped here for hours.

"So you knew the rain was coming," he interjected as she rambled about the delightful scent of freshly milled white pine.

She paused at the diversion but answered him. "The men in Washington got it wrong by half a day, but yes, I knew we were due for a bit of rain."

"The wonders of science," he said pointedly. "How can a good Christian like you even believe in meteorology? Shouldn't mankind's ability to predict the weather disprove God's existence?"

Sophie didn't take offense at his question. With the calm diplomacy he was coming to expect from her, she replied with a confounding mix of logic and innocence. "Climatic events are predicted by analyzing the changes in atmospheric pressure," she replied. "God designed the rules of nature, and we are getting better at reading them. That doesn't mean he isn't the original author."

"But why would the author abandon his work?" he challenged. One of his chief arguments against religion had always been the question of why God, if he existed, would show himself so plainly to some people but stay hidden from others. It seemed unfair and made no logical sense. "Your God seemed to chat quite freely with Moses and Abraham. Why not us?"

"Perhaps he is chatting, and you aren't listening."

Quentin lumbered over to an old bench and sat, stretching out his bad leg and wincing as the blood circulated with greater ease. "Not good enough, Miss van Riijn. There is no logic to it. If God exists, why doesn't he simply appear and tell us what to do? Why do we have to hunt down dusty manuscripts written in languages no one reads anymore and try to guess what they mean? Why doesn't he *prove* he exists?"

He rarely wasted time debating theology with Bible-thumpers who weren't open to reason, but they were trapped here until this storm blew over, and it seemed as good a topic as any.

Sophie seemed a little off-kilter by the question, but after a moment of pondering, she responded. "What if the rain suddenly stopped, the clouds parted, and God appeared in the sky, glowering down at you and ordering you how to behave. You would have no choice but to believe and obey. Your decision to follow his teachings through love would be gone, and you would obey out of fear. There is a pleasing logic to it, if only you'd open your mind enough to consider it."

He was mildly taken aback. "Are you accusing me of being closed-minded?" He was the most open-minded, forward-looking, and rational man in the world. "I have always been willing to consider anything so long as the data and facts back it up."

"But you see *only* with your mind," Sophie countered. "I believe God gave us many ways to experience the world . . . through seeing, hearing, touching, but also heart. When I align my thoughts and actions with the teachings of Jesus, I sense him in my heart, and the entire way I see the world shifts."

"My heart is already too burdened keeping my broken-down body alive to worry about intercepting cryptic messages from Jesus."

"So cynical!" Sophie teased, but she turned to gaze through the broken-out windows. The profile of her face was as lovely

108

as a cameo. What would it be like to see the world through Sophie's eyes? The familiar rasp of envy trickled through him.

Blessed are the pure in heart, for they shall see God.

He looked away. That passage seemed tailor-made for Sophie. It wasn't that he was ignorant of religion. Indeed, he had been exposed to too much of it as he followed his grandfather all over the world from one sacred shrine to another in a bizarre quest for enlightenment. When he was a child, they went to India in search of the Buddha. Another year his grandfather was convinced the golden fleece was real and they hopped islands in Greece in search of it. They never stayed anywhere longer than a few months, as Nickolaas was always eager to seek out whatever lay beyond the next horizon. They saw monasteries in Tibet, walked through tulip fields in Holland, and watched lions in Kenya. "Itchy feet," his grandfather called it. No sooner had Quentin settled into their lodgings in a new city and started befriending the hotel staff than Nickolaas uprooted him to pursue the next spiritual quest.

Sometimes Portia's family joined them on their travels, which was probably why their friendship had been so steadfast growing up. They were two rootless children who understood each other. Aside from Nickolaas, Portia had been the only constant in his life. Their friendship had meant the world to him. To this day, his memories of those faraway sights were tinged by her bittersweet memory.

Portia. Even her name stirred a wealth of painful memories. She had died eight years ago, but he had never been tempted to remarry, for if he and Portia were unable to make a marriage work, how could he trust his judgment a second time?

He looked at Sophie, her face luminous despite the dim interior of the mill as she showed Ratface how the old debarking drum worked. In a way, she reminded him of his younger self, before illness and despair tarnished his world. Hope was a dangerous thing, and he had long since given up toying with it. He needed to keep his distance from Sophie.

It didn't mean he should stand in the way of her dreams. This abandoned mill was not part of the original Dierenpark estate and his grandfather wouldn't care what Quentin did with it. There was no logical reason he should deny Sophie's request to use it to lure the Weather Bureau here.

Sophie and Ratface were giggling over the way a squirrel huddled on a narrow ledge outside the window to keep dry. Their laughter grated on him.

"As soon as it stops raining, we are leaving," he said, cutting off their conversation. "Use the mill however you wish, I don't care. Just stop that infernal tittering before you suffocate the life from me."

The instant his words left his mouth he regretted them. Why couldn't he do something nice for Sophie without spoiling it by being mean? His leg hurt, his head pounded, and he just couldn't tolerate her giddy optimism anymore. The dark clouds of melancholy were closing in again, choking off whatever scraps of happiness he had in his life.

The three of them were trapped in uncomfortable silence until the rain tapered off twenty minutes later. He'd been rude and brusque . . . pointlessly so, but he'd make it up to Sophie by doing everything possible to get one of those fancy climate observatories she wanted located here in the village.

Upon returning to Dierenpark, Quentin summoned Mr. Gilroy to meet him in the orangery, the only place where privacy could be guaranteed. It was annoying to have his grandfather's spy observing Quentin's every move, but at least Mr. Gilroy no longer denied he was Nickolaas's spy. Better still, Mr. Gilroy was occasionally willing to use his considerable talents on Quentin's behalf. He told Mr. Gilroy of Sophie's desire for an upgraded climate observatory and how much Vandermark influence he'd be willing to throw behind the effort to lure the station here. The first order of business was to learn about the man who would be making the decisions.

"Find out everything you can about the director of the Weather Bureau," Quentin instructed. "Where he was educated, what he likes to drink, the name of his wife. Let it be known that I am searching for a scientific endeavor to fund and would welcome his visit at Dierenpark. That ought to get him salivating." A little bribery could go a long way in this world, although Quentin was always careful to disguise such actions as charitable donations or courtesies in arranging key introductions.

"Consider it done," Mr. Gilroy said smoothly.

He remained in the orangery long after Mr. Gilroy left. Facing the others in the main house was too difficult to contemplate right now. Another of the suffocating black moods had descended, draining him of energy and hope. Would it last a day? A month? Impossible to know. He had no understanding of why or how these periods of melancholia swamped him, and therefore was helpless to find a way out.

All he knew for certain was that Sophie was an entirely good person. Entirely kind. If someone of her purity could not rescue him from this dark wasteland, no one could. It shamed him, but when he was in a foul mood like this, it was agony to be near her. She reminded him of his own lost, idyllic youth. Of a world drenched in sunlight, possibility, and endless summer days. Something about her sparked a monstrous hope that he could aspire to more in life than the hard confines that encased his broken body and spirit.

Well . . . enough wallowing. He grasped his cane and rose, wincing against the familiar pain shooting up his leg. It was time to get back to the house and do his duty by Pieter. For now, that meant tolerating Sophie, who seemed to have a magical touch in easing Pieter's endless anxieties. He could endure the glare of her happiness on Pieter's behalf. And if buying Sophie a fancy climate observatory made her happy, perhaps it would help lift his own mood, as well. Even thinking of it brought a smile to one corner of his mouth.

Sophie made him long to be a better man, and that was something he had not felt in a long time.

9

JUNE FADED INTO JULY, and Sophie had never enjoyed herself more as she cooked for the household and mentored Pieter on the roof. The Vandermarks had been here almost a month, and she'd established a tentative peace with most of the men.

All except Quentin, who maintained a stony silence whenever she entered a room. She sometimes overheard him joking with his men, but his humor evaporated whenever he spotted her.

"Miss Sophie, do you want to see the salamander I found?"

Pieter's innocent voice interrupted Sophie's thoughts as she cut steam vents into the top of a newly assembled peach pie. Pieter hovered in the arched doorway to the kitchen, a box clutched in his arms.

Last week she had shown Pieter a mud crab down by the river, turning it over so he could see how the female crab carried a clutch of eggs on her belly. Pieter was fascinated by it, and ever since he'd been prowling the riverbank to collect other reptiles, usually dragging them up to the house for her to admire.

She glanced over at Florence, who was peeling potatoes. "Will you get these pies in the oven? I have a salamander that needs looking at."

The old housekeeper shuffled over to tend the three pies. Between the two of them, they were managing to keep up with the cooking, but just barely. The men in this household had big appetites, and she was getting accustomed to baking three pies at a time.

Sophie followed Pieter to the cozy parlor overlooking the river but drew back when she saw Quentin ensconced at the table, the demolition plan for the second floor laid out before him. Each day, the plan became more detailed as he completed the calculations for the distribution of dynamite. She hated the sight of that plan. The plans for the first two floors were almost complete. With only one more floor to map out, the time for the demolition was drawing near.

"I'm sorry, I didn't realize you were using this room," she said. "We'll find somewhere else to go."

"Not at all," Quentin said. "I'd like for Pieter to join me."

Pieter's fingers curled about the box he clutched. "Do I have to?" Pieter asked, the apprehension plain in his voice.

Even from across the room, Sophie noticed the muscles in Quentin's face tighten. What must it be like for your own son to constantly avoid you?

"Why don't you show your father the salamander, too? It will be a treat for both of us," Sophie said with as much excitement as she could muster.

Quentin pulled some of his drawings aside to make room for Pieter's box. The boy trudged forward, reluctance in every step, but he obediently set the box on the table. Sophie's eyes widened in surprise, for the "box" Pieter carried was a seventeenth-century tea caddy inlaid with hand-carved ivory.

"What on earth?" Quentin burst out. "You're using an antique box to put salamanders in?"

"It was the only box I could find," Pieter said defensively, and Sophie scrambled for a way to smooth over the incident.

"Show me your salamander," she coaxed. "I'll find a more appropriate box from the shed outside, and then I'll be happy to clean up the tea caddy."

The glossy black salamander jerked in panicky motions at the bottom of the box, and sadly, it had already made a mess. Pieter said he planned on releasing the salamander into the window well on the east side of the house, where he was collecting all manner of toads, frogs, and lizards. He brought them water and some of Sophie's cookies every morning.

"I'm not sure they eat cookies," she said.

Pieter smiled. "No, but the bugs do, and they've been eating the bugs."

Sophie was pleased at Pieter's cleverness, but Quentin was still annoyed. "I want that box cleaned up. And you're not to make Miss Sophie do it. You caused the mess, you shall clean it up. That box is a valuable treasure worth more than most people earn in a year, and you've gone and spoiled it."

It bothered her the way Pieter curled in on himself, losing whatever bit of pride he'd gleaned by capturing the salamander.

"It shouldn't matter," Pieter grumbled. "It's just going to get blown up with the rest of the house."

"I don't care," Quentin snapped. "That box was not yours to ruin, and you will learn proper respect and clean it immediately."

Sophie lost interest in the box, dumbfounded at what she'd just heard. "You are going to destroy everything? The contents of the house, too?"

"Everything," Quentin confirmed.

It staggered her. All the furniture, the grand paintings, the antiques filling every drawer and cupboard in this majestic, stately house. Her heart squeezed, thinking of the books in the library that had been her window into the wider world.

"But why? It would be so easy to save the books and the art . . ."

"My grandfather wants everything blown up," Pieter said. "We would get in trouble if we tried to take anything out of the house with us."

"Why on earth would he insist on such a thing?" She held her breath, hoping Quentin would let Pieter answer. Children lacked guile and were sometimes the best source of unvarnished truth.

"This house is cursed," Pieter said, his voice serious. "So is everything in it. We can't take anything out of the house with us or the curse might escape. My grandfather said so."

"Now what kind of person believes in such silly superstition?" she asked, pretending to speak to Pieter but staring directly at Quentin. "It makes no sense to destroy such treasures because of illogical superstition, does it?"

"Perhaps my grandfather's motive isn't based on superstition at all," Quentin replied. "It could be the old man has a perfectly rational desire for wanting the contents destroyed along with the rest of the house. After all, there may be some evidence of a crime he wants destroyed."

Having been raised in New Holland, she knew of the rumor that a fourteen-year-old Nickolaas Vandermark had murdered his father in the river.

"You don't really believe that, do you?" Sophie asked.

"Many people do. After the walls come down, I've been ordered to douse the rubble with kerosene, set it on fire, and repeat the process until nothing but dust survives." A bleak smile curved his mouth. "Quite thorough, isn't he? I wonder what is in this house that he fears?"

There was a bitter twist to his face. Sophie knew Quentin didn't believe in a Vandermark curse, yet he was prepared to carry out his grandfather's senseless demands. How could a man of science and logic let himself be used this way? Did he have no respect for tradition? For the history embodied in this house?

The doorbell sounded. Pieter startled and clutched the box. "Who's that?" he asked in an anxious voice. He scooted closer to Sophie, and within moments three bodyguards and Mr. Gilroy came tromping into the room.

"It's probably just someone from the village," Quentin said, but he shifted higher in his chair and eased his leg off its bed of pillows. "Collins, stay with us. Ratface and Atkinson, secure the other doors."

"I'll go see who it is," Mr. Gilroy said, his voice a soothing contrast to the other men who seemed caught off guard by the unannounced stranger. Is this how rich people had to live? Pieter's anxiety seemed extreme, but the damage done by the kidnappers was a fresh memory for him. Muffled voices came from the front hall, mixed with a little laughter. Surely that was a good sign, wasn't it?

Footsteps echoed down the hallway and an old man, tall and narrow as a beanpole, stepped into the parlor.

"Grandpa!" Pieter shouted, racing across the room and into the laughing old man's arms.

Quentin stood, his face grim. "I don't think this is a good idea."

"Why, it seems someone thinks my visit is a very good idea," the old man said in a good-humored tone, ruffling Pieter's hair but locking a steely gaze on Quentin. He withdrew a bit to look down into Pieter's adoring face. "What do you say, lad? Can a room be found for your old grandpa?"

"You can stay in my room. Please?" The boy's voice brimmed with hope and, once again, Sophie felt a little bad for Quentin. The child was stiff and uncomfortable around his father, but the way he bloomed the instant Nickolaas Vandermark walked into the room was astounding. If Quentin had a beating heart beneath that block of ice, this had to hurt a bit.

"You aren't staying," Quentin said. "Mr. Gilroy can drive

you into the village or he can take you to the city. I don't care which, but you aren't staying here."

"You seem to be forgetting whose house this is," Nickolaas said with a tight smile.

Quentin reached inside his coat pocket and withdrew a sealed envelope. "You gave me complete power of attorney over this house, and I say you can't stay here. We agreed you would give me time alone with Pieter to get reacquainted."

The old man extracted himself from Pieter's arms, his gaze scanning the room. His withered face took on a faraway quality, as though enchanted by the sight of his childhood home. He walked the perimeter of the room, noting the old paintings on the wall and the view of the river out the window. It had been sixty years since he had been in this house, and everything was exactly as it had been the day he left. It must be like stepping back in time. His face carried a wistful smile mingled with sadness as he took in the room. At last his gaze tracked to her.

"You must be Miss van Riijn," he said pleasantly.

Sophie flushed, stunned that he should know her name, but perhaps it shouldn't be a surprise. It seemed Quentin was right about Mr. Gilroy funneling information to the elder Vandermark.

"Yes, I am Sophie van Riijn," she said, dipping into a little curtsy. What was the proper way to greet a man like Nickolaas Vandermark? He was a living legend, and one of the richest men in the world.

Nickolaas reached for her hand, executing a courtly bow and pressing a quick kiss to the back of her hand. "I've heard a great many interesting things about you. We need to have a little chat."

"Not in this house, you won't. I've got power of attorney over this house, and you aren't welcome."

The old man's smile did not waver. "Take me to court," he tossed off over his shoulder.

"Don't think I won't," Quentin said, but Nickolaas was relaxed as he guided Sophie to the settee. After they were both sitting, he patted her knee.

"Tell me about the water lilies in Marguerite's Cove," Nickolaas said pleasantly.

Water lilies? She looked to Mr. Gilroy, accusation in her eyes. She'd confided in Mr. Gilroy because he'd seemed so kind and she longed for a nonjudgmental friend. But his sympathy was merely a ploy to trick her into opening up.

"I can show you!" Pieter chimed in. "They are down by a crook in the river, and they never die."

"I'd prefer to hear about them from Miss van Riijn," Nickolaas said. "There have been lilies blooming in that spot for a long time?"

A trickle of unease curled through her. It was on the precise spot where the dead body of Karl Vandermark had been found. She cleared her throat. "Y-yes," she stammered. "They've been there as long as I can remember."

"And oysters . . . you mentioned that oysters flourish on that spot."

"They do. Yes."

"Fascinating." He withdrew an envelope from his coat pocket and tossed it across the room to Quentin. "I'm revoking your power of attorney. That is a court order signed by a judge. I've got complete control over the house again."

Quentin tore open the envelope, sputtering in disbelief as he scanned the document inside. "I've spent the past three weeks drawing up demolition plans *on your order*. Now you're changing your mind?"

"Quentin, I love your command of the English language. You grasped my meaning so quickly I don't even need to repeat myself. You make me proud."

Quentin stood. "You've been hounding me for years to learn the art of demolition so I could someday blow up this house. When I suggested you simply hire a competent demolition expert, you insisted it could only be done by someone with Vandermark blood. I've tried to reason with you. I've tried to appeal to your sense of history. To Pieter's heritage. To the wanton destruction of precious art and antiquities that ought to go to a museum. Nothing convinced you, but now you waltz in and declare you've changed your mind? I am owed an explanation. Now!"

Nickolaas seemed remarkably calm in the face of the younger man's ire. He simply smiled. "I'd like to learn why water lilies grow in that cove. Perhaps the same reason crocuses grow on my wife's grave?"

"Now I know you've lost your mind," Quentin muttered, collapsing into a chair and rubbing his leg. He looked ready to explode.

Nickolaas turned to look at Sophie. "My wife loved crocuses, and I planted some on her resting spot. Crocuses are supposed to bloom only once per year, but those flowers bloom three times a year without fail." He looked at Quentin with a hint of triumph. "Your vaunted *science* can't explain that. Something magical is at work."

"And someone's mind is clearly slipping into dementia."

"The manners of young men these days." Nickolaas sighed, shaking his head in mock despair and looking at Sophie. "Did you know I raised Quentin from the cradle? His parents died in a hotel fire when he was only a few months old. I took him into my home and raised him like my own son. And after Quentin's wife died and he was incapacitated by the injury to his leg, incapable of caring for young Pieter, who do you suppose stepped in to raise the child?"

"You did, Grandpa!"

He smiled warmly at the boy. "Indeed I did. Of course, I always asked Pieter to call me Grandpa, since 'Great-Grandpa' seemed like such a mouthful. I was sixty-six years old when Pieter was born, a time when men should be basking in their golden years, but I geared myself up to undertake the task of raising yet another child. I had Pieter for two years before Quentin was well enough to take responsibility again. I never asked Quentin for a word of thanks, never asked for a dollar in compensation. All I've ever asked of him was to blow up one house, and he acts as if I had ordered him to reroute the Nile."

Quentin clenched and unclenched his fist. "Miss van Riijn, would you please escort my grandfather to the river and show him the water lilies? Share whatever wisdom you can offer, then he can be on his way."

Nickolaas acted as though he had not heard. "The ancient Egyptians believed the water lily symbolized the eternal cycle of life and death. I think there may be something to it." He reached inside his coat and withdrew a small cloth bag. "Look, I've brought some incense. We can have a séance—"

"Pieter, please leave the room," Quentin said bluntly.

"But Grandpa just got here—"

"I'm not asking again," Quentin said in an implacable voice.

"You won't make Grandpa leave without letting me say good-bye? Because it wouldn't be the first time," the boy accused in a dark voice.

"Out!" Quentin shouted. "Now."

Pieter reluctantly turned around, dragging his feet the entire way out of the room. Quentin waited until the sound of his footsteps disappeared down the hall. He limped to the hallway door and slammed it shut with a force that made Sophie flinch.

"There will be no talk of séances in front of my son," Quentin said in a tight voice. "Nor will there be tarot card readings, fortune-tellers, the casting of horoscopes, or consulting with charlatans. No shamans, palm readers, or voodoo priestesses."

Nickolaas tilted his head back to look down his nose at Quentin. "How about a team of archaeologists from Harvard?"

"What?" That took Quentin aback.

"Archaeologists. Men trained in the study of human history through the excavation of historic sites and careful analysis of artifacts, documents, and other physical remains."

"I know what archaeology is," Quentin snapped. "Why do you want to bring them here?"

Sophie was intrigued, too. This estate had a fantastic history—surely an archaeologist's dream. Every step she took on Vandermark land had once been trod upon by Algonquin Indians, Caribbean pirates, Dutch fur traders, or British soldiers.

Instead of replying to Quentin's question, the old man turned to her. "Forgive me for airing family gossip before you, but I gather you are already well acquainted with this estate and Vandermark history. I needn't tell you that the spot where the water lilies are flourishing is where my father died. I have reason to believe he was searching for something of great value. I want to know what. I want experts brought in to excavate the spot."

Now even Quentin was intrigued. "You think there's something hidden in the river? What?"

"I don't know," Nickolaas said. "But when I was in Amsterdam, I paid a small fortune to buy an archive of Vandermark documents from the seventeenth century. It contained a number of letters written by the original Vandermark brothers, sent to Holland shortly after they arrived in America. One letter included a map hand-drawn by Adrien Vandermark himself. He sketched the cliff, the spot where the cabin had been built, plans for the future house, and the river." Nickolaas leaned forward, the twinkle in his blue eyes vanishing, replaced by a sense of urgency. "And he drew a circle around the stretch of the river where Miss van Riijn says the water lilies are growing. He claimed the waters had magical properties. He said it was a paradise on earth. He believed there was something of great value there. Something worth dying for."

"Or killing?"

Nickolaas's eyes narrowed. "Possibly. In any event, I want experts to look at the site. The house and grounds, too. I want everything thoroughly examined before we return the land to its natural state."

Sophie held her breath, hoping this might be the stay of execution she'd been praying for. Dierenpark was a magnificent estate, and the longer the Vandermarks stayed here, the more likely they were to appreciate that fact.

"I'll agree on one condition," Quentin said.

Nickolaas leaned his head back, peering at his grandson with a speculative gaze. "What?"

"You can't live here while the excavation takes place. You can live in the village or on the moon, I don't care, but you can't stay here."

The steel hidden beneath the veneer of the kindly old gentleman emerged. "This is my house, and I'll sleep wherever I choose."

The door to the parlor banged open. "Don't you make Grandpa leave!" Pieter yelled. "You're always pushing him away, and he's the only person who really loves me!"

"Watch your tone," Quentin warned.

Pieter ignored him, pushing over a tea table and sending a crystal goblet smashing to the ground. "Leave me alone!" Pieter yelled as he tore toward the front door of the house. "I hate you, and I hate this house!"

"Pieter! Get back here!" Quentin shouted, reaching for his cane and following as quickly as he could, but Nickolaas and the bodyguards were faster, the latter sprinting down the hall after the boy.

Sophie stood, twisting her hands in indecision. This was a family squabble and she wanted no part of it, but should she follow? This estate was full of danger for an angry, reckless boy tearing headlong toward the cliff or down the narrow, twisting deer path.

Tact didn't matter when it came to protecting a child. Running to the front door, she saw both Vandermark men and two of the bodyguards standing on the front porch in indecision. There was no sign of Pieter, which meant he probably headed into the woods on the left or the deer path on the other side that led to the river.

"My guess is that he took off for the river," Collins said. With a gesture to the other bodyguard, the two men darted toward the deer path.

Quentin remained frozen on the landing, his knuckles white as he clenched his cane.

"I'm sorry," she whispered. "Pieter didn't mean what he said."

Quentin's mouth hardened, but there was worry in his eyes as he scanned the forests on both sides of the meadow. To her right, she heard the muffled sounds of the men thrashing through the overgrown shrubbery as they headed down the rutted deer path toward the river, a place where Quentin could not follow. What a frustration it must be for a proud man to be locked in helpless immobility while others searched for his wayward son.

"I'll check the woods on the other side," Quentin said grimly as he lurched down the short flight of steps.

"Let him be," Nickolaas said. "The boy just needs to have a little sulk."

Sophie didn't think shoving over tables or yelling hatred at your father counted as *a little sulk*, but she didn't know how rich people behaved. Quentin ignored his grandfather, finally reaching the bottom of the steps and leaning heavily on his cane as he hobbled toward the forest on the left.

"That man has no idea how to deal with a petulant child," Nickolaas muttered. "All he does is scold and bark commands."

From deep in the woods came a loud thump, followed by the panicked cries of a young boy. Then came screams.

"Oh heavens, *the bees*!" Sophie raced toward the path that led to the beehives. The eight-sided hives were kept elevated on a stand, and Sophie had a terrible suspicion that the noise she'd just heard was the entire structure toppling over in the same manner as the tea table.

She followed the shouts to the clearing in the woods, horrified at the cloud of angry bees swarming around Quentin, who held Pieter in both arms. The wooden beehives lay on the ground, covers split open while bees gushed into the air. Pieter sobbed, burying his face in his father's neck while bees covered them both, the furious buzzing ratcheting the sense of panic higher.

Quentin's cane was on the ground, and he lurched toward her in a horrible, lopsided gait but with considerable speed. Pieter screamed and waved his arms, frantically batting at the bees, but Quentin was helpless against the swarm. He held Pieter with both arms, and the bees crawled all over Quentin's face while he lumbered forward. Sophie held a sapling to the side so they could pass, some of the bees still trailing after them.

"I'll run ahead and open the door," she hollered. Quentin nodded, still managing to move with surprising speed as they made it into the clearing before the house.

"Get inside!" she yelled to the bodyguards loitering on the front steps with Nickolaas. The fading buzzing sounds indicated they were outrunning the bees, but a sting pierced her neck and another stung her hand.

Mr. Gilroy saw what was happening and raced to lift Pieter from Quentin's arms, hustling the boy up the steps and through the front door. Relieved of his burden, Quentin collapsed on the landing, but the bees were still at him. Sophie batted at the furious insects, but it had little effect.

"Can you walk?" she shouted.

Quentin was still doubled over, struggling to rise. "I don't know," he gasped. His face was chalk-white except for the bright red splotches from dozens of stings. Squatting down, she propped her shoulder beneath his arm, using all the strength in her legs to push him upright, almost toppling beneath his weight. Mercifully, one of the bodyguards rushed to Quentin's other side, hoisting him up and lifting him over the short flight of stairs. Nickolaas opened the door as they all tumbled inside.

They lowered Quentin to the floor, his body landing with a thud. Pieter clung to his grandfather and cried. There was a sting over his right eyebrow and a few others on his neck, but he hadn't taken nearly the brunt Quentin had. Pieter had been able to bat the bees away, while Quentin had been helpless as he dragged his son from the overturned hives. Sophie had never witnessed such an act of bravery in her entire life.

"I'm sorry," Pieter sobbed. "I didn't know what that thing was. I just wanted to hit something. I'm so sorry."

Quentin still lay on the floor, breathing raggedly. "It's okay," he said, his eyes gentling as he looked at his son. "It's going to be okay."

"But you're all stung," Pieter said. And he was. Quentin had countless inflamed red pricks on his face and neck, and more on his hands. They would swell over the coming days. His skin was chalky and covered in a sheen of perspiration, but he still managed to sound calm.

"I'll be all right," he said. "I would do anything in the world for you, don't you know that?"

Sophie's heart turned over at that confession, for the honesty in Quentin's voice made it impossible to doubt him. The words made Pieter's guilt rip deeper, and the boy cried harder. Quentin glanced at Mr. Gilroy.

"Take Pieter to the kitchen and get those stings treated," he said, not so gently this time. From her position only a few feet away, she could see he was trembling, and both hands were clenched into white-knuckled fists.

The moment Pieter was ushered from the room, Quentin rolled onto his side, turning his face into the floor and rocking back and forth, clutching his leg. It wasn't the bee stings that caused him to writhe in agony—it was his leg. He had fled from swarming bees without the aid of a cane, and now he was paying for it. A shudder seized Quentin's entire body, and he vomited on the floor.

"I think his leg might have broken again," Nickolaas said worriedly. "Go get a doctor. I'll stay with Quentin."

Sophie was frozen, unable to tear her gaze from Quentin's sweat-dampened face, his eyes rolled back in pain.

"Move, girl!" Nickolaas barked, and she sprang into action.

10

IT WAS ALMOST TWO HOURS before Sophie was able to return with Dr. Weir. She had arrived on foot this morning, so it took a while to run to the village, and then locating the doctor at a patient's house took another twenty minutes. He was examining Mr. Cordona's gouty knee and was not pleased when she came bursting inside.

"It's an emergency," she said on a ragged breath. She didn't know exactly what was wrong with Quentin's leg, but she'd never seen such naked agony on any man's face, and it was frightening.

Thank heaven Dr. Weir wasn't the type of person to put any stock in rumors of the Vandermark curse. There were plenty of people in town who refused to get anywhere near Dierenpark, but Dr. Weir had done service in the Civil War, and few things frightened him. It worried her when he insisted on returning to his home to collect a bone saw, but she supposed he knew what he was doing. The bone saw was more than a foot long, with vicious-looking metal teeth along the serrated edge. It was the first thing Quentin spotted when Sophie brought Dr. Weir into the parlor.

"Get that thing out of here!" Quentin snarled, his furious glare locked on the bone saw. He was on a settee, his bad leg propped before him on an ottoman. The pallor of his face made the red splotches from the bee stings stand out more dramatically.

"Now, now," Dr. Weir said as he set his medical bag and the bone saw beside the settee. "No need to panic yet. I just need to examine your leg."

"Not with that bone saw in here."

"I'll take it away," Nickolaas said, emerging from a chair near the fireplace. "Come along, Miss van Riijn. This won't be a pleasant sight."

She was relieved to follow the older man from the room. Nickolaas led her back outside, where the late-afternoon sun slanted long shadows across the meadow. The bees were gone, and if they returned, she would need to use her smoker to calm them and put everything back to rights, although it would not surprise her if Quentin ordered the hives destroyed. It would be a shame, because the bees were one of the reasons this piece of land bloomed in such vibrant health.

Nickolaas headed toward a bench on the far side of the meadow. He moved with surprising agility for a man his age and beckoned her to join him on the bench. From here, they had a perfect view of the mansion, nestled amid the linden and juniper trees.

"It looks exactly the same as when I was a boy," Nickolaas said, his eyes scanning the lines of the old house. "I used to love playing in this old meadow. There were times I was convinced I heard the echo of my ancestors' voices, whispering in the woods. My father said it was only wind rustling in the trees, but I've always wondered."

He propped the bone saw against the bench, its smooth metal gleaming in the afternoon sun. "I don't want to go too far, in case the doctor needs this," he said grimly.

"Forgive me, but what precisely is wrong with your grandson's leg?" She'd always wondered, but it had seemed rude to ask.

Nickolaas gave a sad smile. "It started as a normal break. Quentin slipped on the ice as he was leaving his hotel in Vienna and fractured his shin. It should have been a simple thing, but the bone didn't set properly. A specialist in Berlin recommended the leg be re-broken in hopes that it would set properly. They tried it, but the leg still didn't heal."

Sophie cringed at the thought of having to endure such a painful procedure, especially if it didn't solve the problem.

"Quentin proceeded to visit a parade of medical experts. His leg had become so badly weakened the doctors all agreed the bone was unlikely to ever properly re-knit, and that it was in danger of snapping merely from putting his full weight on it. He suffers regular inflammations and infections in the wounded bone, which plunges his entire body into a fever. They are becoming more frequent and longer in duration."

Was it any wonder Quentin appeared to be in constant pain? Sophie had suffered plenty of cooking burns on her hands, and they always ached for days as they healed. It was a miracle Quentin was able to walk at all.

Nickolaas continued, "You will learn that Quentin puts great faith in science. When standard medical procedures did not cure his leg, he turned to experimental science. Last year was the crowning glory of Quentin's foolishness. He read about a new medical procedure involving transplanting a piece of his own healthy leg bone, grafting it onto his weakened tibia. In short, it was a disgusting procedure in which one part of his body was cannibalized in vain hope it could regenerate in another area."

Sophie recoiled, and Nickolaas gave her a thin smile. "Isn't medical technology wonderful? Quentin certainly puts all his faith in it, and the operation kept him in that clinic for the better part of a year. That was when I took custody of Pieter. Quentin tries to convince himself and Pieter that the graft is working and that it is an example of man's mastery of technology. Despite it all, Quentin remains surly and short-tempered, and instead of learning to respect science, Pieter has learned only to fear his father."

Sophie drew a breath to reply but then thought better of it. She had only known these people less than a month, but she'd witnessed the strained relationship between father and son. Quentin's refusal to tolerate Pieter's fears and superstitions only exacerbated other issues. Perhaps it was no wonder that Pieter preferred to live with a grandfather who showered him with unconditional affection.

Despite the tense cynicism in Nickolaas's tone, the way he clenched and twisted his hands indicated he cared. She noticed the ring he wore, a roughly carved pewter ring, an odd choice for a man of his wealth. She leaned forward to study it closer, for it reminded her of something . . .

"That's the ring from the portrait in the front hall," she said in wonder. One of the grim-faced Vandermark ancestors from the seventeenth century had worn the same ring.

"One of a pair," Nickolaas confirmed. "Both the original Vandermark brothers had just such a ring. One disappeared when Adrien died, but this is Caleb's ring and has always been passed down from father to son. A few years ago, I tried to give it to Quentin, but he wants nothing to do with it. He cares very little for our family's history."

The sun had begun to set when Mr. Gilroy appeared and summoned Nickolaas to attend Quentin's bedside. Sophie had not been invited, and she remained waiting on the mansion's portico as exhaustion set in. At least she could ride home in Dr. Weir's carriage this evening. She closed her eyes and opened her heart to the serenity of Dierenpark. It was easy to slip into a sort of rapt, dreamlike state while surrounded by the sheltering rim of trees.

But it wasn't all paradise. There were restless people here, and the delicate balance could be disturbed so easily. What had happened this afternoon was proof of that. The bees had attacked with ferocity when their world was disturbed. Nickolaas's arrival had brought a new wave of tension into the house. She had always considered Dierenpark the closest thing to paradise on earth, but even this blessed spot seemed plagued by the troubles of man.

She pushed herself to her feet, considering how she could repair the damage. The bees were usually calm at this time of day, and it would be best to get the hives turned upright. She had plenty of gauze netting to protect her skin, and the little tin smoker would further lull the bees into complacency as she did her best to restore their overturned little world back into balance.

Surprisingly, the doctor told Sophie that Quentin's leg was not broken, but he still ordered bed rest and a calcium-rich diet for the next two weeks. Since Quentin was unable to walk up even a single flight of stairs, a bed had been brought down to the formal dining room near the front of the house. The dining table was moved elsewhere, and Quentin rested on a bed installed alongside the Chippendale sideboard. It was an odd sickroom, with a crystal chandelier overhead and a grand oil painting by Thomas Gainsborough on the wall. It showed a sailboat skimming across the sea, bathed in the golden glow of a setting sun. It had always been Sophie's favorite painting in the house. She had never been outside the town of New Holland, but when she looked at that painting, it was easy to imagine setting sail into the great unknown.

Quentin had a table placed beside the bed, loaded down with stacks of books and his demolition plans. Beneath the mattress, he tucked the edges of two cloth sacks from which he could retrieve his drafting tools, correspondence, and reading glasses. Resting across his lap was a contraption with a slanted surface he used as a writing desk, but it could be tilted down in a few quick moves to serve as a meal tray. It made her realize that Quentin was quite accustomed to the life of an invalid.

The next morning, she took extra care in the kitchen. Quentin seemed to dislike her company, but she could show him a little compassion through the preparation of a delicious meal. The doctor's instructions for calcium-rich foods dictated her menu. She made a hearty rice pudding, liberally laced with cream, brown sugar, and a dash of cinnamon and vanilla. Rice pudding was what her mother had always made when Sophie was feeling poorly, and it pleased her to be able to serve the wonderfully comforting dish to Quentin. She toasted cheese atop slices of crusty bread with a hint of garlic.

As usual, people began tipping their heads into the kitchen while she cooked, lured by the aromas wafting through the house. She shooed them away, determined to serve Quentin first.

Nickolaas refused to be shooed away. "The scents from this kitchen have me on the verge of weeping."

She smiled, lifting a pitcher and pouring milk into a tall glass. "If you stir the rest of that cream into the rice pudding, it will be ready. Then we can get our patient served, and you can eat right afterwards."

"It is a bargain," he said with a courtly bow.

A few days ago, Sophie would have been mortified to be directing such a wealthy man as though he were kitchen staff, but nothing was quite normal in this house. They had no servants—only bodyguards. They had no women—only men who had outlived their wives and daughters.

She sighed as she loaded up the breakfast tray. She couldn't solve the problems of the Vandermark family that had been decades in the making, but she could at least serve a healthy breakfast.

Quentin grimaced when Sophie entered his room.

Every ounce of his body hurt, and she was the last person on earth he wanted to see. In addition to the typical pain from his leg, his skin was swollen and ached from dozens of bee stings. The sheets were pulled up to his chest, but his damaged leg lay naked and propped on a pillow above the sheet. A towel-wrapped chunk of ice covered the worst scars, but the entire length of his leg was lumpy from where the muscle and diseased bone had been removed. His brutalized leg was none of her business, and it was humiliating to be seen like this.

"Not a pretty sight, is it?" he said in a flat voice.

Sophie averted her gaze as she leaned over and set the tray on the table across Quentin's lap as if he were a child. "I've brought you breakfast. Your grandfather helped me finish the rice pudding."

"Thank you, but I'm not hungry. Please take it away."

Waves of depression were coming fast and hard today, the suffocating waters closing in over his head, and the only thing he had left was a slender thread of pride.

"I think you'll feel better if you eat something," Sophie said cheerfully. "Shall I fetch Pieter to come dine with you? It always seems so lonely to have no one to eat with. We can pull up a table alongside your bed. Or your grandfather and I can join you, would that be nice?"

"Miss van Riijn, your voice is irritating to me under the best of circumstances, but today it is excruciating. I'm asking for a little peace. If you would please leave, I will be eternally grateful."

He turned his face to the wall, finding it impossible to keep looking at the soft kindness in her face without cracking. Anguish of the soul was so much worse than physical pain. A searching, scorching emptiness filled him, and he was helpless to understand why or how to battle it. And why should he? His son hated him, and the only friends he had in the world were paid servants. The melancholic void expanded, blotting out whatever scraps of happiness were left in his world. He didn't want to break down in front of Sophie. Not Sophie—anyone but her. It would be the final humiliation.

"Would you like the toast first, or the rice pudding?"

"I would just like a little privacy," he said, ashamed of the tremor in his voice. He couldn't cope with her today, not with this suffocating despondency weighing on him. He wasn't even well enough to get out of bed to escape her.

He grit his teeth, praying she'd leave before he was unmanned. Someone like Sophie could have no conception of the gloom that smothered his entire world. To his horror, his bottom lip began to shake.

"For pity's sake, just leave," he managed to choke out. He was running out of time before he was completely humiliated in front of her.

"Sophie, perhaps we should leave," his grandfather said.

"Nonsense," she replied. From the corner of his eye, he saw her dip a spoon into the bowl. "Rice pudding can make anyone feel better, don't you think? Come, I'll feed you."

He snapped. He grabbed the bowl from her and hurled it against the wall, narrowly missing the Gainsborough painting. The bowl shattered into pieces, splattering gobs of rice pudding that dripped down the wall.

Sophie gasped. "That painting belongs in a museum, and you came two inches from ruining it!"

Despair washed over him. Now he was behaving like the child she'd been treating him as, but he couldn't breathe with her in here. He sagged against the pillow, wishing for an oblivion from which he'd never awaken. He covered his face with his hand, desperate not to be seen.

Nickolaas intervened and pulled Sophie toward the door. "Perhaps this would be a good time to step outside for a nice walk, shall we?"

She wasn't giving up. "No! I want to know why he would do something so hateful, so—"

"That wasn't a request, Miss van Riijn." His grandfather's voice carried a note of steel, and apparently it worked. Quentin heard a swish of skirts, and the door shut quietly behind them.

The sun was bright as Sophie stepped outside, Nickolaas close behind. It was embarrassing to be shouted at like that, but she'd done nothing to be ashamed of. They started down the path toward the front gates of the estate, the green scents from the herb garden filling the air. It didn't take long for Nickolaas to get to the point.

"I think it might be best if you stay away from the house for a few days."

Sophie paused, stunned by Nickolaas's statement. "You want me to leave?"

"Not for good, but I know Quentin very well, and you are a hindrance to his recovery. Now, don't look at me like that; you're making me feel like I've just kicked a puppy. All I am suggesting is that Quentin has a dark soul, and your cheerfulness is like acid to him. Until he is well enough to leave the sickbed, it would be best if you stayed away. Perhaps in a week you can return."

She'd never been away from Dierenpark for that length of time. In the past nine years, she hadn't missed a single day of checking the weather station. Someone else could check it for her, but what if the banishment turned out to be permanent? The thought of leaving this little piece of paradise was too painful to contemplate.

"You won't hire some other cook to replace me?"

He smiled. "We can survive without a cook for a few days. Besides, Quentin is more likely to appreciate your return after eating bread and cheese for a while."

She certainly hoped so. She loved cooking for others, but the sight of her mother's rice pudding spattered against the wall made her want Quentin to live on bread and water for a year.

"I suppose I can ask Pieter to take the climate measurements. He's been doing it with me for the past few weeks and knows how."

Nickolaas looked skeptical. "I'm not sure the boy can be trusted with such a task. He's not a very steady lad . . ."

Sophie had tended that weather station as though it were her firstborn child, and it made her nervous to turn it over to anyone, but the task wasn't difficult. All it really needed was someone who would dependably take the readings and send them to Washington. "I think it will be good for Pieter to be trusted with such an adult responsibility. One of the men could carry the message to town each morning, couldn't he?"

Nickolaas gave a concessionary nod. "If you are confident . . ."

The issue of the weather station was resolved, but she still faced the task of persuading Nickolaas to abandon his bizarre compulsion to tear down the house. He'd only arrived yesterday, and this was her first opportunity to begin probing his motives.

"What will happen to the house after the archaeologists complete their work?" she asked.

Nickolaas paused. They had reached the far side of the meadow, and he turned around to gaze at Dierenpark. The grand, stately house looked like it had been sitting in this spot since time began.

The old man's smile was wistful as he stared at the house. "I'll ask Quentin to tear it down, I suppose. I want the archaeologists to answer any lingering curiosity about the history of the place before I wipe it off the map."

"But why?" she pressed. "It's a beautiful house. People come from all over the state to admire it." *And the livelihood of this village depends on it.*

"Those people aren't Vandermarks," he said. "Quentin thinks the Vandermark curse is hogwash, but I know otherwise. It has been spoken of in my family for centuries. My father was on to something when he died. He had learned something very upsetting about this house, and in the end, I think it killed him. If I can't discover the source of the curse, and be confident it has been broken, I will tear the house down. Perhaps that will satisfy whatever gods or demons we've offended. If I can snuff out the curse now, perhaps Pieter and the rest of my descendants will be free to live normal lives."

She shook her head. Her Christian faith prevented her from giving any credence to hereditary curses, but it was plain Nickolaas believed in them.

"Has your life been so very terrible?" she asked carefully. She was walking out on a thin limb here. She had no business prying into deeply personal matters, but if she were to save the mansion, she needed to understand his motivation. "I know your father died an early death, and that must have been terrible for you, but many children lose a parent and don't assume it is part of a lifelong curse."

"So you don't think I killed my father? Many people do, you know." A hint of amusement twinkled in his eyes, and it was impossible to believe he would joke about this if he were guilty of patricide.

"No, I don't think you killed Karl Vandermark."

Nickolaas turned to sit on one of the stone benches angled so one could admire the meadow. "It was difficult after my father died," he said softly. "My parents had been separated for years, and my mother lived in Europe like a princess. I barely remembered her when she returned to take custody of me. Her main concern was securing her access to the Vandermark coffers, for she had an expensive lifestyle in Paris. She kept me completely isolated from my father's side of the family who still lived in Holland, but after I came of age, I sought them out and was able to see why she was so contemptuous of them. My mother was a rare spice, and the European branch of the Vandermark family were genuine salt of the earth. She never had use for such people."

Sophie joined him on the bench, hanging on to every syllable, for she had always been fascinated by the Vandermark history.

"The Vandermarks still living in Holland come from a small village called Roosenwyck," he continued. "They raise goats and make cheese. One of them has a tulip farm that is the loveliest sight this side of paradise. They have some modest investments that allow them to live in nice country houses and send their sons to college, but they never flourished in the princely manner of the American Vandermarks. No, the Dutch Vandermarks are very different. They work the fields and raise their livestock. Their children are healthy, their marriages are life-affirming. They go to church on Sunday and eat family dinners around the patriarch's table. They seem . . . happy."

And that was in marked contrast to the American Vandermarks, with their string of failed marriages, early deaths, and distrustful natures. The Vandermark curse was only a silly legend, but she knew that few of them had been happy. If given the chance, would they trade their diamonds and silks for the homespun happiness of their European cousins?

"And you think tearing down the mansion will make you more like the European side of your family?"

"It couldn't hurt to try. Tragedy has haunted my family since the very beginning of their time in America, and Dierenpark is where it all began."

Sophie closed her eyes, praying she could find the right words to soften the old man's intransigence about this house. "Your father wasn't so very different from your Dutch cousins," she said. "Karl Vandermark oversaw the local timber industry. Sometimes he rolled up his sleeves and helped saw wood at the local mills. People loved him for it. I know the Vandermarks were already fabulously rich from their shipping empire, but your father took personal interest in keeping the New Holland mill operating, even though it probably only represented a pittance compared to the rest of his income. When your father was alive, the pier was used for trading vessels and fishing boats. He employed hundreds of people in New Holland, but it came to an end when your family left the valley."

The old man's mouth tightened. "My father wasn't the heroic saint this town likes to imagine him."

It was an odd comment, but she didn't want to gossip about a long-dead man, she wanted to save Dierenpark.

"Then *you* be the heroic man," she said. "Break the string of bad luck you think haunts your family by some shining act of goodwill. Turn Dierenpark into a hospital or a school. Change the lives of people by doing something astounding. Be a hero."

The old man's face was shuttered as he stared into the distance. Had her words found some spot of softness inside him? It was impossible to tell.

"I think it is time for you to go find Pieter and ask him to take the climate readings," he said. "Whether he agrees to take over the job or not, you need to stay away from Dierenpark. My family needs time alone."

As Nickolaas had predicted, Pieter was reluctant to take responsibility for monitoring the weather station in her absence. Standing on the roof, he eyed the modest equipment as though it had morphed into a dragon he had been ordered to slay.

"What if I don't do it right?" he asked. "Those men in Washington will be mad at me." His face was marred by splotches from the bee stings, but with the vigor of youth, his body was rapidly mending. His spirit, however, had taken another blow, and he was back to the timid boy who feared every move he made was a mistake.

Sophie flipped open the notebook to where Pieter had been recording the numbers for the past few weeks and turned it over to him. "I'm going to sit on this stool and not make a peep while you do the whole thing this morning."

He fidgeted, his shoulders curling in and a mutinous expression on his face. "I don't want to do it. I might get it wrong. We can get Mr. Gilroy to do it."

"But Mr. Gilroy hasn't been with me each morning over the past weeks. Only *you* can do it, Pieter. You know this system better than anyone else in this house. Now, let me watch you take those measurements, and I'll be here to help if you make a mistake."

The boy swallowed hard and stepped up to the hygrometer, scrutinizing the tiny brass dials for a full sixty seconds before writing down a number. After he got moving, he gathered the rest of the data faster. Sophie stood to check his work, pleased to see he'd recorded everything precisely right. She beamed down at him.

"I knew you could do it. You will be so much better at this than Mr. Gilroy. Will you please do this for me while I'm gone?"

"I guess it would be okay," Pieter mumbled. The anxiety in his voice wrung her heart, and she scrambled for a way to breathe a bit of confidence into a boy who seemed to fear the world.

"It's going to be more than okay, honey—it's going to be marvelous. The feeling of purpose you'll have when you see those weather reports published in the newspaper, based on the data *you* provided—that's a feeling of being needed you will never forget. Those reports get printed on the first page of the newspaper, right at the very top corner, because everyone wants to know the weather, right?"

Pieter nodded, a hint of a smile finally turning up the corners of his mouth.

On her walk home, she felt tired, dispirited, and the scent of rice pudding still clung to her. She'd made no progress in saving the house from demolition, and because she'd dared stand up to Quentin, she'd been banished for at least a week while the deadline for the demolition drew closer.

But at least she had made Pieter smile this morning. It was a genuine smile, based on the first hint of confidence and pride in his accomplishment, and that was a very good thing.

Quentin glared at the Gainsborough painting of the sea-scape, the sails of the skiff billowing in the wind. Mr. Gilroy had cleaned up the rice pudding, and now the painting looked pristine against the ivory wall. It had a joyous and exuberant quality. Almost transcendent in the way the light illuminated the majesty of the sea.

He hated it.

There had been a time when he loved nothing more than taking to the sea in precisely that sort of skiff. He and Portia would rise before dawn and slip their sailboat from its moor-ing. Bodyguards followed at a respectful distance, but once he and Portia were at sea, they had no need for bodyguards. Their racing skiff was the fastest in the world, and they were both expert sailors.

They had been best friends since childhood. Portia was two years older than he, but they might as well have been twins the way they grew up. They both summered in Newport, and their families traveled Europe together, giving them a chance to ex-plore their passion for sailing along the sun-bleached Mediterra-nean coasts and the Adriatic Sea. They hungered for adventure, and the sea offered endless realms of pure elation wherever they traveled. Their skiff was so fast it barely skimmed the water as the sails filled with air. They'd spent Quentin's eighteenth summer in Venice, the magical city tucked along the northern shores of the Adriatic Sea.

As long as he lived, that summer would glimmer like a dia-mond in his memory. After a day of sailing, they'd tie up the boat, exhausted and sun-chapped but overflowing with life and exuberance. On days they took to the sea, they were not heirs to great fortunes, they were nomads setting sail for the edge of the known universe.

They sailed during the day, and in the evenings a stream of men came to court Portia. She was beautiful and rich beyond imagination. She was also laughingly disinterested in any of the men who came calling. She wanted the sea, and as the afternoon shadows grew long in the harbor, they pulled their boat into its moorings and explored the city. Always within call were bodyguards hired by Nickolaas, but Quentin and Portia were good at ignoring them.

They bought goat cheese from street vendors, listened to gypsies play mandolins in the distance, and there was nothing that wasn't possible. Portia bought orange blossoms from a peddler and wore them in her hair like a crown of flowers from a Botticelli portrait. As the moon rose, they dined in street cafés with artists and poets, with professors and merchant princes. He felt as if he were at a crossroad. There was nothing he could not do, and the world was alive with hope.

Portia wanted to learn the craft of boat-making and sail a schooner made with her own hands all the way to Canada. He was her best friend and he vowed he would make it happen for her. After they were married, he wanted to spend their first year sailing a boat of their own making around the known seas.

It hadn't worked out that way. Their marriage had collapsed quickly, and Portia avoided him until Pieter's birth finally brought the first hint of softening. They decided to buy a yacht suitable for taking a child and bodyguards with them, and they would try to recapture that lost dream of perfection.

The bodyguards could not save Portia from the tragedy heading her way. Cholera was a horrible disease that crippled some, while others were able to shake it off with little trouble. All the wealth in the world could not save Portia once she'd been exposed to the cholera bacterium.

Portia's final days still tormented him. It shouldn't have ended like that for her. How could she have been so fierce and alive on the sea but collapse in fear as she became convinced she was about to fall victim to the Vandermark curse? "All the Vandermark wives die young," she had said in her delirium. Her restless body twisted on sheets soaked in perspiration, and nothing he could say would convince her she was not destined to fall victim to the same fate. She died three days after falling ill.

The sight of that magnificent Gainsborough painting reminded Quentin that there were days on this earth when it was possible to believe the world would never end, when laughter carried on the breeze and musicians played mandolins in the distance. He closed his eyes, trying to blot out the pain from his leg and remember the scent of orange blossoms and salty air. Of youth and windblown days and the sloshing of water along Venetian canals.

The door opened suddenly. Quentin refused to open his eyes. Only Nickolaas would dare enter his room without knocking.

With a scrape and a thud, a chair landed at his bedside. "You've upset Miss van Riijn."

Of course he'd upset her. That was the point of hurling his breakfast against the wall. He'd been drowning, and all she'd wanted to do was shove rice pudding down his throat. The girl disapproved of anyone who wasn't as blindingly cheerful as she, and how could a person like that know about real melancholia?

He glared at Nickolaas. "And?"

"And I don't like it. Miss van Riijn has insight into this house that I need. Something is going on. My father knew it, I know it, and Miss van Riijn knows it. There is something magical at work here."

A bitter laugh escaped. "Spare me. I've no time for this."

"How do you explain the water lilies that never die?"

"What do you mean, never die? Everything dies."

Quentin listened with drop-jawed disbelief as Nickolaas recounted what he knew about the water lilies, gleaned from Sophie and confirmed by Mr. Gilroy, who had been questioning people in the village. The water lilies were vibrant and abundant, even though the tidal pull of the Hudson forced salty water upstream each day, leaving a brackish taint that ought to make a freshwater plant like a water lily impossible. The water lilies did not merely survive, they flourished. Only during the deepest frosts of winter, when the river was covered with ice, did they disappear, but with the first thaw, as water began flowing again, those lilies rose above the surface, as healthy as though they'd merely been hibernating beneath the ice.

Quentin pondered the mystery. "There must be some sort

of thermal activity beneath the river in that spot," he said. "There are hot springs farther up the river, perhaps there is a similar phenomenon here. Somehow the heat is able to keep the lilies alive."

"And the salt in the water? How do they survive that?"

He crossed his arms and thought. It did seem odd, but surely there was a rational explanation. He was no scientist, but plenty of plant life thrived in salty environments, and these lilies must have adapted to the area over time. "Maybe some sort of nutrients in the soil or water."

"Or magic. There is a thriving oyster bed in that same spot. Oysters have vanished from the rest of the Hudson River, but they thrive in Marguerite's Cove. It is a phenomenon with no scientific explanation."

Suspicion began prickling across his skin. He wouldn't put it past Nickolaas to try to pass off a bunch of folklorists and soothsayers as respectable archaeologists. "And you think the archaeologists you are bringing in are going to find evidence of magic?"

"I have no idea what they'll find, but there's been something unique about this land since the Vandermarks first set foot on it in 1635. It is why they named it Dierenpark, the Dutch word for paradise."

There was nothing special about this piece of land. It was normal for people to endow historical curiosities with a mystical aura. It was nothing more than human instinct to indulge in sentimentality and the longing for something divine. There was a logical explanation for everything in the world, and a few decent biologists were likely to discover an explanation for the peculiar health of the water lilies.

"I'll make a deal with you," Quentin said. "You hire your archaeologists, but I want a team of biologists to examine the same spot in the river. I guarantee they will find a perfectly

147

logical explanation for both the water lilies and the oysters." A rush of competitive spirit surged to life. There *was* something odd about the lush abundance on this estate, but properly trained scientists could provide an explanation.

"What are we wagering?" Nickolaas asked.

"If your archaeologists find evidence of some mystical significance, I'll blow up the house according to your plan. If my biologists can prove a scientific explanation, you agree to quit filling Pieter's head with superstitious drivel. You will instruct him that if he can't see it or touch it, it doesn't exist. You will give up this inane plan to destroy the house."

"It's a deal."

Once they shook on the bargain, it didn't take long to thrash out the details. Nickolaas would contact one of his lawyers in Manhattan to begin hiring qualified experts who could come to the house immediately. It was summer, so most college professors were free to pursue their own interests until classes resumed in September. Everyone would be housed here at Dierenpark. The bodyguards would help fetch and carry and support the research teams in whatever capacity was required. Sophie and Florence would cook.

"The Broeders can provide the teams with a tour of the grounds," Nickolaas suggested.

Quentin shook his head. "I fired Emil Broeder the first day I arrived. He was—"

"You did *what*?" Nickolaas burst out. His grandfather rarely raised his voice, and Quentin was taken aback.

"There's no longer a need for a groundskeeper," Quentin explained. "If you intend to demolish—"

Once again, Nickolaas interrupted him, his voice lashing out like a whip. "Our family has always supported the Broeders. The Broeders have been here since the very beginning, and we are obliged to treat them well. No wonder you've been cursed with a string of bad luck for breaking that commitment. We have an obligation to them."

"Why?" Quentin asked. His grandfather was full of pointless superstition but rarely able to articulate a lucid explanation for any of his wild-eyed beliefs.

"It doesn't matter why, Quentin. All that matters is that Emil Broeder be rehired immediately. I don't care how much we have to pay to lure him back to the house. Get him back."

The determination in his grandfather's voice was pure steel. Over the years, Quentin had learned to choose his battles with his grandfather very carefully. His primary goal was to get his team of biologists to win the wager to save Dierenpark and thus protect Pieter from his grandfather's foolish superstitions. Emil Broeder's employment status was of little consequence to him. "Fine, whatever you want," Quentin said. "I'll get Broeder back, and my attorneys in New York will hire some qualified biologists."

And he would prove to his grandfather once and for all that there was a legitimate scientific explanation for everything in the world.

11

It hurt to be banished from Dierenpark.

The only truly happy days from Sophie's childhood had been spent at the estate where her mother had been the cook. After school, Sophie always headed up to Dierenpark, learning to cook at her mother's side, exploring the grand library, playing with her friend Julia Broeder, or merely wandering the grounds. Sometimes Marten came with her, and together they searched for old Indian arrowheads and ate blackberries straight off the vine. Other times, she came alone and would sit on the granite outcropping that overlooked the river and utter a simple prayer of thanksgiving. It was easier to feel close to God when she was sitting beneath the crystal blue sky and could hear the breeze whispering through miles of verdant green trees. There was peace and abundance at Dierenpark, and she loved it.

But now she was back at the hotel, with little to do other than bring her father endless cups of tea as he pored over the treasure trove of old Vandermark documents he'd salvaged from the bank vault. Almost everything was handwritten in spindly letters, which made for slow going. Most of the records were

151

boring taxation schedules and shipping contracts that chronicled the gradual accumulation of the Vandermark fortune, but a week after her banishment, he stumbled on something that roused his curiosity.

Sophie was pickling cucumbers with the hotel's cook when her father came bursting out of the study. "Emil!" he shouted.

"Shhhh! You'll wake the baby," Sophie said.

"Where is he?" Jasper asked. She could tell from the excitement in his eyes that he must have discovered something important.

"Emil's wife is visiting her mother with the twins, so he is babysitting the little one in his room. I think they are both sleeping."

It was a good thing Emil was back at the hotel. After he'd been fired from Dierenpark, he'd tried to work as a peddler, selling odds and ends to far-flung homesteads, but he always sold his goods for the same price he paid for them. "It would feel like cheating if I asked people for more than what I spent," he said. She and her father both tried to explain the value of his time in carrying the goods to the homesteads, but Emil said he wasn't cut out for overcharging people and gave up the trade.

"Go get him," her father ordered. "He can bring the baby, but the light is poor in his room, and I need to get a good look at him."

Three minutes later, a bleary-eyed Emil stumbled into the room with the baby in tow. Annie was only two months old, and Sophie eagerly reached for her as Emil passed her over. Sophie loved the weight of the baby as she folded Annie over her shoulder, gently rubbing her back.

Her father asked the cook to leave the kitchen and then closed the door. Emil was confused as her father told him to go stand by the window, but he shrugged and stood beside the window, his sleepy eyes blinking in the sunlight.

"Sophie, you've seen the Vandermarks more than anyone

else. Take a good look at Emil's face. Do you see any family resemblance between them?"

Both she and Emil whirled to gawk at her father. Emil's simple friendliness was as different from the Vandermarks as a puppy from a panther.

"Well?" her father demanded.

Emil was a broad-shouldered man with blue eyes and blond hair. He looked like a lumberjack, while the Vandermarks were dark and slender.

"I don't see any resemblance at all," she said. "Why?"

Her father's shoulders sagged, but only for a moment. He turned his eyes to Emil. "Are there any stories in your family about being related to the Vandermarks somehow?"

"We work for them," Emil said, scratching his head. "We've always worked for them. Things have been real good except for . . . well, you know . . ."

Getting abruptly fired and kicked out of their home last month. Every time Sophie was tempted to start liking Quentin Vandermark, she reminded herself of that cold fact to shake her back to reality.

"Father, what is this all about?" she asked.

Jasper pivoted and snatched a document from the counter. "This letter was written in 1695 by Caleb's son, Enoch. Apparently there was tension among the younger generation with the groundskeepers, and Enoch wrote a warning letter to his own son. It says, 'The Broeder family is to be treated well until the end of time. Any Vandermark who fails to look after the Broeders does so at their peril.'"

What odd language. It reminded her of the ominous, metaphorical talk Nickolaas Vandermark indulged in. She wondered if the old man had ever seen the contents of this safe. He was only fourteen when he fled Dierenpark and might not even know about this trove of documents.

But Nickolaas had always treated the Broeders well. Last spring, Emil's sister Julia had been expelled from college over a foolish incident with a dog. Nickolaas Vandermark ordered his attorney to intervene on Julia's behalf to get her reinstated at the school. The Vandermarks paid for Julia's college education and provided a generous wedding gift when she subsequently married that same attorney a few months later.

"That's pretty weird," Emil said with a shrug of his shoulders. "They've always been nice to us. They sent Julia to college. I never asked for anything, but their lawyer sent a nice bank note when the twins were born. Maybe they are just nice people."

Sophie and her father locked gazes. The Vandermarks were *not* particularly nice people. Over the centuries, they'd earned a reputation as ruthless shipping magnates who dominated the world trade of commodities.

"Maybe one of the Broeders saved someone's life?" she suggested. "There was plenty of trouble with the Indians during those years."

"Maybe a bear attack," Emil offered. "Or a snake. It could have been a snake. I've seen them at Dierenpark."

Her father shook his head. "It would have been easier to build a case if there had been a family resemblance. If one of the early Vandermarks fathered an illegitimate child with a Broeder, it could call the entire ownership of Dierenpark into question."

That was an angle Sophie had never considered. In 1695, the country would have been governed by English law, and England had never been overly generous with illegitimate children. She said so, but her father was one step ahead of her.

"What if the child wasn't illegitimate?" he said as excitement gathered momentum in his voice. "What if one of the Vandermarks eloped with a Broeder, and a child resulted? A child that would have a claim to a portion of the estate."

"Wouldn't you have already seen a record of that at the county courthouse?"

"Not if they eloped to a distant town, which is likely."

Sophie patted the back of the baby on her shoulder. Could she be holding a legitimate heir to the Vandermark estate? It seemed incredible, but the Broeders had a long history at Dierenpark, and it was certainly possible for a blue blood to dally with one of the red-blooded servants. Trying to prove something based on a vague reference over two hundred years old would be a staggering task, but it might delay the demolition of the house. If Emil was capable of mounting the charge . . .

She looked at Emil, who was munching an almond cookie while scratching his armpit. She glanced back at her father. "This seems too far-fetched to be able to prove," she said.

"Have you got any better ideas?" her father demanded, and she flinched at the frustration in his tone. Even the baby sensed it and started to whimper. They were all suffering from strained nerves and a sense of impending doom.

She was glum all afternoon while she finished pickling the cucumbers. Her father accused her of being idealistic, but she had a far better chance of landing a climate observatory in New Holland than he had of proving Emil had a legitimate claim to Dierenpark.

Her worries vanished late in the day when Mr. Gilroy arrived with an astounding message.

"Mr. Nickolaas Vandermark requests the immediate return of Emil Broeder and his family to Dierenpark. He apologizes for the misunderstanding and is willing to offer Mr. Broeder a raise in salary to compensate for this inconvenience."

Sophie tried to mask the surprise from her voice. "Did he say why?"

"The Vandermarks have always looked after the Broeders," Mr. Gilroy said. "A simple sense of responsibility for generations of loyal service."

She recalled the warning from the old document: *Any Vandermark who fails to look after the Broeders does so at their peril.* It didn't sound like a sense of responsibility, it sounded like outright fear.

Her amazement was compounded as Mr. Gilroy continued speaking, asking her to return to her duties in the kitchen in order to prepare for a grand wager between Quentin and Nickolaas.

"Two teams of professors are to be hired to research the estate," Mr. Gilroy said. He outlined the terms of the wager, indicating that if Quentin's biologists could produce a scientific explanation for the health of Marguerite's Cove, the house would be spared. Otherwise, Nickolaas retained complete control over Dierenpark and Quentin would proceed with the demolition.

Could it really be true? Hope surged through her as Mr. Gilroy continued speaking.

"A dozen men will be arriving next week," he said. "We need to begin preparing food in advance of their arrival, and we would be grateful for Emil's help in preparing the bedrooms. I gather Quentin behaved less than graciously toward you while suffering his latest setback, and he asked me to apologize and invite you back to cook for the household."

It miffed her that Quentin thought an apology delivered by his butler would erase the sting of her rice pudding splattered on the wall of his sickroom, but she could hardly refuse the chance to return to Dierenpark. Dierenpark held an echo of something infinitely precious that needed to be protected and cherished, and that meant Sophie would do whatever possible to preserve it.

Quentin rose early, gingerly pacing before the windows in his bedroom overlooking the river below. His leg was healing surprisingly well after the incident with the bees, but he dared not move too quickly, for these temporary periods of health rarely lasted long. Until yesterday, his face had been swollen from the bee stings, and he hadn't wanted Pieter seeing him like that. The boy already felt guilty over what had happened, and Quentin's itchy, inflamed face was likely to make Pieter collapse into grief once again.

The marks had almost completely faded now, and he was anxious to leave the room. He eased his contorted leg into his trousers, then tentatively stood, pleased to feel only a twinge of pain. Truly, it was astounding that his leg was recovering so rapidly.

Ten minutes later, he was at the desk in the library, a new set of architectural plans for a bridge in Antwerp unfurled before him. It was pointless to work on demolition plans for Dierenpark, for he fully intended to win his bet with Nickolaas. It meant he had the sheer intellectual joy of returning to the design for a new bridge across the Scheldt River. The diversion to Dierenpark had put him badly behind schedule on the bridge. The patience of the Antwerp city elders was wearing thin, and he needed to complete the design before they kicked him off the project.

As he worked on the design, he actually began to feel healthy again. Perhaps it was the satisfaction of working on the bridge design, or maybe it was something in the air at Dierenpark. With the windows open, a cool morning breeze scented with pine and honeysuckle wafted into the room. The Hudson sparkled in the morning sun, and it was almost mesmerizing in its beauty.

By lunchtime, he'd made solid progress on the Antwerp bridge and didn't even realize he was hungry until Ratface arrived with a tray. Bread and cheese, again. He sighed.

"Miss Sophie is due to return tomorrow," Ratface said. "I'm

already dreaming about that beef stew she makes. And the pies. Oh, and her lemon cake . . ."

Ratface was still enumerating the long list of Sophie's best dishes as he left the library.

Quentin clenched his fists. Sophie's return was going to change things. He wouldn't admit to missing her . . . that wasn't the right word. They were as different as night and day, but he enjoyed her company and wished he didn't.

It would be dangerous to let himself get lured into the bright aura surrounding Sophie. She was sunlight and purity, while he was little better than the angry troll living under the bridge. The fact that he was utterly fascinated by her was of no matter, and he intended to battle the attraction with every weapon at his disposal.

12

THE BEST PART ABOUT RETURNING to Dierenpark was the joy on Pieter's face when Sophie appeared at nine o'clock on the roof to check on the weather station. He was recording data in a notebook balanced on his knees when she stepped onto the widow's walk.

"You're back!" he shouted, startling a pair of sparrows perched on the turret. The notebook tumbled to the planking as he raced to her for a quick hug. "I was afraid my father scared you away for good."

That was precisely what I feared, too. "Of course I came back. Show me how you've been getting on."

Pieter's voice was confident as he showed her his notebook, and she was right to have trusted him with this task. His smile was genuine as he closed the covers on the thermometer and hygrometers.

"It's been really nice, especially since my father has been too sick to leave his room. Grandpa comes and helps me with my readings, and sometimes we play cards with the bodyguards."

His shoulders sagged a bit. "But my father is better now, so all that has to stop."

"You didn't see your father at all while he was recovering?" Quentin Vandermark wasn't the easiest person to deal with, but visiting the sick was a basic tenet of Christian charity, and it wasn't right for a man to suffer in lonely isolation.

"He stayed in his room the whole time, but he's better now. Last night at dinner, he kept asking what I want to be when I grow up. I think he wants me to be an architect like him. I used to want that, but it would be scary if I had to work with him all the time."

"Has he ever said he wants you to be an architect?"

"No. He says I can be whatever I want, so long as I never become an 'idol rich.' I don't even know what that means, but he always says it like it's the worst thing in the world. Does it mean when rich people pray to something?"

She smiled, doing her best not to make light of his confusion between *idol* and *idle*. "Your father doesn't want you to be *idle*. I-D-L-E. Idle means lazy. Without a purpose. Some people are so wealthy they don't need to work, and if they don't have anything meaningful to do with their lives, they drift. I think that's what your father means when he says he doesn't want you to become one of the idle rich."

"Oh. Well, I don't know what I want to do when I grow up."

Sophie had always known what she wanted. The craving to be a wife and a mother was sometimes so bad it felt like a physical ache. It hadn't happened for her yet, and she was beginning to fear it never would, which was why her paltry contributions at the weather station were so vital to her sense of purpose. If she died tomorrow, only her father and the anonymous team of meteorologists at the Weather Bureau would miss her.

She shook away that gloomy thought and smiled down at Pieter. "When are you happiest?"

"When I'm with my grandpa."

The immediate response underscored how deep the rift between Pieter and his father had grown. She drew him to a bench overlooking the river, letting the gentle breeze soothe her as she scrambled for the right thing to say.

"I know your father loves you, even if sometimes he has a hard time saying so, but he showed it when he rescued you from the bees, right?"

"He only did that because he had to."

"He did it because he loved you," she corrected him. "It's because he loves you that he sets rules and teaches you how to live by them."

"But he's so scary. I try, but when I do things wrong or make mistakes, he always catches me at it. Or I get afraid, and he gets mad at me all over again. I'm never afraid of Grandpa."

Unfortunately, she knew exactly what Pieter must be feeling. Wasn't she afraid merely at the prospect of seeing Quentin again? His temper could be so quick and cutting.

She reached over to finger-comb a lock of Pieter's hair that ruffled in the breeze. "My religion teaches me that we must love one another . . . even when it's hard. It's easy to love your grandpa because he is so kind to you, but everyone has goodness and humanity in them. You aren't required to like everything your father does, but you need to be respectful. Look for the good in him, and the love will follow."

"What about the men who kidnapped me last summer?" Pieter challenged. "I could never love them. They kept me in a dark closet and hardly ever let me out. One of them used to fire off a pistol right next to my ear, just to make me cry."

She blanched at the image. When Jesus had commanded them to love one another, had he been speaking about that man with the pistol? How could anyone see something worth loving in such a hateful man? She closed her eyes and opened her heart.

"I don't know why that man was so mean to you," she finally said. "For some reason, making a rich boy cry made him feel better about himself. Perhaps he was once terribly wounded as a child, and it twisted him somehow. He can't hurt you anymore, so perhaps if you can find it in your heart to work toward forgiving him, it will make you feel better. Only a very strong person will have that kind of character, but I think you can do it, Pieter."

Pieter's expression was a combination of hope warring with skepticism. "I don't know, Miss Sophie."

She spoke in her kindest tone. "How do you think the bees felt when you pushed their home over?"

He flinched at the memory. "They were mad, but I didn't want to hurt them. I just wanted to hit something because my father was so mean."

"I know you didn't mean to hurt the bees, but you did," she said gently. "Sometimes cruelty begets more cruelty, and that's what happened when you took your anger out on the bees. The funny thing is that love works the same way. When you try to love, or at least understand your enemies, I think you will be surprised at the way the world looks a little brighter."

She paused to gather her thoughts. She was speaking brave words, but she was equally guilty of assuming the worst about Quentin Vandermark. She had never witnessed anything braver than when he ran toward those bees to carry Pieter to safety. It was shameful, but at that moment, Sophie had been too frightened to move. She stood frozen in place as Quentin staggered away from the hives, and she only leapt into motion when he was well away from the swarm of bees.

He didn't make it easy to see his better side, but she was as guilty as Pieter of overlooking Quentin's finer points, and she needed to look deeper.

Sophie took extra care in preparing Quentin's lunch. She smiled as she whisked a little cream into the fresh pea soup simmering on the stove. Made with chopped leaks and simmered in a rich chicken stock, the soup was a vibrant green shade that always seemed cheerful to Sophie.

"I would be happy to slice the bread," Mr. Gilroy said, nodding to the loaf of rosemary bread cooling on the windowsill. It had been over an hour since she'd taken it from the oven, and it could be sliced now.

"That's very kind of you." It was important for everything to be perfect today. It was irrational, but when she was successful in the kitchen, she felt like she was living up to her calling. Mr. Gilroy seemed to sense her need to succeed today, and he'd been so helpful all morning—fetching ice, mincing herbs, and now he sliced the rosemary bread with the skill of a professional chef.

"Have you ever worked in a kitchen before?" she asked, spooning out a wedge of herb butter into a small dish to accompany the bread.

"I've done a bit of everything over the years," Mr. Gilroy said modestly but didn't elaborate as he stacked the still-warm bread on a plate.

She didn't press him for more information. The soup would cool quickly now that it was in the bowl. She placed it beside the bread and a dish of plump strawberries she'd picked from the garden only a few minutes earlier. Holding the kitchen door for Mr. Gilroy as he carried the tray out, she wished she had as much confidence in her ability to be kind toward Quentin as she did in making a simple bowl of pea soup.

Quentin wasn't going to succumb to temptation. The rest of his household might be irrationally enthralled by Sophie's cooking, but food was nothing more than nourishment, a combination of proteins and starches to fuel the body. Evolution had designed man to appreciate different flavors and textures in order to ensure proper nutrition.

And yet he knew the instant his breakfast tray was delivered this morning that she was back. Why did oatmeal taste so delicious simply because it came out of a pot stirred by Sophie van Riijn? The housekeeper had been making their oatmeal for the past week, and it had been fine. Hot, edible . . . fine, but nothing like what Sophie made. He had tried to analyze the flavors and textures of the oatmeal to pinpoint a reason it was so extraordinary. For the life of him, he couldn't figure out what she did to make it taste so good, and he sent the breakfast tray back after two bites.

But lunch was another matter. He was working in the library when Mr. Gilroy delivered the tray, and the scent beckoned from across the room. He couldn't starve to death merely from an irrational refusal to eat Sophie's cooking. Grabbing his cane, he limped over to the table. It was the scent of the bread that summoned him, but his eyes were riveted on the soup, a bright green bowl of fresh pea soup with a little swirl of cream on the top. He leaned over to sniff.

It didn't smell extraordinary. Just a simple bowl of soup. He lowered himself into a chair, dipped a spoon into the soup, and lifted it to his lips.

An explosion of flavor filled his mouth. It was creamy and soothing and rich and hearty and tasted like every sun-filled day on a grassy mountainside. He closed his eyes, trying to dissect the flavors, but it was hopeless. He swallowed and dipped his spoon in for a second time. And a third. He was going for a fourth when he set down the spoon and paused, trying to figure out why a sense of well-being flooded him. It was just a bowl of pea soup, for pity's sake!

He reached for the note Gilroy had slipped onto the lunch

tray, scanning it quickly. As always, Gilroy could be counted on for accuracy and detail. The butler's precise handwriting listed every activity Sophie had engaged in since entering the house at ten minutes before six o'clock this morning. But all Quentin cared about was the recipe for the soup that Mr. Gilroy had watched her prepare. Freshly shelled peas, chicken stock, some cream, a dash of lemon juice, chopped leeks, a few chives, and salt. Seven ingredients. No magic spice or exotic techniques. Seven simple ingredients found in any kitchen, and yet any king would pawn his firstborn for a bowl of this soup.

He tasted the soup again, closing his eyes to focus on the texture and flavor. There was nothing extraordinary about the ingredients, but the combination transcended the ordinary. He took another bite, then reached for the still-warm bread and the dish of butter. The creamy butter melted into the bread before he could draw the knife away.

He took a bite, thrilled and annoyed that it tasted as good as it smelled. He clenched his hand into a fist, swallowed the bread, then shouted. "Gilroy!" He'd always found houses with bell-pulls for servants presumptuous, but they would be a useful addition to this house. He couldn't afford to stress his leg by hopping up and down to summon guards, and his throat was going hoarse fast.

The ever-present agreeable expression was on the butler's face when he arrived. "Yes, sir?"

"Get her in here," he growled. There was no need to specify who he wanted to see, for Sophie was the only person who seemed uniquely capable of working her way beneath his composure and unsettling his carefully won stability.

Three minutes later, Sophie stood before him, still wearing an apron and wiping her hands on a towel. She glanced nervously at the meal spread out on the table, most of it still remaining.

"Was something wrong with lunch, sir?"

Without a word, he handed her Gilroy's note and pointed to the bottom of the page. "Mr. Gilroy neglected to fully capture the recipe for your pea soup, or perhaps he overlooked a step in the cooking process. What did he miss?"

Her pretty face screwed up as she scanned the note, turning it back and forth to read both sides of the densely written text that recounted all of her movements in the house this morning.

"What is this?" she asked, confusion heavy in her voice. "Was he *spying* on me again?"

"Of course he was spying. I warned you about him weeks ago."

"I thought he was just trying to help! He seemed so nice . . ."

Honestly, she shouldn't have been allowed to leave the nursery if she was this naïve. "Miss van Riijn, I asked you a purely factual question. Please overcome your dismay that Mr. Gilroy continues in his true calling as an accomplished spy and tell me what he overlooked while reproducing this recipe."

"What makes you think he got it wrong?"

Because it was impossible for seven ordinary ingredients to combine into this sublime experience of culinary perfection. "He did. It must have been some kind of seasoning. Was it sage?"

"No," she said, amusement beginning to dance in her pretty blue eyes.

"Some kind of special peas?"

She shook her head. "You're not going to be able to guess. In fact, I'm not even sure you would believe me if I told you."

He narrowed his eyes, savoring the thrill of competition that surged through him. "What makes you think I'm too dim-witted to guess what's in this soup?"

"Because you believe the entire world operates on rational scientific principles, and that is a very limiting quality, Mr. Vandermark. Sometimes there are things science can't explain."

A reluctant smile began tugging on one corner of his mouth.

He tamped it down. "Which rules of chemistry, physics, or gravity does your pea soup violate?"

"If I could answer that question, I'd be limiting myself to your own narrow view of the world," she said with a bright smile.

By heaven, sometimes he really liked this woman. "What's in the soup, Miss van Riijn?" he pressed.

"You won't believe me," she predicted. "And you'll probably laugh at me, too."

"Maybe. Quit stalling and tell me what's in the soup."

It took her forever to parse her answer, looking mildly embarrassed as a gorgeous flush spread across the soft ivory of her cheeks. "It's not an ingredient, but a technique," she finally said. "I love cooking, but more importantly, I love sharing food and serving people. When a person truly loves what they are doing, I think it shows. People can sense that in the meals I serve."

"Love," he said, struggling to keep the mirth from his voice. "You are suggesting that *love* is the mysterious ingredient that makes this soup so good?"

"Didn't I say you would laugh?" She met his gaze squarely even though it looked like she was trying not to laugh herself.

The most astounding thing was that he knew she believed every word she'd just said. She was too transparent and earnest to be fibbing.

He covered his mouth to hide the twisting of his lips. Despite the absurdity of her assertion, it was also charming and delightful, and the irrational attraction he had for her grew each time she came within his line of sight. "I have traveled the entire world, and I've never met anyone quite like you. *Love*," he repeated, his laughter finally impossible to control. "Sophie, I'm glad you love what you do, because this soup is delicious and you're the best cook I've ever had."

For once, her ridiculous idealism didn't annoy him because, quite frankly, he was famished and the soup was amazing.

"There is something I wanted to speak to you about," she said, a hint of hesitation in her voice. He swallowed the last of his soup but was immediately on guard. She was probably about to ask for an increase in salary after his lavish praise of her cooking.

"It's about Pieter," she said.

He set down the bowl and gestured for her to sit at the table opposite him. She seemed reluctant, but after a moment's hesitation, she pulled out the chair and sat. "Go on," he coaxed.

"Pieter did the work for the Weather Bureau while I was gone. He didn't want to do it, but I leaned on him, and he finally agreed. He completed the task every morning without prompting and on time."

"I would expect no less."

She tried not to let exasperation leak into her voice. "It took a lot of courage for him to volunteer his services for the Weather Bureau. He did so with no help or words of praise from you. Don't you think you might tell him you are proud of him? That he is doing a good job? That you love him and are pleased with how desperately he wants to make a meaningful contribution to the world?"

Annoyance began to take root. For the past week, he hadn't stepped outside his room because he feared the sight of his swollen face would upset Pieter. "You have no standing to criticize how I raise my son."

"Pieter is afraid of you, did you know that? You can't raise a child like he is a soldier in the army."

"I'm not raising a child, I'm raising a *man*," he snapped. "It takes more than a little love sprinkled over a cooking pot to do that. And why a childless woman who's never been able to keep a man thinks she is qualified to criticize my parenting is beyond me."

She wasn't so friendly now. Her motions were stiff and

efficient as she placed the cover over the empty bowl of soup and lifted the lunch tray. "Why do you want me to be as dark and cynical as you? Why are you so determined to snuff out whatever light and goodness is in the world?"

"Wishing the world could be like the fairy tales in your story-books won't make it so, Miss van Riijn."

Sophie's chin was tilted high as she carried the tray to the door. "I'm not going to retaliate to your meanness, because I do my best to be kind to every person I encounter. That may seem small to a person like you, but trust me, it isn't always easy. No matter how awful a person is, above all, I always try to be kind."

The *kind* woman slammed the door on her way out.

⌘

Sophie's questions plagued him all night long. *Why do you want me to be as dark and cynical as you?*

She was right. It shamed him, but he *wanted* to dim her happiness. Her effusive cheerfulness scraped against the raw, painful wounds in his body and spirit. She made him feel like cheap base metal compared to her luminous blend of gold and silver. Sophie showed only kindness and compassion to every person in this household, and all he did was launch pointed barbs in her direction, testing to see when she would lose her temper and break.

She wasn't breaking. Maybe it was time to drop his victory-through-venom strategy and try to comport himself like a civilized human being. One who had a beating heart, however sluggish and unworthy though it be. His self-loathing was his own problem, and he needed to swallow it back and become the kind of father Pieter deserved.

Sophie had been right in her accusations about Pieter. Mostly right, anyway. What she didn't understand was that it wasn't spite or disappointment or meanness that drove him to push Pieter so hard. It was fear.

If Quentin died, there would be no one to raise Pieter to manhood. Nickolaas was too old and irrational to do the job properly. Portia would have been an exceptional mother, but she was long dead, so the responsibility was entirely on his shoulders.

He awoke before dawn the next morning to write a note to Sophie. It did not take long, for when one spoke honestly, the words tended to flow.

Dear Miss van Riijn,

As we have previously discussed, I do not believe in God, the hereafter, or anything that cannot be seen or touched. That does not excuse my behavior. You have shown Christian kindness and charity toward my entire household, and my atheism does not excuse me from the rules of common decency.

Even atheists sometimes wish for a talisman to cling to, a shining example that proves there is valor and pure, unalloyed goodness in the world. You are such a person. Sadly, there are times I find it easier to mock goodness rather than be judged small and unworthy in comparison. I have never been particularly proud of myself, but never less so than in the manner I have consistently insulted everything I find admirable about you. I hope you can accept my sincere apology.

Quentin Vandermark

He gave the sealed envelope to Collins to deliver to Sophie as soon as she arrived this morning. He also asked for Pieter to meet him on the mansion's front portico.

There were no proper washrooms in the house, and he brought his shaving kit and a small mirror to prop up on the balustrade of the front landing. He swirled his shaving brush in the mug of soap, staring at the meadow across from the house. It was sur-rounded by ancient linden and juniper trees, making this patch of land feel cocooned from the wider world. Were he a spiritual sort, he might even think this land was blessed somehow.

The front door creaked open behind him. "Did you want to see me?"

The hesitation in Pieter's voice hurt. Quentin began lathering his face but nodded to the morning newspaper folded on the top step. "The professors who will be studying Dierenpark will arrive soon. They'll want to know what the weather is going to be. Can you read it to me?"

Quentin peered into the small mirror propped on the ledge of the balustrade, carefully drawing the blade across his skin. The newspaper crinkled as Pieter unfolded it, sat on the step beside him, and began reading.

"'Decreasing cloudiness today, moderate winds. High tem-peratures in the upper seventies. Tomorrow: expect clear skies.'"

"Clear skies," he said in a casual tone. "Collins will appreci-ate the fine weather as he carts all the supplies here." He rinsed the shaving blade and used a towel to wipe the remaining soap from his face. "The weathermen in Washington wouldn't have been able to make such predictions if you hadn't been here to send them the data each morning. I'm proud of you, Pieter."

Pieter sucked in a breath, and a quick smile flashed on his face. "Miss Sophie showed me how to do it. She knows every-thing about the weather."

Sophie again. The admiration in the boy's voice was ap-parent, for truly it was hard not to be impressed by her. He'd been trying and failing ever since she first waltzed into his life.

"Why do you like Miss Sophie so much?" he asked. Any man

with blood pumping through his veins would find her attractive, but Pieter was too young to notice such things. Was it her cooking? The smile that was never far from her face?

Pieter's forehead wrinkled in concentration as he fiddled with the shaving brush. When the boy finally spoke, Pieter's answer stunned him.

"She listens to me like what I say matters."

His chest squeezed. "And I don't?"

Pieter shrugged but remained silent.

It was humbling, but Quentin knew the answer. He had never treated Pieter with the kind of respect Sophie showed every person in this household. He loved Pieter, but he didn't have Sophie's soft-hearted patience. He was good at lecturing, correcting, berating . . . but treating Pieter as if his opinion mattered? No, he'd never been very good at that.

And he needed to do better.

"Collins and Ratface are making up the beds in preparation for the research teams. They could probably use some help. I heard Ratface threaten to shove Collins into the river if he didn't help turn the mattresses."

"That's not right," Pieter said.

"It's not stopping them. Go on up and see if you can get them to calm down."

Pieter stood, his face unusually solemn. "Above all things, we should try to love one another," he said. "It's in the Bible."

Pieter turned and left, leaving Quentin to stare in stunned disbelief at his retreating back. Since when had his son started spouting off Bible verses like a miniature preacher?

He struggled not to laugh. This was surely Sophie's doing. He'd warned her about proselytizing to his son, but at least she wasn't consorting with palm readers or transcendentalists like his grandfather was prone to do.

And if such sappy little maxims helped put Pieter at ease, he wouldn't quibble. Sophie had made more progress with Pieter in the space of a few weeks than Quentin had managed since the kidnapping last summer. And instead of showing gratitude to Sophie, he'd hurled rice pudding against the wall and mocked her boundless idealism.

He wasn't ready to return inside the house yet. There was something peaceful out here, and it was soothing to him. Soaking up the sunshine and breathing the fresh green scent of the meadow was a balm on his spirit. So was watching those two little white butterflies flitting about the wisteria vines. How long had it been since he'd stopped to savor the natural beauty of this world?

Before long, Mr. Gilroy came driving up the path in the curricle, the morning's groceries on the seat beside him. "A telegram has arrived for you," he said as he passed Quentin on the porch stairs.

Quentin flicked open the card, raising his brow in surprise. Dr. Phineas Clark of the U.S. Weather Bureau had accepted his invitation to come to Dierenpark and would arrive in a week.

Quentin had forgotten about issuing that invitation. The conversation with Mr. Gilroy in the orangery seemed so long ago, before his grandfather had arrived, before his collision with the bees. He was ashamed of the way he'd tattled on Sophie to the Weather Bureau all those weeks ago. He'd just wanted her off his roof and hadn't cared if he damaged her reputation in the process.

Now he cared. Sophie was a rare find: both innocent and strong at the same time. He feared she would someday be crushed by a hard and cynical world, but so far he had been the only one taking aim at her.

Contrary to all his experience, Sophie didn't seem enticed by wealth or aggrandizement, only hopes for attracting a more substantial weather station to New Holland.

And he was going to help her get it.

He glanced up at Mr. Gilroy. "Prepare the turret bedroom. We are expecting a guest."

13

QUENTIN SOUGHT OUT SOPHIE IMMEDIATELY. He still didn't understand her desire to see a climate observatory built in New Holland, but if she wanted one, he would do everything in his power to make it happen. And the first step was to teach her how to impress a man like Dr. Clark.

She was in the kitchen kneading bread. With her hair loosely braided and her sleeves rolled up, she was the picture of timeless femininity, an image so enchanting it ought to be idealized by some grand European painter. Vermeer would have been able to capture the sunlight filtering through the window, illuminating her face as she went about the age-old task of kneading bread dough. She was everything that was good and pure in the world, and all he'd ever done was snarl at her because he was usually in a bad mood.

Blessed are the pure in heart, for they shall see God.

Sometimes he wished he had an ounce of Sophie's purity. It would be nice to see the world through innocent eyes instead of his relentless skepticism.

Sophie looked startled when she noticed him standing in

the doorway. Then dismayed. A normal man might have been troubled by such a reaction, but he was accustomed to people being intimidated by him. He grabbed an apple from the stoneware bowl, aimlessly polishing it on his shirt.

"You were right about Pieter," he said. Her quick, indrawn breath let him know her surprise. "I was wrong to attack you over it."

"Oh, that's all right—"

"It's not all right," he interrupted, perhaps a little more roughly than he'd intended. "You need to quit being so nice when people treat you like that."

"I can't help it." She shrugged. "I *am* nice."

And pretty. And smart. Her practiced hands kneaded the bread dough like a virtuoso playing the piano.

"Yes, you are nice," he agreed. "And you were only trying to help Pieter with what you said yesterday. I should not have lashed out like that. I am sincerely sorry."

"I got your note," she said. "You didn't have to say all those nice things about me . . . but thank you." A gorgeous flush spread across her cheeks, and he wondered if anyone had ever done something nice for Sophie instead of taking advantage of her kindness.

"Tell me about your progress in getting an upgraded climate observatory in New Holland," he said casually.

Her hands stilled atop the bread dough. "I've finished drafting my proposal. I outlined why the Mill Road promontory would be perfect for both receiving information and distributing reports. I offered my own services as a volunteer, in case that makes any difference."

"Why should you volunteer?" he asked. "After nine years of service, they ought to properly hire you and start paying a salary."

"My father thinks they will hire only men, and there's not

much I can do about that. And I don't mind if they don't pay me, I just want to be a part of it all."

"Sophie, if you're doing the same work as a man, they ought to pay you for it. Don't let people take advantage of you."

She gathered the dough into a ball and dumped it into a bowl, covered it with a damp towel, and set it on the windowsill. "I'm afraid they won't hire me otherwise."

Her generosity was admirable, but her screaming ignorance of how the government operated was appalling. She was in desperate need of learning how to navigate the world of business and bureaucrats.

"Tell me why you think the Weather Bureau ought to bring you on board," he prompted.

She took a moment to wipe her hands on a towel while she parsed her words. "Because I want it so desperately—"

"Stop. They don't care how much you want it. They need to know if you can do the job. Try again."

She gave him one of those wounded puppy looks but quickly recovered and tried again. "Because I can be depended upon. No one else will work as hard as me. Or be as loyal. I'll be excited to get up every morning and face the day with—"

"Stop. I sense you are about to blast me with a dose of sappy sunshine."

"Well, yes," she said, looking equal parts amused and bewildered. "But it's the truth! I love my work, and that counts for something, doesn't it?"

Those government bureaucrats would trample Sophie to pieces if she couldn't stand up for herself. He walked around the counter until he was standing directly opposite her.

"Come on, Sophie! Stand up straight and look me in the eye. Tell me that you are the master and commander of that climate observatory. That there is no one in the state of New

York who can operate that office with more efficiency than you. Make me believe it!"

"Shhh . . . your grandfather is taking a nap," she said, but she was giggling and at least seemed to be considering his point. It was going to be a challenge to prop her up enough so she could land a position at one of these newfangled observatories, but a fun one.

"Let's hear it. Dazzle me with your rhetorical brilliance."

"Not everyone can barge in and command attention. I've never been to college and can't help with calculating the actual climate data, but that's only half the battle making these stations work. The real challenge is getting the forecasts out to people so they have time to react."

"And the government isn't doing a good job of that?"

Sophie shook her head and began stemming a bowl of strawberries. "They publish it in the newspapers, that's all. Plenty of farmers don't ever see a newspaper. If I were in charge of communication, I'd deliver the daily forecast directly to the produce markets and post it on the weigh-in tables where everyone will see it. And if a dangerous frost or flood is predicted, I'd utilize the churches to muster volunteers to get the word out."

That was the thing about sappy idealists: Sometimes they surprised you with their ingenuity. Sophie may not have much in the way of formal education, but she had practical insight that bureaucrats in the Washington office building perhaps had never considered.

"I'll help you," he said. "I may not be able to force the government to plant a climate observatory here, but I'll be able to get their attention. Dr. Phineas Clark is going to be in New York soon. I have invited him to Dierenpark."

She gasped. "Dr. Clark? He's the director of the entire operation."

"Which is why a visit would be a good thing, wouldn't it?"

178

"Why are you being so nice to me?" There was a note of suspicion in her voice, and he couldn't blame her.

He drew in a breath to answer, but froze. She looked at him with a combination of hope and . . . admiration? He swallowed hard, uncomfortable with the surge of longing that swept through him at her approval. He must never forget that Sophie was so far out of his reach she may as well be floating among the stars. He made sure his voice was indifferent before he responded.

"Because I like your pea soup," he finally said. "And I want to keep my cook happy."

That morning set the tone for the following days. Sophie was amazed when Quentin materialized each afternoon, coaxing her out onto the back terrace to plan strategies to lure the Weather Bureau to New Holland. He was gruff and demanding as he made her recite the reasons why the Hudson River warranted its own station, but she loved it. He didn't condescend or belittle her expectations. He actually helped her, dragging out old maps from the library and pointing out other promontories on the river that might be a better location.

"You need to research these spots and be prepared to answer why New Holland has more to offer than the competition," he said. Sophie had never realized she ought to include such issues in a proposal. She was thrilled when Quentin offered to review her written proposal as soon as she finished her analysis of all the neighboring towns.

Sophie commandeered one of the tables in the hotel lobby to spread out her papers as she polished the proposal. She picked the minds of her father, the cook, and two of the traveling salesmen for insight into the other villages located on promontories along the Hudson. One of the artists who had been living at the hotel pointed out that other spots had more mosquitoes than New Holland, and a salesman told her that nearby Tarrytown had an unreliable telegraph system. Long after the others had gone to bed, she kept the oil lamp burning as she rewrote the proposal to include details about the affordability of living in New Holland and its easy access to Manhattan. It was two o'clock in the morning when she finished the draft, but she went to bed with a surge of satisfaction for a job well done.

The next morning, she tucked the proposal beneath the bowl of oatmeal on Quentin's breakfast tray then held her breath as she waited for a response.

His reply was delivered less than an hour later. Mr. Gilroy set the proposal on the kitchen counter as she was brewing another pot of coffee. At first she was dismayed to see large X's scrawled through much of her work, but after further review, his strikes, arrows, and insertions made perfect sense. The scribbled notations in the margins sounded very Quentin. *Stop boring your reader with how much you like the work.* And *No one cares how pretty the old mill is.* Most of the comments were critical, but she smiled at the few brusque words of praise. *At last, a glimmer of common sense* and *Good job quantifying the cost of living.*

Oddly, it was his overall assessment at the end that thrilled her the most. *Too longwinded and sappy beyond belief. Clean it up and get better data for Tarrytown, which is your main competition. Show me another version by tomorrow. Good work, but we can do better.*

Quentin was the first person to take her seriously. While everyone else in the village patted her on the head in amusement, Quentin told her *we* could do better. He actually believed in her. Day after day, she and Quentin sat on the back terrace, working to improve the proposal. Each evening, she incorporated Quentin's suggestions and honed her language. With each revision, her proposal grew stronger, and for the first time she actually believed she had a fighting chance to land the climate observatory in New Holland.

Quentin had spent so much time helping with her proposal that she felt guilty at the end of the week when she reported to him in the library to collect her salary.

"I still think you are overpaying me," she said as she tucked the bills into her skirt pocket.

Quentin looked annoyed. "See? Another classic example of you being too nice again. You need to work on that, Sophie. How about making me a nice chocolate cake to compensate for the money you've been extorting from me?"

She winced. "The cocoa powder in this town isn't very good. I'd like to try grinding my own someday, but I've never been able to find fresh cocoa beans. Things like that are hard to get in a village this small." She glanced at the paperwork on his desk. "My goodness! Is this your bridge?"

"The one for Antwerp," he said.

"It's fantastic! I've never thought of bridges as pretty, but I love the arches. Are you really going to be able to put street lamps all the way across it?"

"If the city lets me build the bridge," he said dryly. "They keep threatening to fire me."

"Why would they do that?" It was hard to imagine anyone having the nerve to fire a man like Quentin Vandermark, but perhaps she really was ignorant of the ways of the world.

"They claim I'm overdue with the design. Which is ridiculous. The first delay was their fault over the electricity they asked me to add at the last moment. Besides, they have a perfectly good bridge in place that will suffice until I can get back to Europe and commence the project."

"When was the previous bridge built?" she asked.

"Three hundred years ago. And I'm only five months overdue. That's nothing in the grand scheme of things."

Sophie winced. "Five months does seem like a long time. Then again, trees that take a long time to grow always bear the best fruit."

A bit of humor tinged his face. "Is that one of your fussy Bible passages?"

"No, it's from Molière," she said. "Look, the people in Antwerp have a right to be frustrated. You can't convince me that five months isn't a long time to wait, and if they go with another architect, be gracious and understanding. Above all, we should strive to love one another, for it covers a multitude of sins. And *that* is one of my fussy Bible passages."

When Quentin laughed, it started low and deep in his chest. He usually struggled to keep his face straight, but his mouth would twist in a suppressed grin and his eyes would sparkle. He wasn't nearly so scary when he laughed.

And he'd laughed a lot as he'd helped improve her proposal. It felt good to work with someone who respected her opinion. She could see now that her earlier drafts were juvenile, full of wishful thinking, but Quentin forced her to dig deeper and work harder. Every paragraph of this document was dense with solid reasoning, including the numbers to back her assertions.

The proposal should be professionally typed and bound. The clerk at the courthouse often took in such work, but Sophie left for Dierenpark each morning before sunrise, and it was always well after dinner before she arrived home. The college professors were due to arrive tomorrow, so her time would be scarce. She would ask her father to deliver the proposal for her.

As always, by the time Sophie arrived home at the end of the day, the front lobby of the hotel was crowded with townspeople. In a village as tiny as New Holland, there was little to do in the evenings save gossip at the most comfortable meeting room in town. Her father shared a table with a few of the artists, one of whom was proudly discussing the sale of his work to a gallery in the city.

She rolled the proposal in her hands. The last thing she wanted was to discuss it in public and open herself to another round of teasing from the townspeople, but it took some nagging to coax her father into the privacy of the kitchen. She slid the string off, drew a fortifying breath, and unfolded the proposal on the kitchen work table.

"I'm hoping you can take this document to the courthouse and have it professionally typed for me. I've got my salary from work at Dierenpark to pay for it." *Please ask to read it*, she silently begged.

Her father's brow lowered as he glanced at the proposal, and his shoulders sagged as he recognized what it was. "Not again," he said heavily.

"But it's so much better this time," she replied. "Just read it and you'll see." If she could convince him to look at the second page where her tables of cost data were outlined, he couldn't help but be impressed.

He pushed the document back toward her, sympathy in his eyes. "Why must you do this to yourself? You are setting yourself up to be crushed, and now to throw your hard-earned money down the drain . . ."

She swallowed hard and flipped to the second page. "Look at these numbers! They show that New Holland is ideally situated and has the geography to support the observatory. Father, won't you even look?"

But he had turned away and was heading back toward the lobby. She intercepted him. "I'm trying to help you! I think this plan can succeed. Quentin reviewed the proposal and he says—"

"Quentin? Quentin Vandermark? What does an architect who has spent most of his life in Europe know about the politics of Washington, D.C.?" Her father's voice was scathing, and she took a step back. "That man is flattering you for some unseemly purpose. Mark my words, there is only one reason a man like him would show interest in you."

She flinched. Whatever Quentin's faults—and they were numerous—he never hinted at any improper motives.

"Is it so difficult to believe that he thinks it might work? That he actually respects this idea?" *That he respects me?*

She tried to give him the proposal once more, but her father folded his arms across his chest. "I won't help you make a fool of yourself." The words were gently spoken, but they burned nevertheless.

She swallowed hard. "Never mind. I'll find some other way to get it typed."

14

TEAMS OF RESEARCH SCIENTISTS began arriving the following day. Nickolaas had told Sophie that the professors would be chomping at the bit to study Dierenpark. It was a nationally famous estate but had been off limits to scholars for decades. Every professor to which they'd extended an invitation had accepted the offer.

All morning, Sophie had been welcoming the professors as carriages delivered six biologists, four archaeologists, and two historians to the estate. The historians were rapt with excitement to finally see the inside of the historic Dierenpark mansion. The biologists seemed equally dazzled, repeatedly stopping on their journey up the pathway to admire the abundant wisteria vines or touch fruit dangling from a pear tree. Their distractibility frustrated Quentin to no end, which amused Sophie. Couldn't he understand that these men were curious about the abundance of natural beauty surrounding them? While Sophie fetched cool drinks and fielded a barrage of questions from the professors, Quentin was impatient to get them all inside, holding the front door open and beckoning them with his cane.

After decades of remaining isolated and suspended in time, Dierenpark was once again a grand gathering place of delight and adventure. Quentin's rivalry with his grandfather was out in full force, and he was impatient to get his team of biologists to the river, unlocking the mysteries of Marguerite's Cove. Everyone knew about the wager made between the two Vandermarks, and Quentin wanted the ground rules for the competition spelled out in short order.

After everyone was finally assembled in the grand parlor, Nickolaas arrived to outline the procedures for the coming days. Wearing his finest suit of clothes, Nickolaas stood before the imposing fireplace, framed by an ornate mantelpiece imported from a sixteenth-century castle in Holland. Somber-looking Vandermark ancestors seemed to observe them from the gilt-framed portraits lining the walls. She wondered what those commanding men and white-wigged ladies would have thought of the wager between Nickolaas and Quentin. Had they been aware of the magical qualities of that stretch of the river?

Nickolaas cleared his throat and began outlining instructions for the following weeks. "The water lilies never appear to die," he said, his eyes alight with energy. "There were no lilies on that spot when I was growing up, nor were they there when my father died. I suspect they come and go over time. I have letters from the earliest Vandermark settlers making mention of water lilies."

He reached into his breast pocket and opened a slip of paper. "This is from a letter written by Adrien Vandermark in 1636, and I quote: 'The river is bountiful, but nowhere more so than a cove where oysters grow almost a foot in length and the lilies bloom with a heady fragrance. I sense a divine presence in this land, as though we have wandered into the Garden of Eden. We have no desire to return to Holland, for here is paradise. It is a treasure beyond the words of man.'"

Quentin let out a mighty gust. "Overblown allegorical language common to the seventeenth century," he said. "I don't care about a treasure; I want a soil and water analysis to explain those lilies."

Ever since hearing of the puzzle of the water lilies, Quentin had been on fire to find a scientific explanation. The lilies were a curious enigma, but Sophie preferred to enjoy the beauty of the spot rather than demand a technical explanation and hoped the scientists didn't ruin the cove with their tests and explorations.

"Wasn't Adrien Vandermark the original founder of Dierenpark?" Professor Sorenson asked. He was a world-famous biologist who Quentin had handpicked to lead the scientific research team.

"He was one of two Dutch brothers who laid claim to the land," Nickolaas answered. "He established trade with the English in Massachusetts and built the original cabin, but he was killed by the Indians before this house was built. It was Caleb who built the shipping empire and established trade with ports all over the world. I still have Caleb's ring," he said with a gleam of pride as he held up his hand to display the humble pewter ring. It was the same ring worn in the portraits of every Vandermark patriarch hanging in the grand parlor.

"All that is ancient history," Quentin said. "My concern is what is causing the lilies to grow in water that should be too salty to support them. I will pay five thousand dollars to the first man who can articulate and defend a scientific explanation for the health of the water lilies."

"And if one of the archaeologists finds a non-scientific explanation, or evidence of what my forefathers did to give rise to the lilies, I'll pay double my grandson's offer."

Anticipation rippled through the teams of researchers as they exchanged excited nods.

"Don't get too excited," Quentin said. "The answer to this

paradox will be rooted in science, and I'll match anything Nickolaas offers. Plus, I'll underwrite any expenses to publish your findings in a reputable scientific journal."

Nickolaas raised his chin to look down his nose at Quentin. "Do you *really* want to get into a bidding war with me?"

"Yes, he really does!" the youngest of the professors called out. Professor Byron was a newly minted biologist whose handsome looks and reckless grin were in contrast to the gray hair among the other professors.

Professor Byron's comment was greeted by good-natured laughter, but Sophie knew these men hadn't come here for money. They came because of the rare opportunity to explore one of the oldest estates in America.

Nickolaas folded his arms across his chest and directed his comments to the team of archaeologists and historians from Harvard, a group of bearded men who looked old enough to have been here when the *Mayflower* arrived. "I still have more money than my grandson, wealthy though he may be. Plus, I am open-minded enough to consider things no hidebound scientist can lift his head free of the test tubes to contemplate. I believe the answer to this mystery dates back at least to the seventeenth century. I want my team to look for evidence of some legal maneuver, a feud, and although my grandson may scoff . . . perhaps evidence of witchcraft or a spell that might have affected the land and the family. Miss van Riijn can show the archaeologists to the attic, where you may be able to glean information about my family's history."

Sophie stood to guide Nickolaas's team up the two flights to the warm, dusty attic. When the biologists asked if they might follow, Quentin tried to stop them.

"The answer to this puzzle is in the river, not the attic," he insisted.

"We agreed we would not interfere with their research,"

Nickolaas said. "Let the men have free rein wherever their curiosity leads."

Quentin looked ready to burst with frustration, but all twelve men followed Sophie up the staircase. Resting beneath a mansard roof, the attic had plenty of room in which to stand upright and was stuffed with old trunks, stacks of moldering clothes, and furniture from another era. Weak light from dormer windows illuminated the bare plank flooring, and the stale air swirled with dust motes.

"Are there any estate books?" one of the historians asked. "It would be helpful to know what has been planted over the eras."

"Aside from the gardens, I don't think they ever planted any sort of crops," Sophie said. "There has always been plenty to eat with the fruit trees and wild berries that flourish without any tending on our part. The earliest Vandermarks made their fortune from shipping, animal skins, and timber."

One of the men succeeded in working a lock on an old trunk free and lifted the lid. The leather strapping creaked with age, but the delight on the professor's face was obvious as he surveyed the contents of the trunk.

"These uniforms look like they date to the Revolution," he said in awe. The blue wool coat he lifted from the trunk bore the sash of a brigadier general in the Continental army. Even more fascinating was what lay at the bottom of the trunk. A beaded vest with leather fringe was surely of Indian design. There were other Indian relics, as well. Bone tools, a wampum belt, and a woven mat.

"They look like they come from the Iroquois, but I'm not a specialist in Indian artifacts," the professor said as he lifted an axe, hefting it in his hand. Everyone was silent with wonder. The last time that tomahawk had been handled was probably shortly after the Revolutionary War. How had it come into the

189

Vandermarks' possession? Was it a trophy of war or of friendship? Who had it once belonged to?

Sophie covered her heart, wondering if the pounding could be heard by the professors who seemed as enchanted as she, but she had to prepare lunch and couldn't linger. The men would be able to find their own way downstairs, and she could check back later to see what they'd discovered.

Quentin waited for her at the base of the grand staircase. Leaning heavily on the newel post, he glared at her with impatient eyes.

"Why aren't they following you?" he asked.

"Because there's so much to see!" It seemed a little mean to be so excited since Quentin wasn't able to go upstairs on his own, so she did her best to describe it. "There are trunks from the Revolution, and Indian artifacts. Dresses that look like they could have been worn at a royal palace—"

"That's all very well and good, but if you love this house as much as you claim, you'll do everything possible to assist the biologists in discovering the truth so I can spare the house from demolition. Keep the archaeologists distracted by the pointless junk in the attic, but the sooner my team gets to work in the river, the sooner I win the wager and save Dierenpark."

She glanced up the stairs. "Why don't I dash up there and see what I can do to encourage them to start exploring the river?"

His smile was wintery. "Excellent suggestion."

Quentin closed himself off in the privacy of the library to work on the Antwerp bridge, but it was hard to concentrate knowing the biologists had finally carted their supplies and equipment down to the bank of the river. Had they begun work yet? He wanted to see, but getting down the steep path to the river was impossible for him. He dropped his pencil and clenched his hands, cracking each knuckle systematically. It was frustrating to be trapped at this desk when he craved the chance to wade into the river, plunge his hands into the soil, and help with the investigation.

He pushed away from the desk. He couldn't join the biologists in the river, but perhaps he could at least find a spot to observe. Rumor had it there was an outcropping beneath the terrace that had an excellent view of Marguerite's Cove. He was cautious as he navigated around the side of the house, pushing through a dense screen of spruce shrubs, their piney needles scraping his hands and releasing a crisp scent into the air. Tapping his cane before him, he finally reached the outcropping that jutted from the side of the cliff. The ledge was spacious enough to contain a battered old bench.

As he leaned forward, his eyes widened in surprise. Was that a cannon? The metal was green with age, but the ornate scroll-work around the barrel indicated it came from a long-ago era. It could have been used in the Revolutionary War, or perhaps even further back to when pirates roamed the Hudson. At the very least, it was proof that the outcropping was capable of bearing plenty of weight, and the overhang might provide a place to observe the scientists in the river below.

Bracing his left hand along the grainy wall of the cliff, he wended his way down slowly to the overhang. It had a perfect view of the biologists at work. The river glistened in the sunlight, and for the first time, he was able to see Marguerite's Cove.

It was easy to see why artists would be attracted to the spot. The inlet had a sandy shore lined with cattails and rose mallow, and the water was smooth but for the profusion of vibrant lilies. It must be his imagination, but it seemed he could smell the perfume of the lilies even from this ledge a hundred feet above.

One of the biologists was hip-deep in the river, bent over to scrutinize a lily blossom through a magnifying glass. Two others collected water samples, but the others appeared fascinated with the oysters. He mustn't forget that the oysters were an equally mystifying phenomenon. Sophie insisted that most of the oysters in the rest of the Hudson were struggling to survive, but the oysters on Vandermark land flourished.

It was an enigma. The river should be too salty for lilies, and not salty enough for oysters, yet both thrived. It wouldn't take long for the biologists to come up with a logical explanation for the uncanny health of this cove, and then his grandfather could stop obsessing over curses and supernatural claptrap.

He leaned back on the bench, breathing in the fresh scent that swept through the air. He lost track of time watching sun glint on the river and listening to the voices and laughter from the men below. A sense of calm soothed his spirit. He didn't drift to sleep . . . not precisely, but it was so enchanting and restful it had the same effect. He didn't know how long he lingered on the bench. An hour? Two?

Movement to the east alerted him to Sophie making her way down to the shore from the deer path, a covered basket resting on one hip. From above, he had a perfect view of her willowy figure as she glided toward the scientists. The men wearing caps swept them off, dazed looks of appreciation on their faces as she approached. Even from a distance, he could hear Sophie's laughter carrying on the wind, opening her basket and passing out apples, cheese, and cookies.

He watched Sophie through narrow eyes as she kicked off her shoes to wade into the river. When she hiked up her skirts, he glimpsed shapely calves as she headed toward the oyster beds. She gestured to a spot, and one of the scientists leaned over to pry an oyster free of the reef. She joined him, and soon they had their palms full of the rough oyster shells before heading back to shore. Beckoning the others to gather around, one of the scientists used a pocketknife to pry open a shell then tipped the slimy oyster down his throat to the howls of the onlookers. In short order, he pried another open and passed the brimming half shell to Sophie. She gamely raised the shell to her mouth, tilted her head back, and swallowed the oyster whole while the others clapped in praise.

Quentin's heart darkened. Why was it so easy for some people to be happy? Wherever Sophie went, she carried a buoyant sense of joy that drew people to her. He clenched his fist at the way the youngest biologist, Professor Byron, reached out to clap Sophie on the back. The young man looked like Adonis and had a laugh that echoed off the cliff.

This was hard to watch. Grabbing his cane, he limped over to the cannon, bracing his hand on the sun-warmed metal to get a better view of what transpired below. He wasn't paying these men a fortune to flirt with his cook. It was time to break up the impromptu celebration.

"Sophie!" he shouted, his voice echoing through the valley.

She twisted to look up at him, shading her eyes with one hand and waving with the other. "You've found the Spanish cannon!" she called out. Even her voice carried warmth and happiness.

"Can you join me up here?"

Sophie nodded and tugged on her shoes then scurried toward the footpath, where she disappeared into the forested hillside. A few minutes later, he heard her skirts swishing as she joined him on the ledge.

"Spanish cannon?" he queried.

She nodded. "Spain was a late entrant into the French and Indian War. One of your Vandermark ancestors captured a Spanish ship and took this cannon as loot. It's been here ever since. Why are you here?"

"I wanted to see how the biologists were getting on, but the deer path everyone uses is impossible for me. Is there an easier way down to the shore?"

"Not from the house," she said. "You'd need to take a carriage and pick up the road almost half a mile away."

It was frustrating, but at least he could keep an eye on the activities from this overhang and he liked it up here. The wind tugged at his hair, and he folded his arms, unaccountably nervous. Now that he had Sophie here alongside him, he didn't want her to leave. He wanted to soak up this afternoon and the sense of peace he'd found at this spot. Sophie's company was both exciting and soothing at the same time, a strange combination but an exhilarating one.

"Why do *you* think the water lilies flourish here?" he asked. "You seem to know this piece of land better than anyone else in the valley." And suddenly it was intensely important to know. He was coming to respect Sophie. She was naïve beyond belief, but she was an intelligent woman with amazing insight, and it was getting harder to resist her.

"You'll laugh at me if I tell you."

"Maybe. Tell me anyway."

The tension on Sophie's face eased, and she went to lean against the Spanish cannon, gazing out at the vista before her.

"I think this land is blessed," she said. "I don't know why, but I've always felt very close to God up here, and I'm not the only one who has noticed it. I can tell by the way you're rolling your eyes that you don't believe me, but there are things science can't explain. Your grandfather told me about the crocuses on his wife's grave. They bloom three times a year, and that's not natural."

Just once, he was tempted to let her believe the fantasy. She seemed so charmed by the crocuses it would be petty to disillusion her, but like most things, there was a perfectly logical explanation for the miraculous crocuses on his grandmother's grave. He gave a reluctant smile and told her the truth.

"I pay a gardener to swap out the bulbs every four months."

"You do what?" She looked appalled. "You're tricking your grandfather?"

Putting it like that made it sound worse than it was. After his wife died, Nickolaas plunged into a depression so profound it was frightening. He'd been at odds with his grandfather most of his life, but it hurt Quentin to see the man so buried beneath a suffocating veil of grief.

"My grandfather visited his wife's grave daily, and when the crocuses he planted lost their bloom it hit him hard, as though it was a symbol that his life was over, as well. I feared he might sicken and die. I thought the crocuses would cheer him up, so I paid a gardener to transplant some bulbs that had been kept in cold storage. Forcing bulbs this way is easy enough to do."

"Oh," Sophie said in a voice that lacked her usual spark. She seemed disappointed at the explanation, but wasn't everyone when they learned fairy tales and Santa Claus aren't real? Over the years, his grandfather continued to take such comfort in the sight of those repeatedly blooming crocuses that it seemed cruel to stop. To this day, he paid a gardener to keep transplanting crocus bulbs onto the spot whether Nickolaas was in the country or not.

"Sorry to disappoint you," he said. "There is nothing magical about those crocuses."

She shook off her momentary dismay and looked at him with a new softness in her eyes. "I think it's rather sweet."

He'd been called many things over the years, but *sweet* was never one of them. He had no idea what to say to such a compliment, and he shifted his attention to the river. Oddly, she didn't seem the least bit uncomfortable in the face of his silence. She turned her face to the sun, closing her eyes and breathing deeply.

"I love summer," she breathed. And the bliss on her face made it impossible to doubt. If he were an artist, he'd want to immortalize that look of simple joy.

"Why?" Once again, he felt compelled to know. There were so many layers to this woman, and it was fascinating to peel them away.

"I love all the seasons, I suppose. Spring because it is a time of new life, when the bulbs and berries that have been waiting for a bit of warmth suddenly start bursting with vitality. In the summer the transformation slows, but we work to nurture all the new life around us. And then autumn is a time of reaping the rewards for hard work, for digging in the soil to find the dense, nourishing root vegetables that will sustain us through the winter. It seems like everything sleeps in winter, but it's really a time of renewal and reflection."

Her face carried a combination of joy and wistfulness. It reminded him of something he used to be, when he was young, before he understood how limited and painful his life was destined to become. But that didn't mean he couldn't enjoy this moment, even if it was delivered in the form of an artless village girl who knew how to recognize happiness in the most ordinary of events.

"People have seasons, too," she continued, still keeping her eyes closed but her face turned to the sun. "When Albert died, I went through some dark days. I lost my way for a while. I didn't know if I could find my way back into the light and learn to trust God again."

That surprised him. He'd assumed Sophie's childlike trust was unshakeable. "Isn't doubt forbidden for a Christian?" he asked.

She glanced over at him, an impish twinkle in her eye. "I don't think God dwells on when we fall down. I'd like to think he is more interested in helping us get back up again."

His smile was genuine. Normally he would have teased her for bringing fables about God into the conversation, but the moment was too perfect to spoil with cynicism.

They stayed on that overlook for hours, sometimes talking about the scientists, sometimes about Pieter, sometimes about nothing more important than the differences between black-berries and raspberries.

There was something magical here . . . almost holy, if he were the type to believe in that sort of thing. Sophie's company and her easy forgiveness of his callous behavior was humbling. He didn't deserve it, and tomorrow he might revert to his surly, embittered self. These temporary periods of happiness rarely lasted long for him, but he should enjoy the fleeting glimpse while it lasted.

The sun was starting to cast shadows when Sophie finally pushed away from the cannon. "I need to start preparing dinner."

He wished she didn't. He wished she'd stay here so he could continue to listen to her wax poetic about the simple beauty of an ordinary day. Looking at the world through her eyes was fascinating.

And he wanted more.

15

NEVER IN SOPHIE'S LIFE had she felt so needed. With twelve professors, six bodyguards, and the three Vandermarks, she was cooking morning, noon, and night. No sooner had breakfast been served than she started lunch. Each day, she baked six loaves of bread. She sliced meat and cheese until new muscles began forming in her arms. Pieter kept her supplied with baskets of blueberries and cherries for pies. Walking the two miles to and from the village each day sapped her already flagging energy, and it became apparent she ought to move into the house while the research teams completed their work.

Her father consented only because Florence was there. She and Florence shared a bedroom on the top floor of the house, and Sophie now had more time to spend with Pieter. The boy was fascinated by the biologists and loitered at the river to watch them each day. He peppered them with endless questions about birds and plants and what made the sky blue. Sophie was curious, too. She had never done particularly well in school, but these men seemed to know everything about nature, and she soaked up the knowledge they were happy to share.

No matter how busy her day, each afternoon Sophie found time to join Quentin on the outcropping above the river. He seemed unusually attracted to the isolated spot, spending the majority of every afternoon there. He usually brought a stack of reading material with him, but oftentimes when she joined him the book was splayed open on his lap while he stared off into the distance. The moment he saw her he'd beckon her to join him on the bench and they would speak about everything and nothing during those few enchanted moments of rest.

Meanwhile, the archaeologists had sectioned off land that was most likely to yield historical insight. Of particular interest was the humble cabin where Caleb and Adrien Vandermark had first lived when they'd emigrated to America in 1635. It was the oldest structure on the land, and sections of the surrounding yard were cordoned off for excavation. Using whisks and trowels, they peeled away layers of soil and sifted through the dirt, uncovering broken pipes, old tools, even a rusty flintlock musket. They found the remnants of an old smokehouse that had been abandoned and forgotten by time. Only the rough-hewn rock foundation remained, and Sophie couldn't imagine why it would be of such interest, but the archaeologists were thrilled by the discovery.

"Abandoned structures were often used as trash pits," Professor Winston explained. He was the oldest of all the professors, with stooped shoulders and round glasses, but he attacked the site each morning with the energy of a young man. "You can learn a lot about people by studying what they discarded. It will take months to properly excavate."

Months! Sophie's heart soared at the news, for it meant the house was likely to earn a longer reprieve from demolition no matter who won the bet.

There was little time to savor the relief, though, for as she sat at the work table watching Professor Winston stake out the area to be excavated, Mr. Gilroy arrived with the news she had been both anticipating and dreading.

"Dr. Phineas Clark from the Weather Bureau has arrived," he announced. "He is in the main salon and is waiting for you."

"He's here? And he wants to see *me*?"

"He's asked for Quentin, as well, but he specifically asked to see you, ma'am."

Her heart accelerated, and she felt lightheaded. She murmured a quick prayer, straightened her shoulders, and headed to the front of the house.

Dr. Clark was a rail-thin gentleman with graying hair, round spectacles, and a flawless suit that looked like it had been freshly starched and pressed that morning.

"I understand you have been manning one of our volunteer stations since the beginning of the program," Dr. Clark said as he greeted her.

Sophie wished she'd had the foresight to remove her apron and perhaps tidy her hair. "Y-yes," she stammered. "It's been an honor and a privilege."

She dipped a little curtsy, feeling out of place in the elegance and formality of the grand salon, but Dr. Clark set her at ease as he lavished effusive praise on her efforts.

"My goodness, our bureau could not operate without the dedicated service of people such as yourself. The privilege is entirely ours."

A sense of pride flooded her. Maybe this wouldn't be so difficult, after all. Quentin soon joined them, leaning heavily on his cane but appearing perfectly at ease as he greeted the esteemed meteorologist. He made small talk with Dr. Clark, inquiring about his journey and the politics in Washington. Finally, Quentin suggested they all take a seat, and Mr. Gilroy brought them tea and lemon cake. Sophie poured while Quentin took the lead in the discussion.

"Miss van Riijn has been monitoring the Dierenpark station for the past nine years," Quentin said. "Everyone in the village is impressed with her dedication and attention to detail. I fear I may have caused a bit of unnecessary confusion last June when I sent a message to the Weather Bureau concerning the location of the station at Dierenpark."

Sophie's breath froze. The way Quentin had tattled on her to the Weather Bureau was still a raw wound and she feared his next words.

"The last person to live in this house, Karl Vandermark, was committed to using our fortune to serve the people of this valley. Miss van Riijn and her father, who is the mayor of New Holland, were merely following my great-grandfather's intent by establishing the weather station here on the estate. Miss van Riijn's work initiating and operating the station has been exemplary."

Sophie sat a little straighter. There was no hint of cynicism or mockery in Quentin's tone, no suggestion that she was a naïve, simple soul who couldn't be trusted with a scientific endeavor.

Dr. Clark appeared most agreeable. "Not to worry," he said, his attention entirely focused on the slice of lemon cake he examined on the Delft dish held beneath his nose. "Whoever baked this cake is to be commended," he murmured. "Extraordinary."

How nice he was! Sophie had been living in fear of this meeting ever since Quentin suggested it, but Dr. Clark's gentlemanly demeanor put her at ease. She listened in fascination as Dr. Clark spoke of plans for the upgraded climatological observatories, thirty of which would be built along the East Coast in the coming decade. Each station would have eight to ten employees to coordinate data from the hundreds of volunteer weather stations in the nearby region, and then distribute the results.

Sophie's hope grew as the discussion unfolded. Dr. Clark wouldn't have come all this way if he didn't intend to at least consider her proposal, would he? With Mr. Gilroy's help she had gotten the proposal professionally typed and hoped to present it to Dr. Clark this evening. If the Weather Bureau built one of those new stations here, it would be the culmination of all her ambitions. It would prove to her father and the rest of the village that she was more than a starry-eyed girl who would never amount to more than someone who could bake fine pies.

Late that afternoon, she escorted Dr. Clark to the roof to show him the weather station she'd created and her process for gathering data. He asked all sorts of questions about her work and the Hudson River, all of which she was able to answer with ease. Admiration was apparent in his gaze as he surveyed the river, his clever eyes absorbing every detail as Sophie pointed out the Mill Road promontory, the beauty of Marguerite's Cove, and the clarity of the air here.

"We think the Mill Road would be an excellent location for one of the new climate observatories," she said a little breathlessly. "The people of New Holland have drafted a formal proposal outlining our plan."

"I look forward to reading it," Dr. Clark said politely.

And for the first time, Sophie began to suspect that she was actually going to succeed in planting a climate observatory here in New Holland, and it was all because Quentin Vandermark had faith in her.

The following morning, Quentin walked the grounds with Dr. Clark. An hour remained before a carriage would take the Weather Bureau's director back to the city.

He'd given the director Sophie's proposal last evening, and Dr. Clark confirmed New Holland would be a competitive location for a climate observatory. Quentin wanted another chance to state unequivocally that the Vandermarks would be willing to underwrite the project, provided that Sophie would be part of it. He took Dr. Clark on a brief tour of the grounds to have the discussion. It was hard to find privacy with so many professors conducting research at the estate, so he guided Dr. Clark to a spot in the meadow where they wouldn't be overheard.

The air was redolent with warm earth, sweet grass, and the scents from Sophie's herb garden. A meadowlark chirped in the nearby copse, the birdsong dancing in the air.

"Lord above, look at the carvings on that cabin," Dr. Clark said as the old groundskeeper's cabin came into view beyond an overgrown hedge of bay laurels.

The cabin truly was unique. Begun by the Vandermark brothers in 1635, over the centuries it had been added to and improved by generations of Broeders who tended the land. The skill for carving wood ran in the Broeder family, and over the years, many of them adorned the pillars, railings, and moldings with remarkably lifelike carvings. A lush vine had been whittled along the top railing of the fence enclosing the front porch, with flowers, dragonflies, and squirrels carved into the woodwork. Most impressive were the columns supporting the roof overhang. He recognized a lion, an ox, and an eagle carved into the columns. The only non-animal was a powerful-looking man who was probably supposed to be an angel, given the halo and the wings attached to his back.

"Astounding," Dr. Clark murmured as he ran a hand almost reverently along the carving of the lion. "Who is the artist?"

Quentin shrugged. "No one knows for sure, but my grandfather said they've always been here. The Broeder family has lived in the cabin ever since Caleb moved into the main house. I gather that woodworking has run deep in the Broeder family for generations. The carvings look like they've been done by different artists over the decades."

The features of the ox were more exaggerated and a little

cruder than the delicacy of the lion, a testament to the different men who had lived in this cabin. He shifted at the niggling feelings of guilt that prickled across his skin. He'd terminated Emil Broeder without a second thought, and yet the man had spent his entire life in this cabin, likely adding his own carvings to the menagerie. Emil was a simple man who never aspired to anything more than tending Vandermark land and raising his family. He was glad Nickolaas had ordered the Broeders' return. Even now he could hear Emil's wife inside, soothing a fussy child.

"Whoever carved them must have had a genuine and deep sense of faith," Dr. Clark said.

"How so?" Quentin asked, curious how Dr. Clark could draw such a conclusion merely from looking at a few carvings.

"The animals symbolize the evangelists," he said. "Mark the lion, Matthew the angel, Luke the ox, and finally we have John the eagle. Here they all are, standing in silent witness over this little patch of land. Quite charming."

Quentin was not conversant enough with Christian symbolism to have ever spotted such a detail, for religion had always been distasteful to him. It smacked of superstition and his grandfather's endless parade of spiritualists, palm readers, and soothsayers.

Dr. Clark's footsteps thudded as he mounted the wooden steps to examine another carving above the front door. It was of a dove, her wings extended and surrounded by sunbeams. "Look, the dove has the twig of an olive branch in her beak. The symbol of enduring peace. Absolutely delightful," he said.

Nickolaas had once said there were more carvings inside, but Quentin was reluctant to barge in on the family who had so recently moved back home. Before he could mention it, the door opened and Claudia Broeder stepped outside, patting a baby on her shoulder. She looked bedraggled and tired, but welcoming enough.

"Come on inside," she said. "Emil loves showing off the carvings."

Dr. Clark eagerly followed Claudia inside, but it took Quentin far longer to grasp the railing and mount the steps one leg at a time. By the time he entered, Claudia was showing Dr. Clark the carving of a lamb nestled onto the windowsill.

It was warm in the cabin, and Quentin left the door open to help move the air. He glanced at his pocket watch. Dr. Clark was to catch the midday train back to New York, and Quentin still needed to make clear that the Vandermark support of a climate observatory was contingent on a role for Sophie, but Claudia was still speaking to a rapt Dr. Clark.

"Some people think these carvings are amazing, but I've seen better in the city," she said. She gave a little roll of her eyes. "I think *everything* is better in the city. Emil swears the air at Dierenpark has some kind of calming ability, but I've never felt it. Then again, maybe I've just been too sick and weighed down with babies to notice."

The comment made Quentin pause. He'd certainly felt better ever since coming to Dierenpark, and a couple of the bodyguards had said they loved it here. Which was odd. All of them had traveled throughout the world, but Ratface and Collins had both said they'd never experienced anything to compare with Dierenpark. And yet the other guards shrugged and thought it was nothing special, just a rustic old estate far from the superior comforts of the city. Apparently Claudia shared their disinterest in the natural splendor here.

The squalling from another baby in one of the bedrooms caught her attention. "I'd better go tend to that one," she said with a sigh, disappearing down the hallway. Dr. Clark continued to study the carvings, and Quentin knew this might be his last chance to put in a good word for Sophie.

"The Vandermark family has been neglectful of New Holland since my great-grandfather died," he said, trying to broach the subject with the finesse it deserved. "I am eager to advance scientific progress and would be happy to help fund one of your new climatology stations, provided it could be located here in New Holland."

Dr. Clark's face grew pensive as he continued to study the carvings of dogwood blossoms along the top of a windowsill. "Money isn't our problem," he said. "The government has been generous in funding our initiatives. It is finding trained and reliable men to staff the stations that is problematic."

Quentin resisted the urge to smile at the perfect opening. "Miss van Riijn is both trained and very reliable. I can attest to her care and diligence in overseeing the local monitoring station."

"Miss van Riijn is typical of our volunteers," Dr. Clark said as he ran his palm along a trail of vines carved into the molding of a window. "They are farmers and the like. Simple folk who can be depended upon to submit their reports on time each day, but of whom little *real* intellectual work is demanded. Our upgraded stations will require men with degrees in meteorology and the analytical rigor to calculate thousands of data points. You would be far better served keeping Miss van Riijn making her extraordinary lemon cake. I think that would be a better place for a woman of her aptitude, hmm?"

Quentin's fist clenched around the handle of his cane. It didn't sit well to hear Sophie dismissed so casually, but he could hardly argue with Dr. Clark about the qualifications for a climatologist. That didn't mean New Holland wasn't a suitable location for the station or that there couldn't be a role for Sophie.

"Miss van Riijn has no formal training, but she has an innovative mind that can solve problems. She learns quickly and would be an excellent addition to any team, perhaps in a clerical role."

Dr. Clark cleared his throat and adjusted his tie. "Here's

the thing. Yesterday she showed me the rooftop station and it was clear to me she did not understand the difference between humidity and atmospheric pressure. She mispronounced hygrometer. Someone of her caliber won't be taken seriously by the other scientists, and that isn't good for building an effective team. She is a sweet girl, but so is my golden retriever, and I wouldn't hire my dog, now, would I?"

Quentin stiffened. "You should treat your dog better."

"Ha! No doubt." Dr. Clark continued scanning the wood-carvings spanning the interior of the cabin, but resentment simmered in Quentin. This man was a government bureaucrat who'd clawed his way to the top by currying favor like he had been doing ever since arriving at Dierenpark. Sophie and the other volunteers did the heavy lifting, making Dr. Clark look good with their unfaltering, unpaid service. Quentin wanted to deliver one of those fancy climate observatories to Sophie on a silver platter, but it wasn't something that could be purchased with a bank check.

"I will ask Mr. Gilroy to drive you to the train station. I believe it is past time for you to be on your way."

Nothing Dr. Clark said about Sophie was untrue, but it annoyed Quentin anyway. There was a difference between book learning and life wisdom, and it wasn't until he'd met Sophie that he fully appreciated it. He held his breath against the tightness in his chest. He'd set Sophie up for this failure and didn't know how to break the news to her. This was going to hurt, and he wished he could step in front of the wall of disappointment that was hurtling straight toward her. This was all his fault.

When he followed Dr. Clark onto the cabin's covered porch, a bit of movement from behind the hedge caught his attention. He blanched as he saw Sophie, her skirts kicking up behind her as she dashed toward the house. She carried a basket over one arm, clippings of parsley and rosemary dropping from the basket as she ran. His heart froze. She had been gathering herbs in the garden and overheard every word of Dr. Clark's blunt dismissal of her abilities.

He lumbered down the cabin steps to follow her, but the jarring flash of pain as he landed on the bottom step stopped him cold. He fumbled to grab the lintel post, clenching his teeth and waiting for the spots to clear from his vision. He collapsed onto the bottom step, hoping he wasn't about to pass out. He focused on taking deep breaths until his vision cleared. He'd dropped his cane when he'd grabbed the lintel post and it had rolled a few feet away, but he was as incapable of retrieving it as if it had rolled to California.

"Good heavens, are you all right?" Dr. Clark asked.

"I'm fine, just landed on my leg wrong," he said tightly. "If you could hand me the cane, I'd appreciate it."

Sophie had already darted up the front steps of the house and disappeared inside. Dr. Clark never noticed her as he handed the cane to Quentin, looking down at him in concern. It was a pitying, emasculating look he'd seen far too much of over the past decade. What he wouldn't give to be an able-bodied man who didn't have to fear a flight of three steps. What he wouldn't give to turn back the last sixty seconds so that Sophie wouldn't have heard the belittling of her abilities that confirmed every one of her fears.

But most of all, he wished he hadn't set her up for such a downfall.

Sophie needed to get away, but the house was swarming with a team of biologists at their microscopes, so she did an about-face to run back into the meadow at the front of the house. The archaeologists were on the east side, so she headed west, where the tulip garden was nestled behind a screen of juniper trees that protected the fragile bulbs from the wind.

Whenever Sophie was upset, no place on earth was more soothing than this secluded garden, cocooned by its rim of trees and fragranced by the scent of a thousand days of both happiness and sorrow. It was where she'd come after Marten jilted her. In Albert's final days, this was where she'd walked to soothe her aching heart. Not that the frank words from Dr. Clark in any way rivaled the despair she'd battled after Albert died, but her spirit hurt and it was soothing to look at the ancient juniper trees, their silvery bark weathered and twisted from centuries of wind atop this isolated promontory. These trees had probably been here since Caleb and Adrien Vandermark first ventured onto this land, so they had witnessed plenty of joy and heartache. Their timeless presence helped her put issues into perspective as she tried to walk away the weight of disappointment.

Perhaps an upgraded climate observatory would be built in New Holland, but she would not be invited to be part of the endeavor. She had to accept that.

But she couldn't ignore a patch of blue dahlias that looked like they'd recently been pestered by a squirrel. The soil was turned up, exposing their root bulbs, and their velvety blooms tipped at haphazard angles. Dahlias were the latest-blooming bulbs of the season and should last until autumn if she could repair the damage. Kneeling in the soft grass, she felt the smooth surface of an upturned bulb and, finding no serious damage, she eased the bulb back into the warmth of the soil.

"You'll be okay," she whispered as she nudged damp earth around the abused dahlia.

"Sophie."

She startled at Quentin's voice coming from only a few yards behind her. She guessed he'd seen her fleeing from the cabin, but Dr. Clark's comments were the last thing she wanted to revisit right now.

"I'm very busy," she said without looking up as she moved to the next uprooted bulb. "If I don't get these dahlias tucked back into the soil, they won't survive much longer. Which is a shame. Normally they survive until September, but some squirrel has been pestering them for no good reason. Their bulbs aren't even very tasty. . . ."

She was rambling but dared not stop lest Quentin try to raise the subject of the climate observatory and her foolish dream to participate in the endeavor. As if the Weather Bureau would be interested in a girl who'd struggled all the way through school.

"Sophie, I know you overheard what Dr. Clark said."

Well, that was blunt. She sat back on her heels and peered up at him. "You don't need to look so wounded on my behalf. I should have known I wasn't the kind of person who could be involved with something like this. It was foolish to even try."

Quentin limped to the bench nestled amid a profusion of hollyhocks and gladiolas. "Don't belittle the nine years of service you've given that bureau. Every day. With no recognition and no tangible reward. That kind of loyalty is worth a lot, Sophie."

"Something any simple person could do." She tried not to let bitterness seep into her voice, but this was hard. It underscored how paltry her life had become if the only thing she could point to with pride was her *simple* daily task at the weather station. She turned her attention back to the dahlias, pinching off the dead petals in hopes of encouraging more blooms later in the season.

"What about that St. Peter fellow you Christians seem so fond of? He was a simple man, wasn't he? A fisherman?"

She was surprised he knew that, but Quentin had been to college, so he'd probably learned all kinds of interesting things. "Yes, Peter was a fisherman."

"What about the rest of the disciples? Tax collectors. Laborers. I don't know if any of them were cooks, but I expect you would fit in quite well with those *simple* folk, and history seems to think quite highly of them. And what about St. Paul . . . wasn't he a . . . help me out here." A glint of humor lightened his tone as he looked to her for assistance.

"A tentmaker," she said. "I see where you are going with this, and it isn't helping, and I wish you would please just leave." The way her voice wobbled was embarrassing, and she moved farther away to prop up another dahlia.

"I worry about you, Sophie."

It was the last thing she expected this infamously self-absorbed and cynical man to say, but there was no mockery in his voice. Only a look of gentle concern as he contemplated her from his seat on the bench.

"Why would you worry over me?"

"Because you are so sheltered and vulnerable to the normal slings and arrows of the world. Now calm down, don't look at me like that. . . . I don't mean that as an insult, but I think someone with a little more experience in the world would be able to take this in stride. I lose more contracts to design buildings than I win. That is the nature of the business, but all most people see are the successes, not the countless disappointments and rejections. People like me rarely trumpet our failures. My ego would never survive it."

Once again, a hint of self-deprecating humor lurked behind his gray eyes. When he gave that half-smile and owned his weaknesses, it made him possibly the most attractive man she'd ever seen. Which was so odd. She had no business indulging silly daydreams about a man like Quentin Vandermark.

The last of the dahlias had been put to right, and she brushed the dirt from her hands. She prepared to stand, but his hand shot out to grasp her arm, keeping her in place.

"Don't let that man taint your sense of worth. Maybe you'll never operate a climate observatory, but the mark you will leave on the world will be far more important. Your legacy will be how you soothed a lonely and anxious boy. It might seem a small thing to you, but I think someday Pieter will look back on his summer with you as the most meaningful of his life. Your legacy will be how you extended basic human dignity to a passel of scary bodyguards. How you taught a cynical and embittered man to look at the world through your eyes. You touch everyone around you with kindness and grace, and that has an incalculable effect on the world. Most happiness isn't created by acts of great heroism or prestige . . . it comes from people like you, Sophie. Your legacy of quiet grace and compassion will echo down through generations to come."

Her mouth went dry, and she had no idea how to respond. Her life of stilted ambitions and meager contributions suddenly seemed a little more worthy for viewing it through Quentin's eyes.

"I think that might be the nicest thing anyone has ever said about me." And it was true. How remarkable that this cynical, difficult man recognized a piece of herself even she didn't know was there. She wiped the dirt from her hands and turned to face him. He was only a few inches behind her on the bench, and she reached up to set her hand on his good knee. "I think you might be a very kind man beneath that mask of ice."

He stiffened and withdrew a few inches. He blushed and looked out over the meadow. "Thank you, but I think it would be best if you did not touch me."

"I'm sorry," she stammered. She yanked her hand back as though burned. How embarrassing that he mistook her gesture of friendship, but yes, in a way it seemed as if she was flinging herself at him. It was mortifying and would never happen again.

He stood, fumbling with his cane. "I know you meant nothing

of it," he said without meeting her eyes. "A girl like you would have no use for an old cripple, but I am due back at the house. The Antwerp bridge calls."

She watched his stiff back as he lumbered toward the house.

He was right . . . any notion of a romantic attachment was foolish beyond words. How embarrassing that she had even placed the idea in his head.

She would need to be more careful in the future.

16

THE FOLLOWING MORNING, Sophie met Pieter on the roof to take the climate readings. Dr. Clark's dismissive comments about her intelligence still hurt, but she fell back on Quentin's beautiful defense of her. *You touch everyone around you with kindness and grace, and that has an incalculable effect on the world.*

It was enough. She didn't need the glory of a fancy position at a new climate observatory; she simply wanted to go on cooking for and supporting the amazing work taking place at Dierenpark. The house was alive with the sounds of men at work as they staked out excavation plots, carted mounds of dirt, and lifted out long-abandoned pieces of history from the soil. At the river, the biologists took water samples, soil samples, and plant samples. They brought them to the grand dining room, laying them on long rows of tables that had been set up with rows of microscopes. They compared the samples taken from a few miles upstream, trying to pinpoint microscopic differences that might account for the vibrant health in Marguerite's Cove. Stacks of reference books filled the tables, and Sophie had no idea what they were doing, but she secretly cheered the biologists on.

Not that she wished the archaeologists ill, for every day it seemed they found some new treasure to dust off—but Dierenpark would only be saved if the biologists could identify a scientific cause for the splendid lilies and oysters in Marguerite's Cove.

After the incident in the tulip garden, Sophie hesitated to keep meeting Quentin on the overlook for their regular afternoon chats. The last thing she wanted was for him to assume she was seeking him out in hopes of a closer relationship, but she truly savored their visits each day. And when one of the biologists showed her the largest oyster she had ever seen, it was a perfect excuse to visit him.

She need not have feared Quentin's reaction. His smile was broad and genuine as she joined him on the overlook.

"The biologists found a slew of huge oysters clinging to the underside of a long-sunk keelboat," she said as she handed him the shell. Oysters usually lived only seven or eight years, but these had to be at least fifteen based on the size of the shells. "See how pretty the inside of the shell is?" she said as Quentin took it from her hand.

He tilted it to the sun to see the iridescent shades of pink, blue, and silver on the inside.

"Mother-of-pearl," he murmured as he admired the shell. "I've always found it odd how something so ugly on the outside can hide such great beauty. What happened to the oyster?"

Heat flushed her cheeks. "It was delicious."

"You carnivore," he said in mock indignation. "We find an abnormally long-lived oyster and you can't stop yourself from swallowing it whole?"

She shrugged. "There are dozens just like it in the same spot we found that one."

"I thought you weren't supposed to eat oysters during the summer months. Aren't they more likely to make you sick?"

"They go bad faster if they sit around in a marketplace in the summer heat, but if you eat them straight out of the water, they are fine. Oyster-catchers tell people not to eat them during the summer because it's when the oysters spawn, but we've never had a problem with the oyster population in this stretch of the river. If anything, we've got too many, rather than a scarcity."

"In that case, I want some oysters for dinner."

Sophie listened in fascination as Quentin told her about the first time he'd sampled an oyster. He was twelve years old and Nickolaas had taken him to a Greek island where all the fishermen pulled up their boats and hauled in huge nets bulging with oysters. Rumor had it they would feast on oysters and Kalamata olives under the stars, and Quentin wanted to join them. He desperately wanted to be accepted by the hearty, vigorous men who seemed to take such delight in cracking open the oyster shells. The sight of the pale, glistening blob inside the oyster shell was mildly terrifying, but it was a matter of pride. His grandfather had already swallowed half a dozen oysters, and Quentin had felt like his manhood rested on his ability to conquer his fear.

"I closed my eyes, tipped it into my mouth, and left childhood behind me forever," he said. Sophie laughed at his enraptured expression, and he continued to wax poetic over his first experience with oysters. "It was the cool saltiness of it. It was like tasting the sea and the entire bounty of life it contained."

"I wish I had known you were so passionate about oysters," she said. "I'll make a nice pot of oyster stew for you."

The sound of thudding footsteps came from the ledge nearby, and Pieter came bounding into view. Quentin stood.

"Careful, lad!" he warned. There were no guardrails to

protect over-excited children, but nothing could dampen the excitement on Pieter's face.

"Come quickly," he panted. "The archaeologists have found something!"

A box had been unearthed from the trash pit inside the old smokehouse. It was encrusted with centuries of hard-packed mud, but Professor Winston held it as carefully as he would a newborn baby as he carried it to the work table outside the cabin and then began whisking away the mud with a soft-bristled brush. Everyone in the household gathered around to watch. The biologists left the river, the bodyguards clustered around, and Pieter wriggled through them to get a prime view across the table. And standing beside Professor Winston was Nickolaas Vandermark, watching every movement through guarded eyes.

Sophie glanced at Quentin, who seemed captivated as they all waited to see what the ornate box contained. It was about the size of a loaf of bread and made of dark wood, but silvery flashes indicated it was inlaid with some special material. Still holding the oyster shell in her palm, Sophie suspected it was mother-of-pearl, maybe even taken from the same oyster beds the biologists were studying.

Despite gentle prying, the lid refused to open. Professor Winston grabbed a magnifying glass, kneeling on the ground to be eye level with the box as he scrutinized the lid. Then he set the magnifying glass down and ran his finger across the side of the box.

"It's nailed shut," he said.

A murmur of confusion rippled through the crowd. Putting nails into a box of such beauty seemed a crime. They were crude, rough nails, deeply embedded in the wood.

"Open it," Nickolaas ordered.

218

The archaeologists looked concerned, shifting their weight and glancing at one another. "We try to preserve the historical integrity of artifacts. Opening the box might destroy it."

"It's my box, found on my land," Nickolaas said bluntly. "Open it."

The nails were deeply embedded, and a fine pick was used to scrape the decaying wood from around each nail, creating a hollow where a pair of thin pliers could work in and pull the nails. When the last nail was removed, Professor Winston carefully lifted the lid.

"It's a page of text," the professor said. "I don't want to touch it with muddy hands."

He stepped aside, and an archaeologist with clean hands gently lifted the page from the box. "Just a single page," he said. He turned it forward and backward, confusion on his face. "I'm not familiar with this language. I've never seen anything like it."

Other men lined up to examine the page, each of them baffled by the strange document. The collective knowledge of twelve college professors, speaking over a dozen ancient and modern languages from around the world, was flummoxed by the non-sensical words.

When Nickolaas stepped forward to scrutinize the page, his face went pale. For a moment, Sophie thought he was about to be sick, but he stepped back to allow Pieter to take his place and get a good look. She forgot Nickolaas's strange reaction when Pieter's eyes widened in delight.

"What does it mean?" Pieter asked, his voice brimming with wonder.

"I have no idea, but it certainly looks very old," Professor Winston said. "The printing press dates to 1440, so it can't be any older than that."

Sophie couldn't resist nudging her way through the men to get a peek at the page. It was on thick paper yellowed with age.

She ran her eyes along the first line of heavy black type, under-standing why the scholars were so confused by the senseless text.

Neit mittumwossis nag ne in wunnegen mahtug meechinnáte,
& wunnegen nah en moneaumunneate . . .

She couldn't even begin to pronounce the words that looked like pure gibberish. A few of the sentences were underlined in a firm mark. As she scanned the dense page of bizarre text, her gaze snagged on the one word she recognized.

Genesis.

She caught her breath at the word then stood aside so others could get a look. Excitement rippled through the men as they gathered to examine the page, pointing to the only word that was familiar to them all. *Genesis.*

"Could it be a page from the Bible?" one of them asked.

The format of the text seemed to mimic the chapters and verses of the Bible, and the word *Genesis* at the top made it hard to doubt that it could be anything but a Bible.

"I am fluent in Latin, Hebrew, Aramaic, and Coptic," one of the archaeologists said. "That text has no affinity or derivation from any of them."

Sophie instinctively reached for Pieter's hand, squeezing it. At times like this, she wanted someone to share her excitement.

"Burn it," Nickolaas ordered.

Stunned silence settled over the group, but Nickolaas paced the ground beside the table, dragging an agitated hand through his hair. It seemed sacrilegious to burn anything that even *might* be a page from the Bible, but Nickolaas was resolute.

"Burn it," he repeated. "It's nothing but gibberish, and I won't have anything to do with it."

Sophie looked to Quentin, the only one here likely to coun-termand Nickolaas Vandermark.

"We are not savages who burn books," Quentin said calmly.

"It's not a book. It's a single page found on my land," Nickolaas said. "This is my land, my house, my estate, and every scrap of it belongs to me. I say burn it."

Quentin limped forward, and the others parted as he drew closer to his grandfather. "You and I have a deal," he said quietly. "We aren't burning or destroying anything until we understand what is happening and why. The page will remain with Professor Winston for safekeeping."

Relief trickled through Sophie as the scientists closed rank around Professor Winston. Even the biologists drifted over to stand in front of the professor, who clutched the wooden box with its strange piece of paper inside. Byron, the youngest and most audacious of the scientists, stood with his arms folded across his chest, daring Nickolaas to challenge them. Only the bodyguards remained to one side.

Nickolaas's eyes turned flinty. "Ratface, go get that box," he ordered.

Ratface shifted his weight, uncertainty on his thuggish face. "I don't know if that's such a good idea, sir."

Beads of perspiration appeared on the old man's face. His breath came rapidly, and his gaze darted among the other bodyguards. "Don't just stand there," he stammered. "Someone go get that box. This is an order."

Sophie was relieved that none of the guards moved, and it seemed Nickolaas began to wilt in a strange combination of despair and agitation. He was wrong . . . deeply and profoundly wrong in his desire to destroy something he couldn't understand, but her heart went out to him. He was a proud man being humiliated before all these people who refused to obey his commands.

She stepped forward. "The sun is very hot this afternoon," she said gently. "I've got raspberry tea cooling in the kitchen. Let me help you inside."

Nickolaas hesitated. If she pressured him too much, it would be condescending and destroy his dignity, so she turned to glance at Pieter. "Pieter, you'd better come, as well. You look overheated, too. None of us is used to this much sun."

Pieter looked confused, but Quentin understood. "Run along, Pieter. It's a hot day, and I could use some tea, as well."

All of the archaeologists and scientists remained standing in a protective circle around Professor Winston, but as soon as Pieter scampered toward the house, Nickolaas turned and began to follow with slow, dragging steps.

Immediately after Sophie coaxed him inside, Nickolaas retreated to his bedroom, not even joining them for dinner and refusing a tray. Sophie could think of no reason for his virulent suspicion of the strange bit of text, but she intended to find out, and Quentin was her best way of unlocking the puzzle.

Quentin's leg seemed to ache less when he was outside. Sitting on the front steps of the mansion, watching shadows lengthen across the meadow, it was so serene that it seemed to make the relentless pain ease a tiny bit. It wasn't much, but it was a gift worth having.

He closed his eyes, listening to the rustle of the leaves in the soft evening breeze and the rumble of the men's voices inside the house. Each evening after dinner, the professors gathered in the parlor to discuss the day's findings, then moved on to discuss politics, theater, books, or whatever struck their fancy. Sometimes Quentin joined them, but he could take only so much before the lure of the outdoors beckoned him. The scent from the nearby copse perfumed the air, still warm from the haze of summer.

He had traveled all over the world, but this might be the prettiest spot he'd ever seen. Maybe there was something buried deep in his nature that harkened back to the generations of Vandermarks who had once lived on this precise spot. Perhaps he was tapping into the collective memory that had been handed down through the centuries of his ancestors. It was the only logical explanation for why he felt this profound sense of tranquility here.

Or . . . perhaps there was something to Sophie's belief in a divine being. On evenings like this, so soft and still, it was almost possible to believe the majesty of the world was not mere chance but had been created by a higher power. He scanned the sky, looking for the tiniest hint of God.

Are you out there? Or are we really alone? Why don't you send us a sign?

It would be nice to believe there was something more to the world than what he could see and touch. That they were more than a collection of carbon and hydrogen particles that would grow old, die, and then decay into nothingness.

The door opened behind him, and he immediately knew it was Sophie by the gentle way she closed the door and the swish of her skirts as she joined him on the steps.

"The men are saying you've given Professor Winston permission to take the page to Harvard for translation," she said.

"I did." There was a chance someone at the university would recognize the language, but more importantly, he wanted to get it away from Nickolaas. His grandfather couldn't be trusted to give up so easily. Mr. Gilroy was intensely loyal to Nickolaas, and between the two of them, they were likely to get their hands on the document and destroy it.

"Do you know why it upset your grandfather so much?"

It was a question that had been plaguing him all afternoon. He drew a breath and rolled his cane between his palms. "I think he knows more about this house than he is willing to share," he finally said. "He once said that his father hired a series of translators to go through some old papers found in the attic, and that his father became very despondent after the translations were complete. Karl Vandermark died shortly after."

"What were they translating?" she asked.

"I have no idea. And if my grandfather knows, he's not telling. He's always been very tight-lipped about his father's death."

Which was not surprising. Karl Vandermark had been lionized by almost everyone who knew him. He was wealthy beyond all imagination but still took a genuine interest in running the timber mill. He rolled up his sleeves and learned the trade from the ground up. He mingled with his workers and gave generously to the town.

"Your grandfather once said something strange about his father," Sophie said cautiously. "He said Karl Vandermark was no saint, although everything I've heard about him indicates he was an honorable, hardworking man. The people in the village adored him. Do you know what Nickolaas meant by that?"

It was a fair question, but he didn't want to answer it. He continued rolling the cane between his palms so hard they started to hurt. The silence stretched and became uncomfortable. The tragedies of his family were not something he enjoyed speaking about, but he was as intrigued as anyone about that strange document found this afternoon, and the possibility it was related to Karl's death.

"The people in my family don't tend to live very long," he said slowly. "There is a streak of melancholia that can be seen as far back as our records exist. I've read that physicians are now suspecting this might be a hereditary condition that is passed down from parents to their children. From what Nickolaas has told me about his father, it appears that Karl Vandermark suffered from the dark moods."

"I see," she whispered. "And you? Do you have this condition?" She said the words cautiously, as though she feared the question too personal.

Dark mood was too mild a term for the despondency, the despair, the days he didn't have the energy to lift a fork to his mouth.

There had been no cataclysmic event or day he could point to and declare it the beginning of his long descent into melancholia. It was merely years of oppressive darkness that sapped the joy from his life. The knowledge that nothing endured, and ultimately nothing mattered.

"I suppose I do," he admitted. "I was happy enough until . . . well, the past decade has been very difficult. Altogether awful, to be honest."

"Has it been all bad?" she pressed. "In all that time, was there never a period where you were happy and hopeful?"

His response was immediate. "The day Pieter was born. That was the best day of my life. It was perfect."

"Why?" Sophie asked. "What made it perfect?"

Only a person who had never witnessed the birth of a child could ask such a question, but he wanted to answer her rationally and reached back to analyze those few moments after Pieter's birth and articulate exactly what he felt.

"When I first held Pieter, I felt a surge of love for him. He was so innocent, and I wanted the world to be perfect for him. I felt a sense of new hope. It was like being born again, and I felt like anything was possible if I only reached out and asked for it. I was overflowing with hope and love and the certainty that I had been put on this earth to raise this child."

"And you don't feel those things anymore?" she asked quietly.

He blanched. He loved Pieter . . . but that sense of hope? The belief he could conquer the world merely through the force of his love? No, he hadn't felt that way in a long time.

"Despair is a powerful force," he admitted. For a brief while after Pieter was born, there was a possibility he and Portia could overcome the problems between them and find happiness once again. "I'm afraid my wife and I had a less than perfect marriage," he said slowly. "Portia and I grew up together. Our families had neighboring estates in Newport, and we'd always been friends. Our families traveled together, took the grand tour of Europe together. We shared a love of sailing, and although our friendship was platonic, I always assumed I would marry her one day. There are reasons very rich people tend to marry one another, and it has nothing to do with amassing wealth. I trusted Portia."

She was pretty and smart and fierce. From the time they were old enough to take a sailboat out, they'd shared a love of racing across the sea toward the edge of the known horizon. They should have had a good marriage.

But on their wedding night, Portia had wept, saying he was like a brother to her and sharing a bed would be awkward and horrible. It was something he never saw coming. He was nineteen years old and eagerly anticipating the physical side of marriage, but Portia dreaded it.

Their wedding night was a disaster. Portia knew what to expect of a marriage and was willing to endure it in order to have a child, but their friendship collapsed. She avoided him, no longer even wanting to be in the same room with him. The troubles in the marriage bed reached out to taint every aspect of their friendship.

He'd had such hopes for his marriage, but they were snuffed out quickly. For a fleeting time after Pieter had been born, he'd thought things might get better. After he set their newborn child in her arms, he held Portia, and they both wept in joy. She welcomed his embrace and laughed as he kissed her face and they took turns holding the baby. They had been so happy on that day.

226

It hurt even worse when she rejected him a second time. Like all decent husbands, he had moved into the adjoining suite during her pregnancy and recovery, but when he attempted to rejoin her, she refused.

"If we'd had a girl, I'd have been willing to endure it again until we had a boy, but there's no need now," she explained.

Endure it. Those words still haunted him.

"I learned that sometimes platonic friends don't work out so well in a marriage," he said to Sophie. "It wasn't what I hoped for or expected in a marriage, but it gave me Pieter, so I will be forever grateful."

"What happened to her?"

"Cholera. She died when Pieter was only ten months old. I'll always wonder if it could have been a real marriage if we'd had more time to overcome our troubles."

He shook away the memories, wondering why it was so easy to confide these deeply personal things to Sophie. She seemed to have that effect on people. She was kind and open and didn't have a mean bone in her body.

And she had been good for Pieter. It wasn't until he saw the way Pieter responded to Sophie that he regretted not providing a real mother for the boy. The series of nannies and governesses were employees who were paid to be nice to the child. Sophie did it from genuine love.

Above all, love one another.

The phrase popped into his head without warning. He knew it was one of Sophie's fussy Bible quotations, but she truly lived her faith. He was deliberately rude and mean to her when he first arrived, venting years of accumulated pain and disappointment on her simply because she seemed so cheerful. It hadn't blunted her kindness. She had a gentle dignity in the face of his rudeness, consistently being kind, compassionate, and, in her own way . . . wise.

She would be good for Pieter. She would be an excellent mother. He'd never considered remarriage after the disaster with Portia, but there was something undeniably appealing about Sophie van Riijn. And when one found a treasure, it was only logical to try to secure it for himself.

A flicker of hope flared to life. Sophie was everything he could ever hope for in a woman. He didn't need money or connections in a marriage, he simply wanted a wife who would complete his family. Complete *him*. Maybe it was time to make Sophie more than just his family's cook.

He glanced over at her, but she was staring into the distance in confusion. He followed her gaze, surprised to see a handsome, auburn-haired man heading toward them in the distance. Grabbing the rim of the balustrade, he pulled himself to his feet, Sophie rising at the same time. The man noticed them and waved his arm in a wide arc over his head.

"Hello, Sophie!" he called out.

"Marten?" The confusion in her voice was obvious, and Quentin narrowed his gaze on Sophie's delinquent, one-time fiancé. Dressed in a dapper suit and carrying two traveling bags, he had a reckless smile and a confident air that put Quentin on alert.

"What are you doing here?" Sophie asked, mild reproach in her voice. He was glad to hear it. Any red-blooded man who would throw over Sophie van Riijn for life as a steamship tour guide in Manhattan wasn't worth his salt.

Marten lifted one of the bags. "I've brought tulip bulbs, a special order for Nickolaas Vandermark. Once they arrived, I figured I would deliver them in person."

Sophie crossed her arms, an unusual spark of annoyance on her face. "Bulbs," she said dryly. "You've come all this way to deliver tulip bulbs."

"Not just any bulbs. These are from his cousin's estate in

Holland. Very hard to get in this country, but I was happy to oblige. What's this I hear about a gang of college professors living in the mansion? Everyone in town is talking about it. The butcher says he can barely supply enough beef to keep you all fed."

Sophie reached out for the bag. "Thank you for the bulbs. If you wait a moment, I'll fetch you a tin of cookies to thank you for delivering them, but you'd best hurry if you are to get home before dark."

Marten's grin was annoyingly wide. "Sorry, Sophie. I met that Mr. Gilroy fellow in town, and he said I could stay for a few days."

Quentin narrowed his eyes. The story would be easy to verify, which meant it was probably true. And that meant that either Mr. Gilroy or his grandfather saw some underhanded use for Marten Graaf here at the mansion.

Which meant there was no getting rid of him. Dierenpark had just acquired yet another houseguest.

❧ 17 ❧

THE PAIN IN HIS LEG WOKE HIM. It was a ferocious ache deep in the marrow, running from his ankle all the way up to the base of his knee. Quentin lay perfectly still, the fog of sleep clearing from his brain as he tried to assess the situation and locate what had caused the abrupt worsening of his condition.

He hadn't put undue stress on his leg yesterday. He'd worn the brace overnight as instructed by the specialists in Berlin. The brace was uncomfortable and made sleep difficult, but it spared him the agony of inadvertently rolling onto his leg at an awkward angle. Chronic osteomyelitis was an insidious disease he'd been battling ever since the first surgery on his leg. He hoped this flare-up wouldn't further weaken what was left of his shin bone.

He wished for a fraction of Sophie's faith so that he could pray to a loving God who would magically heal his leg, but he couldn't accept that God would design a complex, magnificent world and then simply abandon it to the ravages of war, famine, and disease. He was learning to respect Sophie, but he couldn't respect her God. Her God either didn't exist or he didn't care, and it was more logical to conclude he didn't exist.

It would be better to stay in bed today. He pushed himself upright and closed his eyes against the pain pulsing throughout his body. Perspiration beaded on his forehead. It was hot in here, and he flipped the sheets back, wishing he knew if this was a simple fever or the beginning of a more serious bone infection.

He lit the kerosene lantern for some reading light. In short order, he snagged the reading table he'd designed to slide across his lap and propped a book atop it. Eventually Mr. Gilroy would come to check on him when he didn't materialize for breakfast. He'd read two chapters on hydraulic engineering when the sounds of laughter from somewhere outside penetrated his concentration. He tried to ignore them, but they weren't stopping.

Grabbing his cane, he nudged the draperies aside to see outdoors. Sunlight flooded the room, making him wince, but as his eyes adjusted he saw two figures swimming in the river, their arms pumping madly as they moved through the water. They were racing, their vigorous kicks churning up white water behind them as they were cheered by onlookers standing on the shore. The swimmers were nearly tied, but one had a slight edge and began to pull away.

Envy snaked through him. How desperately he wanted to be whole and capable of plunging into a cold river and testing his muscles against the current.

The swimmers passed the pier, apparently designated as the finish line. Both men stopped and pushed to their feet, their lungs heaving as they brushed water from their eyes. They were shirtless, their muscles enlarged from the effort, grins on their faces. One of them was Byron, the young biologist. Quentin's mouth tightened when he recognized the other swimmer as Marten Graaf, the idiot who'd jilted Sophie. Marten had won

232

the race, and he clasped his hands over his head with a wide, healthy grin.

Both men waded to the shore, where one of the onlookers tossed them towels.

Quentin straightened when he spotted Sophie among the group. What business did she have ogling half-naked men climbing out of the river? Marten didn't even have the decency to cover his body immediately. Using the towel to rub the water from his hair, he sent Sophie a grin and said something to her.

Whatever he said made her burst out in laughter. The others joined in, and soon Byron and Marten were flicking their towels at each other, playful as schoolboys.

Quentin jerked his cane away, letting the draperies fall back into place and plunge the room back into the dimness lit only by the kerosene lamp.

Envy was a useless emotion. He would give his entire fortune to trade places with either one of those healthy men in the river, but it was pointless to dwell on it. That didn't mean he intended to wallow here like an invalid and let Sophie's one-time fiancé have free rein in his house. He banged his cane on the wall and shouted for Mr. Gilroy. Within moments, his butler arrived.

"Go down to the river and get that young idiot Marten Graaf in here," he growled. "I want to speak with him."

Marten's hair was still wet when he arrived at Quentin's bedroom. He hesitated in the doorway, fidgeting in his ill-fitting suit jacket. This was a man Sophie once loved, a man who broke her heart. He was still boyishly handsome, radiating youthful health and revealing a dimple in his left cheek when he smiled. Quentin pointed where he wanted Marten to stand at the foot of his bed.

The only thing Quentin knew for sure about Marten Graaf

was that his unexpected arrival last night was not prompted by the delivery of tulip bulbs. He sensed Mr. Gilroy's hand in this. Or perhaps Marten was interested in Sophie again, and that would be the worst possible scenario. Sophie was better than the fickle man who shuffled to the foot of the bed, his eyes darting around the dimly lit room, noting the swaths of velvet draperies surrounding each window and the ornately carved headboard imported from an eighteenth-century duchy.

Quentin felt no impulse to put him at ease. Still dressed in his nightshirt and propped up with his invalid's work table across his lap, he was accustomed to receiving visitors from his sickbed and didn't intend to spare this young whelp just because Marten would be more comfortable somewhere else in the house. Quentin was more comfortable here, so this was where they'd meet.

He used a deceptively calm voice. "My grandfather has been purchasing the Vandermark tulips for the last five decades from the Wittenberg Trading Company in Manhattan. They have never personally delivered the bulbs in the past, so it begs the question, why now?"

Marten's face flushed a little. "I share a room with a man who works for Wittenberg," he said. "I volunteered to deliver the tulips as soon as the ship arrived. Wittenberg is grateful for your grandfather's patronage over the years and was happy to extend the service."

Quentin held the younger man's gaze but said nothing in reply. It didn't take long before Marten began fidgeting again.

"And yet I've heard that you capitalize on my family's misfortunes by telling lurid tales to the tourists."

His eyes widened. "Sophie told you?"

No, he'd guessed, but he couldn't blame Sophie for hiding it from him. He had never given her much reason to be forthcoming with him, but he would do better from here on out. Sophie was about to figure into his long-term plans for his family, and he needed her to begin trusting and confiding in him.

"It doesn't matter how I know, but I am notifying you that this house, the pier, and our land are unavailable for use by a private business."

"You might own half of New York, but you don't own the river," Marten said with admirable bravado. "Steamships are earning an honest living, and you have no right to block our access to the river."

As if he needed instruction on nautical law from a puppy. "Like any other duly licensed ship, you have the right to make use of the waterway, but you may not land on my waterfront or make use of the Vandermark pier. Is that clear?"

"It's clear."

"Why did you jilt Sophie?" He fired the question with no warning, hoping to catch the younger man off guard, and he did.

"Young men do stupid things. Letting go of Sophie has always been my biggest mistake."

"What a pity that some mistakes are fatal and can never be forgiven."

A confident gleam lit Marten's eyes. "Have you talked to Sophie about that? Because Sophie is the most loving, forgiving woman I've ever met. She and I are friends again. She knows I regret what happened and forgave me long ago."

Given the joking between the two of them he'd witnessed on the shore not long ago, Marten was right. Sophie desperately wanted children. A home and a family of her own. Now that she was throwing off the veil of mourning for her beloved Albert, she might well turn to a trusted old friend to achieve that dream.

Quentin wasn't accustomed to feeling jealousy over a woman. He couldn't compete with Marten in youth or health or cheerfulness. He couldn't beat him in a swimming match or any other physical challenge.

But he had something Sophie wanted desperately. He had Dierenpark. The estate was still owned by Nickolaas, but the ironclad Vandermark trust required it to be passed down to the oldest surviving son in the family line. He had complete confidence he would win the bet with Nickolaas, and then Sophie could live in this house for the rest of her life if she consented to marry him and be a mother to Pieter. She would be willing to tolerate a lot in exchange for that.

"Don't start weaving any fantasies about Sophie," he warned Marten in a quiet voice. "You've delivered the tulip bulbs; now you can be on your way. I won't have the work of my scientists disrupted by swimming matches or unwanted visitors."

"I'm not leaving."

Quentin raised a brow, not used to being countermanded. "I am breathless to hear how you plan on overwhelming the six bodyguards I have on staff to keep intruders away from my door."

"Mr. Gilroy wants me here."

"Why?"

Marten shrugged his shoulders. "Seems like the old man and Mr. Gilroy think Sophie is getting too much power over you, and they want me to put an end to that." Marten dropped his smug attitude and looked him in the eye. "They probably think I'll be their lackey, but let me be clear. I'm here for Sophie. I know you got her hopes up over that climate observatory, and look how well that worked out for her. You're up to something, and I don't like it. I'm not going to stand aside and let any of the jackals in this house take advantage of her or turn her into a pawn in the strange bet going on between you and your grandfather. Sophie's father agrees with me." Marten's smug grin returned. "So if you want to keep Sophie as your cook, I'm part of the deal."

Marten was whistling as he casually strolled from the room.

Quentin waited until the door closed before flinging back the covers and reaching for his clothes. Today wasn't a day he could afford to linger in bed. He had arrived at a decision about Sophie and had never been the sort to loiter once he made up his mind.

Sophie was growing concerned for Nickolaas Vandermark, as he hadn't been seen since yesterday afternoon when he'd retreated to his bedroom after failing to destroy that mysterious document. There had been an impromptu race in the river this morning, and she feared the raucous outbursts from the spectators might have disturbed those sleeping late, but there was still no sign of either Nickolaas or Quentin at breakfast. It wasn't unusual for Quentin to want to be alone, but it was almost ten o'clock and she worried about Nickolaas. His reaction to that document made her certain he knew what it was, and it didn't bode well.

Walking quietly in the upstairs hallway, she approached the master bedroom, its doorway surrounded by painted white pilasters and topped with a hand-carved pediment. She knocked gently on the closed bedroom door.

"Mr. Vandermark?" she asked. She didn't want to disturb his privacy, but she had the delivery of Marten's tulip bulbs as an excuse to approach him.

Because, frankly, she was anxious. Quentin's statement about melancholia running in the Vandermark family was worrisome, and Nickolaas seemed unusually upset by that old document. If she could coax him into talking about why it bothered him, perhaps she could help ease his despair.

To her relief, she heard shuffling behind the door. The knob turned and the door cracked a narrow sliver to show Nickolaas's eye peering at her through the crack.

"What do you want?"

"I've brought tulip bulbs. I gather you asked for them."

He looked confused. "It's too early to plant tulips. And why would I plant tulips on a piece of land I intend to demolish?"

She tried not to wince at his persistent threat to destroy Dierenpark. "Marten said they come from the tulip farm of your Vandermark cousins in Holland. That you put in a special order for them every year."

The door flung open. Dressed in pajamas, with bare feet and his robe hanging open, the normally meticulous Nickolaas looked bedraggled and unshaven, but a bit of life sparked in his eyes. "Excellent! I am rarely in New York to accept the order personally, so I forgot how early they arrive. Let me see them," he said, holding out his hand impatiently.

She turned over the satchel, and he peered inside, scanning the contents with greedy eyes as he counted the bulbs. "Excellent, excellent," he murmured. "Who brought them?"

"Marten Graaf. He works in Manhattan and must have some connections."

"Tell him I want two hundred more." He closed the door in her face.

She knocked again. "Mr. Vandermark? Perhaps you'd like to come tell him yourself." She had to get him out of this bedroom. He hadn't eaten since lunch yesterday, and she was no closer to understanding why that document rattled him so.

The door jerked open again, but instead of talking about bulbs, he looked at her with accusing eyes. "Mr. Gilroy tells me Professor Winston left for Harvard this morning with my document, and you did nothing to stop him."

She blinked. "I could hardly stop him. Everyone agreed we needed to know more about that bit of text. I'm almost certain it's part of a Bible, but the language is so odd . . . unlike anything anyone has ever seen before."

"You got a good look at it?"

"Not really, but all it took was a glance to know the language is very strange."

"Mr. Gilroy is in the library. I have reason to believe there may be more documents in the same language scattered around the house. I thought they had all been found and destroyed, but apparently not."

She caught her breath, almost certain these documents were what Karl Vandermark had hired translators to interpret.

"I want you to go help him," Nickolaas continued. "You know this house as well as anyone, and I want you to poke through every hiding place or cubby hole. If anything else is found written in that language, I want it brought to me. There's no need to involve Quentin in this."

Sophie couldn't help him. It would be a crime to destroy historic documents before they even knew what they were. Besides, Quentin had hired her to cook and mentor Pieter. She didn't have time to go on a wild chase for documents that may not even exist.

"Why do you care about those documents? You know something about them and aren't telling us. Why?"

"Because it's none of your business," he said in a nasty voice.

Above all, love one another. She didn't understand the torments that drove this man, but they were real, and they were painful to him. Such a man deserved compassion, no matter how rude or blunt.

"I wish you would join us downstairs," she said. "We are having a grand celebration this evening. I'm going to spend the day making the world's best oyster chowder. I'm generally not boastful about my cooking, but on this recipe I feel confident. It would be a shame to spend the day alone up here when we'd rather have your company."

He narrowed his eyes, but she kept pushing.

"You once told me how you admired your Vandermark cousins in Holland because they shared meals together. How can we have a proper meal without the family patriarch?"

The reference to his joyful cousins caused the first real hint of softening on his face, so she continued that train of thought.

"Pieter is going to have his first taste of oysters this evening. He can't stop talking about it, and I know he will want both you and Quentin to be there."

"I'll be there," Nickolaas conceded, then he spoiled the effect by slamming the door in her face.

⁂

"What are these?" Pieter asked, holding up a handful of leeks, their bright green tips flaring out almost like a bouquet of flowers.

"They're leeks," Sophie replied as she mounded the ingredients for this evening's feast on the cutting table. "They are a type of onion but have a softer taste."

"I don't like onions," Pieter said.

"They'll be diced up so small you won't even notice them. And they'll give a wonderful flavor to the chowder, just you wait and see. This will be the best oyster chowder ever served on the eastern seaboard."

Her chowder was a hearty dish made with smoked bacon and thickened with cream and russet potatoes. It would be seasoned with minced leeks, cracked pepper, and an array of fresh herbs. Everything would be fresh and wholesome, and the feast would last until long after the sun went down.

Since finding that astounding bit of text yesterday, the professors felt like they were on the verge of discovering something wonderful. It ignited their curiosity and sent a bolt of energy through the researchers, who were now convinced there was a mysterious history here just waiting to be discovered. And what better way to celebrate than with food? Pieter was bursting with excitement over his first taste of oysters, convinced he was now old enough to sample the delicacy without getting squeamish.

"Marten said it would be better to have the celebration down by the river," Pieter said. "He said that the only proper way to celebrate an oyster harvest is while gathered on a beach. My father can't get down to the river, and he's spoiling it for everyone."

Sophie kept her face calm, although it was spiteful for Marten to share that hurtful detail with Pieter. Marten was terribly threatened by Quentin, who apparently had read him the riot act this morning, although he refused to say what it was about. It was easy to imagine how intimidating Quentin could be, and she didn't want to embarrass Marten by demanding the details.

"We'll eat on the back terrace overlooking the river," she said. "That way, we'll be able to see the fireflies when they come out at twilight. It will be like they are lighting our celebration."

"Okay!" Pieter agreed. It was amazing to see this boy blossom into a curious and normal boy, no longer frightened of the dark or every strange sound. The biologists had taken him under their wing and showed him how they collected water samples, placed dots of water on glass slides, and studied them under the microscopes set up in the dining room. They even provided him with reference books and let him try to identify some of the cell samples collected from the river.

She was dicing potatoes when Mr. Gilroy interrupted her. "Mr. Vandermark wishes to see you. Mr. *Quentin* Vandermark," he clarified.

Sophie kept dicing. "He'll have to wait. Pieter and I have two sacks of potatoes to dice and three sides of bacon to cook."

Mr. Gilroy was smooth, and before she knew it, he removed the knife from her hands and was drawing the board of potatoes toward him. "I am happy to dice the potatoes," he said. "Quentin is waiting for you near the Spanish cannon."

It was alarming how Mr. Gilroy could manipulate the situation with such ease. She propped her hands on her hips, determined this man would not once again get the better of her. "Dicing potatoes? I thought you were under orders to search the house for mysterious texts."

A bit of humor lit Mr. Gilroy's face as he began cutting up a potato with expert hands. "The challenge of serving two masters," he said.

"Can I come, too?" Pieter asked. It was rare for Pieter to seek out a chance to visit with his father, and she couldn't deny him.

It was surprisingly cool outside, and Sophie looked down to Pieter. "It feels like that Canadian front they forecasted has arrived, don't you think?"

Pieter looked at the gentle breeze ruffling the sycamore leaves and then up at her. "The wind is coming from the north," he confirmed with a solemn nod.

"It's steep here, hold my hand as we go down to the ledge."

"I'm not a baby," Pieter mumbled, but he still accepted her hand as they walked toward the outcropping. It was nice to feel needed. All week she had loved cooking for these people and being a part, in however small a way, of the research teams. Maybe she would never run her own climate observatory, but there was still a role for her in supporting the work of others. After all, these men couldn't continue their work if they weren't fed.

A glance at the river showed the biologists busily harvesting oysters into baskets. She hoped she could settle the business with Quentin quickly, for the amount of work still to be done before tonight's feast was staggering. The bacon needed to be cooked, cooled, and diced. She wanted to prepare herbed butter, and shucking oysters required a lot of time, as well.

As the overhang came into view, she saw Quentin formally dressed in a suit jacket with a satin tie, sitting on the bench and fiddling with his cane. She wasn't used to seeing him dressed so formally. It made him look . . . very nice, actually.

"Here we are," she said brightly as she walked the final few steps.

Quentin looked surprised to see Pieter. He pushed himself to his feet and fumbled with his cane. "I . . . um . . . I didn't expect you to bring Pieter."

"I've been helping make oyster chowder," the boy said proudly. "Next we're going to shuck the oysters, and Miss Sophie says I can help. I'm not afraid of oysters, even though they're slimy."

Humor lightened Quentin's eyes. "You sure? Last time I showed you an oyster on the half shell you looked ready to run and hide under your bed."

"But I'm older now. And Miss Sophie says they won't look so awful once they're in the chowder," Pieter said in a voice that still carried a whiff of trepidation. "I'm going to try them tonight. I think I'm old enough now."

She met Quentin's gaze, an amused message flying silently between them. Most people were squeamish about their first taste of oysters, but it would be fun to introduce the boy to the culinary delight. It was going to be a fabulous evening. Everyone here had formed an immediate bond in the quest to uncover the history of the estate. She instinctively wanted to share the moment with Quentin and Pieter, especially given the way Quentin had been so decent to her lately. And the way he was looking at her so strangely . . . like he was anticipating something.

"Pieter, I need to speak with Miss Sophie privately," he said.

"Does that mean you want me to go away?" Pieter asked in a confused voice.

To her surprise, Quentin suddenly seemed tongue-tied. His

gaze darted around, and a flush stained his cheeks. "It means you need to run along for a few minutes while I discuss grown-up business with Miss Sophie."

She couldn't imagine what was making Quentin so uneasy, but Pieter was used to obeying orders and went scampering up the ledge to the house.

"He's come a long way in the past six weeks," Quentin said, still fiddling with his cane and staring somewhere over her shoulder. "Most of that is due to you. You've been very good for the boy."

Compliments from Quentin were as rare as rubies in the sand. "Thank you," she said with a surprised smile.

"I found a Bible in his bedroom."

Her shoulders sagged. So . . . that was why he'd summoned her. He'd discovered she'd failed to slam the door on Pieter's curiosity about faith and was going to interfere.

"He asked if there was a Bible in the house, and I showed him where it was," she admitted.

Oddly, Quentin didn't seem angry. He tugged on his collar and seemed merely a little embarrassed.

"I'm willing to admit I've been wrong about that," he said. "I studied Christianity at college and understand the basic doctrines. The principles aren't bad, and if they bring Pieter comfort, I don't mind him exploring until he is an adult and ready to make his own decisions."

She smiled softly. "What made you change your mind?"

"You."

He couldn't have surprised her more if he sprouted wings and dove off the cliff. For a man so aggressively hostile to religion, this capitulation was stunning. But he still seemed ill at ease. His jaw was clenched and he couldn't meet her gaze, but with jerky motions he gestured for her to sit on the bench.

"You are very good at reading Pieter and his needs," Quentin

244

said as he joined her on the bench. "Before you came, I didn't realize how much he has missed a woman's softness in his life. He lowers his guard around you and becomes curious about the world around him. He is less prone to anxiety over pointless things. I owe all this to you."

"Thank you," she said again, wondering what was prompting this bewildering conversation. He rubbed his hands along the rough fabric of his trousers and cleared his throat. He seemed so nervous that she began to fear his next sentence. Was he taking Pieter and leaving them? His anxiety was contagious, and her stomach clenched and heart began to pound.

"Whatever is bothering you, just say it," she prompted. Anything to break this awful tension.

He took a heavy breath then turned to face her. "Miss van Riijn, I am in need of a wife, and Pieter is in need of a mother. I believe you would fill both roles quite well. Will you marry me?"

She gasped. If she wasn't so appalled, she would laugh, but there was nothing funny about this moment. She'd had three fiancés, and at each proposal she'd believed herself in love, but love was the last emotion she felt for Quentin Vandermark.

He awaited her answer like a condemned man awaited an executioner.

"I can't imagine we would be a good match," she stammered.

He stiffened even further, his spine straightening and his chin lifting. "We're an excellent match," he countered. "You have a genuine affection for Pieter, and your devotion to Dierenpark in unquestionable. If you marry me, you can live at Dierenpark for the rest of your life."

Not a word about love. Not that she expected it from a man as stern as Quentin Vandermark, but she'd never imagined marrying a man without a true and genuine affection. Until recently, Quentin had seemed to actively dislike her.

"That's what you need then, a mother for Pieter?"

"Precisely. As I said earlier, my health is precarious and I need to secure his future. I believe you can provide him with a foundation of integrity and moral judgment. And you could be mistress of Dierenpark for the rest of your life."

His proximity was uncomfortable. She stepped away from the bench, gazing out over the river.

She *would* be good for Pieter. The quick affection that had bloomed between her and Pieter felt almost like being a real mother.

And love hadn't worked out so well for her in the past, had it? All her life she'd longed to feel needed, and Pieter needed her. There would be a lot of advantages to marrying into this family.

She dragged air into her lungs and surveyed the vista before her. She had loved Dierenpark as far back as her memory reached. Marriage to Quentin would mean she could savor the beauty of this breathtaking spot for as long as she lived. It could all belong to her.

It was a perfect day, the sky a blinding blue. The colors seemed magnified, the sound of the insects droning in the nearby flowers strangely loud. The scent of honeysuckle was so strong it seemed cloying, the sunlight so bright it hurt her eyes. She shaded her eyes as she took in the view, dwelling on the idea that it could all belong to her as soon as she spoke the word. All she had to do was marry Quentin, and then Dierenpark would be hers forever. She felt hot and dizzy and overwhelmed.

A movement caught her attention. Quentin rose to his feet, the tip of his cane clicking on the stone as he drew closer.

She would have to be his wife. She couldn't even meet his gaze, and she was contemplating the longest, most intimate connection with a man who half-frightened, half-thrilled her.

It would be a terrible choice. The noise of insects and glare of the sun seemed to fade as she came to her senses.

She turned so she wouldn't have to look at him. "I'm sorry," she said. "I don't think we would suit."

"Why not?" he demanded. "Is it that fool Marten?"

"No!"

"Then why is he here? And don't tell me it was to deliver tulip bulbs, because that's hogwash and you know it."

She turned to face him. "This has nothing to do with Marten. You and I would be unequally yoked."

He blinked, his confusion apparent.

"My faith is what makes me who I am," she said in a shaky voice. "Religion is important to me, and I couldn't be married to a man who did not share that fundamental belief. You would grow to resent my devotion—"

"I said you could teach Pieter the Bible," he said tightly.

"It's not enough. You would eventually resent the way I lean on my faith. Even now, I can see you getting annoyed, as though if you glower enough it will shake me from this position. And I don't want to be the only spiritual leader in a family. I would want my husband to help, to back me, and I will resent it if you can't do that."

"Sophie," he said in a slow and tight voice, as though speaking to a child. "I need you to set aside your whimsical fantasies and think logically for a moment. You want this house. I want a mother for my son. There is a perfect solution if you can be rational enough to take the obvious step."

The temptation that had held her briefly spellbound on the overhang vanished. Quentin was darkness and cynicism. If she tied herself to him, he would dim her spirit and drag her down with him. She wasn't strong enough to save him. Only he could do that, and he had no interest in it.

"I'm sorry—"

He cut her off. "What is it that you want? Whatever it is, I'll give it to you, just name your price."

247

She stepped back. "Money can't buy what I want." All her life, she'd longed for the simple gift of a husband who could be a partner, to help lead her family toward a wholesome and meaningful life. Quentin was not that man.

"I have three buckets of oysters that need shucking," she said quietly. "I won't change my mind, and I implore you not to continue this conversation. It will only be an embarrassment to us both."

She was moving before even finishing the sentence, desperate to put as much distance between herself and this mortifying conversation as possible.

18

IF SOPHIE KEPT THE HEAT HIGH ENOUGH beneath the skillet, the sizzling of leeks and potatoes helped drown out the noise in her head. Two hours after Quentin's bizarre proposal, she still couldn't banish the outrageous thought from her mind, and she lifted the skillet higher, tipping it to keep the vegetables constantly moving in the pan. The bacon renderings she used to cook the vegetables filled the air with a mouthwatering aroma as the dinner neared completion. The kitchen was in full swing, with several bodyguards helping shuck oysters, Florence slicing bread and toasting it with garlic herbed butter, and Sophie frantically preparing the base for the chowder. This was the most important step, getting onions and potatoes to the perfect consistency before stirring in the flour, then the cream, broth, oysters, and a dash of white wine.

Quentin had been dressed nicer than she'd ever seen him. At first she'd thought he'd put on a coat because the day was unusually cool, but now she suspected he had dressed for a proper marriage proposal.

And she'd all but laughed in his face. One might think that

a girl who'd been engaged three times would have a little experience in such a situation, but this had taken her entirely by surprise.

She dreaded seeing him again. She should have been kinder. He had been extraordinarily decent to her over the past couple weeks. He'd been fun to work with as he helped with the proposal for the Weather Bureau. Their efforts had failed, but no one else in the village had bothered to help her, and Quentin not only respected her enough to work alongside her, he picked up the pieces when she fell apart after Dr. Clark's rebuff. Quentin had been kind and decent to her, and in return she'd fled from his proposal as though he had leprosy.

An hour later, the celebratory feast was ready. The sun was beginning to set, and lanterns had been placed all around the terrace. Candles flickered from the tables, which were laden with baskets of warm bread, bowls of asparagus and snow pea salad, and of course, large tureens of oyster chowder. Platters of oysters on the half shell were set out for those who preferred their oysters raw. For dessert she had made a goat cheese tart and strawberry-rhubarb pie.

Professor Byron had brought his violin to the estate, and he played a merry tune as everyone gathered around the tables, serving themselves. It seemed a bit odd to be dining on fine, eighteenth-century china and cut-crystal glasses, but this mansion had hundreds of such place settings. Sophie stood to one side, a heavy, leaded-glass goblet in her hand as she watched people flushed with good cheer filling their bowls and scooping up hearty slices of warm bread.

She feared Quentin would be moody and menacing, but when he appeared on the terrace, his face was devoid of the frustration from earlier this afternoon. Mercifully, he'd changed out of the formal attire and wore a simple white shirt and dark wool pants, leaning heavily on his cane and keeping Pieter close to his side.

250

Pieter kept jumping in excitement, waiting in line for his first taste of an oyster. Nickolaas seemed to have shaken off his strange malaise and was enjoying the sight of Pieter screwing up his courage as the line delivered him to the bounty on the table.

"The taste will be disguised in the chowder, but a real man will eat his oysters raw," Nickolaas said.

Pieter's eyes grew round as he eyed the platter of raw oysters, artfully arranged on the half shells. The plate had been adorned with lettuce leaves and herbs, but only a simple marinade of rice wine vinegar, lemon juice, and a little pepper to season the oysters. The boy's gaze tracked between the tureen and the platter then up to Quentin, who seemed equally amused by Pieter's foray into the world of oysters. Without breaking eye contact with Pieter, Quentin reached for a raw oyster, held the shell to his lips, and tipped it back.

Quentin didn't actually smile, but he came close as his dark eyes lit with amusement and the corners of his mouth tipped up a tiny degree. Still locking gazes with Pieter, Quentin casually tossed the oyster shell over the side of the terrace, where it clattered against the side of the cliff as it bounced back toward the shore.

A smattering of applause greeted Quentin's actions, and Pieter stood a little straighter.

"I want to try it raw," he said.

"Have at it, laddie!" one of the professors urged. The men pulled back from the table so Pieter had a perfect view of the oversized platter. Byron stopped playing the violin, and all watched as Pieter selected an oyster, his eyes growing rounder as he drew it near his face. Finally, he squeezed his eyes shut and swallowed the oyster with a mighty grimace.

The crowd roared with approval. Pieter smacked his lips in distaste but tried to appear brave as he tossed the shell over his shoulder as Quentin had done and then reached for another. The music started again, and everyone served themselves. Quentin patted Pieter on the back.

"Well done, lad, but I hope you won't miss out on Miss Sophie's chowder. I hear it is legendary."

She shrank a little as she leaned against the balustrade lining the terrace. Quentin's voice carried no trace of malice, and he didn't glance her way, although surely he knew she was here. Thank heaven he seemed as determined as she to ignore the mortifying conversation of this afternoon.

Marten joined her at the balustrade. "Your father is worried about you," he said quietly. "He heard about the fiasco with the Weather Bureau."

She dropped her head in resignation. It was going to be embarrassing to confess to her father that he'd been right all along. "It didn't come to anything," she acknowledged. "The director said that New Holland is a competitive location, but I won't be a part of it."

She still hoped they would build an observatory here. It would be a wonderful thing for their village—and wasn't that what she had hoped for all along? But the evening was too perfect to waste dwelling on disappointments. She'd rather celebrate the splendid glimpses of joy when they appeared.

"I made a mignonette sauce for you," she said, nodding to the covered dish beside the raw oysters. Most people did not care for the red wine sauce made with sweet onions and raspberry vinegar, but Marten loved it, and she was happy to make it for him.

"You're the best, Sophie. I really should have married you that one time."

She suppressed a smile. "Yes, you should have."

"Miss Sophie, I swallowed three whole oysters, did you see me?" Pieter said as he came racing to her side.

"Indeed I did." She tugged him against her for a quick hug.

Marten wandered away to sample the mignonette sauce, taking a generous helping and slathering some of it on the warmed herb bread, as well. She met Florence's gaze across the other side of the terrace, the older woman's eyes crinkling in understanding. Sophie had wept plenty of tears on Florence's shoulders during those terrible months after Marten jilted her. How long ago that seemed now. On a perfect summer evening, with candlelight flickering and surrounded by dozens of people enjoying the bounty pulled from the river and the land, her life seemed blessed. Not perfect, but still blessed. It was a joy to see so many people savoring her food, gathered around the table to swap stories and share one another's company.

Mr. Gilroy approached her, his face a polite mask. "Aren't you eating?" he asked.

"Not yet." She folded her arms, watching the others settle in and feast on the meal. "I can never eat at the beginning of a meal. I like to be sure everything is acceptable before I can relax enough to eat."

He gave a knowing smile. "If it came out of your kitchen, I suspect it will be more than merely *acceptable*."

She hoped so, too. Quentin still hadn't tasted her chowder, and she'd worked so hard to be sure it was perfect. Truly, Quentin's opinion of her cooking shouldn't matter. He was sitting with a group of the biologists, listening to Professor Morris discuss his research on the aquatic fly. Pieter sat listlessly beside his father, for once not engrossed by what the biologists were saying.

She leaned her hip on the balustrade, occasionally sipping from her goblet of water and listening to Professor Byron's music. As the sun set, the first fireflies came out.

"I don't feel good," she heard Pieter say to Quentin.

"Perhaps you've eaten too much," Quentin said then turned his attention back to Professor Morris.

"I didn't eat too much, I just don't feel good," Pieter replied. His speech was a little slurred, and Sophie's gaze narrowed. Had he gotten into the wine? Several of the professors had been imbibing from bottles of chilled white wine, but she hadn't noticed Pieter filching any. She pushed away from the balustrade and headed toward Pieter's side.

"What do you mean?" Quentin asked, his gaze narrowing. "What doesn't feel good?"

"My throat hurts. And my tongue feels funny."

Quentin grabbed Pieter's chin and tilted the boy's face to the light of the lantern. Even from a few yards away, Sophie saw Quentin's face go white.

"His lips are turning blue," he said. "Someone go for a doctor."

The music skidded to a stop, but before anyone could speak, Pieter doubled over and threw up onto the flagstones. He coughed and sputtered, dragging air into his lungs with a mighty wheeze.

Only moments later, Marten doubled over and was violently sick, as well.

"I'll go for a doctor," Mr. Gilroy said with uncharacteristic alarm. "Ratface, come with me."

She was grateful for Mr. Gilroy's speed as he saddled a horse and raced from the estate, for within ten minutes, five more men had become violently sick.

Sophie couldn't believe what was happening. The wave of sickness had come so suddenly. One moment everyone was laughing, and the next her world had been upended as sickness swept through the crowd with appalling speed.

Pieter was the sickest. His entire face was blue, and he gasped for breath. He'd been brought into the parlor, where he struggled to suck air into his lungs. He coughed and wheezed, his throat swelling so large it seemed to be strangling him. Quentin held him in his arms, begging him to keep fighting.

Every second was torture. Between Pieter's desperate, wheezing gasps and the panic in Quentin's voice, she'd never lived through such a traumatic experience. She'd already dumped all the oyster chowder on the ground and flung the platter of uneaten oysters over the cliff, listening to the plate shatter on the rocks below.

She didn't care. She'd fed these people tainted food, and impossible as it was to believe, Pieter might die because of it. He could barely breathe. She had been boasting for days about her oysters, and now this precious boy might die. She loitered in the open doorway, twisting her hands and forcing herself to listen to his tortured gasps. She deserved no less.

"Please, Lord," she whispered. "Please open his lungs and make his breath flow. I'm sorry. Please don't make this child suffer any longer, please."

A clattering of horse's hooves declared the arrival of the doctor, and Sophie ran to the front door. A lead weight landed in her stomach when she saw Dr. Weir step out of the carriage, followed by the village pastor. The sight of Pastor Mattisen's white clerical collar, normally so comforting, was ominous and terrifying tonight.

"This way," she said as she led the men to the parlor. There were half a dozen sick men in this house, but only Pieter seemed in such terrible danger.

Quentin looked up, and when his eyes landed on the pastor, his face turned hard. And when he looked at her, there was murder in his eyes.

❧ 19 ❧

QUENTIN DARED NOT MOVE PIETER. The first hint of sunrise was on the horizon, pushing back the darkness with faint traces of purple. The doctor was still here, treating others who'd been clobbered by some sort of illness last night, but thankfully Pieter was out of danger. His breaths were shallow, but regular and no longer labored. The swelling in his throat had subsided.

It had been an allergic reaction to the oysters. Dr. Weir examined the other men taken ill, none of whom shared the same symptoms as Pieter. Those men curled over and vomited, seemed to be weak and clammy . . . but none of them had swollen throats or tongues. None of them struggled to breathe.

Of the two dozen people in the house, all but three had sampled the oysters. If the oysters were tainted, or if Sophie had done something bad to the food, more people should have fallen sick.

Sophie. She'd been so certain in her assertion that it was safe to eat oysters in high summer so long as they were fresh, and at first he'd cursed himself for blindly taking Sophie's word,

257

for her irrational enchantment with Dierenpark made her judgment unreliable. He endured the worst few hours of his life as he listened to Pieter struggle to draw each breath, wishing he could lend Pieter a bit of strength to make his lungs keep pumping, his will to live stronger. If Pieter had died, he would have been tempted to strangle Sophie.

But as the night wore on, it became obvious the problem wasn't the oysters or anything Sophie had done—it was that Pieter had suffered an allergic reaction, seizing up his lungs and sending his body into a radical immune reaction. The quick wave of others who fell ill was a dramatic example of how otherwise intelligent people could be fooled by the power of suggestion, proof that the human mind was capable of believing anything. The assumption that the oysters had been tainted sent panic through the group.

Not that he cared what provoked healthy men to succumb to panic and let themselves believe they were sick. All he cared about was ensuring Pieter's safety.

Now that the terrors of the night had passed, it felt like a physical weight had been lifted from his chest, but he would never forget the desperation of this night. The mind-numbing sense of panic, the howling frustration of helplessness.

And in those moments, he had prayed. He clasped his hands together and sent out hundreds of desperate prayers into the universe, begging for his innocent child to be spared.

Fear had prodded his urge to pray, but the danger had passed, and now . . . now what? As the terror diminished, so did the frantic sense of neediness. Pieter's immune system might have overcome the shock all on its own without any sort of divine intervention.

But he couldn't quite be sure.

He glanced out the window, streaks of pink and purple lightening the rim of the horizon, about to flood the countryside with the pure light of day. The sunrise in this valley was always splendid, but this one captured his attention in a new way. It hinted at a new beginning that was as old as time.

"Thanks," he whispered, just in case there really was a God hovering somewhere in that awe-inspiring sky.

Sophie felt like a sleepwalker as she cooked the pot of oatmeal. It was the same pot she'd used to prepare the chowder, and she didn't even want to touch it, but it was the only pot large enough to serve everyone. She'd taken it out back this morning and scrubbed it with sand and lye, rinsing it over and over, then repeated the process for good measure. Dr. Weir assured her the oysters served last night were fine and she was not to blame for the sickness in the house, but guilt still lingered.

When she went to the larder for milk, two of the professors were behind the hedge, sipping their coffee as they recounted the events of the previous evening. Neither heard her approach.

"She had the dish covered and told Marten she made the sauce especially for him," one of the men said. "She hovered over him and watched him eat then covered it back up because, she said, the raspberry vinegar would attract flies. No one got sick before that dish was uncovered."

"You don't really think she did it, do you?" the other man asked. It was Professor Armitage, one of the kindly old archaeologists with round spectacles.

Sophie leaned closer to the hedge, and the silence was uncomfortably long.

"Rumor has it that Miss Sophie had her wedding dress all sewn, embellished with seed pearls she had sent in from the city," the first man said. "Sewed those pearls on herself. They say she was inconsolable after he jilted her."

There was another long pause as Professor Armitage drew

a sip of coffee. "Well, if she did it, I can't believe she meant for everyone to get sick. Just that Marten fellow."

"Probably," the first man said. "Still, it was a reckless thing to have done. I heard the boy almost died."

Her chest tightened, and she felt lightheaded. Was this what everyone was thinking? Hadn't Quentin looked at her with murder in his eyes? He blamed her for Pieter's illness, even though Dr. Weir assured everyone it was only an allergic reaction, something that would have happened no matter where Pieter sampled his first oyster. She still didn't understand how the others could have fallen sick, since most of them had eaten oysters often and never suffered from such fits.

She drew a steadying breath. These men didn't know her, and God would give her whatever strength she needed to get through this day of whispers and sidelong looks. Walking forward, she rounded the hedge and headed toward the larder.

"Good morning," she said to both men with a wobbly smile. It was the best she could manage. Their coffee cups frozen mid-sip, they watched with flushed embarrassment as she opened the larder door to reach for the canister of milk.

Professor Armitage rose, pushing his spectacles a little higher on his nose. "Can I help you, Miss Sophie?" He swallowed nervously, his Adam's apple bobbing in his thin neck. She didn't know if it was from the embarrassment at being overheard or from suspicion of a scorned woman poisoning the communal cooking pot. She supposed she would find out when breakfast was set on the table.

"No, thank you," she murmured as she retrieved the milk and butter from the larder. The morning was cool, but when she returned to the kitchen, the hot stove added to her nerves as she stirred a little more milk into the pot to loosen the oats. She wished this day were already over.

There weren't many people in the kitchen. It had been a late night for all of them as everyone pitched in to help care for the sick. She dreaded seeing Quentin again but wouldn't abandon the kitchen in case there were special needs for Pieter's care.

"You look overheated," Florence said as she reached for the spoon. "I'll finish here if you go prepare the table."

The old woman meant to be kind, but the last thing Sophie wanted was to wade out among those men, many of whom apparently believed she was willing to poison them all in a spiteful attempt to punish a wayward fiancé.

Conversation sputtered to a halt, and the weight of a dozen men's eyes seared her as she carried a stack of bowls to the table. She set the bowls down gently, but the silverware jangled as she set a basket of spoons in the center of the table. No one met her eyes, and she wanted to flee the house to escape the awful scrutiny.

The distinctive tapping of Quentin's cane and lopsided gait heralded his arrival. Sophie's stomach clenched, and she braced herself for another blast of that furious glare, but his face was calm.

Chairs scraped as everyone rose the moment Quentin appeared. Exhaustion was carved into his face, with grooves around his mouth, and he was still wearing the rumpled clothes from last evening.

"How is the boy?" one of the professors asked.

Sophie held her breath as Quentin reached for a bowl. "Better. He's still sleeping, but his breathing is steady."

"That was a close call," a history professor said. "I prayed for him all night."

"Thank you." Quentin's voice was devoid of the mockery he usually used when discussing religion. "My grandfather is with him while I grab a quick meal. Then I hope everyone will return to their work. There is still plenty more to be done, and loitering in the kitchen won't help the sickened men recover any faster."

With a casual hand, he flipped open the cover of his pocket watch then pierced her with those enigmatic gray eyes. "It's ten o'clock," he said.

And she was unusually late getting breakfast on the table. "One moment, and I'll return with the—"

"Miss van Riijn." Quentin's words stopped her in her tracks. "Yes?"

"It's ten o'clock," he repeated in a pointed voice.

And the table wasn't even set, nor was the oatmeal ready to serve. She was a little embarrassed about that, but Quentin seemed to be driving at something she couldn't grasp. For the first time, a hint of amusement lightened his face.

"It's ten o'clock and you haven't checked the weather station yet," he said.

She sucked in a quick breath. "You're right!" The Weather Bureau urged them to take their readings as close to nine o'clock as possible for the sake of consistency throughout all the stations. Normally she completed that morning task as routinely as rising from bed or combing her hair, but she still had breakfast to serve, and these men must be hungry.

"Run along upstairs," Quentin said. "We can serve ourselves breakfast."

"Thank you!" she said, dashing to the drawer in the sideboard for her notebook of climate data.

The air was fresh and clean on the widow's walk. Surrounded by the serene beauty of this beloved spot, it made the calamity of the previous night seem far away. This was just another day. Another lovely, bountiful day filled with promise and hope and a young boy who was going to fully recover. Her tight nerves unraveled and snapped. She tossed the notebook down, ran to the railing, fell to her knees, and wept.

It felt good to sob it all out. Pathetic, but good.

After her momentary crying jag, she took the daily readings. Her eyes were swollen, so she squinted at the tiny dials, but recorded the measurements as she had been doing for the past nine years. Her handwriting looked small and tidy beneath Pieter's larger, clumsier printing, but she ran her fingers along the numbers he'd written over the past few weeks.

How she loved working with that boy, and how fragile their lives were. Any day could be their last. Pieter was a loving boy, so desperate to please, and she was thrilled she had been granted the opportunity to share this humble task with him.

But she hadn't shared her faith with him. Not really. She'd planted a few seeds and assumed they would have plenty of time to take root and grow. The boy was hungry for meaning in his life, and she had been stingy in sharing her gifts because she was afraid of annoying his father. It wasn't Pieter's fault that he had been born into such an odd family, but for whatever reason, God had planned for her path to intersect with the Vandermarks, and she had more to offer Pieter than teaching him to read a thermometer.

Yesterday, Quentin had asked her to marry him. Amazing, and she still couldn't quite grasp this startling turn of events.

She had been tempted by the house. What woman wouldn't be? But a marriage between herself and Quentin would surely be a disaster. Over the past few weeks, they had formed a cautious truce, but that could snap quickly, just as it had last night when he'd suspected her of feeding tainted food to his family.

No, she didn't need to marry Quentin to share her faith with Pieter. It was painfully obvious that Quentin had no true feelings for her beyond what she could do for his son, and she wanted more from a marriage than that. It was time to head back downstairs and brave the whispers and curious stares of the people who weren't quite sure if she was trustworthy.

She heard the argument before she was even halfway down the hall.

"We're not touching a morsel out of that woman's kitchen," a voice asserted. "If you don't employ a different cook, I'm going back to the city."

"I hired you to find an answer to a specific scientific question," Quentin's ice-cold voice said, "and you are threatening to abandon that quest over pure superstition?"

"The sight of those men doubled over and heaving up their dinner wasn't superstition, that was a fact," another voice said. The speaker was the red-headed man from outside the larder this morning. "If she didn't poison the food on purpose, maybe it was that Vandermark curse we've been hearing so much about. Either way, I want that woman out of here."

Muffled voices interrupted, and it was clear there was quite a battle among the professors. Could this wonderful research all come crashing to a halt because of what had happened last night? She leaned against the wall to steady herself against a wave of dizziness, the plaster cool on her overheated skin.

"Sophie isn't leaving," Quentin asserted, his voice pure steel. "That woman sheds grace and light in every room she enters. Any man with a functional brain would try to catch a fragment of that grace and cherish it, rather than push her aside. I'm not sending her away. Were it in my power, I would cut the moon out of the sky and give it to her on a silver platter."

Her notebook dropped from her nerveless fingers, splatting open on the tile floor. Quentin whirled around to see her standing in the doorway. If he was embarrassed to have been overheard, he gave no sign of it. On the contrary, his eyes that had been sparking with anger gentled the instant he saw her.

She glanced away, rocked by the protective expression on Quentin's face. It shot straight to a vulnerable part deep inside and enveloped her with a sense of well-being. No man had ever spoken so passionately on her behalf, and a rush of wild, electrifying emotions stirred inside.

Her food was untouched on the table, a group of professors watching her through solemn eyes. A few were hostile; most were sympathetic.

Quentin held out his hand, his palm turned up, beckoning her.

In a room full of people, he stood proudly and offered her his support. She placed her hand in his, and a current of strength flowed from his hand into hers. He pulled her closer, and she followed. When she stood alongside him, he slid his arm around her waist and turned to face the group.

"Miss van Riijn stays," he said in a firm voice, daring anyone to deny him. "Anyone who won't take food from her kitchen may leave immediately. She is an essential part of this household, and I won't allow her name to be tarnished by small-minded superstition."

Never had she felt so protected. Standing alongside him made her feel like they belonged together, like they were a team. Even if every one of these scientists pushed away from the table and left the house, it wouldn't matter because Quentin believed in her.

But she didn't want the biologists to leave. Not if they could find a scientific explanation for Marguerite's Cove and save Dierenpark. "Quentin, I'll go if it's the only way—"

"You belong here," he asserted. "More than any of us, you belong at Dierenpark."

He still held her sheltered against his side, and when she looked up at him, the tender affection in his face was overwhelming. He leaned down, smiling softly, his face mere inches from hers. Every instinct urged her to close the space and kiss him, for she wanted more of this compelling attraction.

A clattering came from the front of the house, and footsteps came running toward the kitchen. It was Professor Winston, the man sent to Harvard to find a translation for the strange piece of paper found nailed into the old box. His hair was windblown and cheeks flushed as he held a piece of paper high above his head.

"It's Algonquin!" he shouted.

A bunch of researchers rose, drawing closer as Professor Winston continued rambling in an excited rush of words. "The text is an old form of the Indian language. The librarian at Harvard recognized it immediately."

There was no more talk of anyone leaving as all gathered around Professor Winston to hear what he had learned.

The first Bible printed in America was not in English or Latin or any other Old World tongue. It was the labor of love from missionary John Eliot, who brought the word of God to the Indians of New England, learned their language, and rendered it phonetically into the Roman alphabet. Eliot printed a thousand copies of the complete Bible in the Natick-Algonquin dialect, and in 1663 he distributed them among the praying Indians. The page found nailed into the box on Vandermark land was compared to one of the original Algonquin Bibles in the Harvard library and found to be identical in size, composition of the paper, and font of the text. There could be no doubt. This page was torn from one of the original 1663 Bibles.

Professor Winston said he had left the original page discovered on Vandermark land at Harvard "for safekeeping." No one needed a reminder that Nickolaas might well carry out his threat to burn the page if given the chance. Professor Winston carried an exact copy of the strange text written out in his own hand, using the same stanzas, indentations, and underlining.

"But why was the page nailed into a box?" Byron asked. "Who did it? And why?"

"Impossible to say," Professor Winston answered. "We compared it with an English Bible at the library and translated the underlined passages. It's from Genesis, the part about God putting the mark on Cain."

He gave Sophie the page that had the English translation, complete with the same passages that had been underlined in the document they found. It was from the book of Genesis, shortly after Cain killed Abel, as he stood before God to account for his sin. She read the passage aloud to the group.

"'Cain said to the Lord, "My punishment is more than I can bear. You are driving me from the land, and I will be hidden from your presence; I will be a restless wanderer on the earth, and whoever finds me will kill me."'"

The underlined passages picked up a few lines later. "'The Lord put a mark on Cain so that no one who found him would kill him. So Cain went out from the Lord's presence and lived in the land of Nod, east of Eden.'"

She looked up in bewilderment. "But what does this mean? Who underlined these passages?"

Professor Winston shrugged his shoulders. "The book dates to 1663, but for all we know, it could have been nailed into that box and buried centuries later."

"The nails looked like they came from a seventeenth-century forge," one of the archaeologists said. "And the other artifacts found in the same substrata were all from the seventeenth century. That box was buried hundreds of years ago."

Sophie knew the history of the original Vandermark brothers as well as any local historian. Caleb and Adrien Vandermark had arrived in the country in 1635 and immediately built the humble cabin that eventually became the groundskeeper's home. Adrien was always on the move, forging ties with European settlers as far north as Massachusetts and with some Indian tribes. It was a tragedy when he'd been killed in an Indian raid a few years later. Caleb continued to prosper, building the pier and establishing their shipping empire, sending furs and timber back to Holland. Caleb lived into his eighties and was one of the richest men in America when he finally died in 1685.

The box could have been buried by Caleb, or it could have been one of his sons that survived him, but the question remained . . . why?

Without warning, Quentin plucked the document from her hands. "I'll take that," he said casually, then he pivoted on his one good leg and began limping to the rear of the house.

"You're leaving me here?" Her voice sounded wounded even to her own ears. The confidence she'd felt when standing beside him drained away, and she stared at his retreating back as he hobbled to the far end of the house.

"Anyone who says a single bad thing about Sophie shall be beheaded," he called out over his shoulder as he disappeared down the hallway.

She stifled a laugh. That casual defense was all it took to banish the lingering sense of inadequacy. Quentin knew she was innocent, and the opinion of these men simply did not matter. The untouched breakfast was a clear sign that some of the professors either feared the Vandermark curse or the vengefulness of a scorned woman, but that was their shortcoming, not hers.

Quentin's impulsive surge of protectiveness toward Sophie had surprised even him. It was only a few weeks ago that he was raging at her himself, but that was before he'd discovered the depth of her generosity and good-natured humor. Now he would cheerfully fire anyone who dared breathe an unkind word about her.

Her blunt rejection of his marriage proposal still smarted, for his affections ran deeper than he dared reveal. After the collapse of his marriage to Portia, he'd vowed never again to lay himself open to that sort of unreciprocated emotion, but it was getting harder to repress the turbulent, glorious feelings he harbored for Sophie. He wanted to love and cherish and protect her—all the things a husband should do for his wife.

Even if she wanted nothing to do with him, he still felt compelled to protect her. That was why he took the document away from her this morning. There was something tainted and bad about it, and he didn't like seeing it in her slim, gentle hands. Besides, he suspected Nickolaas knew exactly what the document meant, and that it wasn't good. Nickolaas had once said that in the months before his father's mysterious death in the river, Karl had been preoccupied by strange foreign documents found in the house. Karl had a specialist translate the documents, and whatever he learned was enough to send the man into a profound depression. Ever since discovering that buried box on the property, Nickolaas and Mr. Gilroy had been turning the house upside down on the hunt for more documents.

He found Nickolaas and Pieter in the library. Pieter, still wearing his nightclothes, sat at the desk chair, flipping through the pages of a book. Gratitude surged through Quentin, for although Pieter still looked pale and tired, there was a spark of curiosity in the boy's eyes.

"Feeling better?" Quentin asked, holding his breath.

"Grandpa said I could come help search for more of those strange pieces of paper. He thinks there are still some we haven't found. It's like a treasure hunt."

Sure enough, Nickolaas and Mr. Gilroy had removed entire shelves of books, stacking them around the library in towering mounds that filled the floor space. Dust swirled in the air, and it couldn't be good for Pieter's lungs. Besides, he didn't want Pieter exposed to whatever superstitious rubbish Nickolaas believed was rooted in those letters.

"Pieter, go to the kitchen and get some breakfast."

"Grandpa already brought me a bowl of oatmeal to my room."

"Then go get some fresh air on the terrace. I need to speak to Grandpa."

"Mr. Gilroy will accompany you," Nickolaas said, surprising everyone in the room. Mr. Gilroy was his grandfather's most trusted servant, and Quentin sensed Nickolaas was about to share something very sensitive.

"Certainly, sir." Mr. Gilroy's voice was composed, but he couldn't mask the surprise at being asked to leave. Quentin waited until the door closed behind Mr. Gilroy and Pieter before turning his attention to his grandfather.

"The document is written in Algonquin, although I suspect you already knew that."

Nickolaas fanned the pages of another book and snorted. "I could have told you that the moment it was found. No one asked me."

"You wanted to burn it rather than provide insight into it. Why?"

Nickolaas crossed the room and opened the door, looking both ways as if to assure himself there were no eavesdroppers lingering about. He peered out the windows, as well, before he crossed back to the desk.

"You knew that my father had discovered similar texts shortly before he died," Nickolaas said.

"I suspected as much."

"They were the same. Pages of the Algonquin Bible with underlined sentences. My father wanted to know what they said. There aren't many people who can still read or speak Algonquin, so my father went up to the Natick village in Massachusetts to find someone who could tell him what the documents meant. The underlined passages were always taunting and acrimonious. Bits about men who gain the world but lose their soul. Or how a camel is more likely to pass through the eye of a needle than a rich man is to get into heaven. Nonsense like that. Not very insightful, but it was enough to send my father into a fit of melancholia. He became obsessed with the Indians, convinced that our ancestors must have done something to cheat or swindle them."

"And what do you think?"

There was a long pause, and his grandfather's face was grim. "I think he was right," Nickolaas finally said. "Whatever happened was bad enough for the Indians to hold a grudge for generations. At first it was underlined passages from the Bible, but later they sent letters in perfect English. Apparently, one of the Indian converts to Christianity was sponsored to attend Harvard and had a fine understanding of English common law. After they quit sending biblical passages, they sent legal articles about trade customs and embezzlement. The Indian wrote that "the crime" was long past and could not be corrected by the laws of man, but that the laws of God are eternal, and the Vandermark family would not benefit from Caleb's crime. I think the Indians put some sort of curse on the family."

Quentin scowled. "Not that again—"

"How else can you explain the centuries of misfortune that have befallen our family?"

Ten generations had passed since the first Vandermarks landed in America, and after that much time, it was normal for there to be plenty of tragedies in any family. He spoke slowly and carefully. "Nothing that has happened to our family falls outside the typical trials of life. Money can't insulate us from tragedy, but we've cultivated a streak of superstition that makes us highly attuned to the power of suggestion."

"Only half the story can be uncovered from here in America," Nickolaas said. "When I was a young man, I traveled to meet our Vandermark cousins in Holland. I wanted to know what they remembered about Adrien and Caleb Vandermark, and what they believe is *not* what I know to be true."

"What did you learn?" For the first time in his life, Quentin was intrigued by his family's curious past.

"The village of Roosenwyck wanted to establish a settlement in America and selected Adrien and Caleb to scout out the territory, secure title to the land, and create a village. They were given plenty of money to build a church, a school, and set up trading operations. Other immigrants were supposed to follow later in the year, but a war broke out and the Dutch patroons put a halt to people leaving the county. Years passed, and by the time the ban was lifted, the economy had improved and word was sent to America there would be no additional settlers from Roosenwyck. The Vandermark brothers were directed to welcome any other European settlers who wished to join them."

Quentin could sense where this story was leading. With no additional settlers from Roosenwyck, Adrien and Caleb had no one overseeing how their seed money was used. Caleb continued correspondence with his Vandermark cousins in Holland for decades, and these documents had been collected and stored in the town's archives. Nickolaas had bought the entire archive of seventeenth-century Vandermark letters for a small fortune.

Nickolaas continued with the story. "Caleb wrote to the elders in Roosenwyck that he paid for a fine Dutch church and a three-room schoolhouse. I know from looking at American records that the seventeenth-century church in this village was built by the English, not Caleb. Same with the schoolhouse. Caleb lied and assumed he would never be caught since no one from Roosenwyck was likely to come to America. By then Adrien was dead, so there was no one to be witness to his crime."

Quentin let his gaze roam across the library, with its vaulted ceiling and bank of diamond-pane windows. How much of the Vandermark fortune had been built upon money misappropriated by Caleb Vandermark?

A niggling suspicion began to take root. "Is this why you are so paranoid about finding those old documents? You're afraid one of them will contain proof that the Vandermark fortune was illegally obtained?"

Nickolaas nodded, but Quentin was amazed at his grand-father's naiveté.

"The statute of limitations for embezzlement expired centuries ago," Quentin said. "No one can touch the Vandermark fortune based on a few hundred Dutch guilders that were misappropriated back in the 1630s."

Nickolaas stared into space, cracking his knuckles. "Maybe, maybe not. I think the Indians knew about it, for many of the taunts are in relation to money, but others are to Cain and Abel, and I think there is a reason for that. Caleb Vandermark was adamant that Adrien was killed by the Indians, but I'm not so sure. Something very bad happened on this land, and our family will continue paying for it until it has been made right. That's why I want this house torn down and burned to ashes. I want nothing to do with this house or the land. It was built with ill-gotten funds and has been a curse to our family for centuries."

"Then send a few thousand dollars to Roosenwyck to pay back the money Caleb stole," Quentin said. "Let that be the end of it." Caleb Vandermark had been a brilliant trader, and even if he stole the original seed money intended to found a village, it was a pittance compared to the fortune he amassed through shrewd land negotiations and building a worldwide trading empire.

Nickolaas shook his head. "I think those embezzled funds were only the beginning of the crimes committed on this land. The Indians knew it. My father knew it. A great wrong was committed here, and it needs to be made right. We must wash our hands of whatever Caleb did here and walk away from Dierenpark forever."

For the first time, Quentin was able to see the poetic justice in his grandfather's desire to tear down Dierenpark to its foundation.

Which he would never let happen. There was something special here, something timeless and sacred that he still couldn't quite define. He was starting to sound like Sophie, but yes, there was a purity here at Dierenpark, and so long as he continued to draw breath, he would fight to protect it.

20

SOPHIE'S MUSCLES FELT STIFF as she mechanically went through the motions of preparing breakfast, constantly aware of the men on the other side of the kitchen wall who knew of her humiliation. Ultimately, two of the anthropologists and two of the biologists refused to eat anything prepared by Sophie's hands, packed their bags, and left. At first it was humiliating to see men turning away from the grand intellectual quest at Dierenpark because of her. At best, these men believed the silliness about the curse; at worst, they suspected she was so vindictive as to poison innocent people.

Then she remembered Quentin's stalwart support of her. The conviction in his voice went beyond a man defending his cook. He'd praised her so highly it had made her question his motives in asking for her hand in marriage. Was it possible that in addition to needing a mother for Pieter, he actually harbored tender feelings for her beneath his frosty exterior?

The thought should be appalling, but it wasn't. They had gotten off on the wrong foot and would probably be a terrible match, but the idea no longer seemed as odd as it had the day before. It was . . . well, it was flattering. Quentin was a handsome man, and she loved when she could slip beneath his austere deportment to make him laugh. He usually tried to suppress it, but the straight line of his mouth would tilt at one corner, and then warmth would come into his eyes.

If she doubted that the remaining scientists distrusted her, it was settled when Professor Byron offered to help her make another pot of coffee and Professor Armitage asked for a second serving of oatmeal. She hadn't forgotten that Professor Armitage had been one of the men she'd overheard at the larder discussing the likelihood of her having deliberately poisoned Marten and the others. It seemed he'd made up his mind and decided to stay with the other professors, who continued to speculate about the history of the Algonquin Bible and why anyone would bury a page on the property.

A few minutes later, Marten himself shuffled into the room, looking pale and embarrassed.

"Sorry for making a mess of your celebration," he whispered to Sophie. "I can be a real idiot sometimes."

It seemed to be the general consensus among the people remaining at the house that although Pieter's allergic reaction had been real, Marten's illness had been sparked by the power of suggestion. Nevertheless, he'd been violently ill for hours last night and was bound to be exhausted and dehydrated this morning.

She guided him to a spot at the table. "Can I get you anything? Water? Milk? Do you need help getting to the privy? Don't be proud. I'll help however you need."

He choked back a gasp of laughter. "Sophie, I'm holding on to a sliver of dignity the size of a hangnail. Please don't take it away."

She smiled and kissed his forehead. A piece of her would always adore Marten. He had been her childhood sweetheart,

276

a boy who taught her how to dream, and she had never been the sort to nurture a grudge. She went to the kitchen to fetch him a bowl of oatmeal and wondered why she was not the least bit tempted to rekindle her romantic relationship with him.

Marten simply seemed pale and bland compared to the wonderful complexities she was discovering hidden beneath Quentin's stern exterior. Quentin had said he wanted to catch a fragment of her grace, to cut the moon from the sky for her.

In Sophie's world of workaday tasks and stifled dreams, no matter how long she lived, she would remember those words of admiration.

It was amazing how fast Pieter recovered. Quentin sat on the front steps of the mansion, watching his son play with the assortment of frogs and toads he'd captured. With the resilience of youth, Pieter was down on all fours, scrambling to keep up with the frogs as they continually tried to escape into the overgrown grass a few yards away. Only last night, Pieter had gasped for breath with a face tinged blue from lack of oxygen. Now he chattered to his frogs and tried to coax them to race one another.

Quentin watched with a wistful smile. Had he ever been that young? It was hard to remember past the darkness of the past decade, but what a blessing to relive it through Pieter's eyes.

The door behind him opened, and the heavy tread of a man's footsteps sounded across the porch. It was Professor Sorenson, looking unaccountably nervous as he stepped to the ground and turned to face Quentin.

"I'd like permission to stop studying the oysters," the professor said. It was the last thing Quentin expected to hear.

"Why?" he demanded. "Has my grandfather been harassing you?" Nickolaas seemed more impatient than ever to destroy the house, and whittling down Quentin's team was well within his arsenal of tricks. Two of his biologists had left over the superstitious nonsense about Sophie's cooking, and he couldn't afford to lose any more.

"I have found no obvious explanation for the health of the oysters or the lilies," Professor Sorenson said. "We've compared water, soil, and plant samples against those elsewhere in the river and can see no difference. Someday we may have better equipment to examine the internal workings of a cell, but for now, I can find nothing unique about the physical properties in the cove. Water temperature, salinity, and speed of the currents are no different, either. I'd like the chance to look farther afield."

"What do you mean?"

Professor Sorenson gestured toward the gates at the front of the property. "I'd like to show you."

Quentin pushed himself to his feet, and Pieter sprang up, as well. "Can I come, too?" he asked.

The boy's hopeful voice flooded Quentin with a sense of happiness. It had been years since Pieter had eagerly followed him around, and he held Pieter's hand as the three of them set off toward the front gates.

A piece of him was curious about what Professor Sorenson wanted to show him, but mostly he was enjoying the newfound rapport with his son, listening to the boy talk about frogs and mud crabs. This was how things were supposed to be—a father and son enjoying each other's company on an ordinary summer day.

It was a long walk down the path, and as they drew closer to the front gates, the surrounding stone columns seemed to grow larger and more imposing. It was surely just an optical illusion. Oddly, the gates seemed to serve no purpose, for they were always open. Anyone could come and go at will.

The professor gestured to the stone columns. "The mortar

is in perfect condition," he said. "Emil told me he's never done anything to repair the entranceway over the years, and I should think it would show more signs of age. These old stone gates are just another example of the unusual prosperity at this estate."

Quentin shrugged. "I've traveled all over Europe and seen buildings much older. A well-built structure can endure for millennia."

"How about that old box with the Algonquin text in it? Don't you find it curious that a piece of paper, buried in a wooden box, could be in pristine condition after hundreds of years?"

"What are you suggesting?" Quentin asked.

"It's an enigma," Professor Sorenson replied. "It seems everywhere we look at Dierenpark there is unusual abundance and prosperity."

"Maybe it's magic," Pieter said, and for once Quentin did not stifle the boy. He turned to Professor Sorenson, waiting for him to provide some hypothesis or logical explanation.

Crinkles fanned out from the man's eyes as he smiled down at Pieter. "There is far more to this world than meets the eye," he said warmly. "For all my love of science, I believe there is still room for divine providence. If God could create the solar system and set all the planets spinning into perpetual motion, who's to say he wouldn't spare a little of that ingenuity for a special place here at Dierenpark?"

"You don't really believe that, do you?"

Professor Sorenson looked back at the large entrance gates, scanning them with near reverence in his gaze. "It seems to me that Dierenpark has all the qualities of a utopia. A promised land. Eden, if you will. I'd like permission to begin studying the grounds outside of the river. It seems everywhere I look there are new things of beauty and wonder."

Professor Sorenson would be useless if sent back to the river while his heart was elsewhere. This would mean they would be reduced to only three biologists in the river, and one of them, Professor Byron, was still a puppy barely old enough to be out of the schoolhouse.

Quentin felt he had no choice but to grant the professor's request. Professor Sorenson beamed when Quentin gave his consent, and he bounded back toward the house, his long strides eating up the ground in his eagerness to begin his new project. It would be nice to be able to follow with such energy, but Quentin's leg already was beginning to protest the long walk here, and he nodded to the bench near a pear tree just inside the gates.

"Let's have a sit, shall we?" He exhaled in relief as the weight lifted from his leg. He gingerly stretched it out, breathing deeply as the pressure receded.

"Maybe Dierenpark is the Garden of Eden," Pieter said as he joined him on the bench. "I've already read that part in the Bible, and it says there was a tree of life in the garden and things never got old. Maybe that's why the lilies don't die and the oysters live so long."

"Maybe," Quentin said noncommittally. He wouldn't make that kind of metaphorical leap, but he couldn't entirely dismiss it, either. He looked at Pieter, careful to keep any hint of judgment from his voice. "Do you believe what you are reading in the Bible, then?"

Pieter shrugged. "When I knocked over the beehives and the bees were swarming all over me, I prayed to Jesus for help and then you were there. I think Jesus sent you."

Quentin rubbed the flesh above his knee, wincing at the pain. He didn't want to belittle Pieter's childlike faith, but his name didn't even belong in the same sentence as a man like Jesus.

"I only did what any father would do," he said, rubbing his leg, which was beginning to ache more and more.

"But you did it without a cane!" Pieter said in amazement.

"I've never seen you walk without a cane before, but you picked me up and carried me out of there without any help at all."

Quentin stilled. In the frantic chaos of that afternoon, he'd never realized he had dropped his cane, but he must have, for he'd scooped up Pieter in both arms and carried him to safety. Normally, he couldn't take five steps without a cane, so how had he managed that? Could it have been merely a rush of panic or extra oxygen in his blood that had fueled his ability to walk? Perhaps not.

"Well," he said quietly, "maybe God really was with us that day."

A movement caught his attention, and he glimpsed Sophie headed toward the herb garden on the far side of the house. She had a basket slung over one arm and leaned over to clip a sprig of rosemary. There was a timelessness to the image, a simple beauty that cut straight to his heart. This woman had opened his eyes to so much.

Blessed are the pure in heart, for they shall see God.

He was experiencing the world differently since coming here. Part of it had been a conscious effort to begin seeing the world through the purity of Sophie's eyes, but it was more than that. All his life, he'd prided himself on clear-eyed rationalism. It was a cocksure arrogance that drove him to reject anything outside his realm of understanding. And that had been closed-minded of him.

Sophie had helped open his eyes. He still didn't know what to believe, but she'd taught him that there was more to the world than what could be seen and touched. Clearing his mind of the veil of cynicism, he was learning to see with his heart, and he sensed there was something, or someone, just beyond what he could see. And that someone was waiting for him to come. Beckoning.

The thought was frightening in its immensity. He wasn't

a good person like Sophie. He had never been pure of heart and was unworthy of walking through that gate into whatever glory lay beyond.

But Pieter was. Pieter was pure and innocent and still had a chance. The more time Pieter spent with Sophie, absorbing her wholesome optimism, the better chance his son had to grow up straight and honorable.

"Look, there's a turtle!" Pieter burst out. The boy sprang over a clump of hyssop shrubs to scoop it up, holding it above his head in triumph. "Can I go show it to Professor Byron? Please?"

"Run along." How blessed he was to have this boy in his life. Each day Pieter was blossoming with new interests and curiosities. It was Sophie's doing that Quentin hadn't suffocated the nascent stirrings of faith in his son. She'd given Pieter the freedom to experience the world in a new and different way. With his trusting nature, it had been easy for Pieter to follow Sophie's lead.

Quentin rubbed his chest, the hollow emptiness beginning to ache. How odd that the pain of unbelief had never bothered him until he began to believe.

In these past weeks, he'd had glimpses into a bright and shining world. It had been during those moments when he'd sensed something greater just beyond what he could experience. He wanted to be reunited with something in the universe from which he'd been severed long ago. There *was* more to the world than what he could see or touch. He had a soul that was awakening and alive and that was searching for meaning, for transcendence.

As he sat on that bench with sunlight pouring down on him, a sense of well-being unlike any he had ever known flooded through him. It was a stab of joy, a bittersweet longing that was pointing him toward something—or maybe someone—outside of himself. He closed his eyes to listen for the golden echo, knowing there was a gate he needed to walk through. That gate had always been there, but he'd never opened it to explore what was on the other side.

He didn't deserve whatever it was. He was a small and hard man who deserved none of it—but still the gate was open, beckoning.

He wished he could kneel, but his ruined leg made it impossible. The best he could do was clasp his hands and bow his head. He struggled to find the words, but they came straight from his heart.

God . . . I don't know where I am going or where you are leading me. I can't see the road ahead of me or how it will end. I don't know what you want of me. I'm not even sure you exist . . . but I will keep my mind open to the signals you send. I haven't been very good about that, but I can do better. I want to know you. I want to believe.

What else was one supposed to say in a prayer? His was clumsy and short, but he must have done something right, for the sensation of contentment remained. He wondered how long this feeling would last. He didn't have much experience with happiness.

Sophie would probably tell him not to seek out storm clouds on a sunny day, and she was right. Sophie had been right about a lot of things, and he was grateful he finally had the wisdom to accept it.

As he walked back to the house, he was surprised to see the pastor who'd arrived last night sitting amid the archaeologists, dutifully sifting dirt through a screen at the bottom of a shallow box. Sophie was with him, leaning over the box to pick out remnants of an old Delft platter coming up from the shifting soil.

She smiled when she saw him, loping over to him, her face as bright as the day.

"Dr. Weir has returned to the village, but we are hoping Pastor Mattisen can stay for a few days. He loves history and wants to help us learn more about Dierenpark. Can he stay?"

Quentin glanced over at the thin, elderly man who showed remarkable energy as he sifted the screen box. They were short on men after the departure of the four professors this morning. Besides, Sophie was so eager for his consent, and he liked doing nice things for her. When he nodded, the smile she gave him made his sense of well-being even stronger.

After dinner, Quentin wanted time alone with Sophie, but finding a bit of privacy was a challenge with so many people at the estate. A handful of the professors had gone down to the river for an evening smoke, but there were a few still nursing cups of tea at the dining table. The bodyguards were scattered throughout the ground floor, and Pieter played checkers with Professor Byron in the main parlor. Sophie joked with Marten as they rinsed the evening dishes.

"Let's go down to the Spanish cannon," he said as he entered the kitchen.

"I should stay and finish cleaning up," she replied.

"Let Marten do it. He's been living here free of charge." It sounded a little blunt, but everyone else in this household was working, and Marten's sole purpose seemed to be luring Sophie back into his world.

And that was unbearable. The attraction Quentin felt for Sophie was growing by the hour, especially since this afternoon when he'd accepted she was probably right about some kind of higher power. He couldn't allow his attraction for her to keep growing if he had no chance of winning her, and it was time to find out what she was thinking.

To his relief, she agreed without complaint, even though Marten shot him a surly glare on their way out the back door. Cool air surrounded him as they stepped outside. As always, he held firmly to his cane as he navigated down toward the outcropping, but Sophie let him hold her hand with the other. It felt right to him. It was the perfect phase of twilight, when the air seemed to shimmer with the fading heat of the day. The setting sun colored the sky with a mix of gold and purple, but clouds on the horizon moved in to darken the brightest patch of sky. The combination of beauty and darkness was wildly appealing.

Laughter from the men down near the river drifted up to them. For once, the sound of their happiness did not hurt.

He leaned against the cannon and stared at the river. "I've been thinking a lot," he said. "I think we are more than the sum total of our cells and atoms. We are more than glorified apes."

Sophie tilted her head in curiosity but said nothing as he continued.

"All my life I've been driven by a nagging discontent, a sense that there was something missing. I felt a void. I wandered throughout the world looking for something to fill it. I looked in foreign lands and in professional glory. I looked at people beside me, but I never looked up."

And he wanted to. He wanted to join his life with Sophie and create a family with the same kind of serene confidence she possessed. His first proposal had been clumsy and had taken her by surprise, but she'd had time to think about things. He drew a steadying breath and braced himself.

"Does Marten Graaf still mean anything to you?" he asked.

She blanched. "If you're asking if I poisoned him, the answer is no."

"Don't be ridiculous. I just need to know if you still harbor some hope of resurrecting your relationship with him. He seems open to it." He held his breath. Whatever she said in the next ten seconds would have a profound impact not only on his life, but Pieter's, as well.

"No. I'm lucky that Marten withdrew from the marriage

before we both made a terrible mistake. We were too young to be making that kind of decision."

He was dizzy with relief, and a tiny seed of hope began to grow. "No lingering feelings, then?"

"Friendship, I suppose. Marten and I had been friends forever, so when he decamped six days before the wedding, I felt like I lost more than a husband; I lost my best friend." She paused. "Was that how it was with you and Portia?"

His smile was sad, for yes, he'd lost his best friend when his marriage to Portia had collapsed.

"We should never have married," he admitted. "I realize now how selfish I had been in pressuring her to marry me. Her parents wanted the marriage, I wanted it, our lawyers were giddy over the strength of the alliance. Portia finally consented, but it was a recipe for disaster. We had been good friends but needed something more to make our marriage work." He gave a wry laugh. "An ounce of passion on her part would have been welcome. We never even shared a bed after Pieter was born."

It was so easy to talk to Sophie. He'd never disclosed these mortifying details to another living soul, and yet it seemed natural to share them with Sophie. And the tug of desire he felt for her seemed to be reciprocated. Ever since his defense of her at the breakfast table, she'd been following him with her eyes, a new magnetism humming between them.

"I don't want a reluctant wife," he said. "I want a woman who enjoys being married. Who wants the love and comfort and affection that should naturally happen between a man and his wife. And I want that woman to be you," he said, catching her gaze and holding it. Her eyes widened, but she didn't look away. Closing the short distance between them, and giving her plenty of time to withdraw if she chose, he lowered his head and kissed her.

She leaned in to him, raising her face and kissing him back. To his amazement, she welcomed his embrace. After a marriage of nothing but rejection, it was perhaps the most profound kiss of his life.

"Please, Sophie," he whispered against her cheek. "We could be so good together."

She pulled back a little. "You know I can't marry an atheist." Her voice was so soft he could barely hear it.

"I'm not an atheist," he said. "I don't know what I believe anymore, but I accept there is more to the world than science can explain. I've been closed-minded and deaf to opinions that differed from mine, but I'm willing to learn. I know I need to open my heart and surrender to this power that is calling me. It goes against everything I've ever believed, but I'm ready to be open to it."

Sophie's entire face lightened with hope, and he smiled as he tucked a strand of her flyaway hair behind her ear.

"My leg hurts, but I am used to it," he continued. "Far worse than the pain in my leg is a hollow emptiness I've struggled with most of my life. A nagging discontent. The sense that my existence lacks meaning or purpose. You've shown me a different way of seeing the world, and it feels right." Even saying these words felt right.

"Will you give us time?" he asked. "What I feel for you is illogical and irrational, but it's wonderful and affirming and it's not fading. You've inspired me to find a piece of my soul I didn't believe I had, but it is awakening and coming to life. You've been leading me into a sunlit world I never even knew existed. Don't give up on me yet . . . give us time."

Sophie's smile widened, enveloping him with warmth that made him want to pick her up and swing her in a circle. "Yes," she said softly, "I'll give us time."

As he drew her close, he looked at the glorious, darkening skies above him. The sun was setting fast, and he didn't know how much longer he would live, but he felt as though he was finally pulling into a safe harbor.

21

SOPHIE SOUGHT OUT PASTOR MATTISEN after breakfast the next morning, for if ever she needed spiritual guidance, it was now. After three broken engagements, the last thing she wanted was a fourth attempt if it was destined to failure, but she was so confused. Her earlier relationships had felt easy and natural. Her feelings for Quentin were new and dangerous and tempestuous. She wasn't even certain he was in love with her, so how could she contemplate marriage to him?

The answer came to her quickly. She wanted to marry Quentin because he needed her. She loved the way he seemed so focused on her when they were together, the way he bantered with her and made her feel like she was his equal. Believing herself in love in the past hadn't served her well, so maybe it was time to try something different.

Pastor Mattisen had counseled her through each of her disastrous engagements, especially the last one, when Albert had died and despair had overwhelmed her. During those painful months, she'd confessed everything to him, for Pastor Mattisen was like a second father to her—but a nonjudgmental one. He listened to her heartaches and delicately asked questions that prodded her in the right direction.

She found him at a work table near the groundskeeper's cabin, looking as delighted as a child as he tried to piece together the fragments of a broken pipe.

"This pipe looks like it must have been fired in Delft," he said. "See the remnants of blue and white painting on the bowl? I'll bet the last time someone smoked this pipe he was still paying taxes to the king of England."

"Probably," Sophie murmured, glancing around the area and seeing men at work everywhere she looked. "Could I persuade you to go for a walk with me?" she asked. "Just to the blackberry brambles near the end of the road. I want to speak with you about something."

"Excellent!" he said. "Especially if this means there might be a pie on the way. I've always thought your blackberry pie could make the angels weep."

She hadn't thought to make a pie, but given the look of anticipation on the pastor's face, it would be cruel to deny him one, especially since she intended to dump another load of romantic turmoil on his shoulders. She ran back to the house to fetch some baskets, and twenty minutes later the two of them had finally found a bit of privacy from the people swarming the estate.

"We should pick as many as possible," Sophie said. "The weather reports are predicting several days of heavy rain, so we should lay some in. I'm going to ask Collins to buy more than the usual provisions."

In light of the pastor's age, Sophie hunkered down to gather the berries low to the ground while the pastor worked at shoulder height, although she suspected just as many berries went into his mouth as into the basket.

"Quentin Vandermark has asked me to marry him."

Pastor Mattisen coughed, expelling a berry that shot out into the brambles. "What?" he asked on a choked breath.

When she explained Quentin's need for a stepmother for Pieter, the pastor's eyes narrowed in concern. "Surely you aren't entertaining the notion for that reason alone. Marriage is a lifelong commitment, and young Pieter will be grown soon. What then? Will you still find marriage to his father rewarding if it's just the two of you?"

Her fingers moved quickly through the blackberries as she knocked them into the basket. Yes, she wanted children and hoped to have some of her own with Quentin. Would they still be a good match when that time of life was over?

"I think so," she said hesitantly. "Of course I want children, but I also want a partner in life. I know Quentin has gloomy moods and isn't always the easiest person, but for the most part, he has been very respectful." And tender and protective and funny. Handsome, too. He loved her cooking, and she loved cooking *for* him.

"I heard rumors he was still mourning his wife," Pastor Mattisen said.

Sophie shook her head. "It was mostly a platonic marriage, and his wife never returned his affection. They had separate bedrooms, and I gather it was somewhat contentious." Warmth heated her cheeks, and she picked berries faster. "In any case, once he quit talking about blowing up the house, we've gotten along quite well. I'm not sure how to explain it, but I feel like he needs me."

And that was such a good feeling. All her life, she'd wanted someone to need her—and both Quentin and Pieter did.

"I want to marry him."

She surprised even herself with the sudden declaration, but it was true. Quentin was on his way toward becoming a man of faith. She couldn't doubt the new optimism in his bearing, and she quite liked the idea of settling into Dierenpark alongside Quentin. He was good company. She looked forward to the prospect of having children with him. She was twenty-six years old and had a normal body and spirit that longed for a man's touch. She not only wanted to nurture, she wanted to *be* nurtured, and after last evening by the Spanish cannon, she knew Quentin was excellent at making her feel loved and cherished. It was a new sensation for her, making her long for marriage and motherhood even more than she already had. When she explained these things to Pastor Mattisen, he set down his basket to look at her directly.

"Sophie, you must be careful," he said. "Quentin is in the rush of exhilaration that sometimes overtakes people new to God, and you mustn't rush into a commitment until you know he is a man to whom you can be loyal in good times and bad, for better and for worse. You will be joining your life with his for all time. You will walk alongside him into whatever valleys or sorrows come his way, agreeing to help shoulder the burdens. His money and power cannot release you from these obligations. That is the nature of the marriage covenant."

She turned away to gather more berries. His solemn words looked beyond the thrill of flirting with Quentin on a summer's evening and the joy of motherhood, cutting straight to the heart of what it meant to join her life to another man for all time. She'd much rather savor the excitement of marriage than the awesome responsibilities lurking in the shadows. Pastor Mattisen's counsel wasn't what she wanted, but perhaps it was precisely what she needed to hear.

<hr />

Each morning for the next three days, Quentin awoke with the same burning objective: Prove himself worthy of Sophie's hand in marriage.

It wasn't going to be easy. He'd gotten off to a monumentally bad start with her, and she was still cautious around him. She wouldn't marry him unless he could take the plunge into her world of faith. He didn't know how to prove that he was a new man, but he would try.

Sophie had warned him they were due for a spell of bad weather, and it was here. A front moving down from Canada had collided with a storm blowing in from the ocean, guaranteeing several days of steady rain. The research teams were closeted indoors, making privacy difficult. In a house this big, it ought to be easy to find some out-of-the-way corner, but it seemed whenever she wasn't cooking, Pastor Mattisen was nearby, watching over Sophie like a mother hen. And Marten Graaf was a relentless pest.

Blessed are the pure in heart, for they shall see God.

He needed to stamp out these instinctive resentments and learn the art of patience. Sophie attracted her share of men who wanted to protect her, and he ought to be glad for their vigilance rather than resenting them.

See? His newfound faith was already catching him when cynicism reared its head. While Sophie cooked, he carried the old leather Bible into the privacy of his bedroom. As rivulets of rain trickled down the windows, he soaked in the enduring words of kindness, mercy, and compassion that were the birthright of all people on earth.

It changed the way he related to the world. Having been blessed with a fortune from the moment he arrived in the world, it was time to begin sharing it. Yesterday, he'd wired his attorney to begin the process of donating a bequest to the village of Roosenwyck in Holland to fund some kind of civic charity like a hospital or a school. Perhaps the donation would serve double duty and soothe the guilt plaguing Nickolaas. After all these centuries, it was impossible to know how much of their fortune had been built on the funds embezzled by Caleb Vandermark, but Quentin could pay it back and then some.

After three days of rain, the tempers of the twenty people trapped within the house began to grow short, made worse by Nickolaas's overt rudeness to Professor Winston, the man who had taken the page of Algonquin text to Harvard for safekeeping.

When Professor Winston joined them at the breakfast table this morning, Nickolaas had pushed away from the table and left without a word. Sophie, who had just arrived at the table with two baskets of warm blueberry muffins, had looked wounded as Nickolaas stormed from the room.

Quentin had stood. His grandfather was behaving like a child, and Quentin wasn't going to tolerate rudeness to Sophie or Professor Winston. In the past, Quentin would have let the rift fester, assuming it was a natural consequence of his grandfather's eccentricities. He would have enjoyed watching the drama unfold, with only mild curiosity for how Nickolaas would move the chess pieces to his advantage.

Not anymore. Following Nickolaas into the relative privacy of the library, he tried his most conciliatory tone. "Why the hostility to Professor Winston? You know a historian was honor-bound to protect that document."

"He ought to be *bound* to the man who is paying his salary," Nickolaas replied in a sour tone.

Above all, love one another. Sophie's humble Christian precepts had been burned onto Quentin's mind, and he tried to extend a bit of understanding to his grandfather.

"I don't know why the Indians sent those strange Bible passages to this house, but it's causing you to resurrect a battle begun hundreds of years ago over something no one even remembers. Sophie reports this rain is due to continue for the rest of the week, so we're all stranded here. Can't we abide together in peace? We eat the same food, breathe the same air. Maybe we want different things from life, but we are all brothers."

Nickolaas snorted. "Now you are sounding like Sophie and her Bible-toting pastor."

The comment was intended as an insult, but Quentin absorbed it without blinking. Nickolaas was not instinctively opposed to religion—indeed, he seemed attracted to all manner of outlandish spiritual beliefs. The more exotic and strange, the more Nickolaas liked it. He believed in everything, which meant he believed in nothing. He latched on with the zeal of a magnet seeking true north, but the fascination never lasted more than a year or two before something else captured his imagination. The only constant had been that none of these spiritual quests ever fundamentally changed the way Nickolaas looked at or interacted with the world.

"Why is it that in all the forms of spirituality in which you've dabbled, you never pursued Christianity?"

Nickolaas seemed taken aback by the question, but he considered it carefully, rubbing his chin while staring at the rain pattering against the windowpanes. "I guess because it seems so ordinary," he finally said. "So pedestrian."

Quentin gave a reluctant smile at his grandfather's dismissive assessment. Christianity *was* a pedestrian religion, spread by men wearing sandals who walked across the ancient world driven by nothing more than the awesome power of faith. Sophie was pedestrian, and yet she was the most luminous woman he'd ever met.

If he needed proof of that, it was by the way she blossomed at a simple gift he arranged for her. With enough money and determination, it was possible to find anything in New York City, and three days earlier he'd sent Mr. Gilroy on a very specific quest.

Mr. Gilroy had returned this morning, seeking Quentin

out in the privacy of the library. The butler's hair was still damp from the rain. "The Cohasset bridge has been washed out," he reported as he tossed an oddly heavy sack on the desk. "It wouldn't surprise me if other rivers start flooding their banks."

Like everyone else in the house, Quentin was becoming heartily sick of the incessant rain, but at least his leg was not complaining. Normally, damp weather caused the bone-deep ache in his leg to scream for relief, but not this time. He scooped up the sack and went to find Sophie.

The wide portico at the front of the house was sheltered from the elements, and he coaxed Sophie outside to sit on the bench overlooking the rain-drenched meadow as water dribbled from the eaves. The bench was compact, and her slender frame was nestled close to his. With her layers of skirts and petticoats, not a centimeter of their flesh was touching, but it still seemed agreeably intimate.

The bag Mr. Gilroy had brought from the city was the size of a loaf of bread and quite heavy. He passed the coarse burlap bag to her without comment.

"What's this?" she asked.

"A present," he said, then winced. The presents he'd bought for Portia usually included ropes of pearls or gemstones the size of robin's eggs. A man of his wealth ought to provide something much nicer than a sack of strange-looking pods.

Sophie peeked inside the bag, her face screwing up in confusion. "What *are* they?" she asked, lifting the odd vegetable from the bag. It was a ruddy orange shade, larger than her hand, and looked like an oblong pumpkin. There were four of them in the bag.

"You once said the cocoa powder in this village was bad, and you wanted to make your own. These are cocoa pods, shipped directly from Brazil. If you split it open, you will find fresh cocoa beans inside. Then you can begin your culinary adventure of making chocolate from scratch."

"You remembered!" she exclaimed. Her eyes widened in delight as she held the pod to her nose for a sniff and then ran her fingers along its waxy skin. "It's fabulous. Thank you!"

A piece of him wanted to shower her with expensive jewels and the titles to faraway castles, but he knew such things wouldn't make her happy. Sophie delighted in wading into a river to gather oysters, the challenge of baking the perfect pie, a bouquet of wildflowers, or even a peaceful afternoon on a rain-drenched porch.

She slid a little closer to him on the bench, and he slipped his arm around her shoulders, staring over the verdant green of the meadow and savoring her closeness. He wanted this forever. He was content here, with her. He had been born with sixty million dollars to his name, but he'd throw it all in the dust for this. After a lifetime of wandering the earth and struggling against his fate, he had found happiness in the simple splendor of this glade and alongside this extraordinary woman.

He leaned down to kiss her forehead. "Thank you, Sophie," he whispered. "Thank you for everything."

He had so much to be profoundly thankful for. He was grateful Sophie had taught him to see the world and his place in it differently. His leg felt better than it had in years, and it seemed that against all odds, the last surgery he'd submitted to in Berlin might actually be working. The muscles around the weakened bone still hurt, but instead of the perpetual pain, it hurt only when he put too much weight on it.

Rather than thinking of the success of the operation as a triumph of science over God, something inside him was shifting. Long after Sophie had dashed inside to begin experimenting with the cocoa pods, he sat in the quiet solitude, listening to the rainfall and searching for the spiritual presence he felt hovering just out of reach.

Are you out there? He waited, but no answer came, and he didn't know exactly what he believed—yet his world was opening, expanding, broadening. He was meant to do something with his life rather than wander from city to city, building bridges and counting his money, though he still didn't know what.

And rather than feel dissatisfied, he smiled and looked forward to discovering the answer as the world unfolded in its own time.

❧ 22 ❧

THE RAIN MADE IT HARD for Sophie to get her daily reports telegraphed to Washington. The bridge at the old Cohasset Road was washed out, requiring one of the bodyguards to flag down a steamship to ride into Tarrytown and transmit the message from there. Her messages were arriving late, but at least they were getting through. The massive storm was pouring rain throughout all of New England, so she was certain that plenty of the Weather Bureau volunteers faced similar problems.

Without regular trips into the village for food, the larder was getting skimpy, and Professor Byron offered to go hunting to restock their provisions. "Can you cook venison?" he asked.

"If you kill it, I'll cook it," she said gratefully.

She had already begun the process of turning the cocoa pods into a powder she could use for baking. The first challenge was getting the pods open. None of the kitchen knives was up to the task, and finally Marten smashed them open on the edge of the slate steps behind the kitchen. Inside they found waxy white beans, which the old cookbook instructed her to let ferment in a warm place, turning them several times until the sugars developed on the outside of the bean. Pieter came by many times a day to stare at the beans as Sophie turned them.

"They don't look like chocolate to me," he said.

"Wait until I roast them. I expect the whole house will smell good, and then they will start to look more familiar to you."

She waited three days before she was satisfied the beans were ready for the next step. They roasted surprisingly fast in the oven, and in less than thirty minutes she had cooling cocoa beans that slipped from their husks with ease. Once cooled, they could be ground into cocoa powder. The cookbook advised that the finer the powder, the higher the quality of the chocolate.

All the professors took turns at the kitchen grinder clamped to the work table, the one she normally used only for coffee. She was grateful for their help, for grinding was a lot of work, and the men seemed tireless as they processed the cocoa into a fine powder. It looked better and smelled more fragrant than anything she had seen for sale in the village.

On the fifth day of rain, Quentin did not appear for lunch, which surprised her. Lately he had been dining with everyone, and in an unusually cheerful mood, but she did not let his absence concern her. It gave her a chance to deliver his meal to the library, where he had secluded himself all morning. Stolen moments of privacy were hard to find, but she was glad they would have one.

She tapped softly on the library door before entering. Quentin had been racing to get the design for the Antwerp bridge completed before the end of the month. He was hunched over a mound of papers at his desk, but his eyes softened as she entered.

"Hungry?" she asked as she set the tray before him.

"I should probably eat." It wasn't the effusive praise he normally lavished on her meals, and she glanced at him closer. It wasn't hot, but a fine sheen of perspiration covered his face.

"Are you all right? You're sweating."

He shrugged his shoulders dismissively. "These things come and go," he said, but something in his tone worried her. She drew a chair closer.

"Tell me." If they were going to be married, she had a right to understand the nature of his illness.

She listened as he described the bone infections that still plagued him. Sometimes the infection caused only a simple fever, but at other times, the area around his old wound swelled so much it split the skin open. She cringed at the ghastly thought. Although Quentin spoke in a composed tone, his shoulders sagged a little. It was almost imperceptible, but she was coming to know him very well and sensed his disappointment.

"Things had been going so well lately," he acknowledged. "I'd hoped these periodic infections were a thing of the past and that the bone graft had finally worked. I still think it might, but perhaps these fevers will be with me forever. There is nothing I can do other than wait it out." He smiled softly. "And maybe you could say a prayer or two."

"I can do that." Without thinking, she reached out to stroke a lock of hair that had fallen over his forehead. "Can I see the sketch for your new bridge?"

"Of course."

It was truly lovely, with three brick arches spanning the river and a series of lamps at periodic intervals along the pedestrian walkway. It was hard not to be proud of a man who could design something of such beauty and practical value.

Even as he showed her the design, a few drops of perspiration beaded up and rolled down the side of his face. She swallowed hard. "Are you certain you're all right? You don't look good."

He sighed, but humor danced in his eyes. "Sophie, I haven't felt good since I slipped on the ice outside my hotel in Vienna eight years ago. Lately I've begun to appreciate the distinction between feeling good in my body and feeling good in my spirit."

His hand covered hers, sending a surge of warmth and energy to her. "I've had more happiness, more hope, and a greater sense of purpose in these past few weeks than I can ever remember. Most of that is due to you."

How was it that such simple words could fill her with plea- sure? Never had she felt as appreciated as she did when Quentin spoke words of respect and admiration.

It was impossible to resist him, and she drew closer. "What would happen if I sat on your lap?"

He smothered a laugh. "Forgive me, Miss van Riijn, but I would be in howling agony."

"Oh dear." She averted her gaze in mortification.

He tugged on her hand. "Ask me what would happen if you sat on this armrest, put your arm around my shoulders, and leaned in so I could smell your hair and kiss your neck."

Her eyes grew round, but she was helpless to look away. "Why don't we go ahead and try it out? Like a scientific experiment."

"You read my mind."

"I'm clever that way." She propped her hip against the arm of the chair, close enough so she was snug against his body. From there it was easy to lean down and kiss him. There was a faint smile on his lips, and nothing had ever felt as right and proper as when he turned up his face to accept her kiss.

All his defenses were down. Quentin was warm and giving, with no cynicism or bitterness, just simple happiness as he kissed her back. How amazing that they had been able to see past their differences and become friends. She had helped soften him, but he'd given her the strength and self-confidence she hadn't even realized she lacked until he began propping her up.

He drew away and whispered against the side of her cheek. "Please, Sophie, let us have a chance. We can make this work if you just give us some time."

She'd been waiting her whole life for this. She'd been in love before—childhood crushes and foolish infatuations she'd mistaken for love. She'd been blessed with a wonderful relationship with Albert, but in retrospect, he had been so much older that they had never truly felt like equals. With Quentin, she had a partner. He was not the perfect man, but she was no flawless princess either.

How desperately she wanted this to work. She squeezed his hand. "Yes," she vowed, "I promise to give us time."

They had run out of sugar, and it would be days before someone could get to town to replenish their stock. Most of the chocolate recipes Sophie had seen in Dierenpark's grand collection of cookbooks called for a hefty amount of sugar, but the older recipes used cream, vanilla, and even ground almond meal to sweeten the treat. She'd simply have to make do with an older recipe.

Pieter wanted to help, and as she laid out the ingredients, he fidgeted with excitement. He recounted the fine chocolates he'd had in Belgium and how the taste compared with French chocolate.

"Those are world-famous chocolatiers," Professor Sorensen said from his position at a kitchen stool. "This is our first attempt at a highly complex process, so you may want to lower your expectations a bit."

Sophie flashed him a look of gratitude as she lowered a pot onto the double-boiler. The eighteenth-century cookbook was in French, and Professor Sorenson would be translating the instructions for Sophie, so she considered this a group effort, which took a bit of the pressure from her shoulders. She rarely risked cooking a new recipe in front of such a large audience, but the rain had given them all cabin fever, and helping with the chocolate gave them something to do.

As the aroma of simmering chocolate filled the house, it drew others to the kitchen like a lodestone. They had no proper candy molds, so Sophie used muffin tins, pouring only a quarter inch of the dark, glossy liquid into the bottom of each well. It would take hours for the chocolate to cool enough to eat, which was a disappointment for everyone who had been smelling the tempting aroma for almost an hour, but Sophie still had plenty of chocolate left in the pot.

"I'll whisk the remainder into some milk for a little hot chocolate—how would that be?" she asked. The sentence wasn't even out of her mouth before the bodyguards were scrambling for the teacups. Emil volunteered to brave the rain to fetch a canister of milk from the larder outdoors. By the time he returned, everyone in the house had gathered in the kitchen, and Emil poured the milk into the pot while Sophie whisked. The cookbook warned she mustn't let the chocolate change temperatures too rapidly or it would crystallize. A number of the professors leaned in, shouting instructions and generally making a nuisance of themselves. They might be brilliant educators, but they couldn't hold a candle to her in the kitchen.

"The ancient Mayans believed chocolate to be a gift from the gods," Professor Winston said. "Its creation is the work of alchemy, a transformation of a base material into an elixir fit for the gods. It is the intersection of chemistry with culinary magic."

Quentin also had plenty to say. "Chocolate is the only substance with profound culinary, symbolic, and pharmacological value. It is the queen of the epicurean experience."

"Could you *please* help me lower some of these expectations?" Sophie laughed as she continued whisking. "You're the one who spoiled Pieter with Belgian chocolates—how am I supposed to compete with that?"

"We've got faith in you, ma'am!" one of the bodyguards called from the back of the room.

At last, the proper amount of milk had been whisked into the chocolate, and it had been heated to the correct temperature for drinking. After transferring the first batch into an antique chocolate pot that looked like it had been imported from Versailles, Sophie brought it out to the kitchen table and poured some into a teacup.

"You first, Pieter, since you did such a fine job helping me with the measuring." Pieter wiggled his way through the screen of men, his eyes alight with excitement. The china teacup was warm, and the boy held it gingerly as he took a sip. Everyone watched in expectation.

Pieter's eyes grew round, then his face screwed up so tightly he looked like he was sucking a lemon. Sophie was relieved when he swallowed the mouthful rather than spitting it out.

"It's bitter," he said, smacking his lips.

"Of course it's bitter," Professor Sorenson said. "All eighteenth-century chocolate recipes are bitter. It wasn't until the last century that we've begun polluting chocolate with an obscene amount of sugar."

Everyone wanted to sample the chocolate drink despite Pieter's distaste, but most shared his assessment. They winced, their eyes watered, and they set their cups down.

Emil never did anything by half measures, and he knocked the whole teacup back in one mighty gulp. "Whoa, that will make hair grow on a man's chest!" he said with a violent shudder.

Sophie ventured a sip. It wasn't so bad . . . it was actually rather nice. She took another taste. It had a dark, rich flavor, with layers of complexity that took awhile to surface. The others all watched, waiting for her assessment. After most of them had rejected the drink, she didn't want to appear defensive by claiming she liked it.

Quentin watched her, curiosity on his face as he waited for her opinion. He had placed his own cup down after a small sip, and it was clear he preferred sweetened chocolate, as well.

"I rather like it," she finally said. It took some time to see past the dark chocolate's harsh taste, but she didn't care if others didn't approve, she loved it and knew she would make this recipe again and again.

A few brave men drained their cups, but only Sophie and Professor Sorenson helped themselves to more after their first serving. "I'll make you all a nice peach pie as soon as we can get some sugar," Sophie promised Pieter.

"How about an apple pie, too?" Emil asked. That started a flurry of conversation about which flavor of pie should be the first to come out of the kitchen once the rain let up and it was possible to restock the pantry.

The doorbell rang, startling everyone. Mr. Gilroy set down his cup, and as he headed to the front door, the bodyguards went on alert. Quentin looked only mildly annoyed at the interruption, but she supposed he must be used to living this odd sort of pampered life that was still fraught with its own set of dangers.

Relief trickled through her when she recognized her father's voice. She smiled as Jasper followed Mr. Gilroy into the kitchen, his coat soaking wet and water dripping from the ends of his hair. "Can I offer you a cup of bitter hot chocolate?" she asked him. "There is plenty left, as I have failed in spectacular fashion this afternoon."

Rather than greeting her with a smile, her father's face remained grim as he shrugged out of his coat, shaking water from it and hanging it on a hook in the corner.

"I've come on business," he said. "I found a letter written by a member of the Broeder family long ago. It is sealed and notarized. I have no idea what this letter contains, but I want it opened and read before witnesses so there can be no question of its authenticity."

Sophie caught her breath. It had taken her father weeks to read through the trove of Vandermark documents he'd found in the bank's safe deposit box, but he'd finished that task days ago and had told her he'd found nothing of value. She didn't put much stock in Jasper's belief that the Broeders might somehow be the legitimate heirs to Dierenpark, but he was convinced a Vandermark had once eloped with a Broeder and there would be evidence of it in some government register at a nearby city. He'd gone to Albany last week to begin searching through courthouse records.

Quentin looked only mildly interested, but Nickolaas hadn't torn his eyes from her father since the moment he'd said the name Broeder.

Her father took a sealskin pouch from his jacket pocket, unfolded it, and withdrew an envelope that was yellow with age. "I found this letter written by Harold Broeder at the state courthouse in Albany. Harold was from the second generation of Broeder groundskeepers at Dierenpark, and he put this letter on file at the state courthouse in 1690. The writing on the back of the envelope reads, 'To be opened in the event of my untimely or violent death,' and it is signed by Harold and dated July 9, 1690."

Jasper held up the letter, high enough for everyone in the room to see the old handwriting scrawled across the back of the envelope that was still held closed by a stamp of sealing wax. The ornate stamp of a notary validated its authenticity.

Her father continued. "I want this letter to be opened here at Dierenpark, with witnesses from both the Vandermark and Broeder families."

"I'm here," Emil offered.

Nickolaas looked down his nose at Jasper. "Harold Broeder died peacefully in his bed as an old man. He did *not* die in a violent or untimely fashion. Therefore, the letter is not to be opened."

"That's not for you to say," her father said. "The letter belongs to Emil, as he is the direct descendant of Harold Broeder. Emil? Do you want to open and read the contents of this letter?"

"Um, sure . . . but I can't really read."

Her father slid a thumb beneath the seal. "I'd be happy to do the honors."

"Wait!" Nickolaas exclaimed. "In 1690, this country was still governed by England. Therefore, English law should dictate the inheritance of the letter."

Her father's smile was grim. "You're scrambling. And you are wrong about the law. American law now governs what happens to this letter, and it is quite clear that it belongs to Emil."

Sophie watched the exchange in fascination. Nickolaas clearly feared whatever might be in that letter, but her father suspected it might somehow call the ownership of Dierenpark into question. Quentin's face was tense and alert, watching every move his grandfather made.

"Mr. van Riijn is right," Quentin said. "The letter belongs to Emil, and it is up to him what happens to it."

"I want to know what it says," Emil said agreeably.

Nickolaas winced and turned away, as though he could not bear to see whatever the old groundskeeper had written. Sophie's heart went out to him. She didn't understand his fear and superstition about the past, but his anxiety was palpable.

The room was silent as her father popped the blob of sealing wax that had protected this secret for more than two hundred years. Her father drew a deep breath and read the note aloud.

I, Harold Broeder, am a loyal employee of the Vandermark family but have reason to fear for my life, because my family has been complicit in a great crime. In 1638, shortly after arriving in America, Caleb and Adrien Vandermark had a dispute over money that had been entrusted to them. As a result, Caleb asked my father to murder Adrien in exchange for one hundred pounds sterling, a generous annual salary, and free use of the cabin and pier for as long as the Broeder family lived. My father drowned Adrien in the part of the river known as Marguerite's Cove. Adrien's disappearance was blamed on treachery from the Algonquin Indians, with whom Adrien was known to consort.

Jasper set down the letter, his gaze scanning the onlookers who had gathered around the table. The legend of Adrien Vandermark's murder by the Indians he had tried to befriend had made him a tragic folk hero, but knowing he had been cut down on the orders of his own brother stunned everyone.

Emil looked upset and confused. "I don't understand," he said. "Does this mean Adrien didn't die in an Indian attack?"

"There is more in the letter," her father said, picking up the page.

Driven by greed, my father returned to Caleb over and over for more money, which was always paid. After my father's death, and to my great shame, I continued to blackmail Caleb Vandermark. Although I played no role in the murder, I have benefited from the crime. In his final years, Caleb grew bitter, frightened, and ravaged by guilt. Although not a Catholic, during his final illness he pleaded for a priest to absolve his sins. No priest could be found, and he confessed his sin to his eldest son, Enoch, exhorting him to continue honoring the agreement with the Broeders for fear the shameful truth would defile the Vandermark name.

Enoch Vandermark's patience has grown thin, and attempts have been made on my life. Both our families live beneath a veil of greed and mistrust. To ensure my safety,

*I am sending sealed copies of this letter to the courthouse
in Albany, the elders of Roosenwyck in Holland, and to
Enoch Vandermark. Should I fall victim to the Vandermarks, I beg that this crime be exposed to the light of day.*

"That is the end of the letter," Jasper said, the crackling of
the paper loud as he folded it closed again. For two hundred
years, that letter had hidden a terrible secret. Sophie watched
the men in the room, everyone somber as the news penetrated.
It almost seemed as if the air had been tainted by the saga
of greed and corruption. She had always thought of Adrien
Vandermark as a tragic figure, having been killed by people
he was trying to protect, but the true story of his betrayal was
far worse.

Professor Byron looked sick. "All these weeks I've been working in Marguerite's Cove. I never suspected anything . . ."

Her father offered the letter to Emil.

"I don't even want to touch it," Emil said. "It makes me feel
bad, to know that I come from a family like that."

"You aren't to blame," Quentin said and then looked quickly
to Pieter. "And neither are you. We are all given the free will to
choose what kind of path we want to walk."

"Do you think Adrien might be buried in Marguerite's Cove?"
Pieter asked. "Is that why the lilies still bloom?"

"I don't think we'll ever know," Professor Sorensen said with
a sad smile. "I can find no scientific explanation for the lilies
or the oysters. Your guess is as good as any, lad."

Nickolaas pounced, his eyes alert. "Are you saying you have
given up? That science can't explain what's going on in that
cove?"

"I'm saying there are mysteries that science cannot resolve,"
Professor Sorensen said. "I don't need proof that can be seen
under a microscope to believe there is divinity in the world.

310

That's where faith comes in. If there was proof, there'd be no need for faith, right?"

Professor Byron wasn't satisfied. "There are limits on what science can tell us today, but we are developing better tools all the time. Someday we will have better microscopes and testing procedures. I think someday we will be able to see deeper into a cell. Pull it apart, study its components—"

"I'm not interested in someday," Nickolaas interrupted. "I want to know about today. Do you have a scientific explanation *today* for why those lilies grow on the spot where Adrien Vandermark was killed?"

He looked directly at Professor Byron, the youngest and most confident of all the biologists. Each morning, Professor Byron raced down to the cove with unflagging energy, determined to finally solve the mystery. He'd already asked permission to stay after summer's end to keep hunting for an answer, for surrender simply wasn't an option for him. Even now his inability to produce an answer drove him to wince and screw up his face in frustration.

"No!" he finally admitted. "I can't see a reason, and neither can anyone else."

Nickolaas's smile was triumphant as he jabbed his index finger at Quentin. "You heard them," he said. "Your own biologists agree there is no scientific explanation for the phenomenon. Given the circumstances of Adrien Vandermark's death, it is far more likely there is a supernatural cause for what is happening in Marguerite's Cove. I win the bet."

He set down his teacup, the gentle clink the only sound in the suddenly silent kitchen, and left the room.

"Pieter, go fetch your grandfather and ask him to meet me in the orangery," Quentin said. The orangery had the most privacy of anywhere in the house, and he didn't want this conversation overheard by a multitude of college professors.

"Sophie, I'd like you to come, as well," Quentin said quietly. It hurt to see the wounded innocence on her face as she learned the circumstances of Adrien Vandermark's death. At times like these, he wanted to protect and shelter her. For now, that meant saving Dierenpark from his grandfather's plans.

It would infuriate Nickolaas, but he was *not* going to carry out the destruction of this house. Generations of Vandermarks had been raised to be guarded, superstitious, and distrustful of outsiders, long after the original crime had been forgotten and lost to history. It was time to scrub the lingering taint from the family tree and turn Dierenpark into a source of pride rather than shame. Nickolaas would either agree to the plan or Quentin would take him to court in an ugly battle for the future of their family legacy.

He clasped Sophie's hand and made his way to the orangery, where the rain sounded louder as it pounded on the glass plates. The air was humid and laden with the scent of citrus trees and orchids. An orangery was an ostentatious display of wealth only very rich people could afford. Who needed Peruvian orchids or a climate that could support lemon trees year-round? It was a symbol of the greed that had ultimately led to Adrien Vandermark's murder.

"Are you all right?" he whispered to Sophie, leading her to a bench.

"I'm okay." But the sadness in her voice weighed on him. Adrien's death was hundreds of years in the past, and he didn't want her to spend one second grieving over something for which she had no responsibility.

"That was really terrible chocolate, Sophie."

A bubble of laughter escaped. "Did you think so?"

"I do. But I love you anyway." Her eyes widened in surprise, but it was time for him to admit what was in his heart. He'd hidden behind the excuse that he needed a mother for Pieter, when what he really wanted was so much more.

"I love you," he said again. "I don't expect you to profess any grand feelings for me yet. So long as you give me time, I know I can learn to be worthy of you."

The door opened and he stood, still holding her hand tightly. It was time for his grandfather to get accustomed to the prospect of having Sophie join their family.

Nickolaas glared at him from the opposite side of the orangery. "I won't permit you to back out of the deal now."

"How long have you known about that letter?" Quentin challenged.

"Ever since I bought the archive in Holland forty years ago. The good town fathers of Roosenwyck honored Harold Broeder's request and did not open it."

"And you never thought to tell us?"

Nickolaas walked down the aisle until he stood before them, pretending fascination in the showy blooms of a hydrangea. "My dear Quentin, you've never shown the slightest interest in our family history. I saw no need to expose the sordid details to the light of day."

Quentin gestured toward the main house. "Then why all this?" he demanded. "Why drag all these people here to plunder through the family history, the attic, even the very soil we live on?"

"Because I believe there is a curse," Nickolaas said calmly. "The Indians knew they were innocent of Adrien's death, and they sent us those taunting passages. I think they sent something else along with it. A curse or a hex or such. I want it found and destroyed. I'm not confident that's possible, so it's time to demolish everything."

Nickolaas glanced at Sophie and then back at Quentin. "I'm

313

not blind," he continued. "I've seen the affection you have for her, and I knew she'd pressure you to save Dierenpark. Go back to the village, Sophie." He spoke bluntly but not unkindly. "Marry Marten Graaf and have a dozen babies. Forget Dierenpark. It's time to undo Caleb's crime by abolishing the monument he built on ill-gotten gains. Only then will our family be free of his legacy."

"That's not going to happen," Quentin said tightly. "I believe the source of the curse lies in the twisted way Caleb raised his children. They lived and breathed in the air of guilt and mistrust. That attitude ended up being passed down through the generations. I won't permit it to continue. Pieter is an innocent. At all costs, he must be protected from a fatalistic view of the future."

"That's why I want to destroy the house," Nickolaas said as though speaking to a simpleton. "Dierenpark was born in corruption and can never be anything else. It will stain our family for all time unless it is wiped from the map."

"That's not true!" Sophie asserted, moving a step closer to Nickolaas. "Dierenpark is what you make of it. It can be a millstone around your neck, or you can turn it into something beautiful and sacred. Something that would have made Adrien Vandermark proud."

Quentin gazed at Sophie, pride swelling in his chest. They were thinking along the exact same lines, but he still didn't have legal control over Dierenpark. Nickolaas could hire someone to blow it up tomorrow if he wanted. So Quentin tried another angle.

"How did your father die?"

Nickolaas flinched and looked away. Quentin suspected Nickolaas knew all of Dierenpark's secrets, including the truth behind his father's death, but he kept fierce guard over the past. Given the flash of anguish on his grandfather's face, those hidden mysteries tormented him to this day.

"My father committed suicide," Nickolaas said bluntly.

Quentin rocked back, tightening the grip on his cane lest he topple over. The color had drained from Sophie's face, and she struggled to draw a breath.

"But . . . but he was such a good man," she stammered. The disillusionment on her face mirrored Quentin's own feelings. He knew what it meant to battle melancholia, but he'd always been encouraged by the modest, hardworking example set by Karl Vandermark.

"My father killed himself over *a woman*," Nickolaas said sourly. "He was depressed for months over a doomed love affair. He couldn't marry anyone because a divorce from my mother was impossible. When the woman he loved married someone else, my father wrote a suicide note bemoaning the miseries of his life, took an overdose of laudanum, and died in his bed."

Quentin lowered himself to sit beside Sophie again. Even in the worst ravages of despair, his love for Pieter had always kept him from even toying with the option of suicide. Nickolaas had grown up knowing his father's depression was more powerful than his love for his son. Quentin couldn't imagine the scar that would leave on a fourteen-year-old boy.

"How did he end up in the river?" Quentin asked quietly.

Nickolaas flinched again and turned to gaze at the rivulets of rain tracking down the windowpanes. He seemed haggard, old, and tired.

"I was the one who found him," he said slowly. "At first I thought he was sleeping, but then I saw the note and learned the truth. I didn't know what to do. I had always thought my father was a hero. Everyone in New Holland thought so, too. When I read that note, I was angry and ashamed, but I still didn't want the rest of the village to know what he had done. I burned the note and got old Mr. Broeder to help me carry him to the river. It was easier to let his death seem like an accident than let everyone learn the truth."

To Quentin's horror, his grandfather's lower lip trembled, and his eyes pooled with a sheen of tears before he looked away. Sophie darted to his side, sliding her arm around him and murmuring those soothing words she was so good at.

Quentin closed his eyes, but he couldn't close his ears to the sounds of his grandfather's weeping. The sobs were strangled, coming from deep in his chest as he tried to suppress them. For as long as Quentin could remember, his grandfather had been a crafty old man who delighted in being one step ahead of everyone else. Now he heard the sound of long-buried grief from a fourteen-year-old boy, broken and desperate to cover his father's shame. Was it any wonder that Nickolaas had turned to spiritualists and fortune-tellers who might provide an easy explanation for the tragedy of Karl Vandermark's death?

It was probably Emil's grandfather who'd helped Nickolaas bring Karl to the river, and like other Broeders before him, he had carried the secret to his grave. What a tragic, intertwined history their two families had.

It didn't take Nickolaas long to regain control. "I think my father figured out what had happened," Nickolaas said on a watery sigh. "I don't know if he found Enoch's copy of Harold Broeder's letter or pieced it together some other way, but he'd found copies of those Algonquin texts, and they upset him. He was convinced the Vandermarks were not entitled to our wealth, and that was why he was so determined to work as hard as any other man in the village. I remember in those final days how he tore this house apart, looking through dusty old trunks, muttering about the curse of wealth."

Sophie sat beside Nickolaas, her arm around his back. "I don't believe your family is cursed," she said softly. "You can't change the past, but the memory of what happened here can inspire us all to live a better life."

Quentin nodded. "For hundreds of years, we have been hiding, covering up, and deceiving. Dierenpark is filled with the portraits of people who cared about safeguarding the Vandermark fortune. I am concerned about safeguarding the tattered remnants of my soul. What if we used the fortune we've inherited to do something noble and generous?"

Nickolaas's shoulders sagged. "I have neither the time nor the energy to do that."

"I do," Quentin said with resolve. He had no way of knowing if he'd live another month, a year, or grow to be as old as Nickolaas, but his life was going to have purpose, and it was going to begin at Dierenpark. "I won't destroy the house. That's not the way to change our legacy."

Nickolaas lifted his chin. "It would be best to destroy it. I want it wiped off the map with a dynamite blast loud enough to wake up every Vandermark ancestor in the afterlife and let them see what I think of their estate. I'll burn everything that remains until nothing but dust is left."

Above all, love one another.

Nickolaas was a damaged and wounded man. Quentin needed to accept his grandfather's scars, understand them, and love him anyway.

"If you want a spectacular show that will shake the heavens, I'll commission a fireworks display," he said gently. "And then I will turn Dierenpark into something more than an empty mausoleum, and the portraits of ten generations of Vandermarks can watch it all happen from the walls." As he spoke, he felt a lightness of spirit and a surge of hope powering his body. "Let me turn Dierenpark into something amazing. Let me use it for something that would make Adrien Vandermark proud. We owe it to him, and we owe it to Pieter."

Sophie rose, tears shining in her eyes as she came to stand beside him, slipping her hand inside his own again. He kissed her hand—her callused, scarred, and beautiful hand—and then turned to face Nickolaas again.

Nickolaas sagged but nodded his consent.

23

QUENTIN KNEW before he even got out of bed that he was in trouble. His bed sheets were soaked in perspiration, and the pain in his shin throbbed. The old wound on his leg was warm, red, and swollen. He would need to wrap it, which usually brought some relief, but he couldn't help but feel his spirits sag. For a few weeks, that bit of hope that he might be mending had tasted so sweet.

He stretched his leg, barely able to flex the foot. It was going to be a struggle to get a shoe on today. Sweat rolled down his face as he tugged a sock on, but the first few minutes after waking were always the worst. He'd drink some willow tea, and the savage pain would ease shortly.

There was a gentle tapping at his door, and he hoped it was Sophie. He tugged up the sheet to cover the lower half of his body. "Yes?"

It was Pieter. "Are you coming downstairs?" the boy asked as he entered the room, a hopefulness in his face.

In the past when his pain was this bad, he would shoo Pieter away to Mr. Gilroy or a governess. No longer. The fact that Pieter welcomed his company was a miracle not to be taken lightly.

"What would you like to do today?" No matter what Pieter said, he was going to make it happen.

"It's stopped raining. I wanted to show you my animals. I found some new frogs."

Mercifully, the window well where Pieter kept his collection of salamanders and frogs was only a few feet outside the kitchen door. Quentin dressed and then leaned heavily on his cane as he made his way to the kitchen, drawn by the scent of baking bread, although there was no sign of Sophie. A twinge of disappointment tugged at him, but if the weather held, perhaps he could coax her away for a few stolen hours at the Spanish cannon. Whether he lived for another year or another decade, those magical hours spent with her at the Spanish cannon would glimmer forever in his soul.

The moment he stepped outside it was obvious the weather would not hold much longer. The air was cool, blowing down from the north in a damp chill. The low-hanging clouds were an eerie sort of purple mixed with orange, as if the sky couldn't decide if it wanted to permit the sunrise or concede to the gathering storm.

"Show me what you've got," he said as they approached the window well tucked against the side of the house. Pieter had mounded stones over a wire rack atop the window well. Most of the creatures could probably escape if they chose, but with all the rain in recent days, they were probably happy as a pig in mud down there.

Pieter lifted the wire rack away. "I've got four different types of salamanders. Professor Byron said that there are two hundred different kinds, and I'm going to see how many I can catch. He said that if a salamander gets a leg chopped off, a new one will grow back."

"That would be a useful skill," Quentin said with a laugh, but Pieter was too busy showing him the underside of a turtle to catch the joke. Hiring the team of biologists had been an unexpected stroke of genius, helping awaken Pieter's curiosity in natural science.

He leaned against the side of the house while Pieter continued lifting out various specimens for his approval. The sky was darkening rapidly, and it looked like they were all going to be driven back inside soon. Where was Sophie? Usually she was in the kitchen preparing breakfast by now, but perhaps she'd gone to gather berries in this brief respite from the rain. A pie would be welcome.

Eventually he had admired each of the salamanders, toads, and reptiles in the menagerie. "I need to find another turtle or else this one might get lonely," Pieter said.

The old Quentin would have ordered Mr. Gilroy to go buy a turtle to make his son happy, but with newfound sensitivity, he sensed something else behind Pieter's statement. Perhaps a hint of loneliness? For most of his life, the boy had been deprived of children his own age as they traveled from city to city. Perhaps he and Sophie would have a child of their own. He sensed Pieter would adore having a little brother or sister.

Pieter set the turtle back down, covered the window well, and looked at him with apprehensive eyes. "Did you love my mother?" he asked.

The question stunned him. Pieter had never asked such a question before, and it seemed to come from nowhere.

"Of course I loved your mother."

"Miss Sophie says you didn't sleep in the same bed because Mother didn't like you."

He clenched the handle of his cane and tried to keep his voice calm. "When did she say such a thing?"

"I heard her talking to Pastor Mattisen a few days ago. They

321

were picking blackberries, but I was hunting for salamanders, so I don't think they knew I was there. The pastor said that's how it is for some married people who don't like each other very much."

To this day, the failure of his marriage to Portia was a mortification tainted with shame, embarrassment, and regret. To have his deepest, most private humiliation bantered about in the blackberry meadow was a slap in the face.

"I loved your mother very much," he said, trying to mask the slow burn of anger. "And she loved me, and most importantly, she loved you. Anything you heard Miss Sophie say can't change that—"

His mouth snapped shut as the kitchen door opened and Ratface emerged, dumping a basin of wash water into the yard. Ratface nodded to them both before returning inside, but this conversation shouldn't happen where it could be overheard. There were open windows in the house, and the estate swarmed with people. Sophie should have known that. What business did she have spilling the private details of his life to a stranger?

"Do you know where Miss Sophie is?" he asked Pieter.

"She's with Professor Byron over by the sycamore trees. Professor Byron shot a deer, and he is getting it ready to cook. Miss Sophie is helping him, but they said I had to stay away."

He could well imagine. Field dressing a deer wasn't a sight for tender eyes, and he was surprised Sophie was up for it.

"Marten is helping, too. He said he and Miss Sophie used to go hunting when they were growing up, and it would be like old times. He was laughing when he said it."

Marten again.

A low rumble of thunder sounded from the north, a perfect reflection of Quentin's own dark mood. He pushed away from the house, struggling to hang on to the frayed ends of his temper. "Go inside and see if Mrs. Hengeveld needs help with anything."

The moment the door closed behind Pieter, Quentin set off for the open patch of meadow by the sycamore trees. Anger fueled his steps as he lumbered toward the clearing, heedless of the searing pain shooting up his leg with each lurch. He didn't want to stress his leg today, but the image of Sophie and Marten enjoying *old times* out in the clearing was enough to speed his steps. Had she spilled the private details of his marriage to Marten, as well?

The sight that greeted him was appalling. The deer had been cleaned, quartered, and hung in sections from the limb of a giant sycamore tree. Professor Byron stood a few feet away, still sweating from his labors with the deer. He was shirtless, his bare flesh tanned and gleaming as he grinned at Sophie, who was wringing out cloths and passing them to Byron. There was no sign of Marten.

The professor's trousers were stained and damp from the dripping rags Sophie passed him. "You've got a spot on your back," she said, reaching around to wipe down the professor from behind.

"Don't stop," Byron groaned. "That feels like bliss after being cooped up for days."

"You deserve it," she laughed. "We were likely to starve unless you had braved the wilderness to slay the mighty beast."

Anger burned like acid in Quentin's veins. What an idiot he had been! His rival for Sophie's affections wasn't Marten Graaf; it was Professor Byron. The professor was young, his body vigorous and healthy. He had an intelligent mind and a brilliant future ahead of him.

Quentin's booted feet slashed through the overly long grass, ripping the strands from the rain-softened soil. "Is this your idea of giving us time?" he bit out. "Frolicking half-naked in the field and flirting with another man? Charming, Sophie."

Sophie looked surprised to see him, a gleam of startled reproof in her eyes. "What's put you in such a surly mood?" She faced him squarely, her hands on her hips and challenge in her eyes.

He wasn't about to spill the personal details of his life in front of Professor Byron and his annoyingly perfect, healthy body, but neither was his leg capable of taking Sophie any kind of distance away from the house.

"I need a word alone with Sophie," he said bluntly. "You can clean up in the river."

Byron's smile faded, and he glanced uneasily to Sophie. "I'm not so sure that's a good idea . . ."

"It's an excellent idea if you hope to work at any college in the United States or Europe ever again. All it will take is a brief meeting with the financial office of a college for them to lose all interest in you, and I promise I can make that happen." Anyone with enough money could use the power of endowments to manipulate people, and he was angry enough to threaten it.

Byron still hesitated.

"Go on," Sophie said. "Quentin can be a bad-tempered bear, but I am in no danger. I am quite certain I can outrun him if need be."

It was humiliating to think about, but she was right. Tiny droplets of rain began to fall, and he instinctively clutched his cane tighter. Byron leaned over to scoop up his shirt and a towel, throwing them both casually over his shoulder but keeping his concerned eyes fastened on Sophie.

"I'm going to be ten yards away in the groundskeeper's cabin," he said. "Just say the word and I'll come running."

Quentin glared at Byron's retreating back, but Sophie didn't wait for the professor to enter the cabin before she attacked.

"Is this *your* idea of giving us time?" she challenged, turning his own words against him. "I thought you were trying to be a better man. One with some foundation in decent Christian values instead of growling and flaunting your power."

His eyes narrowed. He spoke quietly, but with intensity. "What I told you about my marriage to Portia was private. I've never told that to *anyone* before you, and you've gone and blabbered the most painful details of my life to your pastor. Pieter overheard everything and wanted to know why I didn't love his mother."

Sophie's eyes grew rounder as he spoke. "I'm sorry," she said. "I needed to talk to someone—"

"He's my son, Sophie. *My son.* Do you know what that means? I'm just barely finding my footing with him, and you've gone and planted that seed of doubt in his head."

"I'm sorry," she repeated. The color had dropped from her face, and she looked sick. "Quentin, please understand, I meant no harm, please—"

"Please what?" he snapped out. "Please keep being patient while you decide if I'm good enough for you? Or please don't fire me from a job that pays one hundred dollars per week?"

She stiffened. "If that's what you think, you don't know me at all." She threw a towel into the bucket and whirled away.

He wanted to call the words back, but it was too late, she was already running. He lurched after her and managed to grab a handful of fabric before she tore away, dashing toward the house. He lumbered forward, his weight propelling him in a desperate bid to stop her.

His shinbone snapped. He heard it . . . like a wet crack of a bat striking a board, just before he toppled over and crashed to the ground. Time slowed . . . this was happening to someone else . . . but then pain blinded him, blazing from his leg to scorch every nerve in his body. The scream sounded like it was coming from a distance, but it was from his own throat.

He twisted and rolled in agony, sensing the grinding of bone fragments shifting in his leg. Wet grass was in his face, dirt in his nose.

Sophie crowded him. She bent over him, talking in panicked

tones, but he couldn't understand her words. All he could sense was a warm gush of blood on his leg. Heat surged through his body in waves. Whatever infection had taken root a few days ago was now flooding his system.

"You're going to be okay . . ." It was Sophie's voice, but she was weeping.

Someone rolled him onto his back. Professor Byron was there, arms sliding beneath him. The pain as he was lifted was agonizing. His head rolled back, and his world went black.

It had been raining for hours, and there was no sign of the bodyguards Sophie had sent racing into town for the doctor. With the bridge over the gully washed out, Sophie could only pray they would get through to Dr. Weir. If the water hadn't risen too high, they could ford the river on horseback. It had been three hours since the accident; shouldn't they be back by now?

Wind sent a surge of rain spattering against the window, and Sophie clenched her fingers together, staring at the front lawn rather than turn around to see Quentin's pale, haggard body unconscious on the bed.

She had been here when they'd cut the trousers from his leg. The image would be forever branded on her mind. Several inches of white bone cut through his skin, jutting out at an obscene angle. The bone graft had broken free. They dared not cover it or try to force it back beneath the skin, and Quentin had been white from blood loss when Byron had laid him on the bed.

"We'll need something for a tourniquet," Byron had said.

Sophie nodded. There was no earthly way such an injury could be healed, but even so, she turned to Nickolaas for permission. The old man looked as if he'd aged twenty years at the sight of Quentin's shattered leg. He nodded.

None of them had ever done a tourniquet, but all they needed to do was bind it tight enough to stop the bleeding. One of the professors brought a braided silk cord from the grand parlor's draperies. As it was tied, Quentin gasped and roused back to consciousness, thrashing on the bed.

Sophie leaned over him, trying to soothe him and block his view of what Mr. Gilroy was doing.

"What's happening?" he gasped.

There was no gentle answer. "Quentin, you are going to lose your leg," she said.

If possible, his muscles seized even tighter. He swallowed. "I know."

The men moved behind her, the mattress shifting as they positioned themselves to tighten the cord even further. Once it was tied and looped, the handle of an axe was slipped into the loop and twisted.

Quentin's eyes rolled back in his head, and he passed out. Thank God.

Hours passed and still the doctor did not come. Sophie had no experience with this sort of illness, but the heat ravaging Quentin's body seemed unnatural and extreme. He was so hot, the intense warmth radiated from him to heat the room. He drifted in and out of consciousness, and Pastor Mattisen lifted him, holding a cup of water to his lips. It was the only thing they knew to do for him.

Twilight descended, sending darkness over the land, but in the distance came a rider on horseback, galloping up the drive. She squinted, but in the gloaming it was impossible to see who it was.

She opened the bedroom door to dash toward the front hall, but Pieter stopped her. He had been loitering in the hall most of the day, but she hadn't let him inside. Quentin's leg could not be covered, and the jagged white bone sticking up from his flesh wasn't something a child should see.

"Is my father going to die?" Pieter asked.

She instinctively wanted to reassure him but couldn't. Squatting down to be on his level, she spoke as gently as she could. "I don't know. It would be nice if you can say some prayers for him. Sometimes God answers our prayers, but not always."

The front door opened, and Ratface appeared, water dripping from his coat and exhaustion on his face. "Dr. Weir is in Boston. We rode to Tarrytown, but no doctor can come until tomorrow."

The strength left her legs, and she would have fallen had Ratface not grabbed her. "You're gonna be all right, Miss Sophie," he said roughly.

But she wasn't. Quentin was in agony, and they didn't even have any proper drugs to help dull the pain.

He was awake when she returned to his room. Night had fallen, and his skin looked ghastly white in the candlelight. "Sophie," he gasped.

She sank into the seat by his bed. "I'm here."

"Sophie, you have to marry me."

She smoothed the sheets across his chest. "We'll talk about that when you're better."

"No," he said, cutting her off. "I'm not going to get better, and you have to marry me now. I can't leave Pieter alone . . ." His voice trailed off, and his gaze tracked to the others in the room—his grandfather, Pastor Mattisen, and three of the bodyguards. "You owe her loyalty," he told the men. "I'm giving her everything. I'm giving her Pieter, control of the estate. You are my witnesses."

The words were directed to Nickolaas. "I agree," the old man said, his voice firm. "I'll see your will carried out."

Tears blurred her vision. How tragic that these two men should finally join forces at this most terrible of moments.

Quentin squeezed her hand. "Sophie, please . . ."

The doctor would not be here until tomorrow. His skin was scorching with fever; his leg was black. It was unlikely he'd be alive by the time the doctor got here. She knew the right thing to do.

"I'll marry you," she said on a ragged breath, and the relief on Quentin's face made her want to weep.

Quentin struggled to stay conscious long enough to get the vows said. Trying to separate his mind from the pain raging in his leg, he issued orders quickly.

"I want everyone in the house to witness this. I am of sound mind. Sophie is to be my wife and my heir. She will be Pieter's guardian."

He feared for Sophie. She was going to inherit control over a fortune, and it would attract a swarm of sharks. After his grandfather was dead, distant relatives would come spilling out of the woodwork. They would try to tear her to pieces, deny his sanity, deny the legality of the marriage itself. As others gathered in the room, he repeated his will over and over. With a pastor and eight college professors to attest to his sanity and the validity of the marriage, it was going to be hard to mount a legal challenge, but he cringed at the thought of Sophie with no protection.

"Ratface," he wheezed. "Look out for her. Guard her."

"Like she is the Holy Grail itself," Ratface vowed in a voice of steel, and if Quentin had had the energy he would have laughed. Sophie collected admirers wherever she went, but she was going to need help after she became his widow.

"I want Dierenpark signed over to her now," he said. "In its entirety. I want no third-cousins or the state emerging to take it from her."

Nickolaas agreed. Terms of the Vandermark trust dictated

the estate go to the oldest male heir, but he wanted Sophie to have legal guardianship over Pieter and Dierenpark until Pieter came of age. She was the only person he completely trusted to do what was right.

One of the professors rigged a wire frame to tent over his leg. They draped a sheet over it so Pieter would be spared the ghastly sight. A ring was produced from somewhere in the house, and the metal was cold in the palm of his hand. Pieter looked frightened and upset, but as soon as everyone was assembled, things moved quickly.

He wished Sophie didn't look so stricken. She deserved so much better, but the pastor stood on the other side of the bed, a large Bible open in his hands.

It was hot . . . so sweltering hot he could barely fill his lungs. He had to fight for every breath. Sophie's narrow hand was cool in his own, and he tugged it until she leaned over him, enveloping him in the scent of pine and lemon. "What is it, Quentin?" she murmured.

"Don't let Pieter be like me," he managed to whisper. "Raise him in the sunlight." If anyone could do that, it was Sophie. She was a bright, radiant light and would know how to guide Pieter into becoming a fine man. One who counted and shared his blessings, rather than jealously guarding them.

"It's time," the pastor said. He nudged Pieter to stand between Sophie and Nickolaas.

The pastor began. Quentin heard little of what was spoken over him, but when the pastor asked if he would love, honor, and cherish Sophie, it was easy to affirm the vow, for he did love her. The muscles in his face eased as she spoke her own vows, because even though he would not be able to raise his son to manhood, he had found someone he loved and trusted to undertake the task. The pastor declared them man and wife, and Sophie leaned over to press her cool lips to his forehead, and it felt like a blessing. He didn't even have the strength to put the ring on her hand. It slipped from his fingers and pinged on the floor, but someone picked it up and passed it to Sophie.

He wished for so much more for Sophie. She wept as she put on the ring, but there was too much to say and so little time. "You were the best thing that ever happened to me," he rasped. "You made me so happy. I am so happy."

"Please . . . Please rest, my dearest," she urged.

He didn't want to rest. He wanted to hold on to this moment forever, even the pain and the heat, for it came along with the joy of knowing he loved and was loved in return. He felt grace showering down on him, a peace unlike anything he'd ever experienced.

Sophie knelt on the floor beside him, clutching his hands between her own. "God is with you, Quentin, no matter what happens. You know that, don't you? Sometimes there are things science can't explain, you understand that, right?" she asked.

He smiled and tried to respond, but there was no more breath left. Dearest, sweetest Sophie . . . all he could do was nod, but he understood. He felt the blessings of grace and knew her words were true.

It was enough. More than enough. For the first time in his life, he was truly and completely happy. Happiness wasn't the absence of pain, it was the joy of life, and in these final moments, he had found it. After decades of cynicism and doubt, love and forgiveness surrounded him. He deserved none of it, but he savored the blessing of peace and quiet joy. Tears leaked from the corners of his eyes. With the last of his strength, he squeezed Sophie's hand.

Joy blinded him. He surrendered.

❧ 24 ❧

THE DOCTOR FROM TARRYTOWN arrived at noon the following day. Quentin had not roused since slipping into insensibility last night, and Sophie prayed his oblivion would last through the amputation.

When the doctor saw Quentin's blackened leg and noted the heat from the fever ravaging his body, he drew Sophie aside. "It might be best to let him quietly slip away. The infection is already full-blown. He is not in pain now, and the trauma of an amputation is unlikely to save him. It will only make his final hours worse."

Sophie looked at the others in the room. Nickolaas, Mr. Gilroy, Ratface—all of them had known Quentin for decades, but now she was his wife and was the only one who could make this decision.

"Fight," she said softly. "Quentin is no coward. He's been battling this injury for years and wouldn't want to give up without a fight." If she doubted her decision, it was banished by the nod of approval from Nickolaas.

She stayed beside Quentin through the entire operation, holding his hand and ready to help should the doctor need any assistance. Quentin did not rouse, for which she was thankful. She kept her eyes averted but could hear the rasp of the bone saw and the grunting of the doctor as he carried out the strenuous task. She heard and smelled burning flesh as the wound was cauterized. Mr. Gilroy passed bandages over and carried away bowls of water. In twenty minutes, it was all over.

"It's in God's hands now," the doctor said as he pulled the sheet over the stump of Quentin's amputated limb.

She bowed her head and prayed.

***

Everything hurt too much to move, but Quentin was used to pain. He kept his eyes closed, trying to assess what was going on in his body. He remembered the tourniquet, but had they actually amputated his leg?

He shifted his thigh. Everything hurt, but . . . he drew a breath and tried to focus. Most of his leg seemed to be gone.

Had he married Sophie last night, or had that been a dream? Light flooded his sight as he cracked his eyes open. She was sitting beside his bed, a book open on her lap. A huge diamond glittered on her left hand. A smile curved his mouth, and a lightness lifted his spirit. He hadn't dreamt it.

"Where did the ring come from?" he croaked.

Sophie startled so quickly the book fell off her lap, splatting open on the floor. "You're awake!"

And alive, apparently. Thank you, God.

The last thing he remembered was a blinding, brilliant sense of comfort. The something—or someone—he'd been sensing these past weeks had surrounded him, and he could no longer doubt. He'd been blessed with a new life, a better life.

He tried to sit up, but the pain splitting his head made him think better of it. The void where his leg used to be was so odd. It made his whole body feel unbalanced and strange.

"How are you feeling?"

"Pretty awful," he managed to say. He glanced down at her ring. "But happy. Where did the ring come from?"

"It was in one of the old jewelry boxes." She covered the ring with her other hand and twisted it with nervous fingers. "Pieter noticed it in one of the portraits downstairs. The grim-faced lady with the white wig and huge dress? She is wearing it in her portrait."

"I suppose my recovery means you are missing out on a chance to be a rich widow."

She slanted a glance that tried to be scolding. "I don't mind."

It seemed she didn't. Dark circles shadowed her eyes, and her face was pale and drawn, but she looked him directly in the eye and smiled.

He had been desperate for the marriage in order to secure a reliable guardian for Pieter. But now it appeared he was going to survive. He had awakened from plenty of surgeries over the years, and this was no worse than the others. It was actually a good deal better. The right thing to do would be to offer Sophie an annulment. Given the circumstances, it shouldn't be too difficult to procure. With an army of attorneys at his command, it could probably be slammed through the legal system within a month. He didn't want a reluctant wife. Never again. He loved Sophie too much to keep her locked in a marriage she had been pressured into by a dying man.

"I'm thirsty," he said, trying to delay the inevitable conversation for a few more moments. She brought him a cup of cool water and he drank, not realizing how parched he'd been until he drained the cup and asked for another.

Sophie was so solicitous, bringing him water and straightening the sheets around him. He'd been an invalid for years and had always resented the intrusion into his privacy, but that wasn't the case with Sophie. Her presence felt right and natural, as though she welcomed the chance to tend him, rather than doing it out of a sense of duty.

"I don't imagine it was the sort of wedding any girl dreams about," he hedged.

She laughed a little at that. "You should have seen the wedding dress I had lined up for my marriage to Marten. It was full of ruffles and had gaudy crystal beads sewn all over it."

He was tempted to groan. Did he really want to hear this?

"But I was proud of my wedding dress when I married you," she continued. "It had grass stains from our argument in the meadow and blood from tending you at the house. It was no glamorous wedding dress, but I am proud of it, stains and all."

She said it in good spirits, but she deserved so much more than a hasty marriage entered into amid a flood of panic and a sense of obligation. He rested the cup on his abdomen and schooled a blank expression onto his face.

"An annulment shouldn't be too difficult to obtain," he said, keeping his gaze fixed on the cup, rotating it in his fingers. *Please no*, he silently begged. For the first time in his life, it felt as if all the stars were aligning, and he wanted Sophie by his side forever. She had guided him into an entirely new world of faith and hope. It wouldn't be the same without her.

"I don't want an annulment."

The relief that washed through him made him dizzy. His gaze shot to hers, and what he saw made his heart swell. She was radiant, smiling at him with a strong, clear sense of purpose in her gaze. No trace of reluctance or regret. She wanted to be his wife.

"Why?" he managed to choke out.

"Because I love you. You believed in me when no one else did. You followed me on a journey I knew you didn't want to take. You truly know me. You know I'm not perfect—"

"You're perfect for me."

"And that's why we should stay married. I love you. I love Pieter. And the three of us belong together. I don't know if you will ever walk again, but we have taken the vows of holy matrimony, in all its joys and heartache. I'm looking forward to our time together, and I don't want an annulment."

She leaned over to kiss him again, and everything felt right. She continued fussing over him for the rest of the afternoon, bringing him cool drinks and straightening the linens. When there were no chores left, she sat beside him and read from a book on her lap, her other hand clasped in his.

Her voice was soothing, but he couldn't pay attention to the words. He stared out the window at the lawn dappled with sunlight, the leaves swaying softly in the breeze. Had there ever been a more beautiful spot than the pristine acres surrounding Dierenpark? It was an alluring dream, a paradise, Eden itself. He wished with all his heart he could give it to her.

He squeezed her hand, and she stopped reading. "We can't keep Dierenpark," he said gently. "Not now that we know how it was built."

Sophie's face was beautiful as she smiled down at him with sad understanding. "I know," she said, even though it looked as if she wanted to weep as she spoke the words. She had spent most of her life here, but this beautiful, shining gem wasn't really theirs, and if they tried to pretend they didn't know how it was obtained, they'd be little better than the first few generations of Vandermarks who hid the secret through greed and guilt.

"It will be hard on Pieter," she said. "He loves it here. He thinks it is the Garden of Eden, but we will find another Eden, for they are everywhere."

And he knew that it was true. Sometimes there were places where it was easier to feel closer to God, and this estate was one of them. But spiritual abundance could be found by anyone willing to search for it, be it in the desert, the city, or an isolated estate on the Hudson River. He hadn't understood that until his mind had been cleaned of the cynicism and doubt that made it so hard to appreciate the blessings surrounding him.

He had his wife and his son. They would find another Eden.

❧ 25 ❧

One Year Later

QUENTIN INSPECTED the carpenter's work throughout the ground floor of Dierenpark, the click of his prosthetic leg marking each step as he surveyed the rooms. He'd gotten used to the clicking, a small price to pay for being able to walk on his own without a cane and without discomfort. His adjustment to an artificial limb had been remarkably easy, giving credence to Sophie's assertion that there was something in the air at Dierenpark that simply made people feel better. He believed her, and it was one of the reasons they both had known exactly what they should do with the grand old estate.

Only forty miles down the river was a city full of suffering people who could never afford prolonged treatment at a clinic. Their pain was every bit as brutal as what Quentin had once endured. He would bring them here to recover in a clean and serene environment at Dierenpark, where they'd have the best medical treatment available.

The doors of their convalescent clinic would open within a month, and the only major project yet to be completed was the installation of new windows. He'd already designed and installed a system for adding electricity to the estate, and Sophie had been working in the gardens outside. Pieter's love of nature continued to grow, and he eagerly worked alongside Sophie as they designed first a new herb garden and then a plot for roses. Pieter was eager to learn everything she could teach him, thriving under the gentle care and attention Sophie showered on him.

The past year hadn't all been bliss. In January, the Weather Bureau had awarded a contract for an upgraded climate observatory to New Holland, and although the town rejoiced at the news, it had been bittersweet for Sophie. It meant the modest station she'd been tending on the roof of Dierenpark would be dismantled and her services would no longer be needed. The prize she'd fought so hard to win had come to fruition, but there would be no place for her in it, and she'd been weepy for the entire week after the news arrived.

A few days later, she'd learned she was carrying their first child, and the entire focus of her world had shifted. A week that had begun with heartache ended with celebration.

Quentin walked to the old diamond-paned windows overlooking the river from the parlor, running a finger along the cool, rippled glass. Sophie wanted to preserve this bank of windows even though all the other old windows were being replaced. He wanted windows that could open to allow wholesome air to circulate through the house, and even now he could hear the pounding of hammers from the carpenters upstairs as sash windows were installed. He smiled a bit, glad Sophie had convinced him to keep this one intact. It was impractical, but it harkened back to the timeless beauty that would always be a part of this estate.

"A letter from your grandfather has arrived," Sophie said, walking into the parlor in her awkward gait. She was in her eighth month but still insisted on coming to Dierenpark each day as the construction continued. They had a fine house in New Holland but would probably always be involved at Dierenpark as it was transformed into a convalescent clinic for the poor.

He gestured Sophie toward the bench beneath the window. "Sit down beside me and let's hear it."

"Brace yourself," she said. "The envelope says he is writing from Egypt."

She settled in beside him and opened the letter, scanning it with eager eyes. Quentin preferred to simply look at her profile, still amazed that this lovely and generous woman was actually his wife.

Besides, he suspected he knew exactly what would be in that letter. Nickolaas's spiritual quest was continuing in full force, but after witnessing the profound transformation in Quentin's life, he'd finally decided to "take a peek" at Christianity. Never one to do anything by halves, Nickolaas immediately set off for Rome to experience the full pomp and circumstance at the Vatican. He wanted the exoticism of the Latin prayers, the incense, the full majesty of seventy cardinals walking in scarlet robes through gilded halls.

Sophie read the letter aloud, which said that although Nickolaas loved the Vatican, he was in the mood for something a little different and had moved on to Africa to find a remote Coptic Christian monastery in the deserts of Egypt, where he was welcomed with open arms. "He says, 'I love the desert! The austerity, the stark sky, the baked landscape, the solitude and stillness. I am thinking of making my permanent home among the brothers.'" Sophie looked up, aghast. "You don't really believe him, do you?"

"Can you see my grandfather becoming a Coptic monk? I expect we'll have another letter within a month from somewhere else, for the charms of a monastic cell won't last for long. Especially now that Mr. Gilroy is no longer there to fetch and carry for him."

Mr. Gilroy, as genteel and shrewd as ever, had lost interest in working for the Vandermarks, and his departure confirmed what Quentin was coming to suspect about Dierenpark. Some people saw the beauty and recognized the peace, the hope, and the gift. Others thought it just another patch of land and moved on. Mr. Gilroy was a fascinating man, but he didn't really belong here anymore.

Sophie was tucking the letter back into the envelope when Ratface came bounding into the room. "You are needed in the front hall at once, sir." Ratface's normally fearless demeanor seemed a little off. His fists were clenched, and his Adam's apple bobbed nervously.

"What's the matter?" Quentin asked.

"I—I'm not sure," Ratface stammered. "But a bunch of Indians have just knocked on the front door. They're asking to see you."

"Indians?" he asked, flabbergasted. Indians had not inhabited this part of the state in over a hundred years.

"Indians," Ratface confirmed. "Four of them. They say they're Algonquin."

Quentin glanced at Sophie. "Maybe you should stay here."

"Nonsense. We've got six bodyguards and twenty carpenters on the property. We are perfectly safe." She swallowed. "I think."

The thudding from a dozen hammers upstairs confirmed her words. He held out his arm. "Come along, then." He followed Ratface as quickly as possible on his artificial leg, grasping Sophie's hand as he walked to the front of the house.

Quentin couldn't believe it, but standing in the foyer of Dierenpark were four bronze-skinned men, looking at him with curious eyes. They were dressed in Western clothing, with proper suit jackets and ties, but each of them had something a little extra. One wore a beaded vest beneath his jacket, and another wore his hair in a braid hanging to his waist. Another wore a feathered earring.

A man about Quentin's age, the one with the feathered ear-ring, stepped forward and offered his hand in greeting.

"You probably don't remember me," he said, "but we were at Harvard together. You were studying architecture, and I was on the other side of campus studying law. I knew you were there, but you were a Vandermark, and well . . . we've never really mixed too well with that branch of the family."

"I see," Quentin said as he shook the man's hand. He didn't remember ever seeing this man before, but Harvard had a long tradition of admitting Indians, so he didn't doubt the truth of what he'd said.

"I am Luke Tanakiwin, lawyer for one of the Algonquin tribes near the border of Massachusetts. These are my cousins. We heard there were big changes going on at Dierenpark and couldn't quite believe it until we saw it with our own eyes. Is it true you have given it away?"

"Mostly," Quentin confirmed. "We are affiliated with a hospital in the city who will send us patients. The estate has been turned over to a charitable trust to oversee its future. I am the chairman of the trust."

"Good," Mr. Tanakiwin said. "Very good. Excellent." His voice trailed away as he scanned the interior of the grand hall. He seemed particularly interested in the portraits of the Vandermark ancestors still hanging in the grand salon. One portrait snagged the strange visitor's attention.

"Do you mind?" he asked and drifted toward the portrait of Enoch Vandermark, Caleb's son. Enoch had a tough reputation, having fought against the British and again during the Indian wars of the 1690s.

"He's got the ring," Mr. Tanakiwin murmured, and the other Indians drew closer to inspect the portrait.

"What ring?" Quentin asked, although he was pretty certain they were looking at the hereditary Vandermark ring that had been passed down to the eldest son in each generation and was now worn by his grandfather.

"One like this," the Indian said, holding up an identical ring. "This one belonged to Adrien. We've gotten kind of tired of taking the blame for his death all these years, you know."

Quentin raised a brow. "Yes . . . a misunderstanding that will be clarified soon. We've had a number of historians visiting the estate, and I expect their publications will set the record straight."

"But how did you come by that ring?" Sophie asked, stepping closer. "May I see it?"

Mr. Tanakiwin handed the ring over. Sophie studied it in fascination and compared it to the ring in Enoch's portrait. "It's identical to the one Nickolaas has," she confirmed. "But how did you get this? I thought Adrien's body was never found."

Mr. Tanakiwin shook his head. "We know exactly where Adrien's body is. He was buried alongside his wife up near the Canadian border. He lived with a tribe of praying Indians for almost forty years after his brother tried to kill him. The ring has been handed down to the oldest white Indian in each generation." A hint of amusement lit his features. "Although after a few generations, we weren't very white anymore."

Quentin reeled back, grasping the staircase post for balance. Had he heard correctly? The Indians seemed to take amusement in his shock.

"Adrien said his brother made a number of attempts on his life before paying the groundskeeper to finish him off, so he saw no point in returning. He didn't want Caleb to forget, though. Every few years he sent his brother pages torn from the Algonquin Bible, but he had no interest in ever returning to Dierenpark. He sent them to remind Caleb of his sin and in hopes that his brother would eventually repent. I guess he never did, since Caleb ended up keeping the money."

"But how did he escape drowning?" Sophie asked. "An old letter we found indicates Adrien was drowned in Marguerite's Cove."

Mr. Tanakiwin shrugged. "He thought he was dead, too, but God must have had other plans for him. The groundskeeper went for a shovel to dig a grave, and Adrien roused and managed to drag himself from the river. He went north to a town of praying Indians, where he fell in love with an Algonquin woman, married her, and had six children." He glanced at Quentin. "So that makes us cousins."

"That makes us *brothers*," Quentin said. He held out his hand, giving more than a cursory shake this time. There was no family resemblance between them. They had a different skin color, different backgrounds, and certainly very different taste in dress, but they were brothers despite it all. Quentin felt an irrepressible grin spread across his face. "I hope you will join us for dinner," he said. "My wife is a good cook."

The celebration that night lasted long after the moon rose high in the sky, illuminating their gathering on the back terrace beneath its shimmering light. The table was filled with platters of steamed oysters, bowls of olives, figs, freshly baked bread, and an array of cheeses from the farm across the road. One of the Indians showed Sophie how to make sweet corn pudding, and laughter echoed across the valley as two families came together after centuries apart.

As the celebration began winding down, Quentin drifted to the far side of the terrace to gaze up at the stars hovering millions of miles above. The awesome sky made him feel dwarfed in a universe so much larger and more profound than he could grasp.

"So you survived," he whispered into the night sky, sensing that somewhere out there Adrien Vandermark looked down on their celebration tonight and smiled.

Sophie drew up beside him, slipping her arms around his waist and gazing up at the sky with him.

"It's nice to know the ending of the story," she said, and he squeezed her hands, even though he knew they were a long way from the end of their story. Ahead of them lay a life filled with purpose and celebration for the time God had given them. Quentin had been a cynical and embittered man, but God had forgiven him and welcomed him to the table, just as Sophie had welcomed him into her life. The world was full of hardness and suffering, but Sophie had opened his eyes to the fact that there were little glimpses of Eden everywhere.

Despite his happiness, Quentin accepted that pain would always be a part of his life. His body still ached on occasion, and debilitating spells of melancholia still sometimes darkened his days. But no matter how bad the pain, he knew the light of dawn would always come again.

Blessed are the pure in heart, for they shall see God.

Quentin had seen God, and he was truly blessed.

Questions for Conversation

1. Marten and Sophie remain friends despite the painful breakup of their earlier relationship. Is it possible to remain friends with someone you once loved romantically, even if they let you down? Why do so few people manage it?

2. Nickolaas looks for spirituality everywhere, but his curiosity rarely lasts long. Do you know people who "shop" for a religion? Is there something worthwhile in sampling other religions? What are the potential problems with it?

3. At the beginning of the novel, Quentin has contempt for all forms of religion based on Nickolaas's erratic spiritual quests. Do you know of people who have soured on religious faith because of an isolated negative experience? What is the best way to respond to such a situation?

4. Sophie loves cooking the recipes that have been handed down to her from generations of her ancestors. Do you have any family recipes you cherish? Is it based on the quality of the recipe or on something else?

5. A major theme of the novel relates to loving *all people*, not just those we deem worthy of love. What are the practical implications of this in your life?

6. Are there any places where you believe it is easier to feel closer to God? What do you suppose gives such places that quality?

7. Why is Quentin so adamant that his son not become one of the "idle rich"? Do you know of any such people? How did it work out for them?

8. At the beginning of the novel, Pieter believes that his grand-father is the only person who loves him, and he fears his father. Should a parent and grandparent have different roles in a child's life? What are the problems and benefits of such roles?

9. Sophie and Marten were supposed to marry when they were eighteen, and she later admits they were too young to be making that sort of commitment. Is there a right age at which to marry?

10. What sort of future do you imagine for Quentin and Sophie? For Pieter? For Dierenpark?

About the Author

ELIZABETH CAMDEN is the author of seven historical novels and has been honored with both the RITA Award and the Christy Award. With a master's in history and a master's in library science, she is a research librarian by day and scribbles away on her next novel by night. She lives with her husband in Florida. Learn more at www.elizabethcamden.com.

More From
Elizabeth Camden

Visit elizabethcamden.com for a full list of her books.

When a map librarian and a young congressman join forces to solve a mystery, they become entangled in secrets more perilous than they could have imagined.

Beyond All Dreams

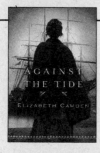

United in a quest to cure tuberculosis, physician Trevor McDonough and statistician Kate Livingston must overcome past secrets and current threats to find hope for their cause—and their futures.

With Every Breath

When Lydia's translation skills land her in the middle of a secret campaign against dangerous criminals, who can she trust when both her life and her heart are in jeopardy?

Against the Tide

You May Also Enjoy...

After being abandoned by the man she loved, Sophie Dupont's future is in jeopardy. Wesley left her in dire straits, and she has nowhere to turn—until Captain Stephen Overtree comes looking for his wayward brother. He offers her a solution...but can it truly be that simple?

The Painter's Daughter by Julie Klassen
julieklassen.com

When Miranda Wimplegate mistakenly sells a prized portrait, her grandfather purchases an entire auction house to get it back. However, after traveling to the Ozarks, they're dismayed to learn their new business deals in livestock—not antiques! While Miranda tries to find the portrait, the handsome manager attempts to salvage the failing business. Will either succeed?

At Love's Bidding by Regina Jennings
reginajennings.com

When Brook Eden's friend Justin, a future duke, discovers she may be an English heiress, she travels to meet her alleged father. Once she arrives in Yorkshire, Brook finds herself confused by her emotions and haunted by her mother's mysterious death. Will she learn the truth—before it's too late?

The Lost Heiress by Roseanna M. White
LADIES OF THE MANOR
roseannamwhite.com

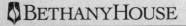
BETHANYHOUSE